COURTESY OF A DEAD MAN

A NOVEL

PERSIA WALKER

ISBN: 978-0-9816023-8-7

For Wesley C. Redding

Detective Sergeant, NYPD

1892–1924

He walked the line when few were allowed to.

This story walks in his shadow.

Dreams built on lies crumble the slowest.
And fall the hardest.

PART I

VAUGHN

1

Crosstown wind cut through her coat. Sharp. Bitter. Damp. Gusts that battered the face and chilled the bone. New Yorkers hurried past—collars up, heads down, shoulders hunched against the night. They were all headed home. Toward safety. Warmth.

She was the only one walking the other direction.

She tried to turn back. Tried to follow them. But her legs wouldn't obey. They carried her forward, step after step, deeper into the dark.

Beatrice Vaughn jerked awake, her heart hammering. She straightened up, gave her head a little shake and rubbed her forehead.

That dream—she'd had it again. The details were already slipping away. The dread stayed.

Where was she?

Not at home in D.C. No, she looked around. She was in New York. In her professor's sublet. At his desk. She blinked. Tried to remember. She was so tired, she'd put her head down for a minute. But she must've fallen asleep.

She shivered, drew her sweater around her. Glanced at the dark night-time streets outside the ground-floor window.

New York made her uneasy. She didn't know why. But lately, she couldn't shake the feeling that if she and her professor stayed too long, the city would collect its due.

Vaughn was everything she appeared to be—refined, composed, cultured—a woman who belonged in literary salons and university halls. But she hadn't started out that way. She'd learned to read the streets before she ever read a book. She still knew what it took to survive.

So New York shouldn't have rattled her.

But it did. It *felt* wrong.

The clock on the fireplace mantel struck nine. Where was he?

She had served as Professor Victor Grayson's secretary for twenty-five years, managing his papers, his life. New York was his calling, not hers.

Grayson was a respected philosophy professor at McAllister, the top Negro university in Washington D.C.—arguably in the entire country. His work centered on the "New Negro" philosophy, a subject that had long defined his scholarly voice and, in private moments, his purpose.

For now, though, his responsibilities extended beyond the classroom. He was in New York as a guest editor for a special issue of *Commonwealth Review* dedicated to Harlem's burgeoning art scene. He was also finalizing a collection of essays based on the special issue, a volume he had titled *The New Voice of Harlem.* Among the colored literati, his name opened doors for some. Closed them for others.

It hadn't gotten him home tonight.

They worked at the magazine during the day. Evenings, they worked here. Tonight, she was working alone.

The sublet was small. A bedroom. A living room. A kitchenette no wider than a bookcase. The furniture was spare:

twin bed, side table, one worn chair, a desk. In the corner, a phonograph waited with a record half out. Books on philosophy, art, politics and history packed the shelves. The space had a certain charm she couldn't deny—but it was still the sort of place a man of rank rented out of necessity, not choice.

And it was a far cry from her tidy little place in D.C.

That Tuesday evening, as always, she'd returned to her own smaller, smellier sublet—scrubbed clean and sprayed with rose water—and eaten alone. Then she'd made her way here, to Grayson's, to finish work that should've been done hours earlier. Tomorrow was already waiting.

She'd sorted through marked-up manuscripts and correspondence the way she always did. Calmly. Efficiently. With the confidence of someone who knew his habits, his quirks and the thoughts he never said out loud.

Two hours in, exhaustion had hit her. She set down her pen. Rolled her shoulders. Reached back and pressed her fingers into the tight place between her shoulder blades.

He should've been back by now.

He'd gone to one of Ernestine Rose's literary gatherings at the 135th Street branch of the New York Public Library. Those meetings pulled in everyone—stars, hangers-on, the hopeful and the bored. Stimulating, maybe. For an introvert like Grayson, punishing. He hadn't wanted to go. She'd told him he should. Now she wished she hadn't. He'd be no good tomorrow. And he wasn't here tonight.

She pushed her chair back and went to the window.

Night fell early in New York in late November. The streets had been dark when she arrived. Now, they were darker. Full of shadows. The kind that made women think twice before walking home alone.

She hugged herself. Rubbed her arms. Just the thought of going out there made her tense.

Don't be ridiculous, she told herself. She'd worked plenty of late nights in D.C.

But there, she'd arranged everything perfectly. Her apartment was close to campus. Close to *him.*

And D.C. was her city. Her jungle. She knew its predators—their haunts, their tells, their approaches. Cement jungles supposedly all shared the same pulse.

This one didn't. Not to her.

She massaged her temples. She should leave.

But she couldn't. Not until she knew he was home safe.

A key turned in the lock. The door creaked open and Grayson stepped inside.

She breathed easier.

He was every inch the gentle scholar. Late fifties. Medium height. Portly. Balding, with a smooth crown and a neat mustache. He projected calm the way others projected power. Soft dignity. Kindness behind the eyes. The quiet that said he'd seen everything and judged very little. He reminded Vaughn of the warmth she used to imagine in someone who would never hurt her—a man who spoke gently because he didn't have to raise his voice.

Cuddly-looking. That was the term that came to mind. Even Vaughn, with her dry humor, would've said so. Maybe it was the deep, warm complexion. More likely, it was the round face and button-brown eyes. Deep down, he resembled the teddy bear she'd never had. The kind of softness a girl pressed her cheek to when the shouting started. Not softness as weakness. But as mercy.

That, of course, was something she would've denied.

She did, however, openly admire the way he carried himself. The quiet authority that came from years in lecture halls, facing down doubters with nothing but intellect and grace. The mild demeanor that masked a razor-sharp mind. The way he could outthink anyone in the room—and often did, though he never said so.

But tonight, the sharpness in his eyes was dulled. The lines around them were deeper, his movements heavier. He moved like a man who'd been wrestling something heavier than conversation. His overcoat was slung carelessly over one arm. He didn't just look tired. He looked worn out.

To her, he looked exposed.

And that, she couldn't stand.

Vaughn rose to her feet. "Long night?"

He set his briefcase down and tossed his coat over the armchair. "Long enough."

His usually immaculate suit was rumpled. And his favorite bow tie sat crooked beneath a loosened collar.

He made his way to the bookshelves and pulled down a heavy tome. Inside it, a hollowed-out space held a small bottle of Dewar's White Label and a single crystal glass.

He poured himself a full two fingers and downed half in one swallow.

That was new.

The bottle had been a gift from a friend who'd smuggled it in after a trip to Europe—God only knew how. This was Prohibition. Grayson treasured that bottle. Usually, he saved it for rare occasions.

Or bad days.

"I've reviewed the letters you need to answer," she said. "The ones that can't wait. The manuscripts that'll need final approval if we're going to make deadline are on your desk."

He picked up the stack, flipped through the pages without seeing them. "You're too good to me."

She'd heard the line so many times before. But tonight, it landed differently—softer, with a hint of regret that startled her.

She eyed him. "Are you all right?"

He took his drink, moved to the window and stared out into the street. His silhouette was still in the amber desk light, shoulders stiff, uneasy. His eyes were sunken, the skin beneath puffy. He hadn't been sleeping.

Grayson was a philosopher, a scholar—not an editor. His guest role at the *Review* was temporary, but the pressure of shaping what was meant to be a history-making issue—a compilation of essays, short stories and other thought-provoking pieces by the day's best Negro talent—was obviously wearing him down.

"You missed Everett Carlisle today."

He finally turned. "He was there? At the office?"

Grayson and Carlisle. Harlem knew the argument by heart. Polite on the surface. Rotten underneath. Grayson could barely stand the man. Something old lay between them. She would have given anything to know what.

Carlisle wasn't a professor. He didn't need to be. Art critic. Theorist. Professional thorn. He even took aim at W.E.B. Du Bois—widely considered the greatest living Negro intellectual in the world.

Du Bois wanted art to do work in the world. Civil rights. Uplift. Leverage. Carlisle wanted art to be free. Free of politics. Free of purpose. Free of Du Bois.

Whether he believed what he preached or just liked being contrary, Vaughn didn't know. She found him a nuisance.

He was loud about white patronage too. Called it "cultural imperialism." Accused benefactors—those who Zora Neale Hurston called "Negrotarians"—of manipulating the very art they claimed to support.

Grayson landed in the middle. He didn't believe the positions were mutually exclusive. "In life, one has to make compromises," he'd say. "Because one does have to eat."

Vaughn agreed. Carlisle didn't. He let the disagreement fester. Nursed it into a wedge. The bitterness calcified. Turned ugly. Now he was taking shots at Grayson's new book. Some people called it honesty. Vaughn called it jealousy.

"You escaped him by a hair," she said. "He stopped by the office right after you left."

Grayson drew an agitated hand over his face and let out a long sigh. The egos and ambitions of Harlem's intellectual elite were a mess to manage. Herding cats. With claws. They were hungry. Anxious. This was their moment, and no one knew how long it would last. The younger ones told themselves there would be another chance. The older ones—like Carlisle—knew better. The clock was running.

Vaughn picked up one of the manuscripts from the pile on his desk. "Still debating whether to print Carlisle's essay?"

Grayson shook his head. "There's nothing to debate."

Just as she thought. He'd already accepted the Barnes piece—Albert C. Barnes on Negro art and its role in America. She'd read both. Carlisle's was better. More colorful. More engaging. More direct. More provocative.

But quality wasn't the issue. And it wasn't her place to pretend it was. Her professor had made his choice. He had his reasons. She didn't need to know them. She simply had to support them. The rest be damned.

If Carlisle got wind of Grayson's choice, the tension would turn vicious. Not just because Barnes was rich, but because he was white—a pharmaceutical magnate who'd made himself an authority on Negro art. To Carlisle, it would be confirmation. Proof that rich white men still dictated the conversation.

She raised an eyebrow. "You need to give him an answer."

"I know." Grayson sighed again. "It's just that... he'll take it as a rejection of him. Not just his work."

Vaughn put the manuscript back down. "Isn't it?"

His gaze cut toward her. Sharp. Unhappy.

She didn't push. Instead, she reached for the appointment book, flipped it open and held it out to him. "Tomorrow. Three interviews in the morning. Meeting with Alain Locke in the afternoon. Then dinner at Margery Davenport's later this week."

Grayson barely glanced at the notebook. "Cancel the interviews."

Vaughn blinked. "You can't just—"

"Cancel them," he said sharply.

She was stunned. He'd never used that tone with her before.

"I'm sorry," he said. "You're right. I can't cancel. Forget I said that."

She hesitated, chose her words. "Professor, you... you do look tired. Maybe you should skip the Davenport dinner. Stay home and rest." She knew he wouldn't. But she had to suggest it. He did such a poor job of looking after himself.

He didn't answer. Just kept staring out the window. Shadows swept over his face with the passing traffic. His silence unnerved her.

"Professor Grayson, I—"

"Bea..." He paused, his voice trailing away.

"Yes?"

"Do you think a man should sacrifice everything for the truth?"

The question stopped her cold. She searched his face. Her response was careful. "That depends. Some truths are more dangerous than others."

He gave a wry, sad smile. "Yes. Yes, indeed, they are."

He drained the rest of his Scotch and crossed to his desk. Set the glass down. Reached into his inner pocket and pulled out a small crumpled envelope. He hesitated—just for a second—then slid it into the top right-hand drawer and locked it.

A letter? A note? She'd never been one to pry. But this time her gut told her she should.

"Professor, if there's anything I can do for you, you know I—"

"No, no I'm fine." He managed another brief smile. "Why don't you go home? You've done more than your share."

The smile was kind. It didn't fool her. Not with that look in his eyes. Not with the way his hand lingered on the drawer.

Vaughn held back a sigh. She'd never seen him like this—so distant, locked in thoughts he wouldn't share. But she knew she wasn't going to get any more out of him tonight. So she reached for her coat. "I'll see you in the morning."

He didn't answer right away. Just took off his glasses and pinched the bridge of his nose. Nodded. "Good night, Bea. And once again, thank you."

She paused in the doorway, turned back. He'd thanked her plenty of times before. He was always gracious. Always thoughtful. One of the reasons she'd turned down every offer—better salaries, better titles, even a proposal—just to stay by his side.

So it wasn't what he said.

It was the way he said it.

It felt—her stomach clenched—like goodbye.

2

The Harlem office of the *Commonwealth Review* was a stone's throw from City College on West 135th. It was crowded and hot—too many bodies and way too many egos.

Writers grouped around desks barely big enough to hold a typewriter and stacks of manuscripts piled high. Poets argued over whether art should challenge injustice—or just exist. Community leaders debated whether the New Negro movement needed artists or activists. Novelists disputed whether fiction should serve the cause—or stay out of the fight entirely. Others argued that any and every work of art produced by a colored man or woman was de facto part of the cause—whether the artist meant it to be or not.

Hot-headed. Hot-blooded.

And all of them chasing the same dream: space on the page.

The *Review* had always seen itself as a forum for the great minds of the age: progressive, forward-thinking, unafraid to tackle the thorny intersections of policy and culture. It was run by well-meaning white men who liked to believe they were on the right side of history. As long as history didn't move too fast.

The *Review* was an offshoot of *The Commonwealth Journal of*

Social Welfare. It carried essays about urban reform and labor struggles. The men behind these publications had built their reputation on essays about reform. About labor. About the so-called "Negro Problem." Most of those pieces were written by men who'd never set foot in a tenement or on a factory floor. Now they wanted a Harlem issue. A whole edition about black art and black thought. And they wanted a colored man in charge of it.

First time they'd ever tried that.

Vaughn saw it for what it was—not generosity, but caution. They knew better than to pretend they understood Harlem. They needed someone who did. Someone who could translate the arguments. Manage the rivalries. Keep the ambitions from boiling over.

Grayson had spent his life writing about philosophy, race and aesthetics. On paper, he was perfect. In practice, he was drowning.

Vaughn had watched him carry the load—splitting his time between the magazine's main downtown office and its temporary setup in Harlem, keeping the work bold enough to matter but not so bold it frightened the money. That was the real fight. Not just selecting the essays and poems that would define the issue, but getting them to print at all. Too much deference to white patronage and the radicals would whisper 'Uncle Tom.' Too much heat and the benefactors would pull their money before the first copy ran.

Somewhere behind Vaughn, a sharp whisper cut through the noise—another argument, this one about poetry versus propaganda. Sorting through a stack of submissions—poetry from Langston Hughes, essays from Countee Cullen and a critique from Alain Locke—she suddenly felt the thrill of being a part of a movement that would outlast them all. No, no one knew how long this marvelous moment would last—or indeed if anyone would ever remember it. But even she, with her desire to go home—back to the rhythm of the staid, but predictable life she'd built in D.C.—even she felt that she was taking part in the making of history.

She let the moment sit with her, let herself feel the quiet thrill of it.

This was history, unfolding in real time. These were the voices shaping the next generation—voices that, decades from now, would be studied, anthologized, dissected in university halls. And here she was, watching it happen—no, helping to *make* it happen.

For just a second, she allowed herself to wonder—would they remember her, too? She wanted to be memorable, to make her mark somehow.

For a moment, she thought about that, how it would be to see her name in the papers.

Then, just as quickly, she shut it down, hard. She knew better than to hope for foolish things like that. Where she'd come from, you learned quick to be realistic, to find your place, defend it and stick to it.

Yes, this was the heartbeat of the Harlem literary movement. But it wasn't necessarily hers. It didn't belong to her. And when she left, nobody would remember she'd ever been here.

Her gaze went to Grayson's office. Through the pebbled glass door pane, she could see him sitting behind his desk, nearly dwarfed by the folders piled high on either side. He was rubbing his temple with one hand, holding a page and pencil with the other.

He wasn't alone.

She knew the visitor. And that meant she knew which manuscript it was. "The Artist as Citizen." By Everett Carlisle.

Carlisle sat across from him, silent but simmering. He always wore the same suit, impeccable, but the cut somehow foreign. She'd heard that he'd lived in Paris. Maybe that's where it came from, not only the suit but the arrogance. Now that he was back, he expected the rest of them to bow down to his returned expat status, his Paris-confirmed *bona fides*. They hadn't. Now he acted like someone who'd been denied something that was rightfully his.

The office door was ajar, enough to let sound travel.

"You still haven't given me an answer, Victor."

Vaughn's pen paused mid-stroke. The usual office noise—typewriters clacking, conversations humming—fell away. She glanced around, saw that others had picked up on that one sentence, too.

For a moment, she considered getting up. Closing the door. It would've kept the others out. Protected her professor's privacy. But it would've shut her out, too. So she stayed put and cocked her ear. Quietly choosing curiosity over courtesy.

A page turned inside Grayson's office. Probably reading something he wasn't really seeing. "I've been busy."

"Too busy to answer a friend?"

A beat. "I read it."

"And?"

A pause. "It's not right for *Commonwealth Review*."

Carlisle gave a short humorless laugh. "Not right? That's what you're calling it?"

"It's too polemical."

Carlisle was bitter. "And Barnes? *His* piece is acceptable?"

Vaughn stiffened. So Carlisle already knew. That hadn't taken long.

Grayson didn't respond immediately. His hesitation was answer enough. "Barnes's article was stronger."

Vaughn felt her pulse tick up.

"It's one thing to reject my work," Carlisle said. "It's another to tell me a white man's is better."

"I didn't say that. I—"

"But it's what you think, isn't it?" Carlisle's voice sharpened. "It's what you think."

Another pause, then: "Yes. If you want to know the truth. That's exactly what I think. Do you want to know why?"

Silence.

"Why are you doing this to me, Victor? I know it isn't about Barnes. Or my writing. What have I done?"

No reply.

Carlisle sounded nearly broken. "What's this really about?"

Another pause. "Do you really have to ask?"

A heavy silence followed. And suddenly, Vaughn understood.

This wasn't about the essay. Or race. Or art.

It was about *them*.

Grayson, sounding tired: "You say you want our people to enjoy artistic freedom. But what you want is impractical, impossible. What you want…is chaos."

"I want our people to be free—free to make our own decisions, not to have to pander to the whims of white folk."

"Please."

Carlisle, angry now, indignant: "So this is what it comes to? You've become the gatekeeper, deciding which voices from our community deserve to be heard? What happened to you, Victor?"

Grayson's tone was final. "This isn't the place for this conversation."

Carlisle let out a soft, pained laugh. "Always hiding behind propriety. That's your answer for everything, isn't it? When the truth gets uncomfortable, just shut it down."

A moment. "You're not speaking the truth. You're just looking for a fight."

"You don't want to admit I'm right, do you?"

Grayson didn't answer.

Then Carlisle delivered the final insult: "You always did like playing it safe."

The door was flung open and Carlisle stalked out. The door slammed against the wall hard enough to rattle the glass.

Vaughn exhaled. She hadn't even realized she'd been holding her breath.

Grayson didn't move. Just sat there, staring at nothing.

She gave him a few seconds alone, then stood, smoothing her skirt, and went in. "Your next meeting is in fifteen minutes."

The pencil snapped between his fingers. "He never could leave well enough alone."

"No," she murmured. "He couldn't."

It wasn't just the man's politics. It was his arrogance, the way he prowled gatherings, playing the tortured genius. Called himself a maverick, when he was really just a jealous outsider, desperate to belong.

Then there was her professor. She didn't always agree with him, but she knew him to be a good man—one who deserved better than having to deal with the likes of Everett Carlisle.

People said they'd once been friends. That some party a year back had reignited an old feud. Whatever happened that night, it hadn't ended in disagreement. It had ended in hatred.

They didn't just dislike each other.

They despised one another.

Back at her desk, she picked up her pen. And smiled.

3

That evening, Vaughn left the office an hour early to pick up test copies from the magazine's printer. She was relieved that the matter took far less time than she'd expected and delighted when she was able to get home and have a few extra minutes to relax and rest her feet.

Ever efficient, she ate a quick dinner and headed to Grayson's apartment. He would be home on time tonight and she was looking forward to reviewing the work with him in private. She took pride in the fact that he valued her opinions, that he cared about her insights and respected her ideas.

For a brief moment, her thoughts returned to the dispute she'd overheard that day. It had further exhausted Grayson. He would especially need her support that evening.

Maybe they would sit down for a game of chess. Grayson was good, but she was better. He didn't know that, of course. She'd refined the art of letting him win. It was worth it to hear him say, *Checkmate, dear Bea. Checkmate.*

She let herself in, hung up her coat on the rack just inside the tiny vestibule and set the stack of prints on the nearby table. The door to the living room was closed. There were voices, two men talking in low tones, music playing in the background. *Some radio play,* she thought. Odd. She'd never known Grayson to be fond of radio plays and one voice did sound like—

"I didn't want it to be like this."

"You made it like this."

Silence.

Then: "You don't have to push me away."

A soft, sad chuckle. "I already did."

Another silence.

Then the first voice: "You don't have to do this."

"For both our sakes, I have to."

Vaughn was only half-listening. She was preoccupied with thoughts of the work that lay ahead and the idea of spending an entire evening alone with her professor. So when she pushed open the living room door and walked in, she did so without hesitation. She looked up, about to speak—then froze.

It wasn't a radio play.

Of course it wasn't, she would chide herself later. *You heard the voices. You should have known.*

The two men stood close, quite close. Grayson's back was partially to her, one hand resting on Carlisle's arm. Carlisle's head was dipped forward, lips parted as if he were murmuring words meant only for Grayson to hear.

And then—

Grayson reached up, cupped Carlisle's cheek and kissed him. Squarely on the mouth.

The room tilted beneath her feet.

She shouldn't have seen it. It shouldn't have happened. Not here, not in his home, not anywhere at all. Not between two men who—by all public appearances—despised one another.

The kiss was long, lingering. It spoke of familiarity. History. Passion.

This was not a mistake. This was not a lapse in judgment.

This had happened before.

Vaughn gasped. The sound was small but it was enough. Grayson spun around, head snapping toward the door. His eyes locked onto hers.

For the first time in all the years she'd worked for him, she saw panic.

"Bea—"

Carlisle stepped back and straightened his posture. He smoothed his face into a mask. But his eyes betrayed him. They still held a spark of fear.

Vaughn stood perfectly still. Then she inclined her head in a barely perceptible nod, said, "Excuse me," and backed out, politely closing the door. She stood in the vestibule a moment, feeling oddly calm. The one clear thought she could manage was that, obviously, there would be no work tonight. Trance-like, she reached for her coat and shrugged into it.

She would go home. Do her fingernails. Maybe even read that book she'd been meaning to finish—the one she fell asleep over every night.

Too tired to read.

Too tired because she spent all of her energy—all of her *time* —here, or there, always at his side, always looking after her professor.

Her professor?

Well. Clearly, he wasn't hers.

Not now.

Not ever.

He—

The living room door yanked open and Grayson rushed out.

"Bea, I'm so sorry. I know you've had a horrible shock. That I owe you an explanation."

"No, of course, you don't." She smiled gamely, held up a placating hand. "You don't owe me anything. If anyone owes anyone anything, it's me. I owe you an apology." She was babbling and she knew it, but she couldn't help herself.

His forehead creased. “Apology?”

“For intruding.”

“Oh, Bea.”

He reached out to comfort her. She turned away. He withdrew his hand and gave a small nod, his way of telling her he understood.

She smoothed her gloves over her wrists, picked up her purse and handed him the magazine prints she’d retrieved from the printer.

“They look fine. Though there is a slight misprint on page twenty-two.”

Grayson hesitated, then slowly nodded. “Thank you.”

Vaughn turned and left, shutting the door behind her.

She did not let herself react until she was halfway home. Only then did she exhale. By then, her hammering heart had calmed down.

Clearly, she would never tell a soul what she had seen. Not because she feared scandal. Not because she feared losing her job.

But because, for the first time, she understood something she’d never allowed herself to see.

That she hadn’t just been loyal.

She hadn’t just been devoted.

She’d been a fool.

4

The dream again. Cold. Darkness. Shadows. Her feet carrying her forward. Unable to stop them. No hope, no goal—just the street rushing toward her, the wind at her back, propelling her toward a destination she didn't want to reach.

No! She wrenched herself awake. Lay there staring into the dark, taking deep breaths, trying to calm her racing heart. No street. No wind.

But the cold was there, damp and piercing. She'd kicked off the blanket. She pulled it back, huddled under it and tried to go back to sleep. She couldn't. She lay there instead, watching the sky lighten. Trying not to think about what she'd seen in Grayson's apartment. Trying and failing.

Grayson and Carlisle.

Together.

The shock had worn off. Somewhat. She had absorbed the initial blow, had pressed it down, boxed it up and buried it so deep she told herself it couldn't hurt her anymore.

Yes, there was a dull, heavy ache. But she'd known worse disappointments. She'd overcome those others. She would overcome this one. She could—and would—*manage* it.

But there was another shock hiding behind the initial one. And it was harder to overcome. Grayson's reaction—that fear in his eyes. *That* stayed with her; it refused to be ignored.

She had known him for twenty-five years. Trusted him. Devoted herself to him. Yet for the first time, she realized:

Victor Grayson had secrets she did not know.

Back at work that morning, Vaughn removed her gloves and hung her coat on the office rack by her desk. Across the room, writers and editors continued their work, oblivious to her inner turmoil. She lifted a stack of manuscripts from her desk, keeping her hands busy, her expression perfectly pleasant.

Grayson arrived a few minutes later.

She didn't need to look up to know it was him—she had spent too many years attuned to his presence. He entered the office briskly, as if determined to prove nothing was wrong.

But Vaughn noticed the little things.

The way he hesitated a second too long before greeting his colleagues. The way he rubbed his temple, as if trying to dispel a thought. The way his eyes edged toward her, then darted away.

He was trying to act normal.

She was better at it.

"Good morning, Professor." The same smile, the same warm expression she'd always given him.

Grayson blinked, as if surprised to see her. He gave her a quick nod—"Morning, Bea"—and disappeared into his office without another word, closing the door behind him.

She assumed his nervousness, his tension, the slight tremor in his hands were about Carlisle. About the kiss. About her having seen it. She told herself she should let it go. If he wanted to keep his distance, fine. If he didn't want to talk about what she'd seen, then that was fine, too.

But the more she saw of him that morning, the more she realized: this wasn't just about her. Something else was troubling him. Something deeper. She had seen him anxious before—before lectures, tense debates, major editorial meetings.

But this was different. This was a preoccupation.

Then she remembered: the note. The envelope he'd hidden in his desk. She'd seen it then—the worry, the preoccupation.

The secrecy.

Her hand went to her mouth. Had someone else found out his secret? Seen what she'd seen? Had someone…sent him a warning?

The thought gripped her. She saw it all so clearly.

He wasn't afraid because she'd seen him and Carlisle together. He'd already been afraid well before that.

Her hands curled around the pages she was holding, knuckles pale. Her professor was being blackmailed. The certainty settled in her like a stone. It explained everything—the note, his anxiety, his distraction, the way his eyes darkened whenever he thought no one was looking.

She set the manuscripts down and smoothed the edges. Glanced at Grayson's office. The pebbled glass blurred his form, turned him into a washed-out specter of himself. He sat, head bowed, lost in thought. If someone was threatening him, he wouldn't tell her. Of course, he wouldn't. He kept so much to himself.

She leaned on her desk, hands clasped, elbows resting on the stack of manuscripts, and reflected. If Grayson wouldn't tell her the truth, she would have to find it herself. She'd seen where he'd placed the note, had watched his hands slip it into the drawer, had heard the quiet turn of the key locking it away. If she wanted answers, she was quite capable of finding them on her own.

She told him she was stepping out for lunch. Technically, she was.

She smoothed her gloves as she walked briskly down the street—not toward the small diner she frequented, but toward Grayson's sublet. She had timed it well. She'd already provided Grayson with a packed lunch. That was routine on days like this when he was too busy to leave the office. He had back-to-back meetings with writers and editors this afternoon. So she had at least an hour. Plenty of time.

She adjusted her hat, a woman with a goal.

Once at his apartment, she removed her gloves, set them down on the entry table and headed straight for his desk. He'd placed the envelope in the top right-hand drawer. Locked it. A trivial detail. Annoying, but nothing to worry about. Locks could be persuaded. She hadn't done it in a while, but as her mama had once told her, this particular skill, once acquired, was one you never quite lost.

And she'd always been good with her hands.

A moment of careful, deliberate maneuvering and—click.

She exhaled slowly, then slid open the drawer.

There it was. The envelope. She reached for it, fingers nimble, drew it out and smiled.

She opened the envelope and pulled its contents free.

The notepaper was creased, handled. The message typed. Simple, direct.

"You've threatened to reveal my secret. Should I reveal yours? My silence, however, won't come cheap."

It mentioned a dollar figure. And it was signed with the letter "C."

She stared at it. Her pulse didn't quicken. It slowed. Because this...*this* was exactly what she'd expected to find.

C. For Carlisle.

Of course.

She could see his bitterness in the phrasing. Her professor

had rejected Carlisle's essay—rejected *him*. So now, Carlisle was doing what bitter men did. Make threats. Demand money.

Retaliate.

Vaughn gave a grim smile. She had been right. She'd always been right. About the menace Carlisle posed. He wasn't just angry. He was spiteful. Petty. Dangerous. And here was the proof.

But the sense of satisfaction didn't last long. A cold anger took its place. How dare Carlisle! *How dare he!*

She slid the note back into the envelope and placed it exactly where she'd found it. Then, with the same methodical movements, she locked the drawer again, ensuring that everything appeared undisturbed.

She stepped back. Straightened her coat. Lifted her gloves from the entry table. And left.

Outside, chill air hit her face. The streets looked normal enough—traffic, people hurrying home, nothing to see. But Vaughn sensed an undercurrent. A tension both familiar and foreign. Her awareness of it was so strong that it pushed aside thoughts of Carlisle and Grayson.

New York had a pulse, and right now it ran fast and wrong. The rush of it tugged at her, the way a hard wind pushed at your back when you're not ready for it. She couldn't see the danger, but she felt it—sharp, insistent, already steering her where she didn't want to go.

She set her jaw and shrugged it off. Determined, she walked on. Her mind focused on the matter at hand.

Everything was clear now. It was time to stop pretending. She loved him. Had loved him before, loved him still and always would. Nothing would change that. Fighting it was pointless. Better to accept it—and carry the ache to her grave.

As long as ye both shall live.

Words from wedding vows. Words she would never exchange with him.

It was a dream she'd never dared admit to having. Now it didn't matter. She knew why it would never come true. The clarity hurt. But it beat the slow poison of hope.

That was one side of it. The other?

Her professor was in trouble. Deep trouble.

Which meant he would never be able to cast her aside.

She gave a small, quiet smile.

He would need her now—for the rest of his life.

5

They walked along Riverside Drive, past bare trees and iron benches. The air was crisp but not cold. Vaughn tucked her hands into her coat pockets and looked toward the horizon. A fine mist drifted over the Hudson, softening the jagged New Jersey skyline on the opposite side.

The noise of the city was muted here. They were in their own private world. It was the perfect place for confidences. She had suggested the walk that Friday evening, hoping to relax him, reassure him. He'd been surprised but readily agreed.

Grayson had been quiet since they left the office. She let him be. The silence between them wasn't as easy as it once was, but it wasn't uncomfortable yet. She meant to keep it that way.

She waited until they'd settled into a rhythm before speaking. "You know, you never have to worry about me saying anything."

Grayson paused, turned to look at her. "I never thought I did."

"Good." A small smile. "But just in case, I wanted to reassure you."

A pause.

"Thank you." Quiet relief, nothing more.

They walked on.

A breeze stirred the river. Damp stone. A hint of salt. A tugboat chugged along in the distance, trailing a thin line of smoke. It all looked so very peaceful.

This walk along the Hudson was the one place in New York where Vaughn felt at ease. That tight knot she felt elsewhere—here, she could feel it loosen. Here, she could breathe.

It was the river itself. She felt drawn to it. Calm on the surface, but churning underneath. Currents strong enough, quick enough to drag you under. Dangerous. Yet mesmerizing. Alluring. Almost impossible to resist.

She glanced at him. "It must've been difficult for you and him."

A moment of hesitation.

Grayson looked down, gave a quick nod. "Yes. Yes, it was."

She noticed his use of the past tense.

Another pause. Then, he gave a self-deprecating chuckle. "You know, it's strange."

"What is?"

"That we've worked together for so long. Yet I know so little about you."

"There isn't that much to know."

"Oh, I'm not so sure about that. I sense that deep down, beyond that quiet exterior, there's a fascinating human being, just waiting to be discovered."

She was, for the moment, stunned. Was he one of those men who swung both ways? Even if he was—and she couldn't believe he would be—this was unexpected—this sudden interest in her. It was unsettling. A few days ago, she would've welcomed the attention, come as close to being ecstatic as she could be. But now? Now, she had to wonder: was he genuinely curious about her—or just probing to see if she had any secrets worth knowing, now that she knew one of his?

"I know that you're loyal, steadfast."

She donned a smile. "Then you know all there is to know."

"Did I say modest? We can add that to the list."

Despite her unease, she felt faintly flattered. It felt good to be seen, acknowledged. "But you're not satisfied."

"No." He went on, slower now. "I know you're from D.C. That you put yourself through school. That's it."

His clumsy persistence amused her. "If you want to know more, why haven't you asked?"

"I don't know." He gave a small shrug. "I suppose I always thought..."

She didn't help him.

"You've always been so...private. I never wanted to intrude."

"That's wise." She met his eyes, her gaze steady, knowing. "Prying can be dangerous."

He blinked, startled.

She nearly laughed. She'd never believed anyone could actually look like a deer caught in headlights.

She did now.

She let him squirm, then offered mercy. "I'm joking. Mostly. But seriously—what did you want to know?"

He gave a soft huff of a laugh. It wasn't quite relief. She saw it then—that jolt in the eyes. Subtle, but unmistakable. He'd caught a glimpse of the real Vaughn. Not much. Just enough to know there was more to her than he'd ever guessed. And that he didn't know how deep it went.

A rookie mistake. She cursed herself for it. How many years ago had she sworn to never show him anything real? Not even a glimpse. She knew better.

So now she adjusted. Reined herself back in. Dimmed the smile. Put that light back under a rock. Became, once more, the woman he knew. The ghost he trusted. The secretary. The confidante. The one who asked for nothing and gave everything.

By the time he spoke again, she could already see the doubt forming—maybe he'd imagined it. Maybe he'd read too much into the moment.

"Tell me about your family," he said. "Big? Small?"

"Big. Three brothers, two sisters."

"Close?"

"We were. Once." A pause. "Not anymore."

He gave a thoughtful nod. Left space. An inviting silence meant to coax more.

So she told him her story. About how her parents had died young and how she'd raised her three younger siblings. She told it with gentle wit and modest candor, downplaying the hardships, easing the edges.

It was all lies, of course.

She didn't tell him that two of her brothers, Leland and Roger, had died in prison for crimes they hadn't committed. Or that the third, Benny, died when his best friend wrapped their car around a tree. She didn't tell him about Marnie, strangled by her husband in their kitchen while their children slept. Or Louise, who hated her for reasons Vaughn preferred not to dwell upon.

Why should she tell him anything? What business of it was his? Of anyone's? He wasn't entitled to the truth. No one was.

Besides, he was only half-listening. Something in his expression had shifted. Just slightly. Like a man who had always assumed the lock was on his side of the door—and was beginning to realize it wasn't.

Grayson nodded. "And you never married?"

A wistful smile. "No."

She did not mention the two proposals. The one she'd accepted and the one she'd turned down. She almost never thought of the first, but every now and then she did think of the second.

He was the only good man, other than Grayson, she had ever

known. A coal miner in West Virginia, with rough hands and soft eyes. *I love you, Bea. Won't you marry me?*

She'd refused. She would not be a miner's wife. A life of coal dust and constant struggle? No, thank you. She wanted better. *Deserved* better. She didn't desire glamour but she did require class. So she'd left, sure she was right, sure she'd never look back. Or that he'd give her reason to.

But he'd surprised her. Had dragged himself out of the dirt. Gone back to school. Gotten his degree. Built a life. A good one.

Now, he was a business owner. Sold mining equipment. Made a right good living. Had married the woman he met months after Vaughn left. Had built her a fine house with a big view, given her a diamond ring, two kids, grandkids and a car to boot.

That woman was sitting pretty.

And Vaughn? With all of her dreams? How had she ended up? In a tiny kitchenette with a view of a wall. No ring. No kids. Not even a lousy car.

All of it flashed through her mind in an instant. She just shrugged and said, "I suppose I'm married to my job. But that's okay. Look what it gave me. All these years with you."

Grayson looked like a man who knew he was bleeding but couldn't find the wound. His habitual politeness kicked in. "And I'm grateful for that. I really am."

They walked in silence.

What he did next surprised her—the topic he returned to. Later, she'd wonder if he thought that sharing might win her sympathy. Or distract her. Or buy him something he couldn't name.

He began tentatively. "You asked about…about me and him. I guess I should tell you."

"You don't have to."

"No, I know I don't. But you're the only one I can talk to. The only one I can trust."

She looked at him, relieved to know he understood that. "You've known each other for a long time?"

"Since McAllister. I met Ev my second year. He was—" He smiled. "Brilliant. Arrogant. Infuriating." A small chuckle. "I liked him immediately."

She matched his wry smile with one of her own. She was a good listener. Always had been. And he, as always, felt comfortable talking to her—even about a secret that had obviously pained him for years.

"We spent every moment together. Nights in the library, arguing over books. Walking through campus till dawn. He had this way of getting under my skin and I let him." His voice softened. "I think I loved him then. And he loved me."

He glanced over at her. Just briefly. As if to gauge whether he'd made a mistake.

But her expression didn't change. No judgment. No surprise. Only quiet interest.

He let out a breath, faint and guarded.

It hurt to see his look of relief. After all these years—after everything she'd done for him—didn't he know by now? That nothing he said could change how she felt about him? Not now. Not ever.

"So what happened?" she nudged. "What drove you two apart?"

Grayson hesitated. "Reality." He stared out over the water. "It was 1906. Our last year. And Ev...he was reckless. Too bold."

A pause.

"He kissed me. Not in private or off the quad. But in broad daylight. And they caught us."

She said nothing. But inwardly she felt a kick of revulsion, flashed on the kiss she'd witnessed in his living room.

"He was expelled."

Vaughn blinked, brought back. "Expelled?"

"You could almost say within the hour."

She feigned surprise. McAllister was a conservative institution. It had to be to survive. The code of behavior was strict. Much of it was unwritten. Yet everyone knew it. Knew the urgent need to abide by it. That to do otherwise was foolish. Suicidal even.

"So he was asked to leave, but you—"

Grayson gave a quiet, humorless laugh. "I would've been, too. But I...I denied everything. Put it all on him. I let him take the fall."

Interesting. This was a side to him she'd never seen. She didn't blame him for what he'd done—or failed to do. It was, after all, a matter of survival.

He fell silent, bit his lower lip. "I didn't see him again for nearly twenty years."

"Until last year."

He nodded. "At one of Ernestine's events. It was—unexpected. A week of nostalgia. Then...everything else."

A pause.

She waited.

"I tried to end it," he said. "For his sake. For mine."

"And did you?"

A beat.

"No."

She saw it in his eyes. The pain. "You still love him."

Grayson looked down and nodded. "I'm afraid I do. I never stopped."

She already knew this, of course. She had already decided she had no reason to be jealous. She was the winner here, not Carlisle. She was the one who stood beside Victor Grayson, day in and day out. The one he turned to.

And yet.

It hurt to hear him say those words. To again be hit—hit hard—with the fact that it wasn't her he'd chosen. Had never been.

Never would be.

She trudged along beside him, her steps steady, her expression composed. Inside, the ache bloomed—slow, familiar, dull.

He sighed. "I never thought I'd be telling you any of this."

She gave a gentle, reassuring laugh. "That's what friends are for."

He smiled, grateful. "Thank you."

They walked on, the Hudson stretching out beside them, ever more placid on the surface, the currents gaining strength underneath.

As the cold wind blew, Vaughn looked ahead. Her steps were unhurried, her face calm.

It had taken her more than a minute to pack away the pain. To flatten it back into the lockbox where she kept old griefs. More than a minute to reach that cool, calm equilibrium she so valued.

But reach it she did.

She now had everything she needed.

6

On Saturday, the day of the Davenport dinner, Vaughn picked up Grayson's rented tuxedo and delivered it to his apartment. Then she returned home. Now, she moved through her place with quiet efficiency, setting things in place for the evening ahead.

Her dress, a silk of deep burgundy, hung smoothly on its hanger, headband, pearls and gloves laid out beside it. A list of last-minute errands was on the table, the ink still fresh.

She glanced at the clock. Plenty of time. She'd never been one to rush. Everything would be in order.

She would make sure of it.

She retrieved her coat, grabbed her list and started out, walking with purpose but no urgency. The evening air was bracing. New York pulsed with its usual energy. For once, she felt safe. No dread. Nothing.

Later, she would know better—that the absence of unease was itself the warning.

But that came later.

For the moment, she was in fine spirits, just zipping along, taking care of one errand after the other. She stopped first at a small grocer's on Seventh Avenue. Exchanged brief pleasantries with the owner and picked up a few household essentials—a new tin of coffee, a small bundle of fresh herbs. Nothing unusual. Nothing out of place.

Second stop: a pharmacy. She spoke briefly to the pharmacist, placed a request for a tincture. By the time she left, she'd purchased the bottle of bitters, along with several strands of cherry licorice (her favorite sweet) and a jar of Josephine Baker's Bakerfix for her hair.

Back in her apartment, she set the groceries on the kitchen counter, then went to get dressed.

She had already mentally mapped the evening's events.

The guest list was predictable. The dinner would begin promptly at eight. Drinks would be served immediately upon arrival. (People like Davenport always had stores of alcohol, all supposedly purchased before Prohibition took over.) And Grayson would drink. Of course he would. He always did at these gatherings. There would be dinner. Lots of rich food. He would overeat. And then, with his delicate stomach...

She sighed. As for herself, she would be poised, observant and—as always—protective.

She applied the Bakerfix, slicked down her Eton crop till it gleamed, worked those curls pasted to the forehead and cheek until they formed perfect semicircles. She did her makeup, just a touch, enough to honor the evening.

Then it was time to dress. She slipped the dress over her head, loving the feel of it as it flowed down her body. Smoother, in some ways more intimate, than a lover's touch. She drew on the silken gloves, fastened the delicate pearl buttons, admired their sheen in the bedroom light.

She checked her reflection. Josephine Baker's signature hairstyle. How did it look on her? The short sleek do *was* a bit daring. So was the dress, with its beaded pearls and subtle shimmer. But she'd decided to do something different tonight. Be someone else, if only for a while.

She met her own gaze in the mirror. Held it.

She was composed.

Ready.

Margery Davenport was all pale elegance and precision, with the kind of face that had never stood in a breadline or weathered a hard wind. Fine-boned, immaculate, carrying her refinement like a rule no one else had been taught. Her hair was a shiny jet black and set hard into place, her lipstick a dark, rich red against an ivory complexion.

Her eyes, large and a deep dark blue, missed nothing. Wherever she sat, the chair became a throne, her cigarette holder a scepter. One brow arched. Conversation thinned. People paid attention. And when she smiled—always on the right, never by accident—it meant she had already decided how matters would end.

Her party was in full swing by the time Vaughn and Grayson arrived. Davenport greeted them with polished warmth and swept them into an elegant tour of the elegant rooms of her elegant Fifth Avenue mansion. It was all marble and velvet, a showcase of wealth and quiet power, calculated down to the very last brick.

Even the air was rich. Smoke from Turkish cigarettes and Cuban cigars coiled through a cloud of Chanel No. 5, bourbon, and the sharp tang of gin. Lots of bad jokes and polite laughter; the ruder the joke, the harder the laugh. Slow, honeyed notes of a jazz piano slipped between conversations. Smooth enough not to draw attention. The player was tucked away somewhere—heard but not seen.

It was an exquisite affair, as expected. The widow Davenport was a well-known patron of the arts. Her fortune had built galleries, funded exhibitions and financed more than a few struggling poets and painters. This gathering, like all of hers, was a bringing together of old money and new genius—established intellectuals rubbing elbows with up-and-coming artists, downtown patrons exchanging knowing glances as they checked out the brilliance of uptown's brightest minds.

Langston Hughes was deep in conversation with Zora Neale Hurston near the fireplace. Augusta Savage, nearby, chatted with a journalist from *The Crisis* about her latest sculpture. Across the room, a trio of young painters argued over whether Aaron Douglas's latest mural was too political for its own good.

Vaughn stayed close to Grayson, watching as he accepted handshakes and greetings. His usual grace was intact—but something was off. His posture was too rigid, his smile fixed, eyes wary.

Then she saw why.

Across the room, Everett Carlisle was watching him.

What was he *doing here?*

It wasn't as if he was looking for a patron. Had Davenport actually invited him? Or had he crashed the party—Davenport too polite to show him the door?

The next two hours progressed peacefully enough—the conversation was civil, the atmosphere pleasant. But Vaughn remained on edge. Carlisle's gaze tracked Grayson's every move. Politeness, like a lid on a slow-boiling pot, could only contain trouble for so long. At some point, it was bound to boil over.

And it did.

It started, predictably, with a discussion of art—a natural

occurrence at a gathering where patrons and artists met in a careful dance of opportunity and obligation.

Jean Duval, an up-and-coming painter popular with white collectors, had been speaking about his latest commission. The project had received mixed reviews. Some praised it as progress; others damned it as pandering.

"You can't have it both ways."

Carlisle's voice, loud and strident, cut across the room. Heads turned.

All but Grayson's. He was standing nearby, his back to Carlisle, and chatting with Vaughn and Jessie Fauset. At the sound of Carlisle's voice, Grayson audibly sighed. Vaughn caught his eye, gave a subtle nod toward the door. They both knew what was coming, the trouble on the way. But Grayson wouldn't run. It would seem cowardly. She knew it. So did Fauset, who raised an eyebrow but said nothing.

"Victor." Carlisle's voice found Grayson, heavy as a thrown stone. The professor stiffened but didn't turn around. The room fell still.

"I say, Victor. Yoo-hoo! *Please*. You're the wise one here, the great philosopher. So perhaps you can explain to us mere mortals the solution to a perplexing contradiction." Carlisle lifted his gin glass in mock salute. "How free can a man be when he's bought and paid for?"

Grayson closed his eyes, clenched his jaw, but still didn't turn around.

Carlisle, however, refused to be ignored. "C'mon, man. C'mon. Share your wisdom. You always say you support artistic freedom. Freedom from white approval. Freedom from political agenda. Freedom from the cause itself." He raised his arms and swept the room from right to left. "But then, in the next breath, you're all for white folks throwing money at our artists."

Grayson gave in. He turned, an Old Fashioned in one hand,

the other hand shoved deep into his pocket. Vaughn flashed on two gunslingers squaring off.

"I don't dispute the danger," Grayson said. "But a man's got to live. He's got to eat. Pay his bills."

Carlisle swayed slightly. His smile was cold. "Is that what it is now? Living?" He looked around the room, daring someone to challenge him. "All this compromise—this polite bowing and scraping—you call that freedom?"

Across the room, Davenport's gaze sharpened.

"So, you think," Grayson said, "that our artists should refuse a commission if it's—?"

"I think," Carlisle said, voice rising, "that if Mr. Charlie or Miss Anne"—here, with a drunken but courtly nod toward Davenport—"is dictating what we create, then it isn't freedom. It most certainly isn't art. It's mere..." He hiccuped. "Advertising."

He looked around. He was standing in a room full of the very people he was savaging. Yet he apparently expected them to agree with him. None did.

"C'mon, people. Be honest. Whose message do you think this one is delivering?" He pointed to Duval. "His own? Or that of the man paying him?" He jerked his thumb at the silver-haired, obviously wealthy man standing nearby.

Duval opened his mouth, but Davenport appeared at his side and hushed him with a stage whisper. "Better not."

Duval hesitated, unsure.

She patted him on the shoulder. "Just let them slug it out, dear. Trust me. This has nothing to do with you."

Vaughn heard them. By the look on their faces, everyone else had, too. Everyone but Carlisle, apparently.

He stood center stage, glass in hand, jabbing a belligerent finger at Grayson.

"You're the one who says we need to be free—to create without white hands shaping our work. Yet you defend this?

Selling our souls one painting at a time?" His words were slurred.

Grayson shook his head. Less the gunslinger now, more the weary professor dealing with a recalcitrant student. "You're confusing survival with surrender. They're not the same."

Carlisle laughed, the sound bitter. "You tell yourself that. Helps you sleep at night, I suppose."

Grayson's fingers tightened around his glass. "This isn't the place."

"Of course, you'd say that." Carlisle gave a sullen little smile. "Not the place. Not the time." His eyes flashed with anger. "It never is, with you."

The guests shifted uneasily. Davenport said nothing, but the look she threw Carlisle could have cut glass.

Carlisle abruptly laughed, tossing off the moment like a man who didn't care what he'd broken. "Ah, but why spoil a lovely evening with ethics?" He turned to their hostess with a dazzling smile. "Margery, darling, I do hope you have something stronger than gin."

The conversation resumed, but the mood had curdled.

Grayson looked pale, shaken. Vaughn wanted to go to him, but he held her off with a small shake of the head. Then he found a table, took one long swallow of his drink, then another —fast, like he needed it—and set his glass down. Carefully. Deliberately. He gave Vaughn a slight, tired wave—just a curl of his fingers—before he turned and headed toward the rear garden. Vaughn started after him, but Fauset caught her arm.

"Let him go. He's grown. He can handle this on his own."

Vaughn gave a worried frown. "Yes, but perhaps I can—"

"Jessie's right, dear." Davenport slipped in beside them. "Let him be."

Vaughn was outgunned. She forced a small, reluctant smile. "Fine."

Fauset roped her arm through Vaughn's and steered her

toward the powder room. "Let's freshen up a bit." She gave Vaughn's Eton crop an approving look. "Suits you. I thought about it myself, but I don't have the head for it."

She drifted into cheerful chatter. Vaughn let herself be drawn along, but her mind stayed on Grayson.

She glanced back once. Davenport hadn't moved and she, too, was following the professor with her eyes.

Grayson seemed oddly quiet for the rest of the evening. Withdrawn. Preoccupied. Barely able to keep up his end of the conversation. A quiet fatigue blunted his usual acuity.

Finally, he sagged down onto a chair and asked for a glass of water. Vaughn fetched it, but he had trouble holding it—had to grip it with both hands. After two sips, he passed it back to her.

Then he held his hands out, staring at them. "I can't—" His voice was a hoarse whisper. "My hands. I can't feel them."

Vaughn moved closer, peering at him. "Professor?"

He swallowed hard. "Really. It's nothing. I—" He gasped and lurched forward, clutching his chest.

"Oh, dear Lord, Professor Grayson—"

"It's okay. Really." He tried for a smile, but it twisted into a grimace. He closed his eyes, sucking in air and when he opened them again, fine beads of sweat shone on his forehead.

Vaughn produced a handkerchief, bent close and dabbed them away. "I really think—"

"It's nothing. Just a little heartburn. No offense to the cook, but I think those oysters did me in."

But his breathing was shallow, his color gray.

He murmured something about needing to use the facilities and made a move to rise. But when he stood, his legs buckled and he dropped back down.

"Professor?"

With visible effort, he tried again, pushing himself upright. Vaughn stepped forward to help, but he raised a hand to ward her off. A mistake. His balance faltered. He caught himself against the back of a chair, fingers digging into the wood.

Someone called his name. "Is he all right?"

Carlisle, she thought. It must've been clear—painfully clear—to everyone that Grayson was ill. Yet it was Carlisle, despite all the cruel things he'd said earlier, who called out, expressed concern. The only one who did.

She noted the irony and glanced over her shoulder. The room was too warm, too close, too full of eyes. She had to get Grayson out of here now. Before Carlisle—or someone else—stepped in.

Her focus narrowed to the man she had loved for twenty-five years. His lips were pale, his breath shallow. Yes, it was getting bad.

She heard movement behind her—someone approaching. She didn't turn. If it was Carlisle, she didn't want to encourage him. Let him stand there—and watch. He didn't have the right to do more than that. Whatever he felt—remorse, worry, guilt—it didn't matter. She was the one here. The one Grayson needed. She wasn't about to let Carlisle cause confusion—not now. Not when every second counted.

Grayson swayed again.

Her hand steadied him. "I'll take you home."

"No, I-I'm fine. Just give me a moment."

She knew that tone. Not pride, but modesty. That old reluctance to cause trouble. It was, in general, an endearing quality. But this was not the time for it.

They needed to go.

Suddenly, he pitched forward. For a second, it seemed he might be sick. His throat worked as he swallowed hard, forcing it down. Eyes closed, breathing ragged, he fought for control.

After several long seconds, he straightened. Drew himself up. His hand stayed on the chair for support.

Just in case.

He'd conquered it, whatever it was. But for how long? His breathing was labored, his face pasty. Something was clearly wrong.

"Professor?"

He looked at her. Nodded faintly, murmured. "All right. Thank you, Bea."

She gave a reassuring smile and slipped her arm through his. "Of course."

And together, they left, Vaughn guiding him through the crowd, proud to let the others see how much he needed her.

7

The cab ride home was mostly silent. Every now and then, Grayson let out a raspy breath. Vaughn sat beside him, one gloved hand on his shoulder, the other resting on his forearm.

Streetlights threw haunting shadows across his face—his features drawn with pain, his hand pressed to his gut. Despite the cool air, sweat slicked his forehead.

Still, he insisted he was fine.

At his building, he waved off the driver's help and forced himself upright, steady, in control. But he struggled to make it those few steps to the door. Vaughn had never liked the fact that he'd sublet a street-level apartment—too exposed to busybodies peering in—but now she was grateful for it. In the state he was in, she never could've gotten him up the stairs alone. And now, with the cabbie gone, there was no one to help.

She put his arm around her shoulders, got him inside the building and managed to half-drag him across the lobby. At the apartment, she had to have him lean against the door frame while she fumbled for the key. When the lock gave, she again tried to help him. But he braced himself a second longer, then shoved off and stumbled inside.

One hand around his shoulder, the other under his elbow, she steered him to the living room armchair. He dropped down heavily, gripping the armrests, breathing hard.

Vaughn slowly peeled off her gloves and set them on the desk. She took in the unnatural tightness in his jaw, the slight tremor in his hands. "You should've let me take you to the hospital."

Grayson let out a weak laugh, shaking his head. "No. I've caused enough trouble."

"Oh, Victor," she said. "You've never been any trouble."

He closed his eyes for a moment, then leaned his head back, lips parted for air.

She started for the hall telephone. "You need a doctor."

Grayson barely heard her. He clutched his stomach, his fingers trembling. "Oh, God."

Vaughn froze, her face fixed in a mask of worry.

He grimaced. Then he opened his eyes and looked at her apologetically. "Sorry. I didn't mean to ruin your evening. It was just me being greedy." He closed his eyes again against the pain. "Those damn oysters. They were so good. But I should've known better. My stomach never could tolerate them." His voice was weaker now, looser. And his eyes were bloodshot.

She hurried to the bathroom. Ran a cloth under cold water. She was only gone a few seconds, but he was practically unconscious by the time she got back. His eyes were closed, the rise and fall of his chest so shallow she could barely see it.

She pressed the cloth against his forehead. And he let her. He was too weak to resist. For twenty-five years, he had kept her at arm's length. Now he had no choice. He had to rely on her.

"You need water," she said, rising.

"No." Grayson's head lolled to one side. "I... I just need to rest."

His breathing faltered—stopped. She stared at him. Then, suddenly, his chest heaved upward in a desperate, ragged gasp. For a second he looked like a man drowning, struggling in a sea of air. Then his body sagged. His breath rattled out in a broken groan. His eyes opened—clouded now, unfocused.

That was when she saw it. The moment he understood. The moment he knew.

Her heart thudded, her throat tightened—but she forced herself to stay calm.

Her professor. He was dying.

She fell back a step, overwhelmed by the grim reality of it. All the years they'd spent together collapsed into a blinding flash of memory. All that time. Gone by. So fast. And now—

"Bea." He beckoned weakly with one hand. "Come. Please."

She hesitated, then sank down by his side.

Grayson's fingers grasped at hers, the grip faltering. "I'm s-sorry."

Her gaze went over him, taking in every beloved feature. "For what?"

"For taking you for granted. For… keeping you from the life you deserve."

She shook her head, smiling softly. "Oh, Victor. I never felt that way."

"I know." His lips twitched into a smile, small and sad. "And for that, I thank you. For putting up with me. For…everything."

She laid her hand over his. "Don't talk like that. Just rest."

But his eyes, clouded though they were, held something deeper.

Finality.

"Promise me something," he whispered.

"Anything."

For a moment, that old hope resurfaced. Was he finally going to see it? Would this be the moment he'd realize—?

His hand tightened weakly around hers. "Tell Carlisle I'm

sorry. For everything." His voice was barely a breath. "I was wrong. So. Wrong."

Her heart broke.

He still didn't know.

And now, he never would.

Twenty-five years. And his last conscious thoughts were of *him*.

Vaughn swallowed hard and hushed him gently. "Don't worry about that. Rest now."

But he wouldn't let it go. "Promise."

She nodded. "Of course. Now, please. Rest."

He gave a faint nod. Closed his eyes.

His fingers slackened in hers.

She sat there for a long moment, studying him. Overworked. A weak heart. And now this. He wouldn't last long if she didn't act—and act soon.

She laid his hand at his side, then rose and crossed to the hall telephone. After placing her call, she moved quickly to his desk, unlocked the top right drawer and reached inside.

The note.

She flipped it open to confirm it was the right one, saw the C. *Carlisle*. He'd caused her professor so much pain. Threatened him. Humiliated him. He would pay for that. She would see to it.

She slipped the note into her pocket, returned to Grayson's side, and sank down beside him once more. His breathing was ragged now.

"Don't worry. The ambulance will be here soon."

She reached up and stroked his cheek—the first and only time she'd ever dared to touch him so intimately. His eyelids fluttered, but there was no other sign he was aware of her presence, much less of her caress.

She straightened his bowtie. Smoothed his lapel. Her fingers, moving deftly, slipped inside his inner jacket pocket.

A final adjustment. A final pat.

A final goodbye.

Vaughn sat with her hands folded in her lap, spine rigid, expression composed. Harlem Hospital's waiting room stretched wide around her, too large, too quiet. The air smelled faintly of old bleach and iron. High ceilings loomed overhead, their edges lost in shadow. Amber pendant lamps hung from long brass chains, casting small, warm pools of light on the mosaic tile floor, but leaving the corners of the room in dusk.

The benches were polished wood, dark and gleaming, hard under her hands. Tall windows lined the far wall, black and bottomless, framing the night outside like gaping mouths. She could feel the pull of them if she looked too long. A sense that if she stared too deep, she might fall straight through, vanish into the dark.

Only the clock marked the silence. It was a heavy-faced device with bold black numerals. Its minute hand jerked forward at uneven intervals with a sharp nerve-grating click. Time didn't flow here—it lurched. Dragging her with it.

Little more than an hour ago, she'd been surrounded by light, warmth, laughter. Now she sat alone amid shadows, in this chilly silent space. Left to wait, to contend with a sense of inevitability.

Footsteps on tile. The soft creak of leather soles.

She looked up. A man in a long white coat approached her. Dignified, early fifties, thin, with wire-rimmed glasses flashing under the lamps. His name, Gerard, was stitched on his chest pocket.

"Miss Vaughn?"

Her fingers closed around her purse so tightly the frame bit into her palm. She saw his lips move, but his words seemed to come from far away.

"I'm sorry. Professor Grayson is gone."

A breath. A pause.

"It's really… over?"

Gerard nodded once.

Vaughn blinked, hard. She had known. Of course she had. And yet some stubborn part of her had still been waiting. Still listening for some other verdict.

Lyrics reached down through the years, carried by her mother's voice.

"What am I gonna do with all that love now?

"What am I gonna do?"

Her mama used to hum that song, washing dishes late at night.

"Gonna put it in that box where it belongs.

"That's what I'm gonna do.

"Back in the dark where it belongs.

"That's what I'm gonna do.

"And make sure it don't never leave no more.

"That's what I gotta do."

That voice came back now—quiet, worn, and right on time.

She sat a moment longer. Remembering. Thinking.

Then she closed her eyes and pushed those old spirits away.

She had to live in the present. Accept it.

Her professor was gone.

But the permanence of it was too much, too overwhelming. Her mind shrank back from it, groped for something solid. Funeral arrangements to make. Letters to write. Practicalities she could control. No relatives to deal with. Logistically, it would be simple.

"I'll take the body," she said. "See to it personally."

Gerard looked taken aback. Maybe he didn't understand that practicality was her shield.

Then again, maybe he did.

A shadow of sympathy crossed his face. As if he sought words to comfort her but knew from experience how useless such words would be.

Instead, after a moment's hesitation, he shifted his stance. Glanced toward the door.

"We can't release the body. Not yet."

A slow blink. A frown. "Why not?"

"There are…questions."

The clock jerked forward again. *Click.*

She frowned deeper. "Questions?"

"Yes." He adjusted his glasses, a small weary motion. "I've already called the police."

The words jolted her. She stared at him, uncomprehending.

"The *police*?"

"Yes."

Her voice came out quieter now. "Why?"

Gerard pinched the bridge of his nose, closed his eyes and took a slow breath. "When he was brought in, we assumed it was heart failure. But…" He shook his head. "Something isn't right."

She blinked. The waiting room stretched wider, colder.

"What do you mean?"

He hesitated. A longer pause this time. Then: "His skin showed an abnormal mottling. And his fingernails—"

"What about them?"

"There are faint striations under them. That's inconsistent with a typical cardiac event."

Inconsistent with. She couldn't believe what she was hearing. He couldn't possibly be implying—No. *No! NO!* This was all wrong. It couldn't be. It was—

"Are you sure?"

His careworn eyes regarded her with concern. "He had no history of heart trouble. None. I spoke to his doctor in D.C.

Woke the man up from a sound sleep. He told me Professor Grayson had the heart of a healthy man half his age."

She stared at him.

"I'm sorry," he said. "But his symptoms don't fit."

Vaughn felt herself telescoping away, suddenly dizzy. She gripped the bench with one hand and shook her head, as if to clear it. But the heavy lamps above swayed in her vision.

"B-but what does this mean?" A realization hit her. A thought, sharp and unwelcome. "Does this mean an *autopsy*?"

"I'm afraid so."

The very thought of anyone cutting up her professor, slicing him open like that… It sickened her.

She pressed her purse tighter against her knees, struggling for something—anything—to argue.

"But that's so unnecessary. He went to a dinner party tonight. He'd been drinking. Maybe it was too much. He even said the oysters didn't agree with him."

Gerard frowned. "That may be. But if it was alcohol—or food-related poisoning—then that's all the more reason for us to investigate. However…" He paused and the words came heavier. "Given the symptoms, we suspect it was neither."

Silence fell again. Thick. Absolute.

The clock jerked forward. *Click.*

Gerard met her gaze. Steadier now. Final. "We're treating it as possibly suspicious."

Vaughn forgot how to breathe. Her nails dug into the wood of the bench. She was sitting, but it didn't matter—the room still tilted. The black windows across from her yawned wider.

Possibly suspicious.

Not a stroke. Not a heart attack.

But something intentional.

She willed herself to think clearly.

Her professor would've wanted to go out peacefully. No fuss. No muss. Unfortunately, it hadn't quite happened that way. Not with this doctor turning what should've been a quiet passing into something more. Something darker. But if that's how it had to be, so be it.

They would still blame Carlisle.

Blame him if it was a heart attack. Blame him if it was something worse. Either way, he would soon stand in the line of fire. She would make sure of it.

The waiting room door creaked open.

Vaughn turned sharply. A man's shadow stretched across the mosaic floor ahead of him—long, dark, reaching.

Then he stepped into the light and filled the space. Everything else shrank.

A professional. In a trench coat over a business suit. Visiting a hospital waiting room. This late at night. Sharp eyes—eyes that swept the room like spotlights on a manhunt. Eyes so deep-set and cutting that when they locked on her, Vaughn felt their impact.

A cop. But not just any cop.

A detective.

A man who had come looking for something.

No. Some*one*.

8

He was tall. Not towering. But with the kind of posture that made people look twice. Broad-shouldered, hat in hand. A man who didn't need to speak to be heard.

She'd seen plenty of men like him growing up. Men who belonged wherever they chose to stand. Mostly cruel. Corrupt. Who didn't follow the evidence. Who decided a man's guilt, then twisted the evidence to prove it.

But this one—

This one was different.

For one thing, his skin was damn near as dark as hers.

A colored cop.

Nathaniel Redding. The first Negro detective sergeant in New York City. A man who had climbed the ranks in a force that had no intention of making room for men like him.

Only last month, the *Harlem Chronicle* had run his photo and a piece on him. Sung his praises. Said he was *"a man as feared as much as he's liked."* Seeing him in person, she didn't doubt it.

The article might've been right. But that photo? It hadn't done him justice.

His face was all angles. A strong jaw. High cheekbones.

Heavy, arched brows. A nose straight as judgment. Full lips, firmly set. Nothing about him invited familiarity. Everything about him commanded attention.

Vaughn met his gaze. She sensed the sharp intelligence, the quiet calculation. This was a man who'd made a career out of stepping through other people's carefully constructed lies.

The fog cleared—fast. Her mind moved. Making connections. Going back over what she knew, the way Carlisle had attacked Grayson—first at the magazine, then at Davenport's house.

If this was going to be considered a murder, then the detective would be looking for a motive—and a killer.

She would help him find both.

Gerard excused himself and walked over to Redding. The two men conferred, Gerard glancing her way now and then. Finally, Gerard left and Redding started toward her.

"Miss Vaughn." He introduced himself.

She nodded. Once. "Detective."

He sat down across from her. "My condolences on the death of Professor Grayson. I'm just here as a matter of procedure."

"Are you saying the police are always called in when..."

He smiled briefly. "When the cause of death is questioned, yes. But nine times out of ten it amounts to nothing."

"I see."

"I understand you were with Professor Grayson when he fell ill."

"Yes."

"Tell me what led up to it. Were you out? At home?"

"We were at a dinner party. A gathering at Mrs. Davenport's—"

"Margery Davenport?"

She watched him make a mental note. What would he take from it? That the kind of people—the very fine, refined people

—Davenport had at her house didn't poison one another? Or that if one of them did, he'd better not look too close?

He nodded for her to go on.

She took her time. Went into her purse for a handkerchief. Dabbed at her eyes—not because she needed to. Her eyes were dry. She felt numb. Frozen. That's the way she'd always reacted to shock, to loss. Sometimes, she wished she could cry. But she couldn't. The greater the pain, the deeper the grief, the colder she became.

Never let 'em see you cry. That's what her mama had told her, right before she closed her eyes and died.

But Vaughn knew that sometimes it paid to do just that, to let them see you cry—or think they did. Like now.

"He was fine when we arrived, but sometime after dinner, he started feeling sick. Tired. Dizzy." She hesitated, dabbed again. "Actually, it might've started during dinner. He seemed a little shaky even then."

"Explain."

"Well...he had this...tremor." She held up her right hand.

Redding said nothing. But she knew he was storing it away. It struck her that he carried no notepad. He didn't need one. The article had mentioned that, had said his mind was like a camera. And right now, his eyes never left her face. Every word. Every twitch. Every glance. He was recording it all, filing it away, frame by frame.

Vaughn clenched her handkerchief, balled it up. "Later, he looked like he had a stomach ache, you know? I suggested he let me take him home. He insisted he was fine, but when he stood —" A small, almost imperceptible shake of the head. "It was clear he wasn't."

She described Grayson's symptoms—the paleness, dizziness and delirium, much as she'd described them to Gerard. Redding didn't interrupt.

"We took a cab," she said. "By the time we reached his

apartment, he was worse. I begged him to let me bring him here, but he kept refusing. Thought it was something he ate. The oysters, maybe. He always had a weak stomach for shellfish."

"So, if he got ahold of something, it must've happened there, at the party."

She wasn't sure whether he was speaking to her or thinking aloud. "Yes, I-I guess so."

He reflected. "Professor Grayson had a lot of admirers. A lot of people who looked up to him."

"Yes. Yes, he did."

"But a man like that—he must've had a few enemies, too."

Vaughn's lips pressed together. She looked down at her handkerchief. "Yes. Mr. Carlisle. Mr. Everett Carlisle."

Carlisle had been ever present. Ever demanding. The man wanted his essay published—needed it published—and when he learned that Grayson wasn't going to oblige, he turned ugly. Vaughn had seen it coming. She'd warned Grayson. But as always, he'd insisted he could handle it.

He couldn't.

She told Redding about the argument at the magazine office. How it flared again at the party. How Carlisle had attacked Grayson—not with fists, but with words. Hard ones. "The things he said. They were…cruel."

"Did other people hear this argument?"

"Oh, yes. It was in front of everybody."

Redding's dark eyes narrowed. "Do you think Mr. Carlisle was angry enough to want to harm Professor Grayson?"

Vaughn hesitated. Then, a soft, almost regretful, "I don't know."

Redding hit her with a gaze that made most people squirm. Not Vaughn. Her eyes remained wide and hollow with grief. The look of someone devastated by loss. Someone with nothing to hide.

Redding gave a small nod, as if he'd satisfied some question.

"This man, Carlisle. How long had he and the professor known each other?"

Vaughn folded her hands in her lap. "Since their college days."

"What college?"

"McAllister. They were students together."

Redding nodded slowly, turning that over. "Old friends, then."

"Old *acquaintances*." A small correction, but pointed. "They were close once, I believe. But that was a very long time ago."

"What came between them?"

Vaughn looked down. "I really couldn't say."

The answer came too quickly and too neatly.

But Redding let it stand.

He reached into his coat pocket and withdrew an envelope. He checked the contents, then held it out for her to see.

The note.

Vaughn did not blink.

"This was found in Professor Grayson's pocket." He unfolded it for her to read.

She looked it over, frowned. "I've never seen it before. What is it?"

Redding tilted his head. "It's somewhat threatening, don't you think? And that initial C at the bottom."

"Yes, I-I'd agree. It does seem to be—"

"Did you ever have the sense the professor was being blackmailed?"

"No." She shook her head, quick.

"That someone was threatening him? Or that he had a secret he'd pay to keep?"

"No, *no!* Of course, not! Professor Grayson was a most respectable man. Men like him, they…"

"They what, Miss Vaughn?"

Her fingers worked the handkerchief in her lap. She hadn't noticed how tightly she was gripping it.

"Well. They do have secrets. But they're respectable ones. Like…he enjoyed a glass of rye now and then—as many fine men do."

Redding's gaze dwelled on her. She had the feeling he was looking right through her. But all he said was, "I see."

He folded the note, tucked it away. "I appreciate your time, Miss Vaughn. And I'm sorry—genuinely sorry—for your loss."

She gave a small, sad smile. "Thank you."

"You'll stay in town?"

The way he said it, so easy-like, it could've been a question. But she knew it wasn't.

"Of course."

He put on his hat. Tipped it once. Walked away. Footsteps slow. Deliberate.

Vaughn watched him go. She was alone now, with nothing left but grief and rage, anger and loss. The thought settled in her chest, heavier than expected.

Her professor was gone. And one man was clearly to blame.

Everett Carlisle. He'd haunted—*hunted*—her professor. Relentlessly. Remorselessly. Clung to him like a curse. Threatened his reputation, his very future. All for what? Pride? Possession? Spite?

Selfish. Reckless. Destructive.

Well, her professor was beyond his reach now. But Carlisle? He was within hers. And she'd make damn sure he was hunted just as mercilessly as he'd pursued the man she loved.

If she played her cards right, that detective—Redding—would help her. She'd planted the seed, pointed him where she wanted him to look. He was sharp. He'd find what she meant for him to find.

And if he didn't, she'd make sure he did.

She was so lost in thought, she didn't notice Redding

hesitate at the door, then turn back. Didn't register his presence until he stood near enough to cast a shadow over her.

Her heart kicked.

"It's late," he said. "Nearly one in the morning. Let me take you home."

She blinked. "That's not necessary."

"Maybe not." He tipped his hat back. "But it is common courtesy. Common sense."

She hesitated. Her thoughts pulled in two directions. Accept and risk more time under his scrutiny. Refuse and face those godforsaken streets alone.

She folded her handkerchief. Pulled on her gloves. Buttoned them at the wrists. "I appreciate it, Detective." A pause. "Just this once."

Redding nodded as if he'd expected nothing less. Then he shifted slightly. Yawned—a slow, lazy stretch of jaw and breath.

Vaughn noted it with faint disdain. How he didn't even bother to cover his mouth. Where were his manners? Well, that certainly knocked some of the polish off his shine.

He pushed open the door, held it for her. She stepped around him like a woman walking past a grave.

Shoulders squared. Spine straight.

Her grief wrapped in steel.

Just this once.

PART II

CARLISLE

9

The knock came hard, steady. *Bam! Bam! Bam!* Everett Carlisle stirred, disoriented, the pounding in his skull syncing with the sound at the door. He groaned, rolled onto his side, and pulled the pillow over his head. The knocking didn't stop. Just got louder. More demanding.

What the hell?

He glanced at the clock on the dresser. Who the hell would have the nerve to be knocking on his damn door this early on a Sunday morning?

Had to be the landlord. Bitching about the rent. Two weeks overdue. Well, hell's bells, he'd already told him he'd have it next week—when *Commonwealth Review* paid him for the article.

Oh, yeah. It came rushing back to him. He wouldn't be getting a dime because that sonuvabitch had rejected the piece.

Bam! Bam! Bam!

He opened his eyes with a sigh, forced himself upright, eyes heavy, mouth dry from last night's liquor. He stunk, his room stunk, of stale smoke, cold sweat and dirty laundry. He swung his legs over the side of the bed, planted his feet on the cold wood floor, scrubbed a hand down his face.

Bam! Bam! Ba—

"All right! All right! I'm coming, damn it. *I'm coming!*"

Whoever the fuck it was, he was gonna give 'em a piece of his goddamn mind.

He pushed himself to his feet, shuffled across the room and yanked the door open. His mouth was already open, curse half-formed. But the angry words died on his lips.

"Who the fuck are you?"

A stranger stood in his doorway. Well-built, well-groomed, shoulders filling out what looked like a helluva nice overcoat.

Carlisle knew clothes. Even groggy, he could peg quality and price. That suit wasn't rich-man flash—it was professional. Purposeful.

So. Not from that cheap-ass landlord.

Still. Nice rags didn't give this mutherfucker the right to be banging on his damn door this early in the morning.

Before he could ask again, the stranger gave a name. Showed a badge. A detective's badge.

Carlisle blinked. A cop? And a *colored* one at that? And did he say, *Homicide?*

Redding stepped inside. No hesitation. No invitation. Carlisle let the door hang open a moment before shutting it.

The detective slow-rolled through the room like he owned it. Quiet steps, shoulders square, back straight as a firing line. Not swagger, exactly. Something older. More trained.

A soldier once, Carlisle thought. Still carried himself like one.

And unhurried. Taking his time.

Redding took in everything—the books stacked high, the empty glass on the nightstand, the typewriter, manuscripts, overflowing ashtray on the desk. Carlisle tensed as Redding moved to the bookcase, pulled a slim volume free, flipped it open. French poetry.

Carlisle folded his arms. "You make a habit of walking into people's rooms and reading their books?"

Redding read, closed the book, placed it back. He moved to the dresser, picked up a small framed photograph. Carlisle and another man, cheek-to-cheek at a Parisian café. Dainty. Intimate. Next to it, another photo. This one of Carlisle alone, in costume for a drag ball. Lipstick faint in the black-and-white print.

Redding's face gave nothing away as he placed it back.

Then—finally—he turned, and Carlisle felt himself pinned under the cop's gaze. A flush of heat crept up his neck. He knew how he looked, like a bum: the ripped stocking cap, the stained undershirt, the twisted suspenders he hadn't bothered to straighten.

"Rough night, Mr. Carlisle?"

"Better than some. No worse than others."

Carlisle padded across the room to his desk. He grabbed a battered silver cigarette case—dented, scratched, just holding together. Like him. He pulled a cigarillo free, tapped it against the wood desk. "So, tell me, who died?"

"Did I say someone had died?"

"You said you were from homicide."

"Grayson. Professor Victor Grayson."

Carlisle went still. Stared at Redding. Then his eyes edged away. He flicked open his lighter, brought the flame to the tip, hands trembling. The cigarillo glowed as he inhaled. A long drag. Controlled. He let the smoke curl through his nostrils before releasing it into the stale air.

"Victor...dead." A verbal shrug. "Sorry to hear that."

"You seem awful calm for a man who just lost a friend."

"People die all the time, Detective."

"But you were friends."

"Were we?"

"You weren't?"

Carlisle's jaw worked. "Let's just say we had...history."

"Good? Bad? Indifferent?"

"Never…indifferent."

"When did you last see him?"

"Last night. At a party. But since you're here, I assume you know that. So you should also know that he left before I did. He didn't look well, but he was still very much alive."

"Let's not get ahead of ourselves. Tell me about the party."

Carlisle rolled the cigarillo between his fingers. "It was a party. People talked. Drank. Some of us danced, some of us argued. Some of us took full advantage of Madame's hospitality, went off somewhere and got fucked. Others, like me, just got piss-ass drunk."

He tilted his head. "What part do you want me to elaborate on?"

"I heard that you two argued."

A shrug. "Yeah, we had a difference of opinion. So what?"

"It wasn't the first time?"

"No. And it probably wouldn't have been the last, but…"

"But what?"

"Let's just say I'd hoped we'd reach an understanding."

"Did you?"

"I think so." He paused. "Then again, maybe not."

Redding waited.

Carlisle didn't fill the silence.

"What was this understanding about?"

"Nothing major. Just an item I'm writing for *Commonwealth Review.* Vic wanted edits. I agreed to make 'em." He gestured toward the typewriter. "Over there. See?"

Redding glanced at the desk where the article lay. Red marks bled across the original. The first page of a new version was rolled onto the typewriter spindle.

"Did he promise to accept it if you made the changes?"

"I don't know about your business, but nothing's ever promised in mine."

"Tell me about the argument you had at Davenport's."

"I didn't say we argued."

"The negotiations, then."

"What can I say? We had words."

"What exactly were these words?"

"Nothing you haven't heard already."

Carlisle held his gaze. The detective had nothing. He aimed to keep it that way.

Redding gave him a hard look. Then he brushed past Carlisle to the dresser and yanked open the top drawer. Carlisle straightened up, pulse quickening. The detective pulled out Carlisle's toiletry bag, rifled through it and threw it to the floor. Items spilled out and rolled across the floor. Redding grabbed a bottle of cologne from the dresser top, uncapped it with a sharp twist, held it to his nose, then tossed that down, too. It hit the floor hard but didn't break.

Carlisle wanted to rush over. To tell this damn cop to stop. But he knew better. His fingers tightened around the cigarillo, then loosened by force of will.

"What're you looking for? Maybe I can help."

Redding didn't glance up. "Poison."

A muscle jumped in Carlisle's cheek. He watched, silently fuming, but now also terrified, as Redding went through every drawer, pawing through Carlisle's meager wardrobe. He said nothing as the detective ransacked his closet, checked every pocket, even inside his shoes, sometimes tossing things to the floor, sometimes kicking them to one side.

Finally, it was too much.

"Stop!" Carlisle ran a hand over his head. He didn't have much. He couldn't stand to see what little he had treated that way. "Stop," he said more quietly. "Look, I haven't done anything. I certainly didn't kill him—if that's why you're here. I didn't even know—"

"You didn't even ask how he died—because you already knew."

"No!" Carlisle sagged. "It's because I didn't *want* to know." He gazed at Redding. "There's a difference. And you know it."

Redding's nostrils flared and Carlisle realized something he should've known all along—that the cop's cool exterior was merely a cover for a simmering intensity underneath.

Redding pulled something from his pocket. An envelope, crumpled. He removed the contents, a slip of folded paper. Opened it, held it up in front of Carlisle's face.

Carlisle's heart hammered. A lump jammed his throat. How'd this cop get his hands on this note? How'd he found it?

If you reveal my secret, then I'll reveal yours.—C.

"You recognize it?"

Carlisle forced himself to swallow. Flicked ash. Pretended disinterest. "Should I?"

"You tell me."

Carlisle took another drag. Exhaled slowly. "Never seen it before."

"Look again."

Carlisle forced himself to meet Redding's gaze. "Like I said, it's not mine. You need me to say it another way?"

"It was found in Grayson's pocket."

Carlisle felt sick. His head was pounding and his mouth felt dry. But he forced a smile. "Sounds like your problem, not mine."

Redding tapped a finger against the bottom of the note. "Let's talk about that C."

"You want a list of every person in Harlem with that initial?" Carlisle waved a lazy hand. "Countee Cullen, Charles Gilpin, Claude McKay, C. J. Walker. Hell, I think your own commissioner's name is Callahan, isn't it?" Outwardly calm, he smoked again, exhaled. "That all, Detective?"

Redding slid the note back into his pocket. "For now."

He left.

Carlisle stood there for a moment, a knot forming where his

stomach should be. Then he went back to his bed, dropped down, shoulders slumped. The mask of defiance fell away.

He pulled the bottle from under the bed. Hands shaking. Bottle straight to mouth. A swallow. He grimaced. Bootleg rye. Cheap. Raw. Nothing like Paris. Just another reminder of how far he'd fallen.

He gagged down several swift and necessary swallows. Wiped his mouth on the back of his hand.

That's when he heard them. Out in the hallway, footsteps. A heavy tread, uneven gait. Growing louder.

Carlisle didn't move.

10

Redding stood at the base of the Davenport house steps, staring up at its pristine facade. White stone, elegant lines—everything about it declared that its owner never had to worry about the world's uglier edges.

He climbed the steps, rapped twice with the brass knocker, and took out his badge to present it.

A white-haired brown-skinned butler opened the door. His eyes dipped to the badge, then to Redding's face, and he froze for a half-second. The butler's eyes said what his training wouldn't let him—that he was seeing something new in this old world: a Negro detective with a badge, standing at the front door like he belonged there. A flash of pride quickly masked. Lips pressed together to hide a smile. Then, the butler stepped back, opened the door wide and gave a small bow.

"Mrs. Davenport is expecting you."

He led Redding through a grand foyer lined with oil paintings. The butler's steps were silent on the polished marble. The house smelled of roses and cedar, of wealth lived in but never flaunted.

Redding was reluctantly impressed. Wealth without

ostentation. Elegance without clutter. The kind of money that didn't need to prove itself.

But what preoccupied him more was the woman behind it. Was she one of those rich people whose interest in his people's culture was merely a passing fancy? Or did she care, really care, about the artists she supported?

He'd asked around before coming. Heard she was controlling, that she had the best interests of her artists "at heart." But how far would that concern extend when she learned that one of her guests had been murdered, the method possibly administered right under her roof? Would she duck for cover or stand firm?

He'd been warned to treat her with all due respect—a warning both unnecessary and insulting. He'd accepted it without a murmur. Privately, he decided that nothing—neither her social standing nor her money—would keep him from finding the truth.

Margery Davenport stood by one of the bay windows in her drawing room, a cigarette in a long stiletto holder balanced between her slender fingers.

Redding made a quick assessment—knowing full well she was making one of her own. Davenport was no society ingenue. She was established. Her parties mattered. She knew how to orchestrate a scene, how to protect reputations, how to turn charm into a weapon and use it without leaving fingerprints. He figured she had a past—likely discreet, probably interesting. Women like her usually did. He put her in her late forties, maybe fifty at most. Old enough to know better. Still sharp enough to play the game.

Her expression was mildly curious—but not concerned. Maybe she'd dealt with law officers before. Maybe to intervene for some reckless artist caught with liquor or drugs, or in the wrong bed at the wrong time with the wrong person.

"Detective Redding," she said. Not surprised. Not rattled. But the wheels were turning behind her eyes.

"Mrs. Davenport."

She gestured toward the gleaming silver service set on a nearby table. "Can I offer you coffee?"

"No, ma'am."

She nodded once to the butler. He disappeared without a word. She sat down and gestured for Redding to do so, too. She poured herself a cup—hands steady, movements practiced. Controlled, but not quite relaxed.

Redding waited. She was bracing for the blow. He'd seen it before.

Finally, she turned. Still measuring. Still in control.

"All right. Who's in trouble this time? Goodness, I do hope no one's made a fool of themselves beyond repair."

"No, ma'am." He paused. "I'm here about Victor Grayson."

Her eyes widened, brow furrowed. The cup, raised halfway to her lips, stopped short. "Dr. Grayson?"

"Yes. I was told he attended a party here last night."

"Yes, yes, he did, but—" She set the cup down, studying his face. "Detective, what is this about?"

"How did he seem during the evening?"

"How did he seem?" She frowned. "Well, he was his usual charming self. Engaged in conversation, enjoyed the meal…" Her voice sharpened. "Has something happened to Victor?"

"Did you notice any change in his demeanor as the night went on?"

"Change?" She straightened. "Well, yes, actually. At some point, he became quite unwell. Pale, unsteady. His secretary had to help him leave—Detective, you're frightening me. What's happened?"

"Did he eat the same food as your other guests?"

"Of course he did. We all shared the same meal." Her

composure was fraying at the edges. "Please, tell me what this is about."

"Mrs. Davenport, I'm afraid Professor Grayson is dead."

She froze. Her face drained of color. When she spoke, her voice was barely above a whisper.

"Dead?" A pause. "Was it his heart? A stroke?"

"We're still determining the cause."

She absorbed this, her gaze distant for a moment. When she looked back at him, her eyes held genuine sorrow—but also sharp awareness. "Still determining… That's rather vague. What exactly does that mean?"

"It means we have questions about how he died. Did any of your other guests report feeling ill? Either during the party or afterward?"

Now her control wavered just slightly. A quick intake of breath. Her hand moved to her throat, then dropped.

"No. No, everyone else was fine."

She paused, studying him. "But you already know that, don't you?"

Redding said nothing.

Her eyes narrowed, mind working. "If no one else was ill…" A beat. " And it wasn't his heart or a stroke…"

Another beat.

"You think someone meant to harm him."

Still no answer.

Her voice dropped. "You think he was poisoned. On purpose."

She stared at him.

"And you think whoever did it was here. At my table."

"We're investigating all possibilities."

"But that's why you're here. Because you believe his death is connected to my gathering."

"I'm here because I need to understand what happened last night."

Her fingers drummed once against the arm of her chair. "Detective, you must understand—my gatherings attract a certain caliber of people. People who value discretion."

"People who value their reputations."

"Yes. And people with resources to defend them." Her voice carried steel beneath the silk. "I trust you appreciate the delicacy of the situation."

"Mrs. Davenport, a man is dead. Delicacy takes second place to justice."

"Of course. But surely you understand that accusations—even unfounded ones — could ruin innocent lives."

There it was. The velvet threat. He could've backed down. He didn't.

"Are you more concerned about finding a killer or protecting your social standing?"

Davenport's eyes widened. For a moment, she just looked at him.

Yes, ma'm. I said what I said.

She started to say something, then paused. Recalculating. Recalibrating. Finally she forced a little smile.

"I'm simply concerned about ensuring that whatever occurred is handled properly. With appropriate…care."

"Then help me understand what happened."

She pressed her lips together, clearly weighing her options. "What specifically do you need to know?"

"Start with who was here. What you observed. Anything unusual." It was an easy question, the kind Redding used for difficult interviews.

She answered promptly. "There were fifteen guests. Authors, artists, a few patrons. It was meant to be an intimate evening." She paused. "Though there was some…tension."

"What kind?"

"Artistic differences. The sort of spirited debate one expects at such gatherings."

"Debate? You mean polite disagreement—or going for the jugular?"

"It's rather brutal of you to put it that way."

"Then correct me."

Her fingers tightened almost imperceptibly around her cigarette holder. "Let's just say that one of my guests turned out to be...more provocative than expected."

"Mrs. Davenport."

She crossed one leg over the other. Took another draw from her cigarette.

Redding waited.

She said, finally, "Detective, I've hosted dozens of dinners. Writers, musicians, politicians—they thrive on performance. On being heard. Sometimes they go too far. But that doesn't mean they mean harm."

"I'm not interested in their intentions. I'm interested in what happened."

Her gaze sharpened. "And if I say nothing?"

"Then I'll keep asking until I find someone who will."

A long silence.

"Very well." She exhaled, the smoke rising in a delicate plume. "But I expect discretion. These are private matters involving private people."

"That depends on what you tell me."

She had a poker face. But he would've bet she was calculating the odds. People in her situation always did. Then, with a faint sigh, she settled back, drew a breath—and began.

Dinner had been splendid. Rich. Indulgent. Five courses, including a decadent Oysters Rockefeller drowning in butter, parsley, breadcrumbs. French wine flowing—most of it smuggled, some from her private cellar. The result was as intended. Conversation had been polite. Convivial even.

But for some, the superficial civility was just that—superficial. Like black ice. Smooth and thin and deceptive. And so very easy to punch through.

Davenport had been hosting salons long enough to recognize when a man was pretending to enjoy himself. And Carlisle—he was pretending.

She didn't often doubt herself, but she was beginning to see the mistake in inviting him. He wasn't the spark she'd hoped for —he was a fuse. She'd considered showing him the door, but men like him never leave quietly. He'd make a scene. And scenes had consequences. For her. For him. For everyone watching.

He laughed, he charmed, he tossed out provocations—challenging the patrons to acknowledge the power they wielded over the artists they so graciously "supported."

"You manipulate them. Of course you do. C'mon, man. At least be honest about it."

A few chuckled. Some squirmed. An increasing number shot her glances begging for rescue—or urging her to act. *Do something.*

But just when it seemed he might go too far, his gaze would drift.

Toward Grayson.

And Grayson—well. He'd begun the evening as himself—poised, at ease, accustomed to this world of quiet power. But now, something was off.

She caught it at dinner in the way his jaw muscles worked. In the slight tremor of his hand as he set his glass down.

Across from him, a guest—a professor from Columbia, well into his third brandy—gave a knowing look.

"Christ, Grayson, you look like you've been at this since noon."

A few soft chuckles.

Grayson managed a tired smile. "Nothing of the sort." He lifted his glass slightly, as if to prove his control. "Just the one."

His tone was easy, unbothered. But Davenport saw the way his fingers tightened around the glass, the careful way he set it down. As though he did not trust his grip.

As the evening wore on, his movements slowed. His forehead shone faintly in the candlelight, glistening with a thin layer of sweat. Twice, he rubbed at his temple, blinking as if clearing his vision. Another guest noticed, made an offhand remark about the rich food, the strong wine.

Grayson gave a tight smile. "Yes. Perhaps that's it."

After dinner, Davenport invited the men to sit by the fire in her library for Havana cigars and contraband liquor. A chance to repair old relationships, cement new ones.

Grayson, however, slipped away.

Davenport watched him go. He was an introvert, so she wasn't surprised to see this stepping back from the crowd, this retreat into himself. He needed the quiet, the distance. Most of all, no doubt, he needed to escape Carlisle's gaze.

Vaughn started after him, but Davenport and Jessie Fauset dissuaded her. Fauset managed to lure Vaughn into the powder room.

Which meant Vaughn didn't see what happened next.

But Davenport did. She saw Grayson slip through the garden doors. Saw Carlisle follow.

She took another sip of wine, weighing her choices. Respect their privacy? Turn away? No way. It was *her* house. And some moments were too rare to pass up.

She set her glass down, moved to the doors and slipped into the garden. Cold air stung her bare shoulders, sharp after the warmth of the dining room. She shivered, but only briefly.

Despite the years she'd lived in the house and the many hours she'd spent in the garden, it always caught her off guard. Its beauty. Its solitude. Ivy-covered walls enclosed the space, cloaking it in monastic silence. Stone paths curved between statuettes and topiaries, each lamp-lit turn designed for secrets, for promises of discretion—promises that were often broken.

Davenport moved carefully, the crisp night air tightening her skin. Ahead, Grayson and Carlisle stood on the edge of lamplight. They faced each other in profile, their expressions half-lost in shadow. Both handsome, elegant—dashing, even—in their tuxedoes. The air between them crackled with raw, repressed energy, thick and electric.

Even from a distance, there was no mistaking the pain in Grayson's eyes. Or the yearning in Carlisle's. He was the one driving the conversation, speaking adamantly, making forceful gestures.

Carlisle stopped, his arm raised in mid-gesture, and glanced up, in her direction. Had he sensed her presence? Still standing in shadow, she darted behind one of the topiaries. Stood there, her bare back pressed painfully against the sharp leaves, breath held tight.

Would they catch her? Her heart beat heavily.

But after several seconds, the men resumed their conversation. And Davenport inclined her head to listen.

The cool night air delivered their voices clearly. Carlisle's came to her first. Tight, but low. Controlled, but only just.

"Who decides what's acceptable, then? You? Or men like you? Men who've given up without a fight? Or is it the white men writing the checks?"

Then Grayson's response. "This isn't about the magazine and we both know it."

A humorless laugh. "No, I suppose not."

A beat of silence.

She peered around the topiary to see them. Their body language spoke louder than their words.

Carlisle, standing too close, aggressively close.

Grayson, straight-backed and holding his ground, exhausted

but resolute. "You attacking me in public—that won't change anything. It's just embarrassing for everyone else."

"That's the difference between you and me, Victor. I don't choose my words for the comfort of others."

"Maybe you should."

Davenport held her breath. She had known Carlisle for years. Had seen him passionate, furious, drunk. But this—this was different. His voice held a rawness she'd never heard before. A desperation barely concealed beneath the sharp edges of his words.

Carlisle's hands curled into fists but he kept them at his side. His tone was bitter, something dangerous twisting inside it. "If you do this, I swear, you'll regret it."

Grayson started to answer, then apparently decided not to bother. He'd had enough. He walked off, hands shoved deep into his pockets, shoulders hunched against the cold.

Davenport, fearing that he would see her, drew back. But he veered off, took a different path and disappeared into the shadows. She leaned forward again to see Carlisle, still standing there, still watching where Grayson had been moments ago.

Then, in one last burst of anger, frustration, helplessness, he dashed his glass to the ground. The sharp smash rang out across the garden. Shards scattered, glittering in the moonlight. And the dark amber liquid spread across the stone like blood.

The silence that followed was absolute.

Davenport had seen men break things before. Usually, they were careful to have an audience. To make a show of it. But this —this was not performance. Carlisle had forgotten himself.

He stood there, chest heaving, staring down at the wreckage. His breath fogged in the cool air, sharp and uneven.

And then—he stilled.

Davenport didn't move, didn't speak. But she knew the exact moment he sensed her presence. Slowly, his head turned. Their eyes met across the garden and for a half a second, she saw it—

something naked, something raw. Shock? No, not quite. Embarrassment? Perhaps. Rage? That was closer. And then—like a candle snuffed between fingers—it was gone.

Carlisle straightened. Rolled his shoulders back. Smoothed his lapels. The mask slid back into place. A slow smile curled his lips, but it didn't reach his eyes. "Enjoying the show, Margery?"

Davenport came out from behind her cover. She wasn't afraid, but she was wary. "Not particularly."

Carlisle let out a breathless laugh, sharp and bitter. He pulled out his cigarette case. The silver glinted in the lamplight as he flipped it open.

Davenport's gaze dropped to his hands. The faintest tremor. A shake, there and gone before he steadied it. He struck a match, exhaled a slow stream of smoke, filling the space between them.

"Whatever that was, Everett, you should be careful where you let people see it."

Carlisle tilted his head, assessing her. Then he grinned, slow, lazy. "Careful, darling? In what world have I ever been that?"

Davenport held his gaze a moment longer. Then, without another word, she turned and walked back inside.

Davenport picked up her coffee cup again, this time taking a small sip. "Satisfied?"

"Did anyone else witness this?" Redding asked.

"Not that I know of."

Redding considered that. "You said Carlisle followed him into the garden. Did Grayson seem to expect it?"

"No. But I don't think he was surprised by it."

"Like that type of thing had happened before?"

"More like it was inevitable."

Another silence.

"And after that? How did Grayson seem?"

A slight hesitation. Then, "Like a man walking toward his own funeral. Calm on the outside, but his eyes…" She paused. "I think he knew something was coming."

"Something?" Redding rubbed his chin. "Or someone?" He steepled his fingertips, leaned forward and leveled his gaze at her. "Carlisle. What can you tell me about him? His background, his habits?"

She gave a wry smile. "Ah, that one! He *is* a bit of a cipher, isn't he? No one seems to know much. But I can tell you who might know something. Julius Hayward."

"The bookstore owner?"

"You know him?"

"Heard of him. Who hasn't? He's Harlem's 'Keeper of Secrets.'" He made finger quotes.

She laughed. "Yes, well, he and Carlisle were in Paris together. He'd be the one to talk to. If anyone knows him, it's him."

"Good." Redding nodded to himself.

Watching him, she said: "You believe Carlisle did it."

"Do you?"

Davenport's lips tightened. Not offended, but troubled. "I don't know. I only know what I saw."

"And I appreciate you having shared it." He stood, adjusting his coat. "Thank you. You've been very helpful."

She followed him to the door.

He turned at the last moment, hand resting on the knob. "Oh and before I forget—I'll need a full guest list."

She barely paused, but the shift in her expression was noticeable. "Detective, this wasn't a backroom poker game. My guests included some of the best people in New York. I doubt any of them—"

"I still need the names."

She stiffened, folded her arms. "And if I refuse?"

"I'll be back. And next time, I won't be asking."

She looked him up and down, as if to say, *Who are you to give me orders?*

Any other day, that measuring look might have bothered him. Today, he didn't have the time.

"Mrs. Davenport—"

"Fine. I'll see what I can do." She dropped her arms. But the worry in her eyes lingered. "What about my name? The newspapers. The damage. If they get word—"

"It won't come from me."

A nod. A faint sigh. Clearly, she would make a call—or two—the minute he left. The wheels were already turning. People to contact. Strings to pull.

He doffed his hat, ready to go.

She reached out to stop him. "Detective."

He turned back, less patient now.

She stepped closer, eyes meeting his—hers, cool and somber; his, dark and unwavering.

"Murder has its own mind, doesn't it?"

A pause.

"In what way?"

"It doesn't stay in the streets the way people expect it to. It moves up. Finds its way into places where people like to think they're safe."

Redding studied her. Weighed her words. Then gave a slow nod. "Have a good afternoon, Mrs. Davenport."

Her gaze searched his. "You, too, Detective." A beat. Then, more quietly: "There is one more thing—" She stopped herself.

"Yes?"

She shook her head. "No. Never mind. It's probably nothing."

"You're sure?"

But she only smiled—tight, indecipherable—and closed the door.

11

The bookstore sat on 131st Street and Fifth Avenue just past a newsstand selling week-old copies of *The Chicago Defender* and a barber shop where men swapped stories between haircuts. A light drizzle had begun to fall, tapping gently against the storefront windows. Redding pulled his collar up as he approached the entrance. The painted sign above the door read:

Hayward's Books & Curiosities

Julius C. Hayward, Proprietor

A thin layer of dust coated the window, but the books inside were arranged like offerings—Langston Hughes, Alain Locke, *The Souls of Black Folk* propped open to a well-worn page. *The New Negro* tucked close by, a slim volume of *Baudelaire* in the original French wedged between them.

The bell above the door gave a soft chime as Redding stepped inside. The shift in atmosphere was immediate. The air smelled of old paper, pipe smoke and something faintly sweet—clove, maybe. The street noise faded to a murmur. It was like stepping into a place where the world outside barely mattered.

Bookshelves stretched floor to ceiling, their contents arranged in a way that made sense only to the man who ran the place. The counter sat toward the right, beneath a hanging lamp that cast a warm glow over the workspace. A silver phonograph spun something smooth and slow, a jazz melody so low it barely touched the edges of silence. The muted brass and low, rolling piano chords created a sense of elegance tinged with melancholy. Perfect for a space where words mattered, where thoughts unfurled slowly.

Two women in cloche hats browsed poetry. An older gentleman in a worn suit read intently by the window. Toward the rear, a young man—early twenties, hair neatly conked—was taking inventory. He held a notebook, his pen moving in quick, careful strokes, an open box at his feet.

An older man sat behind the counter, his face lit by a banker's light. Silver hair slicked back. High cheekbones. Strong profile. Well-groomed, well-dressed, a bit dandified. He held a fountain pen, studying a large book laid flat before him. A ledger from the look of it.

Hayward, Redding guessed.

The older man scribbled a note, nodded to himself, then glanced up from the pool of lamplight—and clocked Redding. As he shifted, the light caught his eyes. A dull green, odd and unsettling. Then a change.

Redding sensed it, the moment of recognition. Not for the first time, he wondered why he'd agreed to that newspaper profile.

He approached the counter. His broad-shouldered silhouette fell across the polished wood surface, stretching over the open ledger and cutting across Hayward's handwriting.

Hayward closed the book gently, ran a hand over the worn leather. He picked up a cigarillo from an ashtray, relit it and took a slow drag before exhaling toward the ceiling.

Redding felt those green eyes taking his measure, checking the flesh against the legend. He'd learned to wait it out.

Hayward's gaze traveled north, then south. Took in

everything from Redding's hat to the tips of his worn but polished shoes. And it lingered long enough in-between to convey appreciation, not mere assessment.

"A man like you doesn't walk into a place like this unless he's looking for something—and I do admire a man who knows what he's looking for. What can I do for you, Detective?"

Redding sighed. "That article in the *Chronicle*, right?"

"The very same."

Redding leaned on the counter, glanced around. "You've got a fine selection."

"I should. It's my business to know what's worth reading." He gestured toward the window display. "Tell me, are you the sort to appreciate a soft sonnet? I'm thinking you're more of a hard prose man."

Redding chose to ignore the subtext, again. "I'm the sort who appreciates an answer when he asks a question."

"So this is business. Not pleasure?"

"It is indeed."

"Homicide, right?"

Redding nodded.

"Well, well." Hayward's eyes filled with curiosity. He arched one eyebrow, then leaned forward, supple as a cat. "By all means, ask."

"I'm looking for information on a man who had strong opinions about Professor Victor Grayson."

Hayward's eyes narrowed. "So it's true. The good professor is no more." A somber nod. "Tragic. He was a good man."

"It's possible not everyone agrees."

Hayward gave a dry chuckle. "That's true of any man worth remembering." Then he made the connection. "And your little visit here today, does that mean that his passing, shall we say, *n'était pas tout à fait naturel?"*

"C'est la question du jour."

Hayward inclined his head. "You speak French?"

"Enough to get by."

A mischievous smile. "I bet you get by in a lot of places. Hm-hmm. I bet you do."

Redding stayed on task. "Everett Carlisle. Word is, if you want to understand him, you're the one to talk to."

"That right? Must've been a slow news week."

"I didn't come here looking for headlines."

"Good. 'Cause I don't hand those out."

Redding pushed aside a growing irritation. "Look, I'm just trying to figure out where he fits."

"And you're already sure he does?"

"It's beginning to look like it."

Hayward took a long drag, exhaled toward the ceiling. "I've known a lot of men lose their souls chasing ghosts."

"And I've seen a lot more railroaded 'cause folks stayed silent when they should've spoken up."

"You're saying Carlisle's under suspi—"

"I'm saying if you've got anything worth saying, now's the time to say it. Before the story sets—and people stop listening."

Hayward's hand hovered over the ashtray, the cigarillo burning low between his fingers.

"Ev's seen his share of trouble. Some of it 'cause he trusted the wrong people. A lot of it 'cause he never knew when to leave well enough alone."

"So you two aren't close?"

Hayward grunted. "That man's driven me crazy more times than I can count. Still does. But that doesn't mean I wouldn't go to bat for him."

He stubbed out the cigarillo and stood.

"Jimmy," he called to the boy in the back, "watch the register."

Then he turned to Redding. His look said this wasn't charity. "You want to talk about Ev, let's do it upstairs. Just don't expect easy answers. Man's complicated."

The study above the shop wasn't just for books. It was a sanctuary—a space curated, lived in, shaped by years of collecting. A liquor cabinet stood against one wall and a faint trace of rum lingered in the air. A chaise lounge sat near the window, draped with an indigo shawl so fine it might've come from Marrakesh. The bookshelves here were filled with first editions and private correspondences, some stacked neatly, others scattered, as if recently thumbed through. On one of the shelves, a framed map leaned against the wall. Not of Harlem. Or even New York. But of the Caribbean. With Barbados at its center. Old, hand-colored, the kind that got passed down.

Hayward gestured toward a chair. "The thing is, men like Ev, they don't make themselves easy to know."

The two men sat.

Hayward exhaled a thin stream of smoke, regarded Redding. "Where'd you like me to begin?"

"The beginning is always good."

"Well, that would be McAllister. We were tight back then. Victor, Ev and me." He paused. "A drink, Detective?"

The two men's eyes met. Offering a cop a drink during Prohibition wasn't casual. It was a test.

Redding said nothing.

Hayward rose, crossed to the cabinet. Drew out a dark bottle, beautifully etched and heavy. Uncorked it. Poured. One glass only.

Redding said nothing.

Hayward returned to his chair. Set the bottle down. Held up his glass. The rum caught the lamplight, deep and amber. He glanced at the cop.

Silence was the answer.

Hayward took a slow sip. "Ev was smart. As smart as Victor. Maybe smarter. But he had a mouth on him. Always angry.

Always spoiling for a fight. So when the accusations came, people were ready to believe the worst."

"What accusations?"

"Why, of plagiarism. What else?"

"Go on."

"Y'see, Victor was the golden boy. Ev? The troublemaker. Too loud. Too vocal. Too in-your-face. So when two of their papers looked too much alike, whose name do you think they put on the wrong side of the ledger?"

"Carlisle's."

"Right. The thing is, they had it backward. Victor borrowed from Ev. Not the other way around. Deadline crept up, Victor panicked. Ev, trying to be a friend, said, 'Here. Use mine. They'll never know.' He pulled Victor's butt out of the fire."

"But the similarities were caught."

"Sho 'nuf. Of course, Ev denied it. Said he'd never do such a thing. But he did not, would not, blame Victor."

"So, he took the fall."

"And Victor let him."

Redding let that sink in. He thought of Vaughn. W*hat came between them?* he'd asked. *I really couldn't say.*

She'd known. She must have known.

An old betrayal. An old wound. But was that enough for a motive? After all this time? And that garden argument Davenport described—it still didn't quite make sense.

Hayward went on. "McAllister kicked him out. Put his ass on the street. No ceremony. No second chances. It wasn't just the stain on his name. It was the betrayal. That's what haunted him."

Redding frowned. "You're sure about this?"

"Oh, I'm sure. First of all, Grayson barely admitted there'd ever been anything between them. And he stayed away from, you know, us folks. Was scared someone would find out. If one of us did hear enough to ask about him and Ev—and not many dared—he'd say Ev was asked to leave 'cause he had kissed him in public. That he himself didn't want to have nothing to do with him. But Ev wouldn't leave him alone. He'd say Ev was too obvious. Too...out there. *Outré*. That Ev had brought it all on himself."

Hayward paused. "What he'd never say was why Ev couldn't find steady work for the next twenty years. A public kiss gets you expelled. Plagiarism follows you to the grave."

Hayward fell quiet, lost in his memories. Redding absorbed what he'd learned.

It should've been them against the world. Two sharp, ambitious young men, both working twice as hard for half the chances. McAllister was a Negro college, established to educate colored youth, tomorrow's colored leaders. But it wasn't a birthright—it was a battle. Grayson and Carlisle had made it through the doors, past the gatekeepers, past every whispered doubt about whether they belonged. And when one faltered, the other should have steadied him.

Instead, when one had found himself pushed to the edge, the other had let him fall. In later years, Grayson had chosen to portray himself as a tragic lover. Not a cold opportunist. The lies people tell themselves—and others—to survive. Maybe Grayson had even believed this one himself.

Outside, a car horn blared faintly in the distance. The soft crackle of the phonograph reached them through the floorboards, the needle catching on a groove before sliding past it.

Hayward swirled the amber liquid in his glass. Redding, watching him, wondered how Hayward really felt about Carlisle. Despite his avowed liking for Carlisle, the bookstore owner was helping to build a case against the man, turning Carlisle from a mere person of interest into a suspect. Then again, Hayward had said not to expect easy answers.

"So," Hayward said. "That gives you your grudge. The one you'd have dug up anyway, so there's no use hiding it."

"It doesn't explain murder."

"Glad you see that it doesn't."

Redding waited a beat. "Do you think he did it?"

Hayward considered it. "I think," he said, "that men like Ev don't go quietly. And they don't forget."

"That's a pretty damning answer."

Hayward shrugged. "I hear they call me a Keeper of Secrets. I wouldn't disagree with that. But knowing a man's sins doesn't mean I know his crimes."

Redding gave a slow nod. "All right, then."

Hayward took another drag. "Victor moved on. Built a career. But Ev? He had doors slammed in his face, one right after the other. He'd move a foot ahead, get pushed back a mile."

Hayward paused and for several seconds there was silence. Then he roused himself. "After McAllister, Ev drifted on down to Philly. Thought he could start over. But that's when the pushback really began."

12

"Ev still had ideas. Still had fire. And for a while there, he believed he could do some good."

Hayward exhaled smoke, tapped ash into the tray.

"He took a teaching job. A colored school in Philadelphia. Thought he could shape young minds, build something. He gave those boys everything he had. Made them read books, essays, things their parents had never heard of. Made them *think*." Hayward let out a small, ironic laugh. "Problem was, that's exactly what the men running the school *didn't* want."

"Vocational training?"

Hayward nodded. "Booker T. Washington's model. A school for trades, not ideas. Conformity, not creativity. They wanted to produce young men who could swing a hammer, lay a brick. You know, boys with practical skills. Not highfalutin' do-nothins'. Not boys who thought they were the next Du Bois or, God help them, Karl Marx."

"Ev didn't see it that way."

"Not at all—and he let them know it." Hayward's voice turned wry. "He was a brilliant teacher. But you can't teach kids to question the system when the system's footing your bill."

The ending was predictable. "How long did he last?"

"A year. Maybe less. He was already walking on thin ice. He undermined the headmasters in front of students. Encouraged them to challenge what they were told. Parents started complaining—why wasn't their boy learning to be a tailor, a mechanic? Why was he coming home talking about poetry and labor unions?"

Hayward swirled his drink. "Ev had no patience for 'go along to get along.' He told them their school was teaching obedience, not education."

Redding raised an eyebrow. "So diplomacy is not his strong suit."

Hayward let out a soft chuckle. "That's Ev."

A pause. Then Hayward's expression shifted. Just slightly. "Then came the whispers."

"From McAllister?"

Hayward nodded. "Word got out about his expulsion. Someone had a connection, dug up the old plagiarism charge. And that? That was all the administration needed." A small, knowing shake of the head. "Ev was already a problem. But now, he was a problem with a stain on his record. They didn't fire him outright. Just made it impossible for him to stay."

"Forced him out."

"Let's just say, when he left, there was no farewell."

Redding nodded. "How'd he take it?"

Hayward leaned back, stretching his legs out. "How do you think, Detective?"

Redding said nothing.

Hayward smiled, slow and thin. "He got angry. And then he got even angrier."

The jazz from below barely reached them now. It was just a low hum under the crackle of the phonograph. But Redding was sure it was Fats Waller.

He eyed Hayward. The man's willingness to talk surprised him. Hayward was too smart not to realize what he was doing. That with every anecdote, every detail, he was nudging Redding toward a shift in attitude, turning Carlisle from a fellow worth revisiting into the fellow worth arresting.

Hayward took another sip, then set his glass down. The heavy crystal base made a soft thud against the wooden table.

"Boston," he mused. "Now, that was a mistake." He glanced up at Redding. "Ev went there thinking he could play the game. That maybe, just maybe, he could fit somewhere. Prove he was more than McAllister's castoff. I suppose that was Victor's gift, wasn't it? Even when he wasn't around, he still managed to shape Ev's goddamn decisions."

Hayward's lips curled around Grayson's name. Dislike? Disapproval? Definitely something there.

"Ev landed a job at *The Beacon Standard* in Roxbury. Was supposed to be the best Negro paper in the city. Fierce, fearless, never pulled a punch."

Redding knew the type of paper. Black-owned, white-hot rhetoric. Boston had its radicals, same as Harlem.

"Editor was one of those Trotter men—name was Langford. Born with a fire in his belly and a memory for slights. Called himself a defender of the race and he was, but God help you if he thought you were getting too much attention."

In other words, territorial, Redding thought.

"He brought Ev on to edit copy," Hayward said. "Tighten up columns, smooth the sermons, trim the fat off the poetry. At first, Langford liked him. Said he edited like a razor. Quick, sharp, clean."

Redding could see it—Carlisle hunched over a battered desk,

sleeves rolled, red pencil in hand, trying to keep up with his own convictions.

"But it didn't stay that way," Hayward said. "Ev wanted to shine, not just help other people do it. So he started working late. Wrote up some pieces. Offered them up. They were good. Again, Langford liked them. Started running them on the front page. Letters started coming in. People quoting him at rallies, slipping his lines into Sunday sermons."

"That's when the trouble started."

"And how. Langford didn't say anything at first, but you could feel it. That man did not like to share his pulpit."

"And Ev didn't know how to lay low."

"No, he didn't." He paused. "And then came the Bell piece."

Redding raised his head. The name sounded familiar. "Isaiah Bell? Farmhand. Down in Holmes County?"

"Yup. Supposedly said the wrong thing to a white woman. They dragged him out of his shack, beat him raw and hanged him from a tree at the county fairgrounds. Left his body there till sunup. Ev had a source down there—a cousin, I think. Got the names. The sheriff. The magistrate. A member of the state house, no less."

He gave a humorless laugh. "Ev wrote it like a war report. Cold, clear and furious. No flowers. No euphemisms. Said Boston had no right to sit smug while this happened in the country's name. Said, and I quote, 'The tree that bore Isaiah Bell is watered by every editor who calls for patience and every northerner who shakes his head but does nothing.'"

Redding gave a slow exhale. "And they printed it?"

"They tried. Langford agreed to run it. But the minute the typesetter read it, word got out. Printer's shop caught hell. Men started calling, saying they'd torch the press if it ran. Irish boys from Southie. Veterans. Even a couple of flat-foots stopped by. Offered some 'friendly advice.'"

"Langford caved."

"He ripped the plates out himself. Told Ev it would be suicide to print that story. They'd lose every advertiser, get blacklisted by the unions and maybe lose the office, too. But he didn't just kill the piece. He blamed Ev for the fallout. Said he'd gone rogue. Claimed he'd never approved the final version."

"That true?"

Hayward shrugged. "Does it matter?"

Redding got it. Carlisle had done everything right and it still turned to ash. He found the story, wrote the truth, told it right and got knifed by the very institution that claimed to want fire. He was brilliant, but brilliance wasn't enough. He gave them what they said they wanted and when it got too hot, they left him standing in the flames.

"Carlisle told Langford to go to hell. Walked out the same day. No severance, no thanks. No other paper in the city would touch him. Langford made sure of that. Said he was unstable. A firebrand who didn't listen. Ev tried to get the piece printed at a smaller outfit out in Cambridge. The editor liked it—but his print shop burned down the night before it was set to run."

Redding gave a knowing grunt.

"They said it was wiring," Hayward said. "Funny how the wiring only burned the linotype room."

Redding shook his head. "And then?"

"Well," Hayward reflected. "Let's just say that Ev had a way of finding people who burned just as hot as he did."

"The Communists."

"Yes, indeed. For a time."

Redding tilted his head. "You say that like you didn't approve."

Hayward shrugged. "I say that like a man who read Ev's letters. He liked all the talk about a revolution. The rhetoric, the fire. But in the end, that's all he thought it was—was just talk. And they wanted him to say what they wanted him to say. For man like Ev, that's never going to sit right."

Redding got it. "So he left."

"He walked. Before they could show him the door."

Downstairs, Jimmy had changed the record. Not Waller anymore. Armstrong. Redding thought he knew all the recordings, but he hadn't heard this one. Reflective, mournful in parts, with Louis' famous trumpet doing a solo that pierced right through the noise. Melancholy. But beautiful. Grace in the sadness. It felt right for Carlisle's story—talent and truth met with silence and fire.

Hayward's smile faded slightly. "Boston didn't have room for a Negro too smart for his own good. He had no job. No prospects. And that's when the whispers from McAllister caught up with him."

"Plagiarism."

Hayward inclined his head. "It didn't take much. Just a mention of it. A rumor, passed from one room to another. The business with Langford, then that outfit in Cambridge had already made things difficult. The word about the plagiarism, that made them impossible. Nobody wanted him. Couldn't risk it. Propriety and all that."

Redding shook his head. "So, another city turned its back on him."

"Boston was never his city. Just another stop along the way."

"What did he do then?"

"What every nigger with more pride than options does if he can swing it—got the hell out."

"And went where?"

Hayward took his time answering. He picked up the bottle, poured another measure, then finally said, "Paris."

Redding wasn't surprised.

He flashed on his own days in the City of Light. Paris. Beautiful after the war—bruised and battered, but still standing. Still singing. The French had called men like him heroes, bought them drinks, treated them like men. For colored American soldiers, their whole experience with the French had been a revelation. A taste of freedom and respect they'd never known back home. Plenty stayed. He'd thought about it too.

"That's where he hoped to finally find belonging?"

Hayward let out a short, humorless laugh. "If only."

13

"You ever been over there?" Hayward asked. "To Paris?"

"Yeah. For a couple of months."

Hayward nodded to himself, like a man seeing a piece fall into place. "After the war?"

"Hmm-hm. After the war."

Nothing more.

Hayward looked down at his glass. "Figures."

Redding caught the shift in Hayward's eyes—the recognition, maybe even respect.

Paris meant different things to different men. For Ev and his kind, it was an escape. A haven. For Redding? It was something else entirely.

Redding remembered Paris lit up with victory—the shouts, the handshakes, Dipper Mouth Blues swinging out from smoke-choked cafés. Being hoisted on shoulders. Drinks pressed into his hand. Women tugging him into dance.

But even then, he'd seen the edges. Once the parades ended and the struggle resumed—the day-to-day battle just to survive—that welcome would thin.

In time, it might fade altogether.

He could've stayed, maybe. If he'd had a trade. A skill. The French didn't bar you for the color of your skin—but they didn't hand out work for nothing, either. Most of the brothers who made it stayed because they could play a horn, paint a canvas, dance or sing. That's what the post-war world had room for. He didn't have any of that. And he hadn't come that far just to scrape by in someone else's city.

He was young. Strong. Still believed the fight wasn't finished.

Paris had been a stopover. Nothing more. A place to pass through before heading back to a country that called him a hero one minute and a problem the next.

That summer. He'd been one of thousands of colored soldiers who came home proud in their crisp uniforms. Many were met with blood and fire. Washington. Chicago. Charleston. Elaine. The summer of 1919. The Red Summer.

He'd lived through it. Survived it.

Now, here he was. In another city. Fighting a different kind of battle. A different kind of war. But still a soldier.

Hayward let out a breath, rough around the edges. His gaze flicked to the ceiling, like he was watching something invisible there.

"Mo-mart," he said—the affectionate shorthand colored artists used for Montmartre, the gritty Parisian neighborhood that was their home away from home. "Jazz on the breeze. Anise on every breath. Smoke curling from the cafés, men talking about art, about revolution—sometimes about nothing at all." He was almost wistful. "A man could get drunk just standing still."

Sort of like now, Redding thought. He let Hayward's rum do the talking.

"For us, it was a dream. No color lines. No 'whites-only' signs. No back doors. Just talent and nerve. That's what they said, anyway." Hayward's smile was twisted, small and dry. "Ev believed it. Thought it could be his city. And for a while, maybe it was."

The smile faded. Hayward took one long draw on his cigarillo, then stubbed out the butt.

"Ev got work easy enough. The expat papers liked his fire—his sharp critiques, his willingness to put knives in backs. And the artists? They liked his praise when he gave it. Even the white ones. Especially them." Hayward swirled the rum in his glass. "Nothing a certain kind of white man likes more than a smart Negro calling him a genius."

"So, he had a voice."

"For a time." Hayward took a slow sip. "Wrote for small presses. Translated plays. Ghostwrote when he had to. Smoked and drank in cafés with men who thought they were making history."

"Where did the interest in art come in? I don't see the connection."

"Paris. Maybe even a little before, but it came into focus over there. Painting. Sculpture. He was good, actually."

Redding raised an eyebrow. "I didn't peg him as the artistic type."

"He wasn't. Not at first. He was angry. Restless. Fighting everything. But over there, he started to shape it. Tried to make something with it."

"Tried?"

"He didn't have the training, the backing. No patron, no stipend, no community. Just the hunger and the need."

Redding could well imagine.

Hayward's fingers tapped against his glass. "But you know what his real problem was? He wanted to do everything. He was everywhere, trying to do it all. Couldn't fully commit to one thing." Hayward shook his head. "He couldn't afford materials—or a stable place to stay."

"Tough situation to be in."

"Well, he did have Pierre. He was French. Older. Sophisticated. Got Ev into the right rooms. The right circles."

Redding caught a subtle shift in tone.

"It was the first real thing Ev had since McAllister." Hayward turned the glass slowly between his fingers. "And Pierre loved him." A beat. "God help him, but he did."

Ah. The sound of a man who'd danced to that particular song and paid the band plenty.

"But Ev had a temper." Hayward's mouth flattened. "And the kind of love he knew? It burned everything down."

"So, it ended badly."

Hayward let out a snort. "Is there any other way?" He took another sip. "The Frenchman left him. Ev didn't take it well. He never did. When someone left, he made sure they knew what a mistake they'd made."

Hayward's eyes grew distant. "After that? Paris turned on him. The critics took out knives. The editors refused his calls. The salons—the ones that had once feted him—they started acting like they'd never heard his name. And then," Hayward paused, "the whispers started."

"About?"

Hayward met his gaze. "Boston."

Of course. Even across an ocean, a man's past could still reach for his throat.

Hayward set his empty glass aside. "It didn't happen overnight. But it happened."

He lit another cigarillo. "Some men leave places. Some places leave them first." Hayward shrugged, palms up. "So, when the wind changed, when the doors slammed shut, Ev did what he always did."

Redding guessed. "He left town."

"Sure did. This time, he came home." Hayward's eyes narrowed against the smoke. "And that's when he found out what those years in Paris had cost him."

14

Carlisle wanted to slam the door in the landlord's face. Took all his strength not to do it. Took even more to smile, to lie, to say, "I'll have it day after tomorrow."

Marchetti was short, square and ugly. Had a face that made a bulldog look pretty. Right then, that face was mean. "You got till noon, you hear me?" He jabbed a thick dirty finger at Carlisle in the chest. "Noon tomorrah. Or you and your trash'll be out on the street. Got it? "

Get the fuck away from my door!

That's what Carlisle wanted to say. To bare his teeth and growl it. To tap Marchetti with a fast right hook and knock him flat. The words sat on his tongue, barbed and hot—but he bit them back. Barely.

Instead, he nodded. Watched Marchetti roll away, round shoulders beefy under his shirt. Saw him take out his pocket watch and check it, like he was already counting the hours, the minutes, till he could get rid of Carlisle and find a new tenant, a *paying* one.

Carlisle couldn't hold it in anymore. He slammed the door,

hard. Slumped against it. Closed his eyes. Clawed his hands down his face. Fists clenched, breath shallow.

Finally, he opened his eyes and looked around—really looked—startled to see it as someone else might.

The place was a wreck.

Ashtrays overflowing. Clothes draped over a busted chair. Empty bottles lined up under the radiator like bowling pins ready to fall.

What the hell was he doing here? How had it come to this? And was he really fighting—*scrambling*—to hold on to this dump?

He rubbed the back of his neck, stumbled forward and dropped onto his cot. He thought of all the rooms in all the cities—D.C., Philly, Boston, Paris. Some good. Some better. A few damn near fine. And now, this? Was this how it ended? Would he die here? Alone?

He'd heard the stories—bodies not found till the stench hit the hallway. New York was full of endings like that. Would his be one of them? His chest hitched. He let out the breath he hadn't realized he was holding. Shook his head. This wasn't the time for existential wondering. Or philosophical meandering. Or any of that shit. The real question was: how the hell was he going to make rent?

The envelope from *Commonwealth Review* lay unopened on the floor—thin, flat, useless. He didn't need to read it. Not after the blowout at Grayson's office. He knew what it said. Rejection. Not just of the piece—but of *him*.

And then like a fool, he'd gone and lit up the man in front of everyone at Davenport's party. Now, Grayson was dead. And a cop had come sniffing. If things didn't break his way, getting the rent might be the least of his problems.

He thought of the poem he'd roughed out. That stupid poem, packed with images he needed to get rid of. That wouldn't help him now. That wouldn't leave him alone.

Paris, Paris, you were sweet as sin,
Golden wine and silver streets and love let in.
Doorway kisses, café smoke, a hand in mine—
Lord, I thought that kind of living was a sign.

They called my name in rooms I'd never known,
Said, man, you got a gift, you ain't alone.
For one sweet season I believed it true—
That I could be the man I always knew.

But promises, they rot like fruit left in the sun.
What felt like forever, baby, was barely begun.
You gave me just enough to make me want the rest,
Then left me with your memory pressed against my chest.

Paris, Paris, why'd you have to lie so good?
Made me feel like maybe I was understood.
Now all I got is what I can carry in my mind—
Half-lies, half-glory and the ache they left behind.

I know I ought to bury you, put you in the ground,
Stop listening for an echo of that old sweet sound.
A man who feeds on memory is a man who dines alone,
But these tired bones of mine won't leave well enough alone.

Lord, I've thought about the quiet.
Thought about the peace.
Thought about the one sure way to make the wanting cease.
But I ain't got the guts and maybe that's my curse—
To keep on living hungry, which is somehow even worse.

So I reach back for those streets, for that golden light,
For the weight of someone beside me in the night,
For the sound of my name said like it meant something
fine—
Paris, Paris, you were never really mine.

But Lord have mercy, when the cold comes creeping in,
And the walls press close and the bottle's wearing thin,
You're all I've got to keep the darkness back—
A fool's warm fire on a fool's cold track.

He sat there, stilled, and closed his eyes and let those memories of better days, those half-lies, warm him. Then the train roared past. And just like that, he was back in that room in Harlem.

More memories then. Of his return, driven by fear and longing. Foolish, perhaps—but he'd felt hope. Now, he wondered what the hell he'd been thinking.

The IRT train groaned to a stop, steel grinding against steel. The final shudder jolted Carlisle awake from a half-sleep, the kind that left a man feeling like he'd been dreaming with his eyes open. He inhaled, rubbed a hand down his face, then reached for his bag.

The door hissed open. A rush of Harlem air spilled into the car—chilly and moist, edged with the bite of late autumn. Beneath it, faint but unmistakable, was the city's scent—damp stone, wet leaves crushed under hurried footsteps, the acrid bite of coal smoke drifting from chimneys. It wasn't Paris. Not by a damn mile.

And for that, he was grateful.

He stepped onto the platform, the weight of his bag dragging at his shoulder. 125th Street. Bodies moving everywhere. It had been years. For a moment, he just stood there, letting it hit him.

A woman in a cloche hat and a fur-trimmed coat clutched a kid's hand, urging him along. Men huddled near the stairwell, collars turned up against the wind, their voices low and quick. The distant wail of a saxophone floated down from the street. Probably, a performer playing for change.

Carlisle adjusted his grip on the bag's strap. Felt a rush of excitement, of relief and belonging. He'd had some last-minute doubts about leaving France, of abandoning the life he'd struggled to build there. On the whole ship ride back, he'd had to fight those qualms, squelch that little voice that said, *Turn back.*

It'll be all right, he'd told himself. *The moment I'm home, it'll all be fine.*

Now here he was. He allowed himself the smallest of smiles. He'd been right, damn it.

To get outta there.

To. Get. Back. Here.

He started up the steps. The rhythm of the city swept down to greet him. The sharp scent of frying fish. The clang of streetcars. A preacher's voice riding the wind.

With each step, the sounds grew sharper, clearer. The heavy clack of polished shoes against the pavement, and voices, hundreds of them, layering over each other like an orchestra tuning up before the show. It was alive, electric, moving at a pace that didn't wait for anyone to catch up.

At street level, Harlem hit him full in the chest. Brown faces everywhere. He hadn't realized how much he missed that.

Lenox Avenue was a river teeming with life. Newsboys shouting, smoke curling from sidewalk grates, women in furs laughing with men in polished shoes. A Victrola crackled from a second-story window. Chestnuts roasted in a pan beside a shoe stand.

The current of pedestrians moved fast, too fast to be sentimental. Nobody looked twice at the man with the duffel.

He breathed it in. Deep. He was back. In his city. Among his people.

He'd made the right call. Paris had been a fantasy, a fever dream. But this? This was real. This was home.

He felt triumphant. For the first time in a long time, maybe things were going to go well for him.

A group of young men passed him, fresh-faced, laughing, tossing jabs at each other. Sharp suits. Shoes still shining. They hadn't yet learned how easily hope could be crushed.

He'd looked like that once.

How long, he wondered, had it taken before he stopped?

The thought soured the moment—but only a little. He still had something left in him. He still could turn things around.

There were cards he could play. For one thing, he had Paris on him. That magical mystical glow that was bestowed on any American who could say he'd spent time there. The stories he could tell and the gossip! Ooh, la-la! Drop a few names and toss off a few French phrases. Dish it out with a dash of *le snobisme français* and he'd come off golden. Welcome in the best drawing rooms.

He chuckled and sucked in a deep breath. Puffed his chest out proud like a rooster. Then a thought came a-pecking—clipped his wings, killed his strut.

If life was so grand over there, someone might ask, then why was he back here? If Mo-mart was all that, someone might say, why hadn't he stayed? Had something gone wrong in paradise?

How would he answer? The air left his lungs. His chest deflated.

Would they suspect that Paris had ended the way things always did for him—with doors slamming and backs turning? Would they know he hadn't returned in triumph—but because he had nowhere else to go?

He shoved the thought aside. Pulled his coat tighter. Lifted his chin.

And started walking.

Not toward the clubs. Not toward any old haunt.

Toward Hayward.

He still had a little money, but not enough. If Harlem had changed its rules, he needed someone who knew the playbook.

Hayward would know. He always did.

But was he still there?

Carlisle cut east along 125th, slipping into the current—past shop windows and shoeshine boys shouting for a dime. Then north, up Fifth. The air shifted block by block, but the beat of the city stayed steady.

Somewhere along the way, the skies opened up and the rain came down. He swore the rain moved with him. It was like he had a personal cloud above him.

The story of his life. The only answer? As always: keep moving.

By the time he reached 131st, the rhythm had settled inside him. And the rain had drenched him.

Hayward's shop waited—tucked between a newsstand and a record store. Light spilled from the upstairs window, soft and steady, like it always had.

Hayward was still here. Still holding space.

The sight of it steadied him. But then another doubt crept in.

Hayward might be there, but was he still a friend?

They'd seen each other in Paris. Kept up a correspondence for a while. But that had faded. Carlisle had let it fade. He'd gotten caught up—swept into his affair with Pierre, into the attention, the reach. He'd forgotten who he was. Forgotten who his real friends were. Forgotten what it meant to be one.

Now, he was back. But could he expect to be welcomed? Maybe the door would open and nothing would be the same.

A pain struck—sharp, deep, right through the chest. Like a hand had reached in and squeezed.

Maybe he should duck into a speakeasy. Get a drink. Just one. To delay what came next.

He fingered the coins in his pocket.

But no. He was done with delay.

More to the point—he couldn't afford it.

He adjusted his bag and crossed the street.

He'd come too far to stop now.

15

"You were already back from Paris," Redding said.

"Oh, I'd been back," Hayward replied. "Didn't stay but a year. That was more than enough for me."

"Didn't like it?"

"No, I loved it. It was everything folks said it would be—fun, vibrant, full of life. But it wasn't home. You understand?"

Redding did. More than he cared to admit.

He was almost ashamed of how much he'd missed the States. Not the laws or the threats. Not the Miss Annes or Mr. Charlies. Not the constant darts of humiliation that flew at you from every direction. By all logic, he should've stayed gone. Should've taken that freedom, that peace France offered and let America vanish in the rear view window. But he hadn't. Because despite everything, he missed her.

He missed grits done right, bacon strips served crispy and sweet potato pie cut ragged from a church supper tin. Missed the crack of a bat in summer and the holler from a stoop two doors down. Missed the kind of talk you only got at a barbershop or after church—the kind that told you exactly who you were and where you stood.

In short, he missed his people.

Most of all, he missed his family back in D.C. Not just their presence, but their history—the fights, the silences, the stories passed over kitchen tables and back porches. Missed the bickering and bone-deep loyalty, the way his sister could cut him down with a look and still pass him the biscuits. A letter could only hold so much. A photograph, even less. He didn't want to live right up under them—but he didn't want to live with an ocean between them either.

Then there was the patriotism. It was emotional. Irrational. It didn't make no kind of sense. And it was what bewildered him the most. He had every reason to leave America behind. But he loved her. She was his, goddamn it. His, as much as anyone's. And he wasn't about to give her up, hand her over.

"My place was in Harlem," Hayward continued. "And this bookstore—this is my legacy."

He looked around, let his gaze rest on the shelves, the papers, the treasures he'd gathered and tended over the years. This bookstore was his passion, his calling. The pride he felt in it was quiet, but clear.

"I checked out the scene in Mo-mart," he said. "It was hot, all right. And I'm glad some of our folks have found what they need over there. But it wasn't for me. Like I told Ev—my roots are here. And I'm not about to let nobody chase me away."

The rain intensified outside, drawing Hayward's gaze to the window. Redding watched the storyteller's mask slip—revealing not nostalgia, but a harder truth beneath. The cold tap of water against glass had taken him back, washed away the present, leaving only the sharp edges of a memory that wouldn't stay buried.

"You know, it was on a night just like this that he came back. Cold and wet."

"When was this?"

"'Bout a year ago." Hayward's fingers traced the rim of his empty glass. "I remember it. Hard to forget it."

That was the night the past came knocking—soaked coat, tired eyes and nowhere left to go. Carlisle, back from Paris, standing at the edge of the only door he dared try.

Hayward's gaze swept over him, taking his time to make up his mind. Not surprised. Not welcoming, either.

Carlisle gave a half-smile, the kind a man wears when he's not sure if he's about to be let in or put out. "You're not gonna offer a man a drink?"

Hayward took a slow drag from his cigarillo, taking in the changes—the thin face, the hollows under his eyes, the years etched in places they hadn't touched before.

Carlisle was a fool, always had been. And now, here he was, on his doorstep, hoping for a handout. Broke, bruised and banking on a friendship he hadn't bothered about in years.

What the hell.

Hayward turned and walked inside. Carlisle mutely followed, closed the door behind him, dropped his bag. Behind the counter now, Hayward leaned in, said nothing, just pursed his lips. Carlisle stood there, arms crossed, hugging himself.

Hayward's gaze met Carlisle's—and in those eyes, he saw it. Not pride. Not swagger. But fear. Shame. The look of a man who'd run out of road.

Damn, Hayward wanted to say. *What did they do to you over there?*

Instead, he exhaled a long stream of smoke, watched it curl between them. Then he tapped out his cigarillo, slipped a hand into his pocket, pulled out a lighter and silver case. He flicked it open. Took out a joint. Held it between his fingers, eyeing it.

This was some of his best. Good. Clean. *Pricey*. He wasn't about to give it to just anybody.

He looked at Carlisle—*shivering like a stray in the goddamn rain*—and offered it.

Carlisle hesitated—just for a second. The relief on his face was almost pitiable. Then he took the stix, rolled it once before bringing it to his lips. Hayward lifted the lighter, the flame flickering to life. He held it steady. Carlisle leaned in. Their fingertips brushed against one another.

A beat. A pause.

A silent memory neither acknowledged.

Carlisle pulled back, inhaled deeply, smoke curling through the space between them.

Only then did Hayward reach for the bottle and the glasses he kept behind the register after hours when he worked alone.

He poured a drink, slid it across the counter. Carlisle caught it mid-slide, lifted it slightly. Not quite a toast. More like testing the waters.

"Not like the swill you were drinking with Pierre," Hayward said.

"It'll do." Carlisle knocked it off in two swallows, wiped his mouth with the back of his hand. "Thank you."

Time for questions. Maybe some answers. "So, what happened?"

Carlisle let out a breathy laugh, short and humorless. "The prodigal son returns."

"I see that. But why?"

Carlisle hesitated, looked down at his glass. "You know how it is. All that freedom. All that art. So much damn inspiration, a man could drown in it."

"And yet here you are."

Carlisle flinched.

Hayward gave a wry little smile and poured himself a drink. He didn't believe in stripping a man of his last scrap of dignity—

especially not one already running on fumes. The reefer, the pause before the pour—small signs, but clear. He wasn't going to turn Carlisle away.

And Carlisle knew it.

Still a fool. But not a coward. And not done yet.

Over the next few weeks, Carlisle reacquainted himself with Harlem. He found work—Hayward didn't know what kind and Carlisle didn't say. But it earned him enough to let him move out, get a room of his own. Somewhere.

Still, he dropped by. Often.

One night, nursing a drink, Carlisle let out a quiet chuckle, shaking his head. "Everything's bigger now. Bigger. Brighter. The lights, the clubs, the money. Harlem's grown fat while I was away."

Hayward rolled his glass between his fingers. "Some parts, yeah. Other parts, not so much. Point is, while you were gone, we built something here." He glanced at Carlisle. "I'm not saying you were wrong to leave. But the folks who stayed? We fought for something. You didn't."

Carlisle bristled. "So what, Harlem doesn't take back its own?"

Hayward set his glass down with a quiet clink. He was silent, thoughtful. Then, finally: "That depends."

"On what?"

"On you."

Carlisle looked puzzled. "Say what?"

"Are you back for good, now? One of us, or what?" Hayward's eyes met his. "You tell me, Ev. You tell me."

16

It had been nearly a year since Carlisle came knocking. "Why do you think he's been so—"

"Unhappy since he's been back?"

Redding nodded.

Hayward took a moment. "I've been thinking about that, thinking about it a lot. Ev left Harlem when it was still becoming. When it was on its way. When he came back, he found a Harlem that had *arrived*.

"The clubs are bigger. The parties, wilder. Everybody who was gonna be famous is famous. Even the intellectuals—the ones who used to fight over scraps—are getting invited to Fifth Avenue.

"And Ev? He wasn't here to fight for his place. He wasn't here when Harlem built itself. Now, he's just another man trying to slip back in."

He leaned back, shaking his head. "He'd never admit it, but I think he misses Paris. And I think the regret set in within weeks of his coming back."

Redding tilted his head. "What does he miss?"

"The illusion of freedom. Even if it wasn't real, it felt real—

and that meant something. The cafés, the conversation, the late-night arguments about art and philosophy. The language.

"Even though he was an outsider, there was a kind of elegance—even a sense of superiority—that comes with being an expat in gay Paree. Just the fact that you made it out of here —to *over there*—gives a certain kind of prestige. Back here, he's just one of us. No different from every Tom, Dick and Harry trying to make ends meet.

"Then, there was Pierre, the man he left behind. Even though it ended badly, there must've been moments that felt true."

Hayward paused. "At the same time, sometimes, I wonder—does he actually miss Paris? Or just the idea of what Paris was supposed to be?"

Redding slowly nodded, watching Hayward through half-lidded eyes. He gave it another beat. Then leaned forward, voice shifting back to business.

"I'd like to return to McAllister for a moment. We've talked a lot about Carlisle," he said. "But you knew Grayson, too."

Hayward stilled. "Everyone knew Victor."

"Not like you did."

Hayward shifted uneasily.

"So," Redding said. "Did you stay in contact with Grayson over the years, the way you did with Ev?"

Hayward's eyes registered the nickname in Redding's mouth, that small familiarity landing like a gentle probe against a tender spot. A slow exhale. "No."

"Why not?"

A shrug. "It just didn't happen."

"You never saw him? Not once?"

"I didn't say that. I said we weren't in contact."

"There's a difference?"

"Damn straight there is."

"You run a bookstore. Grayson wasn't just a highly respected professor. He was a well-received author. You mean you never had him in here, to do a reading, to talk about his books?"

Silence. Then an admission, followed quickly by a denial: "I may have—but that's not the same as keeping in contact."

"Still, you must've heard things. You are, after all, Harlem's Keeper of Secrets." A bit of honey to make the medicine go down.

Hayward's gaze dipped to the floor, stayed there a second too long. "Yes, well, Grayson, for all intents and purposes, wasn't a Harlem resident. He was only up here on occasion, to deliver talks—or do special projects."

A soft veering away. "And when he was here, did you hear anything? Rumors? Threats?"

"Against Victor? He wasn't the kind to make enemies."

Redding raised a brow. "We are talking about a man who was murdered."

Hayward glanced at him sideways. "Fine. If you count the people who envied him his success, then..." His voice trailed away.

They both knew who sat at the top of that list.

Redding reached into his coat pocket, pulled out the envelope and the note inside it. He didn't hand it over. Just held it out, let Hayward see the creases, the clean cut of the typewritten words, the lone initial at the bottom.

Hayward, the muscles in his jaw tense and bunched, read the brief note. Redding caught it—the moment Hayward's gaze landed on the "C." The bookstore owner's fingers tightened on his glass.

"You recognize this?" Redding asked.

Hayward slowly picked up his cigarillo, exhaled smoke through barely parted lips. Then he held out a hand. "Let me see."

Redding handed it over.

Hayward ran his thumb over the paper. It was standard

stock, nothing remarkable about it. His gaze traced the words again, lingered at the bottom.

"Hell of a thing." He passed it back. "I'd like to help you, Detective, but I've never seen it before."

"No? It's got your initial at the bottom."

Hayward smiled faintly, but there was no humor in it. "Mine and that of another ten-, twenty-, maybe a hundred thousand other men in this city. Hell, half the men I know got a C somewhere in their name."

"Including Carlisle," Redding said softly.

Hayward's eyes met his, then shifted away. A slight pause in the rhythm of his breathing.

"Yeah," he admitted, with a sigh. "Including him."

They sat in silence for a beat, smoke curling between them.

"Grayson and Carlisle. Were they in contact all these years, just like you and Carlisle?"

"I don't know, but I don't think so."

"Then when did they re-establish contact? Was it because of this special issue of *Commonwealth Review?*"

"No, it happened before then. Last year, in fact. Not long after Ev got back. They ran into each other at a literary salon."

"By chance?"

"Well, now that you ask, I'd have to say no, it wasn't."

"Go on."

"Ev found out Victor would be there. Made sure he was, too."

"Why?"

Hayward made a palms-open gesture. "Hell if I know. Maybe he thought he could mend things."

Or settle a score.

"You do know your friend's in a bad spot."

Hayward exhaled slowly. "That, Detective, is nothing new."

"This time it's worse."

Hayward tapped ash into the tray. "So what are you asking?"

"What would he do, if cornered?"

Hayward turned his glass in his hand, watching the slow swirl of liquid. Then, quietly: "Run."

Redding gave a small quick nod. That's what he figured.

Hayward lifted his eyes. "It's what he does, Detective. It's what he's always done."

Redding put away the note. His gaze drifted to the window. Outside, the late afternoon had faded into evening. The light drizzle had intensified into a steady rain, drumming against the glass with growing insistence. The sound deepened Redding's sense of isolation.

Inside, the shadows in the room were lengthening. Redding realized he'd lost track of time, of how long he'd been sitting there. His gaze returned to the bookstore owner.

The way Hayward told it, Carlisle came home because he had no choice. But Redding had another explanation.

Carlisle hadn't just come home. He'd come back for Grayson.

Further uptown, on 145th, the same rain tapped steadily on the gutters as Carlisle lit a cigarette with shaking fingers. He stood outside his rooming house, coat collar turned up against the night. It was cold in the drizzle, but somehow his little room felt colder. Wetter, heavier. Out here, at least, he could breathe. He didn't feel like he was in prison.

Not yet.

That detective—that bastard—meant business. Once upon a time, he would've been proud to see a colored man climb that high. Proud and happy.

But not now. Not like this.

That cop had all but said he was looking to pin Grayson's death on him.

Grayson. Dead.

How many times had he wished for it, prayed for it? Just so the ache might ease. How many hours had he wasted imagining the moment, how it would feel—to have Grayson gone and him finally free?

How the hell had he been so goddamn naive?

And now that cop was after him.

Should he run? Pack what little he had, slip away before the questions turned sharper? Before the walls closed in?

Paris crossed his mind again. Not the Paris where everything fell apart, where the dream rotted slow and quiet. But the other one. The one he preferred to remember. The one he'd wanted it to be.

But it was too far away, too expensive. And let's face it. He was too old, too tired. And it was too damn late. The brick wall behind him felt like a tombstone. He leaned against it, gave in to a shiver. Exhaled. Smoke rose into the Harlem night.

He'd stay. He'd never been much of a gambler, but this time, he'd let the chips fall where they may.

17

He sensed the tilt the moment they put him in the chair. One chair leg was shorter than the other. He instinctively tried to adjust himself, to shift his weight, but every move caused the chair to rock, to deliver a jolt.

The tilt was deliberate. Had to be. A little psychological trick. To rag the unlucky slob who had to sit there.

He tried to sit still, to endure the chair's unrelenting tilt, but his body betrayed him. He shifted his weight again and the sharp tilt beneath him sent a jolt straight up his spine. Every movement, every shift, made the room tilt even further. He couldn't escape it. Couldn't hold still. The damn chair mocked him, just like everything else in his life. No matter how hard he tried, it would always remind him that the ground beneath him wasn't steady. Not anymore.

The best solution was to sit forward, his hands clenched and placed on the table. But every now and then his right hand would pat his pants pocket. He couldn't help it. Had to reassure himself that the folded bills he'd managed to scrape together were still there. Of course, they were. But they were a cruel joke now—money meant for rent, now useless behind these walls.

Hours earlier, he'd been counting those same bills on the street outside Hayward's shop, relief washing over him. He'd pulled together just enough to satisfy Marchetti, to keep his meager possessions from being tossed onto the curb. All that desperate scrambling.

Please, Lord, he prayed. *Don't let it turn out to be for nothing.*

The night before, he'd found a card game in the back room of a tailor's shop on Lenox, the curtain drawn tight, the wood stove glowing low. A bottle passed hand to hand, the cards slick with wear, the stakes small but brutal. He played close, careful. Let the others talk themselves into folding. When he left, he had the beginnings of what he needed, but he was still short.

By the time he made it back to his room, it was three in the morning. He collapsed and slept late. Dragged himself out to scrounge up the rest of the rent. First stop: the pawn shop. The broker was no friend—just a man marking Carlisle's descent.

This time, it was the cufflinks. Rose gold with jet inlay, a gift from Pierre, the only thing Carlisle had managed to hold onto through the last financial collapse. He didn't want to think about what Pierre had paid for them, only what they'd meant.

The broker barely glanced up. Turned the cufflinks over with calloused fingers. "Three fifty."

"They're worth twenty times that."

"Take it or leave it."

Three bucks fifty. Carlisle walked out sick.

He started walking. Found himself in front of Hayward's bookstore. Told himself not to think. *Just go in and get it over with.*

Hayward looked up from his ledger, took in Carlisle's appearance. "Early for you, isn't it?"

Carlisle's rehearsed speech vanished. Instead, he simply put what he had on the counter. "It's the rent. I'm short."

It was an old song. They both knew how to play it.

Hayward didn't say a word. Just opened the register, counted out bills and slid them across the polished wood. "I don't mind giving it to you, but it's a loan, you hear? I want it back. You got that?"

Carlisle nodded, folded the bills and tucked them into his wallet. "Yeah, I got it. I'll pay you back. I promise."

Hayward grunted, then went back to his ledger. Carlisle lingered. Took in the lines in Hayward's face. They were deeper now, set in places where exhaustion tended to settle. It struck him that Hayward no doubt had his troubles, too.

As for the cash, he knew what Hayward was doing. Offering a lifeline without calling it one. Pretending it was a loan, that Carlisle would find a way to repay him. It was Hayward's way of saying he still believed in him.

Problem was, Carlisle no longer believed in himself. He wished he did. Wished he felt confident that he'd someday be able to pay Hayward back—not just for this but for all the other kindnesses he'd shown him.

But the way his life was going, that would never happen.

So he murmured, "Thanks," and stepped outside into the cold. Relief passed through him. He could still make it. Get there in time. Pay the rent.

He paused to count the bills. The cold bit at his fingers. He didn't care. He finally had enough. He'd get to keep his room, his typewriter, the unfinished manuscript—everything.

He didn't notice the crunch of tires on frozen gravel, didn't look up until it was too late. The squad car rolled to a stop beside him. Two white cops got out, their expressions stone-like.

"Everett Carlisle?"

His throat constricted. "Yeah?"

No explanation. No nothing. They just shoved him into the back seat. Begging didn't help. Nothing helped.

Now, he sat in an interrogation room, collar open, suspenders off-kilter. Cold sweat gathered at his back as his fingers kept returning to his pants pocket, as if the money there might somehow still save him.

He didn't know how long he'd been sitting there, but he knew it was too long. If he didn't find a way to get out of there, noon would come and go, and Marchetti would have his way.

His throat felt dry, but he didn't reach for the water glass they'd left him. Experience had taught him to touch nothing.

Instead, he stared at the walls, the grime, away from the lurid light that made his eyes burn. He could feel the cold creeping in, not just from the air, but from the room itself. It was bone-cold, the kind that gripped deep.

He eyed the grating on the window. What the hell had he done with his life? To end up here. A prisoner of his own damn decisions.

But it was the smell that got him. It hit him in his gut, low and nauseating. Stale smoke, old coffee, and something else. Oh, yeah, the sour stench of desperation. His stomach turned, but he didn't let it show. He'd learned long ago that fear was a scent pungent to any hunter.

The lamp overhead flickered again. Bare and glaring, it hung low from a thin, rusted chain. Its harsh light beat down on him —mean and merciless. Did what it was meant to do: make a man feel trapped.

Carlisle held up a hand to block out the glare. But it cut through his scrawny fingers with the sharpness of a blade. Squinting, he could just make out the silhouette leaning against the wall. Arms folded, one boot to the wall, his outline darker than the shadows around him.

A soldier's stillness. Not casual—controlled. Like a sniper who could wait all night for the shot and not flinch when it came time to take it.

It was that detective, Redding. He was behind this. He was the one who could cause him to lose it all—his room, his work, what little he had left.

"Detective, could we do this later? I promise to come back. It's just that I've got some personal business to take care of. It's urgent and—"

"Let's talk about that fight at *Commonwealth Review*." Redding pushed away from the wall. Walked over to Carlisle.

Carlisle felt his heart thump. "The *Review?* What about it?"

"The way I hear it, you didn't take rejection too well." Redding circled the table, slow.

The light threw shadows that were far and long. They crawled up the table, dark fingers reaching for him.

Carlisle forced a shrug. "A rejection? You do realize I get those weekly? Sometimes daily even."

"That many, huh? Then I gotta wonder—what made this one so special?"

Carlisle worried his bottom lip. *Noon,* Marchetti had said. *You and your trash'll be out on the street.* It must be close. Damn close. But he could still make it. If—

"Listen, I gotta go pay my rent. I promise to—"

"Witnesses say you were angry. Furious. That you accused Grayson of being afraid of your ideas. Called him a coward."

Carlisle gave a weak smile. "If you hauled in every writer who ever called an editor a coward, you'd need a stadium."

"Maybe. But how many end up on the wrong side of a murder investigation?"

Murder. Investigation.

Carlisle went still. Murder wasn't just a word. It was a door, closing.

"A small tantrum," he said. "Done to impress all those long-nosed Sallies in the room." He paused. "Every writer does it once."

"You stormed out. Slamming doors. That sound about right?"

How to convince this cop to let him go? "Look, if I were going to kill a man, it wouldn't be over a damn magazine rejection."

Redding stopped behind him. "That's the thing. This wasn't about the rejection. It was about something older, much older. And whatever it was, you brought it to Davenport's party."

Carlisle felt the chill penetrating. It wasn't the cold, his thin clothes, his malnourishment. No, it was the quiet feeling, growing by the moment, that this room, with its filthy grated windows, wasn't just a place—it was a sentence. A quiet little death sentence.

"I don't know—"

Smack. A fat folder hit the table hard. Carlisle jumped.

Redding gave a slow nod as if satisfied. "A lot of people saw you take your shot at Grayson. A beatdown, front and center."

"People exaggerate."

"Multiple witnesses. More than a dozen guests."

"Half of them drunk. Too sauced to remember their own names."

"And yet, somehow, all of them remember *you.*"

"Well, I've always been memorable."

Carlisle forced a chuckle. But inside, he could feel the walls closing in. The minutes were ticking by. And he was nowhere near getting out of there.

"Detective, seriously. My rent, I—"

Redding scraped a chair out, swung it around, and sat. Arms folded on the backrest. "Then, there's what happened in the garden."

Carlisle's stomach clenched. *Davenport. Damn her.* "Look, I don't know what that crazy lady—"

"You mean your hostess? That the lady you mean?"

Carlisle clamped his jaw shut.

"You told Grayson: 'If you do this, I swear, you'll regret it.' What was he gonna do, Ev?"

Silence.

"You weren't arguing about art anymore, were you?"

More silence.

Finally, Carlisle, trembling, lifted his chin. "Two men. Too much gin. Too much history."

"History?"

Stillness again.

Redding leveled his gaze at him. "Tell me about it."

Carlisle felt it. The hope drain out. Like a bell inside him, ringing flat.

He wasn't getting out in time.

Now he had to focus on getting out at all.

"You're reaching, Detective."

"Am I?"

Carlisle swallowed. "If I killed every man I ever argued with, Harlem would be empty." *Wrong thing to say,* he realized. He'd just admitted it—to being combative. Argumentative.

Angry.

Redding pushed harder. "Grayson's been on your mind a while now, hasn't he? Long before the blowup at *Commonwealth Review.*"

"I don't know what you mean."

"I mean McAllister."

Carlisle froze. "Th-that…was a long time ago."

"Not long enough. You never forgot. Never recovered. He ruined your life, didn't he? And you've been bitter ever since. Carried it like a monkey on your back. Finally got tired of it. Hell, I know I would've."

"I—"

"So, you came back. Gave up that big-ass life in Paris, came back to good old Harlem, just to track him down."

"I—"

"And you tried—really tried—to claw your way into his world. But they wouldn't have you. *He* wouldn't have you. That rejection? That wasn't about your writing. That was him saying no to *you.* Kicking you to the curb. And he did it in front of *everybody.* Every living soul in that office heard him take you down."

"No—"

"So you decided to take *him* down."

"No!"

"To humiliate him. Tear him down in front of his people. In front of those rich white folk who backed him. The same ones you so desperately want to back you."

"No. You got it all wrong. I—"

"And when that didn't work, you took him back in time. Back to when he messed you over. You told him he owed you. But he shook that off. Then you told him he'd regret it. And he. *Still.* Said. No."

At first, Carlisle said nothing. Then, chest heaving, he dragged a hand down his face. "Fine. What if I did. So what?"

"So now...he's dead."

Carlisle paled. "That's a hell of a thing to lay at a brother's feet."

"And that ain't all."

Redding pulled out the blackmail note and slapped it on the table.

Carlisle stared at it. Horror crossed his face.

"Go on, Ev." A slow nod toward the note. "Tell me about it."

Carlisle's hands shook. He clasped them together. "I told you. I've never seen it. Don't know nothing about it."

"That's funny." Redding picked up the note, studied it as if he was really seeing it for the first time. "Cause it's got your initial on it." He pointed to it. "That *is* your initial, isn't it, Ev? That 'C'?"

Carlisle's lips parted—then shut.

"So, you do recognize it," Redding said.

Carlisle's shoulders, already hunched, caved just a little more. "No."

"You were angry. Felt betrayed. Thought you'd make him pay."

"I didn't."

"So you sent him this little note here—"

"I—"

"And when that didn't work, you finished him."

"No."

But the word was more a protest than denial, and weak. His breath hitched. His eyes welled. He pressed his fingers against the shape in his pocket.

The folded bills. Still warm. Now useless.

He pictured Marchetti's face, smug and mean. The door to his room cracked open.

All that scrambling.

None of it mattered now.

"You'd better start talking." Redding's shadow fell long across the table. "And you'd better start now."

Carlisle exhaled, head sinking. He wasn't angry. Just tired. Worn down to the bone.

He thought of the clothes Pierre had bought him. The cologne. That one bar of soap from Paris he'd never used, just kept for the scent and the memories. He thought of his typewriter, bought second-hand and certainly battered, but still beloved. The articles he was editing. The novel he'd finally started.

They'd all be gone now.

Scattered across the sidewalk. Picked over by strangers. Swept into the gutter.

His memories. His work. His name.

Gone.

And now, most likely—his freedom, too.

He wanted to give up, to let this cop frame him. But the same stubborn streak that had refused to let him give up, give in before, reared up.

Carlisle drew a deep breath. His lips parted—

Then came a knock at the door.

18

Redding turned, irritation flashing across his face. He was close. He could feel it. Carlisle was cracking, bit by bit and now—this interruption.

"Yeah?"

A young uniformed officer stuck his head in. "Capt'n wants to see you."

"But I'm right in the middle of—"

"What can I say? The captain says he wants to see you—and I think he means now."

Redding gritted his teeth, flexed his hands. He glanced back at Carlisle. The man's face was pale, drawn tight. Clearly, he'd been on the edge of breaking. This delay would give him time to collect himself, to steady his nerves. To come up with more stories. More lies.

Shit.

"You want some coffee?" he asked Carlisle.

The man nodded, almost absently.

Redding grabbed the case file and headed for the door. "Get him a cup of joe. Black," he told the uniformed cop before brushing past him.

The precinct was loud, all jangling phones, shouted orders, boots scuffing the cracked tile. But inside Captain James Egan's office, the racket hit a wall and died. Only the tick of a battered clock marked the time, slow and steady as a funeral drum. The room reeked of tobacco, cologne and pizza. All of it cheap. All of it old.

Egan sat behind his desk like a man rooted to the earth, thick from neck to knee. His gut rode high and hard against the battered wood and he was proud of it. His silver hair was slicked to one side, flat against his pink scalp. His ice-blue eyes, small and sharp, pinned a man in place better than any badge or sidearm.

He wasn't alone.

Lieutenant Sturgis "Brutus" Benedict lurked off to one side, all slab shoulders and hanging fists. A freight engine in human form, running on grudge and badge authority. The kind of man you sent in when a warning needed to leave bruises.

Redding entered. "Captain?"

Egan nodded toward Benedict. "You know the lieutenant."

The two officers acknowledged one another with a nod.

"Sir," Redding said.

"He and I," Egan began, "we've been discussing the Davenport case."

"The what, sir?" Redding frowned, hoping the captain's words didn't mean what he thought they meant.

"Oh, I'm sorry." Egan waved a dismissive hand. The gesture was heavy, slow, like a man swatting flies he considered beneath him. "I meant the Grayson case. It's just that… Well, it's starting to seem like the Davenport case to me."

"I don't understand," Redding said, but he did. He understood quite well. Had sensed what was what the minute he stepped in the door. Davenport wanted this mess swept up and tucked away before it could stain her carpets. And her needs now took priority.

Over justice.

Over proper procedure.

Over everything.

As for Grayson, the man who'd lost his life? He was now no more than a footnote in his own murder file.

He felt Benedict's gaze on him, the smirk lurking at the corner of the lieutenant's mouth. Redding felt a quiet fury begin. The thought that this thug—that he and the captain—had been "discussing" the Grayson case behind his back galled him. Inwardly, he called them both every name in the book. Outwardly, he clasped his hands in front of him, the case file tucked protectively under one arm, arms pressed tightly to his sides.

Egan leaned forward, elbows on his desk and stared up at Redding. "We're getting pressure from the top. People are nervous. This ain't just some back-alley killing. This happened at Margery Davenport's house." He paused. "She's been making calls. To all the right people. Important people."

Redding nodded. "I understand, sir."

Egan's gaze sharpened. "Do you? 'Cause I'm not so sure you do."

He yanked open a drawer and took out a folded sheet of paper. "You went to see her, didn't you?"

"Yes, sir."

"Demanded—not asked—demanded she turn over a guest list. Like you thought you had the right."

"Yes, I—"

"Well, she did."

Egan held up the typed list of names just long enough for Redding to catch a glimpse.

Redding felt a surge of relief. He started to extend his hand.

Egan tore the list clean down the middle. Then again. And again. Until it was nothing but jagged scraps.

He tossed the pieces into the brass ashtray on his desk, flicked open his lighter and touched the flame to the pile.

The fire caught fast. Blackened edges curled inward. The paper twisted, smoked and collapsed into gray ash.

"There." Egan clicked the lighter shut with a snap that sounded final. "That takes care of that."

He ground the ashes down with the flat of his lighter until there was nothing left but dust.

Redding pressed his lips together, jaw tight.

"Let me make something clear to you, Detective," Egan said. "You do not embarrass people like Margery Davenport. You do not leave fingerprints on her walls. And you don't go kicking over rocks unless you're told. You forget that and you're done—and not just here."

Benedict chuckled from his corner. "Or worse."

Egan dusted his hands, brushing off the last of the ash. He rose, slow as a landslide. His gut nearly nudged the desk toward Redding.

"Now, I called you in here 'cause I need some good news. We need to make this go away. But quick."

The office seemed smaller with him standing. More airless.

Egan came around the desk and stopped a foot from Redding, that high gut leading the way like a battering ram.

"I told them I have my best man on it. And I'm gonna give you a chance to prove that." He smiled, thin and humorless. "So now, I need some good news. I called you in here, hoping you'd give me some."

"I'm making progress. But Captain, that list—"

Egan held up a hand. "You never saw it. Never heard of it. Will never speak of it again."

He lowered his bulk on the edge of his desk. The wood groaned under him. "I'm told you have a suspect—a perfectly fine one, practically made to order—but that he's still walking free."

Redding checked his anger. "Actually, I have him in interrogation. I was just—"

"Good. Very good. So I can expect you to wrap this up any minute now?"

"The thing is, I—"

"That was not a question, Detective."

Benedict chuckled, low and mean. "Davenport wants her Negro parties scandal-free, huh? What a goddamn tragedy."

Redding realized his hand had tightened into a fist and relaxed it.

"The evidence is there." Egan ticked the points off with thick fingers. "We have motive. Opportunity. Even a goddamn note. What else do you need?"

Redding breathed in, breathed out. "A confession."

Benedict scoffed. "Then break him."

Redding ignored him, kept his focus on Egan. "You know as well as I do, sir, that a broken man will confess to anything. A confession gotten like that? It's not worth the paper it's written on."

Egan narrowed his eyes. "You questioning my methods, boy?"

There it was. That word and all the contempt it conjured. Meant to put him in his place. To reduce him, in one fell swoop, from a grown man to a child. It didn't matter how many cases he closed, how hard he'd worked to pull himself up the ladder. How many awards he earned or medals got pinned on his chest. It would never matter, not to men like Egan. They'd clap you on the back one minute, slip a shiv between your ribs the next.

Redding met the captain's gaze, held steady. "No, sir. Not questioning. Just making sure we don't get sloppy." A pause. "I've met Mrs. Davenport. She's an honorable lady."

"She wants it done fast."

"I'm sure she also wants it done right."

Silence. Tense and coiled.

Egan broke it. "You have two hours. Two. After that?" He jerked his head toward Benedict. "I let the lieutenant take a crack at him."

Benedict's grin widened, slow and satisfied. He cracked his knuckles. "Guess I better get my hands warmed up."

Egan glanced back at Redding. "It's been a while since the lieutenant here has had a chat with one of your suspects, hasn't it?" His smile was laconic, easy and full of malice. "I'm sure you'd like to keep it that way."

Message sent, message received. Benedict's methods weren't just rough—they were ruthless. Redding could feel the man's stare, heavy and smug.

"Yes, sir."

Benedict shifted, rolling his shoulders. Big hands. Slow movements. A man who liked to take his time.

"You're excused, Detective."

Redding left, head swimming. Two hours. That's all he had to get something real. Because if he didn't?

The next time he saw Carlisle, he might not recognize him.

He crossed the squad room without looking left or right, the case file clenched tight in his hand. The noise washed over him —phones, laughter, the scrape of chairs—but it barely touched him.

Two hours.

Less now.

Because he knew damn well they weren't going to let him use all of it.

19

Redding slipped back into the interrogation room. Carlisle sat cuffed to the chair, a cup of coffee sitting on the table, untouched. Hands clasped, ankles crossed.

Redding was relieved to see that signs of him cracking were there. In the shoulders. The tightness in the jaw.

Redding pulled out a chair. Sat. "You're out of time, Ev."

Carlisle swallowed but said nothing.

Redding tossed the folder down between them. The slap of paper against wood made Carlisle flinch. Redding flipped the folder open, pulled out the note, let it rest between them. Carlisle's gaze landed on it. Held there.

"Tell me again how this wasn't you."

Carlisle shifted, just slightly. "I already did."

Redding leaned in. "The captain wants this case closed. Every minute you stall, every second you hem and haw, the worse it's going to be for you."

"Is that supposed to scare me?"

"It should."

Carlisle paled, just slightly.

They went back and forth like that. Words sharp, the pauses sharper. Each feint and parry bleeding the minutes dry.

Redding flicked a glance at his wristwatch. An hour gone already. One left.

He needed to figure Carlisle out. The man was holding out like a pro. Like a man hardened by multiple run-ins with the law.

But that wasn't him.

What was the source of his resistance? He should've broken by now. He should've—

Redding straightened up. He understood. He should've seen it before. It was staring him right in the face. Carlisle was—

A sharp knock at the door.

Redding turned, frowning. The door creaked open. It was the young officer again.

"Your wife's on the line. Says it's urgent."

Redding frowned. That didn't make sense. She never called him here. "Did she say what it was about?"

"Nope. Just kept asking for you."

Redding hesitated. Something was off.

But if it was his wife—if something had happened—he couldn't ignore it.

His fingers curled into a fist against the table before he grabbed the file and stood. He pushed past the officer and headed toward the bullpen. Reached his desk, yanked the receiver off the hook.

"Yeah, hon? I'm here. What is it?"

Silence.

He pressed the phone to his ear. Nothing. No crackle, no voice.

He jiggled the switch hook. "Operator?"

A pause, then a crisp, professional voice came on the line. "Yes, this is the switchboard."

"This is Redding. You patched a call through for me—from my wife?"

A longer pause. Then: "No call came through for you, Detective."

Redding's grip tightened on the receiver. His jaw clenched. "You're sure?"

"I handle every call, sir. No one's rung for you all night."

Realization hit him. It had been a trick. To get him out of the interrogation room. His head snapped up, suddenly aware of the men standing around, watching him. One cop flicked ashes into a tray, observing him with barely concealed amusement. Another leaned toward his partner, murmuring something under his breath.

Redding's gaze cut toward the interrogation room.

No!

He slammed the receiver onto the cradle and barreled back down the hall. He shoved past desks, ignoring the smug glances from the other officers. His heartbeat thundered in his ears as he reached for the handle—

And threw open the door.

Carlisle was on the ground. Benedict loomed over him, fist clenched, breathing hard like a man who'd been enjoying himself.

Blood spattered the floor, a smear of it trailing down from Carlisle's mouth, where his lip had split open. One of his eyes was already swelling, the deep purple bruising creeping in fast.

Carlisle coughed, trying to push himself upright, but his hands trembled, fingers curling against the pain.

Redding's stomach churned. "Get the hell offa him!"

Benedict turned, wiping his knuckles with a slow grin. "Didn't hear you knock."

"What the fuck are you doing in here? I had another hour."

Benedict glanced down at Carlisle. "Figured I'd help move things along."

Redding stepped closer. "Get out. Now."

Benedict calmly wiped his knuckles on a handkerchief. "Fine. Do it your way." He stepped past Redding, bumping his shoulder as he went. Then he leaned in, close and gripped Redding's shoulder. "But don't take too long. Captain wants this wrapped up. And next time?" His hold tightened, just enough to let Redding feel it. "You don't get a warning."

The door shut behind him.

Silence.

Redding let out a slow breath, forcing the anger down. He turned toward Carlisle. Carlisle sat still as stone, his eyes barely open. His right hand—fingers bent at an awkward angle—trembled against his knee.

Redding crouched down next to Carlisle. Then, quietly, "Ev."

Nothing.

Redding reached out. "Ev."

Carlisle jerked away, as if expecting another hit. Redding's stomach twisted. Carlisle's breath hitched. Carlisle's eyes opened, barely, and for the first time, his gaze lifted. It was unfocused, hazy with pain. But there was something else there, too.

Defeat.

Redding kept his voice low. "Can you move your hand?"

Carlisle swallowed, then shook his head.

Redding took a quick visual inventory of Carlisle's injuries. Possibly a broken eye socket, maybe a broken rib, definitely broken fingers. "You need a doctor." Redding started to get up to go.

Carlisle's good hand shot out, grabbed the detective. "D-don't leave me here. Not with them."

Redding took a moment. "I got to. But I won't be gone long. I promise." He gently removed Carlisle's hand from his arm.

Carlisle gave a soft grunt. "No, of course you won't." He closed his eyes, and with a sigh withdrew into his world of pain.

Redding got to his feet. Less than an hour left.

And now?

Now he had to make sure that whatever came out of Carlisle's mouth was the truth—and not something beaten out of him.

He turned and left, throwing open the door with just enough force to make it bang against the frame.

He had a fight ahead of him.

Because now, this wasn't just about a case.

This was about making sure Everett Carlisle survived it.

Redding pushed through the crowded bullpen, the scent of blood still fresh in his nose. His strides were tight with frustration. He itched to grab Benedict by the collar and slam his face into the nearest desk, but that wasn't going to help Carlisle—not now.

It took him less than a minute to find Egan.

The captain was behind his desk, sleeves rolled up, hunched over a report. He didn't look up when Redding entered.

"Carlisle needs medical attention."

Egan let out a slow breath, finally glancing up. "I warned you, didn't I? Told you to break him. You had your shot."

"That wasn't a break. That was a goddamn beating."

"That's the way things get done."

There was a knock on the door. Egan bellowed, "Later." He looked at Redding, said, "And you're still here."

"At least keep him alive long enough to make it to trial."

Egan appeared to consider it. "Well, I guess I could call in Dr. Evans. He'd patch him up. That's the best I can do."

"Call him in when?"

Egan's gaze sharpened. "When it suits me."

"Not good enough. I need Evans here now."

"*You* need?" A slow, malignant smile. "We're not here to serve *your* needs, Detective." Egan let out a slow breath, sat back and adjusted the belt containing his gut. "Anyway, I don't see the urgency."

"No? He's barely upright. His fingers are broken, his eye socket's swelling and I suspect his ribs are broken."

Egan was unmoved. He picked up a pen and tapped it twice against the desk. "You want him patched up so you can finish your little chat, is that it?"

"I want him conscious enough to answer my goddamn questions."

Egan raised his eyebrows, inclined his head. "Fine. I'll see what I can do. But I warn you, Evans is a busy man."

"Not too busy for this. One more thing."

Egan sighed. "What now?"

"We keep Carlisle in holding. Here. And you tell Benedict and everybody else to stay the hell away from him. No transfers to the Tombs."

"Why not?"

"Because that'd be a death sentence and you know it."

Egan shrugged. "It'd save the taxpayers some money. What's wrong with that?"

"Not much. Just that if Carlisle dies in your custody, this whole case will blow up in your face. You think Davenport's making calls now? Wait'll she sees those headlines. '*Star Suspect in the 'Davenport' Murder Case Dead While in Police Custody.*' Strung up or beaten to death. A supposed suicide. You think she wants her name associated with that? She's spent time and money building a reputation for supporting colored artists. You let one of them get beaten to death in a police cell? She becomes the woman whose pressure led to a lynching."

Redding watched the truth of his words sink in.

Egan's jaw tightened. They both knew what would happen. The Negro papers would call Carlisle's death a tragedy—and the white ones would turn it into a spectacle. White people who opposed Davenport would use the death against her, say it served her right for having 'niggras' in her home. And the colored? They'd blame her for bringing down the weight of the law on one of their own, for not caring enough to ensure his safety.

Still, Egan resisted. "She wants it solved quick—"

"She wants it solved clean. She damn sure doesn't want a scandal."

Egan's eyes narrowed. Then, finally, he grabbed the phone. "You'd better give me what I want, Redding. A goddamn confession or I swear I'll—"

But Redding wasn't there to hear the rest of it.

He was already moving, already out the door.

20

Everett Carlisle had suffered a good number of beatings in his life. In Philly, Boston. Even in Paris. Men everywhere liked to take out their petty bigotry by making him their punching bag. And he'd learned to take it, to hide the pain, roll with the punches.

But he'd never been beaten quite like this. It wasn't just the physical pain—bad as it was, he could handle that. No, it went deeper. Cut deeper.

Right down to his soul.

His eye pulsed, ribs throbbed, each breath a stab. The fingers on his right hand—he didn't even want to think about them.

The good thing about feeling pain, he told himself, as he always did in these situations, was that he could still *feel* it. That meant he was still alive. Still breathing.

But if he didn't talk now, he might soon not be able to.

He gazed at the detective through his one good eye. "Show me that note again."

Redding pulled it from the folder, unfolded it and slid it across the table.

Carlisle picked it up with his left hand—the only one that still worked. His fingertips traced the creases. An ugly note with an ugly message. But it was something that Victor had touched, had held in his hand.

"Where'd you find it?"

"On Grayson's body."

Carlisle nodded to himself. "Then it's the same one all right."

"So you do recognize it."

"Yeah—but not because I wrote it."

"Explain."

Carlisle inhaled deeply and grimaced at the pain. "Victor showed it to me. Asked me about it. I told him it wasn't from me. But he already knew that."

"You're saying he knew who it was from?"

"Yeah. Someone at McAllister."

"Why would another professor write him such a note?"

Carlisle's grip tightened around the paper. "Victor found out the truth about him."

"What truth?"

"I don't know the details. Victor wouldn't tell me. Just said that it was bad, real bad."

"And who is this person?"

"Mercer. Name is Clive Mercer. He's faculty research coordinator. Victor said Mercer was up to no good and Mercer found out that Victor knew about it."

"Up to no good? What does that mean?"

A painful shrug. "Not sure. Victor didn't tell me. Not all of it."

"So the note?"

"Was Mercer's response."

Redding sagged back in his chair. Carlisle couldn't tell if Redding believed him or not. But he was gratified to see the detective rub a hand down his jaw and sink into pensive silence.

But then Redding gave him a quick, probing look. "Man, are you jiving me? Cause if you are—"

Carlisle sat up fast—too fast. The chair rocked, giving him a nasty jolt, and his ribs screamed in protest. "No. No jive." He grimaced and panted, open-mouthed, at the pain. "Why the hell would I lie now?"

"Then tell me something else."

"What?"

"Why would Grayson trust you with this? Why not someone else?"

Carlisle went still. That one question went to the heart of it, didn't it? That one question required an answer that would reveal it all. "Because..." He forced himself to swallow. "Because I was the only person he could trust with it."

Redding's expression didn't change, but his body shifted—a fraction, but enough. "Say that again."

Carlisle closed his eyes. The answer was so obvious—so deep in his bones—that for a moment, he couldn't believe Redding didn't already know it. He stared at the detective, forcing the words out.

"Because his secret was mine, too."

Redding tilted his head, eyes narrowed. His silence forced Carlisle to say the unspeakable.

"We were lovers, man. We were lovers."

The words sat there between them. Heavy. Irrevocable.

Carlisle held his breath, expecting something—judgment, disgust, maybe even amusement. But the cop only nodded, as if Carlisle's revelation was no great surprise. As if he'd already guessed it and only needed confirmation.

Redding stared past Carlisle. Just sat there.

The clock on the wall ticked. Ticked again.

Finally, Carlisle felt Redding's gaze move back to him. Felt the detective's probing stare. And he had the feeling he'd had before, that in a world of men, this man was a hunter, but that this time he, Carlisle, might not be the prey.

Then the hunter said four words, four that brought Carlisle some sense of relief. It wasn't much, but it was something.

"Tell me," he said, "about Mercer."

PART III

MERCER

21

He'd messed up. Failed to follow his own golden rule: know your victim. Now that failure had blown up in his face. A man was sitting in stir who didn't belong there—might die there, because he'd lowered his standards. Had been too quick, too willing to take the easy way out.

He hated cops who did that. Lazy. Sloppy. Short-sighted. Or just plain burnt out. He'd be damned before he ended up like them.

But this was worse than lazy. He'd had his doubts about Carlisle and buried them. The powers-that-be needed it to be Carlisle and he'd obliged: served up a colored man neat and clean, no fuss, no muss. He'd bowed to the system in a way he'd vowed he never would. Had told himself he was following the evidence. What he'd done was follow orders—and called it detective work.

So he was backtracking now. Going where he should've started: Grayson's apartment.

Vaughn let him in without a word.

She was composed, but her eyes were shadowed. "I don't suppose I can stop you from doing this."

"No, ma'am."

She stepped aside."The living room's this way." She gestured toward the open sliding doors.

Redding stood on the threshold, taking it in. The air smelled faintly of pipe tobacco and old paper. A reading chair sat in the corner, a blanket folded neatly over one arm. The place was neat, restrained. Much like the man himself.

Redding turned back to her. "You said this was a temporary rental."

"Yes, we're here just for as long as it takes him—would've taken him—to edit the special issue we were working on."

Redding took in the array of books and odds and ends. "So most of these things, they're not his."

"No." She shook her head.

Redding nodded to himself. "Was he troubled the last few days?"

Vaughn hesitated, then nodded. "Yes."

"How troubled?"

"Enough that he wasn't sleeping."

"Any other signs?"

"No. Not really. Just... Well, at times he seemed incredibly preoccupied."

"Did he tell you what was bothering him?"

"No. He wouldn't say anything. He knew I would've done anything to help him. I told him that. But he wouldn't tell me what was wrong—just said he appreciated my being there."

Redding made a mental note but didn't press. Instead, he turned his attention to Grayson's writing desk.

The drawers were unlocked. Redding worked through them quickly—stacks of letters, personal and professional. An unopened bank statement. Editorial notes relating to the lineup of content for the journal.

Then—something different. Correspondence from McAllister's accounting office.

Redding flipped through the letters, brow furrowing. The letters were dry, the language formal. But the contents? They were fire.

Grayson had been fighting accusations of fraud—allegations that he'd been falsifying travel expenses, claiming reimbursements for trips he never took.

Redding turned to Vaughn and held the letters out to her. "Did you know about this?"

She frowned, stepping forward to take them and quickly read the text. Her eyes widened and mouth slowly opened. Shock, yes, but something more. Something deeper.

"No." A quiet, almost disbelieving whisper. "I-I never saw these."

Redding observed her. "You're sure?"

"I would have remembered." She looked up, something wounded in her gaze. "He told me everything. Or at least, I thought he did."

Redding said nothing.

Vaughn exhaled, still staring at the letters. Then, slowly, she handed them back to him.

"I thought it was the journal," she murmured. "The special issue. The pressure to get it right. I thought that's what was weighing on him." A beat. "But this?" She shook her head. "He didn't tell me."

Not doubt. Not disbelief.

Grief.

Redding set the letters aside and went back to work. Nothing jumped out—until he found the notebook.

Leather-bound, worn. Grayson's handwriting—tidy, precise. Grayson was a man who wrote in all capital letters. Notes from meetings, more thoughts on the articles in progress.

And near the last few pages: detailed passages.

JET CONFIRMED SCHOLARSHIP DISCREPANCIES. SAME THREE NAMES. MERCER'S TOUCH ON ALL. FOUND THE

SOURCE FOR THE FINAL PIECE. MD WILL CONFIRM IN WRITING. NO DOUBT NOW.

Redding read the entry again. Twice.

Grayson had found something. Not a hunch. Not hearsay. Proof. The kind men kill to bury.

He turned to Vaughn. "Did the professor have a friend or associate named 'Jet?'"

She frowned, shook her head. "No. Why?"

MD. Two letters. Could be a name. Could be a place.

"Maryland. Any reason he'd go down there? Know someone? Have business?"

Another shake of the head. Slower this time. "Not that I know of."

Redding gave the room another look. His gaze landed on the filing cabinet. He nodded toward it. "You have the key?"

She glanced at it, her brow pulled tight. He could feel her resistance—quiet, tight-lipped. She didn't want him touching any of it.

Still, she opened the desk drawer, took out a key and handed it over. No words. Just that closed mouth and lips pressed into a tight line.

Redding put the notebook down. He unlocked the cabinet and started rifling through. Donor letters. Financial reports. Travel claims.

Then—

A gap. A folder missing. Just enough space to tell him someone had gotten there first.

He shut the drawer and took both the notebook and the stack of correspondence.

When he turned, Vaughn was still there, arms folded, watching him.

"Was he really murdered?" she asked.

"We're still waiting on the M.E.'s report, but given what we know so far, I'd say, yeah."

Her eyes grew hard. "Then find who did it."

Redding tucked the paperwork under his arm and gave her a nod. "I'll do my best."

Clearly, it wasn't what she wanted to hear but she'd have to accept it. Another curt nod. The grief was still there, but sharper now. Shaped into something that could cut.

"I'll see myself out," he said.

He turned to go, but she reached out, touched him lightly on the elbow.

"You didn't ask me about Professor Mercer. Why not?"

"You said you didn't know about the allegations against the professor. Or his suspicions. I figured—"

"What? That I wouldn't have anything to say?"

She didn't mean just about Mercer. And they both knew it.

"Do you?"

"I just don't want you distracted from the person you should be focusing on. Everett Carlisle. Remember what—"

"I remember. Everything you said. Trust me, I do. And if Carlisle's the one, then digging into Mercer only strengthens the case."

"How?"

"By tearing down anything the defense might try to float at trial."

She tilted her head. Considered that. "Oh. I see."

Then she smiled.

"Like playing chess, isn't it? Thinking several moves ahead."

"Yeah." He didn't smile. "It's just like that."

He reached the vestibule before her voice stopped him.

"Detective?"

He turned.

"He was a good man," she said. "Better than most."

"Then he deserves the truth."

He stepped out and closed the door before she could say anything more.

The notebook was heavy in his pocket. He had a better picture of Grayson now, of a man accused of fraud who'd found evidence of something bigger. Something that got him killed.

That missing folder. It sat in his mind like a gap in a smile.

Whoever took it knew what it meant—and who it could ruin.

The small cramped office of *Commonwealth Review* was busy, but oddly muted. People were going about their work, but the atmosphere was devoid of energy. It was almost as though people were sleepwalking through their tasks.

Grief? Redding wondered. Shock? Likely both.

He followed Martin Jacobs, the editor-in-chief, to Grayson's office. Jacobs had told Redding on the phone that he'd be happy to cooperate, but in person he was sullen, irritated.

"Make it quick," Jacobs muttered.

Redding pushed past him without answering.

This office was smaller than the one Grayson had at home. It was Spartan, efficient. Just a desk, with a phone and two chairs. Shelves lined one wall, stacked with past issues of the magazine, a dictionary, and typed pages. The desk held more stacks of manuscripts, along with an inkwell and pen. The air smelled of dry ink and paper dust.

Redding started with the obvious—the desk drawers. The top drawer held paperclips and a half-used bottle of ink. The second drawer had copies of correspondence—letters exchanged with contributors, editorial notes. He flipped through them quickly. Nothing about Mercer.

Redding tapped the desk twice with his fingers, thinking. He hadn't expected to find a conclusive clue—that would've been too easy—but he had hoped for something.

All he'd found was absence.

But absence can itself speak volumes. Whatever Grayson had been facing, he'd been careful to keep it out of his workplace.

Redding left. Clearly, Grayson had buried his truth somewhere else. But where?

22

The precinct had that restless energy of shift change—uniforms heading out, detectives settling in, phones ringing with fresh complaints. Then there was the radiator in the corner. It was clanking and hissing, full of complaint. Listening to it, Redding thought it was as tired as he was.

He pulled the report from his typewriter and set it aside. Braced his elbows on his desk and rubbed his eyes. It had been a long day—too long—and he was more than ready to go home. But he wasn't done. Not yet.

He picked up the receiver and had the operator put through a call to McAllister. The connection crackled faintly before a clipped, professional voice answered.

"McAllister University, Faculty Offices."

Redding shifted slightly, adjusting his grip on the receiver. "Professor Clive Mercer, please."

A pause. The faint rustle of paper.

"One moment."

A few beats of silence. Then—

"This is Professor Mercer." The voice was smooth,

cultivated. Even over the line, it carried the confidence of a man used to being listened to. "How may I help you?"

"Professor, this is Detective Nathaniel Redding with the New York City Police Department. I'm investigating the death of Professor Victor Grayson."

A pause—brief, but there.

"Ah," Mercer said, his voice settling into something lightly sympathetic. "A terrible loss."

Too smooth. Redding had heard that tone before—from men who were quick on their feet, careful with their words.

"As part of my inquiry, I'm speaking with people who knew him," Redding continued. "Your name came up."

A fraction of a second too long before Mercer replied.

"Victor and I were colleagues. I wouldn't say we were particularly close. But still, I'd be happy to assist in any way I can."

"I'd like to meet with you. Would your office at McAllister be convenient?"

"Of course. Tomorrow afternoon. One PM. Does that suit you, Detective?"

"I'll see you then."

"I look forward to it."

The line clicked. Redding set the receiver down, stared at it for a long moment.

Cooperative. Efficient. And way too smooth.

Most people hesitated when they received a call from a cop. Especially when that cop said he was investigating a death. They stumbled, processed it. Even those with nothing to hide had to think about it for a second.

Not Mercer. He'd answered like a man expecting the call.

Redding sat back, considering.

That was either the mark of an innocent man.

Or a man who wanted to sound like one.

The holding cell smelled of sweat, stale air and rust. Weak light flickered from the overhead bulb, throwing long, sharp shadows against the concrete walls. The cot in the corner was barely more than a slab with a thin, scratchy blanket tossed over it.

Carlisle sat on the edge of it, upright, but with effort. His right eye was swollen, a dark purple mess, and his lip had split again where the stitches hadn't held. His fingers—two of them wrapped and stiff—rested lightly against his knee. He wasn't cuffed anymore, but his wrists still bore the deep red imprints.

Redding stepped inside. The door clanked shut behind him.

Carlisle didn't look up at first. Just sat there, hands folded, staring at some fixed point in the distance.

Redding stepped closer. "I'm leaving town."

Carlisle's brow barely lifted. "That right?"

"Going down to D.C."

"Congratulations. Hell of a time for a vacation."

Redding didn't smile. "Following that lead you gave me."

Surprise shifted in Carlisle's bruised face. Surprise. Even hope. Maybe. "Mercer?"

Redding gave a single nod.

Carlisle exhaled, with a slight grimace. "You think it'll make a difference?"

"It's the only shot you've got."

Carlisle took that in. "And what happens while you're gone?"

Silence.

They both knew what the real question was.

"I'll be back before you know it."

Carlisle's gaze held his for a long beat. Then, just once, he nodded. Small. Barely there.

That was as close to trust as he was going to get.

Redding didn't waste time on reassurances. Didn't bother with promises. He just stepped back and rapped twice on the bars. The guard swung the door open. Redding started out, then paused and glanced back.

Carlisle was watching him. They said nothing. They both knew what was at stake. Redding held the look for a second. Then he turned and was gone.

When Redding got back to his desk, he sat for a moment, thinking. Then he picked up the phone and had a call put through.

One ring. The line clicked open.

"I need to talk to you about the Grayson case."

Silence. Then: "I wondered when you'd call."

23

Dark wood and law books. The trappings of a life David McKay had never asked for but had settled into all the same. His Strivers' Row townhouse was all limestone and high ceilings, burnished hardwood floors and polished brass and exquisite marble fireplaces. It spoke of solid money and the dreams realized through his father's relentless drive.

Redding never failed to be amazed that a colored man owned it.

As Redding understood it, McKay's feelings were more… ambivalent. The delicate touches reminded McKay of his mother, a gentle, elegant woman. But the bones of the place—its stone and mortar—those spoke of his father's unyielding ambition.

McKay had once told Redding: "My old man wasn't just a businessman, he was a kingmaker. He thought power came with the right address. But this house—these walls—can be as much of a prison as a home."

That one comment told the story: the drive that had carved out this space in a white man's world and the burden of expectations that had nearly crushed the son who inherited it.

McKay had walked away from it once, from his father's dictatorial demands, from his place among Harlem's elite—that suffocating world that bestowed privilege on the few while binding them in golden chains. He'd stayed away for years, until death called him back.

As a civil rights and criminal defense attorney, McKay was still one of the best. But scandal had tarnished his reputation. Every now and then, he'd hear from a friend. But for the most part, only gossipmongers and curiosity-seekers darkened his doorway—along with the truly desperate. He took their cases—the lost causes, the ones no one else would touch, where the clients could rarely pay. He was always searching for something that mattered—a means to redemption, maybe, for what he saw as a failure that would haunt him for the rest of his life.

He and Redding had a shared history. They'd both served in the 369th Infantry Regiment under French command, side by side in the Champagne-Marne and Meuse-Argonne offensives, where they bled in the trenches. That meant that when Redding called, McKay answered.

McKay now sat behind his father's old desk, tie loosened, sleeves rolled up to his elbows, listening.

Time was burning. Redding didn't waste any more of it—he laid it out. "Got a man locked up for a crime he may not have committed and the brass is about to let the system eat him."

McKay already had some basic knowledge of the case—all of Harlem did. He let Redding talk, nodding here and there, making space for the facts to settle.

"What do you need from me?"

"I need you to keep him breathing long enough for me to do my job." Redding explained that he was headed down to D.C., to follow a lead.

"The minute I step away, I know one of them hard boys is gonna try to pull something. I can feel it in my bones. If Egan gets impatient, if Benedict decides to have another *chat*—Carlisle could be dead before I even step off the train."

"I don't disagree." McKay paused. "This trip you're planning. Your chief, he signed off on it?"

"Well," Redding said with a half-smile. "Put it like this: sometimes you gotta jump first and look later."

"Do you now?" McKay nodded slowly, an old wise man in a younger man's body. "Well, I say that may be true for a white man but it's never been true for a colored one."

"Amen to that. Problem is, I can't just sit on my hands while they railroad an innocent man."

A pause. "You do realize what you're risking, don't you?"

"I do."

"You know what the department does to colored officers who step out of line—even for a moment."

"I do, indeed."

"You talked to the missus about this? 'Cause what you're planning—"

"I've got no choice."

"It could destroy both your lives."

"It's about Carlisle living or dying, about finding a good man's killer."

"It's about your career, your reputation, maybe even your badge. If your captain finds out? He could kick you off the case. Most likely would. Egan's the type to take it even further. You could find yourself suspended, reassigned, or worse."

"This case is worth it, goddammit. It's worth it."

McKay said nothing. Just watched him. The clock on the wall ticked once, twice.

"I'll represent him. But what you really need is someone in that station house who can keep an eye on him. Step in if things turn ugly. You telling me there's no one down there you trust?"

"There's one," Redding said. "John 'Blackie' Blackwell. He

and Lanie Price cross paths more than most. He looks out for her."

"And for you?"

Redding held his gaze. "He'd do what's right."

"Then call him."

"He's out of town. Working a case."

A beat.

"So it's just me."

"Looks that way."

McKay said nothing. Then he reached for his pen. "Give me the details."

24

Penn Station's vast concourse stretched overhead like a cathedral to American progress, its steel-and-glass ceiling catching the early morning light. Redding moved through the crowd, mentally rehearsing his questions for Mercer, details of Carlisle's confession still fresh in his mind. Around him, porters called out destinations, shoes clicked against marble floors and the deep rumble of locomotives vibrated through the stone pillars.

He found his platform, boarded the Congressional Limited and walked toward the back. First coach. Second. Past the seats a man could buy with money—and lose with geography.

There were no permanently designated "colored cars" leaving New York. But once the train crossed into Maryland, matters changed. South of that line, the railroad observed segregation law. If you weren't seated in one of the rear coaches by then, a conductor would stop beside you and see to it.

Redding wasn't in the mood to be rearranged in public. Not today. Not with Mercer on his mind.

He chose the rear coach from the start.

The seat leather was worn but clean—the Pennsylvania

Railroad maintained certain standards. He settled by the window, draped his coat over his lap and tipped his hat forward to claim a slice of privacy. The train lurched into motion. Manhattan's steel canyons slipped past, then faded into the clear light of morning.

The train rattled south through New Jersey, steel wheels grinding against the tracks in steady rhythm. Outside the window, the city blurred away. Brick and steel dissolved into stretches of open fields and flickering towns.

The sunlight caught the Delaware River as they crossed into Pennsylvania, its surface like hammered copper.

Carlisle's words about Grayson had shifted focus in the case, but not in the way most would think. It wasn't about their relationship—that was just another secret in a city full of them. No, what mattered was how Grayson had stumbled onto Mercer's scheme: by being accused himself.

And the case, it wasn't just about who wanted Grayson gone.

It was about who needed him dead.

Redding thought of the blackmail note, the most damning piece of evidence yet. A single typed page, with the letter 'C' at the bottom. Everyone assumed it stood for 'Carlisle.' But it could just as easily stand for 'Clive,' couldn't it? As in Clive Mercer.

Redding mentally reviewed his notes. The university's accounting office had accused Grayson of padding travel expenses, claiming reimbursements for trips he'd never taken. But Grayson had fought back, demanded to see the claims—and found his signature on forms he'd never filed. All of them had crossed Mercer's desk.

The train crossed the Maryland line.

Redding looked up and saw more colored passengers entering the car, passengers who'd been sitting further forward. They came in one at a time at first. Then in twos. Men lifting valises. Women carrying coats. Empty seats filling up fast.

This was why Redding had walked past the earlier cars at Penn Station. He stayed put. The train rolled on toward D.C. and his seat stayed his.

In a small university where every dollar was watched, counted, fought for, Mercer's position was perfect cover. Faculty research coordinator—the man who processed every grant, every stipend, every travel claim.

When Grayson started digging, he must have found more than just forged signatures.

He'd found proof of something bigger.

Redding stepped out of the cab, his feet hitting the gravel path. McAllister University. The place had history, purpose. It was etched in the red-brick buildings, the white columns, the arched windows. The kind of grandeur that could make a man feel small—but also proud.

He walked past Jeremiah McAllister Memorial Hall. Its clock tower reached for the sky, a beacon for every colored man or woman who ever dared to dream big. The Booker T. Washington Chapel stood to his left, marble steps gleaming. He could almost hear the whispers of the great minds who once spoke there.

Oak and elm trees lined the shaded paths. Students milled about, their chatter mixing with the rustling leaves. Redding felt a tug of envy, but also hope. He'd never had the chance to walk these paths, to lose himself in books and debate. But seeing these young faces, eager and determined, made him believe that change was coming. Slow, but inevitable.

The main quadrangle was a sea of green, dotted with clusters of students. They laughed, they argued, their voices carrying. Redding couldn't help but wonder what it would've been like to be one of them. To have had the chance to sharpen his mind against the best and brightest.

But as he approached McAllister Library, with its fancy columns and decorated front, his thoughts shaded darker.

All this shine, did it hide something rotten? Resentments, betrayals, frustrated ambition gone awry. He assumed there were tensions. There had to be.

Of course, none of that was new. Just the progressive types butting heads with the old guard. The same story was playing out in Harlem.

But what about the troubles Grayson had hinted at in his journal? Mismanaged funds? Donor influence? What about *that?*

He paused before Linley Hall, the university's main administration building. It was surprisingly modest in appearance, a two-story structure of red brick and ivy. Modest or not, it cloaked and protected the university's beating heart. Not its classrooms or libraries, but its money, secrets—and power.

He climbed the steps, his mind on Mercer. He knew next to nothing about the man. But in that brief phone call, he'd heard the slick, oily cunning of a con man.

So, yes, Mercer was capable of fraud.

But was he capable of murder?

The lobby smelled of varnished wood and old paper. A directory flanked one wall—black letters behind glass, framed in tarnished brass. His eyes skimmed the list. Philosophy Department, Third Floor. He didn't linger. A guy reading the directory was a guy who didn't know where he was and that was the last thing he could afford to look like.

He climbed quickly, moving with the easy confidence of a man who belonged, who knew where he was going.

The third floor stretched out before him, a quiet corridor lined with heavy wooden doors. Sunlight slanted through tall windows. It made the brass nameplates gleam, showed him the door he was looking for:

PROF. VICTOR GRAYSON
PROFESSOR OF PHILOSOPHY

He didn't have permission to enter, hadn't bothered asking for it. The university would have said no and he didn't have time for a fight he'd lose.

Now, he glanced up and down the hall. Empty. He pulled out his picks, worked the lock. The door gave with a soft click. He stepped inside, shut it behind him.

Tobacco. Leather. The smell of a man who thought books could change the world.

He stood still, taking it all in. Twenty-five years of academic life, packed into a single room.

A heavy desk off to the right, loaded with stacks of paper—syllabi, lecture notes, essays. A half-empty tin of tobacco blend beside a worn pipe rack. Framed photographs linking deep-set windowsills: Grayson in Paris, Grayson with students, Grayson shaking hands with men just like him—learned, respected, esteemed members of the exclusive Talented Tenth.

For Redding, relief hit first—they hadn't cleared his office out. Then the harder truth: Too much everywhere. Not enough time. And no clue what he was even after.

He drew a breath. Fifteen minutes. Maybe less.

He started with the desk.

The top drawers held the expected clutter—pens, paper clips, rubber bands, ink bottles. The middle one, correspondence. The bottom, locked. His pulse quickened as he picked it. Click.

Old faculty minutes. Class records. Nothing recent. Nothing damning.

His gaze swept the room. The space was suffocating in its

fullness, an entire career frozen in time. African masks stared from between bookshelves. The kind brought back by scholars and collectors, the kind that found their way into libraries, salons and Harlem drawing rooms—reminders of a heritage both distant and deeply felt.

On a side table, a framed photo—Grayson and a companion, the Arc de Triomphe behind them.

Above the desk, a painting by Henry Ossawa Tanner. Large, striking. Possibly valuable. A copper astrolabe, green with age, perched on a stack of philosophy texts. Near it, a glass case of ancient coins bearing a brass plaque inscribed "Pompeii."

Everything spoke of connections—of a life richly lived and now, suddenly, cut short.

But Redding couldn't afford to get lost in the details.

Time was burning.

The filing cabinet next. Teaching materials. Research notes. Letters from colleagues. Nothing hidden.

The clock on the wall ticked steadily. Ten minutes gone.

He turned back to the room. If he were Grayson, where would he hide something he didn't want found? The books maybe? Hollowed out volumes? A classic hiding place. But damn, there were so many—hundreds in fact. Too many to go through.

A door slammed in the hallway.

Redding froze. Voices. Close.

He turned back to the room, eyes moving fast. The books, the tobacco tin, the painting—especially the painting. Large enough to conceal an envelope, a folder, something Grayson didn't want found.

He strode toward it. His fingers had just brushed the frame when—

"Just what do you think you're doing in here?"

25

Redding turned. A short, portly man shaped like a bowling pin stood in the doorway, wearing a bow tie and an expression of bureaucratic outrage. Some department secretary, no doubt, the kind who wielded his tiny authority like a cudgel.

"This office is supposed to be locked."

"I'm Detective Redding, NYPD. I'm investigating—"

"You have no business here." The man's expression tightened, beady eyes sharp with suspicion. He jerked his arm up and pointed down the hallway. "Out. Now. Before I call security." The motion was stiff, unnatural. A scarecrow warning off scavengers.

Redding wasn't impressed. He'd dealt with plenty of gatekeepers before—petty officials who thought bluster could substitute for actual power. The smart move was knowing when to push and when to walk away.

He was there without permission. An argument would've ended up in a report to his captain. So, he walked away. The secretary's indignant spluttering followed him down the hall.

The search had come up empty. He wasn't surprised. He'd

known that was the most likely outcome going in. Still, it stuck in his craw.

He hadn't expected to find Grayson's evidence—not outright. The man had been too careful to hide something so potentially damaging to the university in his own office, on university property, where it could be discovered and destroyed. But a clue? That was different. That was possible. And deep down, that's what he'd been hoping for.

Maybe it was still in there, hidden or left right out in the open, waiting.

That's what burned. The thought that he might've missed it, looked right at it and not recognized it.

And now, by the time anyone granted him official access—if they ever did—it would be too late. The space would be cleared out, sanitized, everything of value gone.

His one shot at the office—blown.

But he was not done yet.

The anteroom of the Faculty Research Office held three desks—two on one side, in front of a window; one on the other. The third sat before a door, the only other door in the room. A young woman staffed each desk, pounding typewriter keys like her life depended on it. The place resembled a chapel—dark wood, frosted glass, almost meditative—but sounded like a telegraph office.

Redding headed for the desk guarding the door—the inner sanctum.

The woman on duty looked to be in her forties, amply built and punctiliously groomed. Auburn hair in perfect marcelled waves. Freckles scattered across her face. No makeup except for a precise touch of lipstick. Though it was midday, her shirtwaist dress could have been fresh from the iron. Not a wrinkle, not a hair out of place. She was crisp as morning frost. She was typing, a quick staccato rhythm, eyes fixed on her steno pad.

The nameplate on her desk read 'Julia E. Turner.'

"May I help you?" She didn't bother to look up. Her Georgia lilt carried both warmth and warning.

"Detective Redding, NYPD. Here to see Professor Mercer."

Now she did look up. Green eyes took his measure. "Oh my, I *am* sorry, but Dr. Mercer had to step out rather unexpectedly. Urgent business, you understand."

"When do you expect him back?"

"Now that's difficult to say. These matters can be quite unpredictable."

"I see." Redding said. "Must have been quite sudden. We had an appointment."

"Yes and isn't that just unfortunate?" She picked up pencil and flipped to a fresh page in her steno pad. "I'd be happy to take a message."

"Actually, I'd prefer his contact information. This concerns an ongoing investigation."

"Oh, dear. I do wish I could help." Her smile was honey-sweet. "But university policy strictly prohibits sharing personal details of our faculty. Even with law enforcement—unless they have proper jurisdiction and documentation that is."

"You mean a warrant?"

"Why yes, that would do. But you haven't presented one — which tells me you don't have one. And being NYPD, you're out of your jurisdiction anyway. So I rather doubt you can get one, can you?"

Redding felt a trace of annoyance, but set it aside. "Well, in that case…" He pulled out his card and scribbled a local phone number on the back. He placed the card precisely in the middle of her desk.

She picked it up, read it.

"When Dr. Mercer returns," Redding said, "Please have him contact me." He paused. "It's about Victor Grayson."

She froze. Her eyes shot back to his. For a moment, it looked like she stopped breathing. Then, she relaxed and smiled a smile full of Southern charm. "Of course. You have yourself a good day now, Detective."

Redding tipped his hat. "You too, darlin'. You, too."

Her eyes widened and a soft flush crept up her cheeks. He turned and left.

She was good. He'd give her that. Professional. Controlled. But that reaction to Grayson's name—it confirmed what he'd suspected. Mercer wasn't just out. He was avoiding him. And his secretary wasn't just being difficult. She was running interference.

So, Mercer was nervous. Good. Nervous men made mistakes.

The Accounts Office smelled of ledger paper and fountain pen ink, with undertones of the leather-bound volumes that lined the walls. Through the window's wavy glass, afternoon light fell in distorted patterns across the meticulously organized desk of Mr. Harrison Whitfield.

Whitfield was tall and rail-thin, with skin the color of well-oiled walnut and a precise ring of white hair that made his baldness seem intentional rather than inevitable. His high cheekbones and aquiline nose gave him an aristocratic air that his careful movements and crisp bow tie only enhanced. He sat ramrod straight behind his desk, hands folded atop his green felt blotter—the only item on an otherwise spotless mahogany surface save for a brass nameplate, telephone and banker's lamp. Everything positioned with precision.

"Most unfortunate business, this matter with Professor

Grayson." Whitfield's accent carried hints of both British precision and Georgia warmth. "He was, as I'm sure you know, one of our most distinguished faculty members."

"Then you knew him well?" Redding said.

"I had the pleasure of processing his expense reports for the better part of fifteen years." Whitfield's lips curved into what might have been a smile. "In accounting, Detective, that's as close to intimacy as we generally get."

Redding settled into the straight-backed wooden chair across from Whitfield. "Then you must've noticed when things changed."

"Changed?" Whitfield's eyebrows lifted. "I'm not sure I take your meaning."

"The fraud allegations."

Discomfort shadowed Whitfield's eyes. "Ah. Yes. Most regrettable situation."

"I'd like to see those expense reports."

"I'm afraid that won't be possible." Whitfield's tone remained courteous but took on an edge of steel. "University financial records are strictly confidential."

"Even in a murder investigation?"

"Even then, Detective. Without proper documentation—a warrant, I believe would be required—I cannot share private institutional records."

"What about the records Grayson himself requested?"

Whitfield was thoughtful. "That was different," he said after a moment. "It was internal to the institution. He is, unfortunately, gone now. And I'm not at liberty to discuss any faculty member's financial dealings."

"Not even to catch a possible killer?"

Whitfield blinked, paled. "You're saying–You're sure–I heard it was a heart attack. Or possibly a stroke. Nothing like—"

"The official report isn't in yet. But we can't wait for that. If it is what we suspect it is, then…"

"I see." Whitfield fell silent. His gaze traveled to the window, to the rolling hills beyond it and stayed there. Finally, he sighed, turned back to Redding.

"Detective," Whitfield paused as if searching for the right words. "You must understand. McAllister's reputation—our very existence—depends on the trust of our donors, our faculty, our community. If word got out that we were sharing private financial information..." He spread his hands in an elegant gesture of helplessness. "The damage would be considerable."

"More considerable than a murdered professor?"

Whitfield's eyebrows drew together. After a moment, he nodded, giving in. "Professor Grayson came to me, yes. He was...troubled by certain discrepancies."

"What kind of discrepancies?"

"I've already said more than I should." Whitfield's hands tightened. "But I will say this: Professor Grayson was a man of principle. When he noticed something amiss, he pursued it. Thoroughly. Relentlessly." He sighed. "Perhaps too relentlessly."

"What does that mean?"

Whitfield shook his head. "I'm sorry, but I can't say more."

A bell tower struck the hour in the distance. Redding rubbed his chin, thoughtful, then decided to take the plunge.

"Do you believe his inquiry had anything to do with his death?"

A moment of silence.

"I couldn't say."

"Did he ever mention Clive Mercer by name?"

Whitfield was quiet for a long moment. "I cannot discuss other faculty members."

"No, of course you can't."

Redding sighed, closed his eyes briefly. Another door. Another wall. He'd gotten used to them over the years, but they still took something out of him. He had one more visit to make before catching that train back to New York. One more chance to make this trip worthwhile. And he had to hope—just hope—that nobody at McAllister was going to pick up the phone to tell his captain that he'd come down here. He stood, adjusting his coat.

Whitfield rose and extended his hand. His grip was firm, and he held Redding's hand a moment longer than necessary. "I do hope you understand my position. I simply cannot give you what you want. Not without a warrant."

Redding looked Whitfield in the eye. They both knew he couldn't get one—not without explanations he couldn't give, conversations he couldn't have.

"I understand perfectly. You say you're protecting the university, Mr. Whitfield. You're not. You're protecting the rot within it."

Whitfield's hand came up. "No, I—"

"Thanks for your time."

Redding walked out. He couldn't afford to waste another minute.

26

The row houses of Faculty Hill, modest yet stately, rested under the long shadows of late afternoon sun. Brick facades glowed amber under the slanted light. Redding climbed the worn stone steps to a well-kept Victorian with a polished brass knocker and leaded glass panels flanking the door.

A woman answered. Steel-gray hair swept into an elegant knot. Gracious, reserved. Southern, he guessed, from the way she held herself.

"Detective Redding. Right on time. My husband's waiting for you in his study. Please, come in."

The foyer whispered middle-class money and upper-class taste. The Fitzhughs were doing well on a McAllister salary: a Persian runner on hardwood, ancestral portraits in gilded frames. There was warmth too, signs of real living beneath the posh and the polish. Fresh flowers in a crystal vase. A man's hat set askew on the rack.

She hung Redding's coat and hat, then led him down a book-lined hallway and knocked once before opening a heavy oak door.

Harold Fitzhugh, professor of French literature, stood up

from behind his desk. Medium height, soft around the middle, with a neatly trimmed mustache and gentle eyes behind round spectacles. A man more likely to quote Montaigne than shout over a classroom, he had the air of someone who believed curiosity and civility could solve most problems.

The study reflected the same spirit—books stacked neatly along the walls, corners softened by wear. A brass letter holder with Islamic designs caught the light, an impressive piece. Then there were the carved African figures. A jade Buddha. Artifacts from abroad shared space with framed photos and student thank-you notes. Redding recognized one of the pictures. He'd seen it in Grayson's campus office—the image of Grayson standing with another man in front of the Arc de Triomphe. That man was Fitzhugh and the photo held pride of place on the literature professor's desk.

"Detective." Fitzhugh stepped forward and shook Redding's hand. "I imagine you've had a long day."

He gestured toward one of the leather armchairs by the fireplace. "MaryAnne's made coffee. And if you're hungry, I'm told the cake is fresh."

As if on cue, she returned with a silver tray—delicate cups, a pot of coffee and what looked like fresh pound cake.

She set the tray on the table between the chairs, movements fluid and sure. "I'll leave you gentlemen to your discussion," she said and started out.

Fitzhugh touched her arm. "Stay a moment, dear. You knew Victor, too."

She glanced at Redding, who nodded, then took the nearby chair, smoothing her skirt. Her presence somehow made the room feel both more formal and more intimate.

Fitzhugh poured the coffee himself. His hands, careful with the silver pot, moved like a ritual. "I understand you've spoken with Harrison Whitfield."

Redding accepted the cup. Used it to mask his irritation.

He'd left the Accounts Office only fifteen minutes ago—just enough time to walk here. But word had already gotten around.

"I see news travels fast."

"Not news, Detective. Whispers. Which, in a place like this, can be far more effective."

"Is that why we're talking here in your home? Instead of at your office?"

Fitzhugh shrugged. "I simply thought this would be more comfortable." A sip of coffee. "How'd it go with Whitfield?"

"He was…let's say, carefully unhelpful."

"That's him, all right." A knowing smile. "He guards the university's secrets as if they're his own. He means well, but it does make certain conversations more difficult." He held his cup at eye level, regarding Redding over the rim. "And now you're here. Did you ever meet Victor?"

"Never had the pleasure."

"A shame. You would've liked him. Or not. He inspired strong opinions."

"From what I've heard, I'd agree." Redding set his cup aside, ready to ask his first question when Fitzhugh cut in.

"You've come a long way to ask about a man you never met."

Redding didn't like it when the questions ran the wrong way. But sometimes it paid to let the other man talk. He'd take control when he was ready.

He shrugged. "I'm a cop. That's what I do. Every victim deserves answers."

"But most don't get them. They don't get a cop chasing a lead from city to city." Fitzhugh's eyes weren't quite distrustful. Cautious, maybe. "What makes this one matter to you?"

"Why? Doesn't it matter to you?"

"Of course. But what I want to know is whether—"

"You can trust me."

Silence.

Redding relented. "Listen, I've got a man in custody. But I still have questions."

"Doubts."

"A responsibility. To make sure an innocent man doesn't fry when another man's guilty."

"Everett Carlisle." Fitzhugh took a sip, nodded. "Yes, I heard."

MaryAnne threw her husband a look. Redding caught it, but didn't know what to make of it. He continued.

"It's my understanding that Grayson suspected someone of padding his travel expenses. Someone with access to those records. Someone who could make those accusations stick."

A pause. Then Fitzhugh gave another nod. "That's correct."

"Did Grayson come to you with his suspicions?"

Another pause. An even slower nod. "He did."

"What exactly did he tell you?"

A long pause here, so long that Redding wondered if Fitzhugh would answer. He did.

"Well, at first, he wouldn't say a thing. But I could see he was worried. Stressed. I kept asking what was wrong. He kept brushing me off. But finally, I guess it got to be too much. He broke down. Desperate. Said the university was accusing him of fraud. Him, of all people. After all the years he'd put in. They were willing to keep it quiet, he said, if he paid the money back. Otherwise, they'd have him arrested."

He set his cup down. "I tried to calm him down. He didn't want to be calmed. Said he'd told them they were wrong, but they wouldn't listen. They insisted he'd submitted expenses for travel that never happened, been reimbursed for trips he never took, He'd demanded to see the records they had against him. They didn't even want to give him that. But finally, they did. And that—that's when he saw them. Claims with his signature. Payments directed to an account he didn't recognize. It wasn't just a mistake. It was deliberate. And once he realized his name was being used like that, he knew someone had been doctoring records for a long time."

"Did he have a name?"

Fitzhugh hesitated. Then, with quiet certainty: "Yes. But he wouldn't share it until he was sure. He wanted evidence before he made accusations."

"Did he find it?"

Another shared look between Fitzhugh and his wife. "He came to me about three weeks ago. By then, he wasn't just troubled. He was...afraid."

"Of what?"

"He said he'd found something. Something bigger than just padded expense reports. Systematic theft, going back years. Money meant for students who needed it most. Looked like the deeper he dug, the more he uncovered. Missing scholarship funds. Grant money that vanished. A whole system of theft, hidden in plain sight."

"Did he have proof?"

"He said he did. But he was careful. Said he needed to be absolutely certain before he made any formal accusations." Fitzhugh paused. A look of regret crossed his face. "The last time I saw him, he said he was close. Just needed to confirm one final piece."

"Somebody must've been helping him, don't you think?"

Fitzhugh frowned, as if the idea hadn't occurred to him. "Now that you mention it, I guess so. Somebody who had access." He thought again. "But I can't imagine who would've taken that chance, run that risk."

"Couldn't be Harrison Whitfield, could it?"

"No way on God's green earth would that man ever do such a thing."

"Not openly, no, but secretly?"

Fitzhugh considered it. "Maybe. But I doubt it." He thought some more. "And now that Vic's gone, if it was Whitfield—or whoever it was—I'm sure they've gone to ground. You're never going to get them to talk."

Redding rubbed his chin. "Yeah, I guess you're right." He frowned. "You said he finally gave you a name?"

Fitzhugh gave a single nod. "Yes. Mercer. Clive Mercer." He paused, glanced at MaryAnne. She gave him an encouraging nod, mouthed the words, *Go on. Tell him.*

Fitzhugh continued. "You see, Vic never trusted Mercer. Not from the jump. Couldn't understand how Mercer had inveigled his way into such a position of power and trust. But he only started worrying for his safety when he began digging into the finances. He came to suspect that Mercer was siphoning funds from multiple sources—scholarships, travel grants, even faculty stipends."

"And what did Grayson plan to do about it?"

Fitzhugh's mouth tightened. "He wanted to force Mercer's hand. Confront him privately. Demand he step down or confess. I told him it was reckless. But Vic thought he could handle it."

"Did Grayson go through with it, the plan, and confront Mercer?"

"He did. He told me he gave Mercer an ultimatum. Either fix the problem or face exposure. Vic was a logical man. He thought logic would make Mercer back down. Instead, it made him desperate."

"And that's when Grayson got scared."

"Yes."

Redding let it settle. Across from him, MaryAnne reached over and gave her husband's hand a gentle squeeze. A small gesture but significant.

Redding thought of his own wife, Lena. He missed her. Wanted to get back to her.

"What about Mercer—did his behavior change?"

Fitzhugh inclined his head, frowning thoughtfully.

"Generally, I don't pay much attention to his activities. But after Vic came to me, I started worrying. Maybe Mercer had been using my name, too. Maybe I should do some investigating of my own."

"Did you?"

"No, Vic said not to. Said there was no reason to go exposing myself. Suppose I did uncover something? The Accounts Office was taking the position that you were guilty till proven innocent. He said to wait. Let him finish his investigation. I tried to argue with him, but he wouldn't listen. Told me to leave it alone." A pause. "I wish I hadn't."

"Harold, don't say that." MaryAnne regarded her husband with compassion. "You know you both were also trying to protect this university."

Fitzhugh just shook his head.

She turned to Redding. "You have to understand something. About McAllister. We're not just a university. We're a family—and a symbol. Every scandal, every hint of impropriety—it doesn't just damage us. It damages what we stand for: hope. The chance for our people to rise. Not by proving we belong—because we've already done that. Many times over. We've paid our dues. Our ancestors laid the foundation. And now, here, we get to build what they were never allowed to finish—something of our own. At McAllister, minds are sharpened. Our history is honored and no one's asked to make themselves small to fit someone else's idea of their worth."

Fitzhugh looked at her the way a man looks at his compass—like every decision, every challenge, every ambition made more sense because he had her at his side.

He turned to Redding. "She's said it better than I ever could." A pause. "Since Vic died, I've done what I could. Quietly. Through contacts. Eyes that know how to look without being seen."

Redding could well imagine. He thought about how quickly

Fitzhugh had learned of his trip to the Accounts Office. "And these contacts, what are they telling you?"

"Little bits of nothing. But together, they form a pattern."

"Specifically?"

"Mercer has started coming to work early. Leaving late. He's been digging through the archives. And after he leaves, some of those old records...they're gone."

"He's covering his tracks."

"I believe so."

Good information. But it was all smoke. Nothing solid. Nothing strong enough to land Mercer behind bars.

Then again, they'd had nothing solid against Carlisle either.

Except that blackmail note. A note that could've come from Clive Mercer just as well.

As for motive: theoretically, Mercer's motive was as strong as Carlisle's. If it could be proven. And that was a hell of a big *if*.

MaryAnne cleared her throat. "Any word on when Victor will come back to us? For the funeral, I mean."

Redding shook his head. "No, not yet."

She nodded, glancing toward Fitzhugh before returning her attention to Redding. "I suppose you've spoken to his secretary?"

"Yes. I take it you know her?"

"Of course, we, uh..." She hesitated. Another glance between her and Fitzhugh, brief but telling. "We were acquainted."

Acquainted? Fitzhugh and Grayson had been friends for decades. Yet the two main women in their lives were merely 'acquainted?'

"She appears to have been very devoted to Professor Grayson," he said.

"Yes. She was."

"Always there?"

She nodded. "You might even say..."

"Possessive?"

"Well, let's just say she's never encouraged friendships. She made it clear, from the beginning, where the boundaries were."

"I used to tease Vic about it," Fitzhugh said. "Told him she guarded him like a lion at the gate."

MaryAnne gave a thin smile, picked up the coffee pot. "May I refresh your cup, Detective?"

Redding glanced at his watch. It was getting late. He needed to grab some dinner before his train. "Thank you, but no." He paused, then looked at Fitzhugh. "Did Professor Grayson ever keep anything at home? Any files, notes—anything that might've been left behind?"

Fitzhugh nodded. "He was meticulous. Always kept copies of important documents."

"Do you have a key to his home?"

Fitzhugh nodded again. "Yes."

"Would you be willing to let me in? Tonight, before I head back to New York?"

Fitzhugh hesitated. "Maybe. Is it legal?"

"It's…necessary."

"Oh," Fitzhugh nodded. "I see." Another moment to think it over. "All right, I will." He had a new thought. "By the way, I assume you reached out to Mercer."

"I did. But there was…a bit of a mixup."

"I bet there was." Fitzhugh gave a grunt. "He ducked out on you, didn't he?"

"I'm sure we'll catch up sooner or later."

Redding stood. Fitzhugh rose, too.

MaryAnne went out and returned with hats and coats. Redding thanked her. The two men started toward the door. MaryAnne's voice stopped them both.

"Harold." She beckoned to him.

He went back to her. They conferred in low voices. He glanced at Redding. Then looked her a question. *You're sure?* She nodded. Fitzhugh still looked unsure. She rested a hand on his shoulder, smiled reassuringly. Redding heard him say, "All right."

Then to Redding, Fitzhugh said: "Hold on a minute. There's something I should show you."

He crossed to his desk, opened the brass letter holder Redding had admired. "Vic and I picked this up the last time we were in Paris. He got it for me."

Redding, a bit bewildered and more than a bit impatient, said, "Yes, it's nice."

Fitzhugh gave a faint, sad smile, one hand resting on the letter holder. Stayed that way for several seconds. Then he drew himself up, performed a bit of sleight of hand. The bottom panel slid back. A single envelope was revealed.

He lifted it out. "Vic told me if anything ever happened to him, I should turn this over. Not to the authorities, necessarily. But to the right person. Someone who'd actually do something with it." He looked at Redding. "Someone who'd care."

His voice had softened. "I never opened it. He didn't want me to." He walked back to Redding, hesitated and then finally, held it out. "But I've got a feeling he left exactly what you need. And I think he'd want you to have it."

Redding hefted the letter in his hand. Whatever was inside, had it cost Victor Grayson his life? He tore open the envelope, unfolded the single sheet inside.

"Well?" Fitzhugh asked.

Redding half-turned away. Read. His brow furrowed. He flipped the page over—nothing on the back. Read it again, slower this time.

"Detective? What does it say?"

Redding's jaw tightened. He folded it carefully, slipped it back into his pocket.

"Come on," he said. "Let's go."

Dusk had settled over Washington by the time they reached Grayson's residence, a modest townhouse on a quiet street. Fitzhugh's key turned smoothly in the lock. The door opened with a soft creak, releasing the stale air of an empty home.

"I should stay," Fitzhugh said. "Just in case someone comes by, asks questions about you being here."

Redding nodded, understanding the real reason—this was Fitzhugh's way of protecting his friend's space, of bearing witness. "Just let me work."

The home office was larger than the one at McAllister, but somehow more intimate. Here, away from academic pretense, Grayson's true character emerged. Books still dominated—philosophy texts in multiple languages, literature, history—but they were arranged with less formality. Some lay open on his desk, others had scraps of paper marking passages, as if their reader expected to return any moment.

The desk itself was wide and generous, of old polished wood. A blanket lay folded across the reading chair's arm. Photographs of Grayson and Fitzhugh and sometimes with MaryAnne were placed on the shelves. A small crystal Eiffel Tower. And African masks on the walls, carvings on the window sill. *From Benin,* Redding thought. He'd seen masks like that in his wife's art history books.

An oversized Trojan horse chess set sat on a side table, its large, ornately carved pieces frozen in place.

"He loved chess," Fitzhugh offered from his position by the door. "Said it kept his mind sharp."

Redding moved methodically through the drawers, finding much the same as he had on campus—correspondence, lecture notes, daily minutiae. But here there were personal touches: a half-finished letter to a friend in Atlanta, theater tickets from shows in New York, a scandalous gay novel hidden beneath more respectable texts.

An antique map of Paris hung above the desk, corners

curling with age. Beneath it, a collection of postcards from former students—some dating back decades, others more recent. All thanking him, praising him, sharing their successes. Grayson had obviously been a man who had shaped lives.

"He kept everything," Fitzhugh said. "Every note, every thank you. Said it reminded him why the work mattered."

Redding paused at the desk. A half-empty cup of tea, now dust-filmed. An open journal, the last entry unfinished. The pen laid precisely parallel to the page edge—a final, unconscious act of order.

He found nothing that pointed to Mercer, nothing that revealed where Grayson might have hidden his evidence. But he found something else—the portrait of a man who lived deliberately, who built his life around principles and purpose.

The kind of man who would have been thorough in gathering proof before making accusations. And who would have made sure that proof survived him.

Redding straightened, shutting the last drawer. "We're done here."

Fitzhugh lingered a moment longer, his hand resting lightly on the doorframe. Then he nodded and they left Grayson's sanctuary to its silence.

27

Redding stepped off the streetcar and adjusted his coat against the evening chill. The streets of LeDroit Park were quieter than downtown. The houses here belonged to the city's colored middle class—doctors, lawyers, academics and the occasional journalist. It was a neighborhood where pride resided in polished brass door knockers and carefully swept front steps.

He had stopped by earlier, when he first arrived in D.C., long enough to let his younger sister, Ida Mae Redding, know he was in town and would be using her number for any messages. They hadn't had a real conversation then—just a few quick words in the doorway before she had to get to work and he had his own stops to make. This visit was different.

Ida's house was a modest two-story brick row home, narrow but solid, with a small front porch barely large enough for two chairs. Light spilled from the front window, softening the edges of the night. It was the house she and Redding had grown up in, the house she held onto after their parents passed and her brother moved north. Its familiarity was both comfort and burden.

He hesitated before knocking twice. The pause wasn't about the cold. It had been too long since they'd actually talked.

Footsteps inside. Then the door opened and there she was—younger than him by a couple of years but always carrying herself like she had something to prove. She looked him up and down, not cold, not warm—just assessing. Then, with a short shake of her head, she stepped aside.

The vestibule was small and practical. A coat rack stood to the right of the door, its hooks worn smooth by years of use. A small table stood next to the coat rack. It was a slender piece with just enough space for the heavy black phone and a small notepad to jot down messages. The phone's black receiver reflected a glint of street light filtering through the glass. This was where urgent news lived, where telegrams from relatives and nighttime calls about births, illnesses and bad news had always arrived.

Beyond the vestibule, the parlor opened to one side. A sofa and two chairs faced the fireplace. Framed photographs rested on the shelf above it: their parents' wedding portrait, Redding in uniform, Ida's graduation photo.

A narrow hallway led back to the kitchen, the heart of the home, where Ida spent most of her evenings and the scent of simmering beans now drifted faintly. The kitchen door opened onto a small yard, hemmed in by fences shared with her neighbors on either side. Upstairs were two bedrooms and a bath. Each was simple and functional, their windows overlooking either the street or the alley.

It wasn't much, but it was Ida's—and that meant everything.

"Well, you're on time. That's something," she said as he stepped inside.

"Trying to do better." Redding took off his hat, hung up his coat on the vestibule rack.

She shut the door behind him. "We'll see about that. You hungry? I was just about to start supper."

"Depends on what you're cooking."

"Beans and rice. Cornbread, if you're nice."

"I can be nice."

She gave a small, knowing smile, leading him into the kitchen. The scent of onions and salt pork spiced the air and she moved with the efficiency of someone who had done this a hundred times over. Redding scrubbed his hands in the sink, then settled at the small table. He watched her stirring the pot for a moment before speaking.

"You still at the *Capital Tribune?*"

"Yeah."

"How is it?"

She didn't look up. "Same as always. Fighting to stay open, fighting to get the truth printed. Fighting the Bureau breathing down our necks."

That got his attention. "You're sure they're watching you?"

She turned, giving him a look that said he should already know the answer. "Nate, they've been watching all of us. The way things are going, they'll come knocking soon enough."

He bit back the words that wanted to come. The most he dared say was, "Little sister, be careful."

"Says my big brother, the detective working in one of the most racist, back-stabbing departments in this here USA."

"Can't help it. I love you. You the only baby sister I got."

She softened, just a little. "Yeah, I know. I love you, too."

She nodded in return. Silence between them with the comfort of an old coat—worn, familiar, carrying weight neither of them wanted to unpack just yet.

Redding grabbed a glass from the counter, filled it from the tap and took a slow sip. He stood, arms crossed, watching Ida as she moved around the kitchen. The warmth of the stove, the familiar smells made the years fold in on themselves. For a moment, the past and present blurred together and it was their mother he saw standing there instead, stirring that pot with the same easy rhythm.

Something in his chest tightened. He knew better than to ask, knew exactly how it would go, but the words slipped out anyway.

"You get the money I sent? For the headstone?"

Ida's stirring slowed for just a second before she answered. "Yeah. I got it."

The warning was there in her tone, just below the surface. Still, he pushed. "And?"

"And it's there." A little muscle in her jaw flexed. "White stone. Good carving. Mama would've liked it."

Redding was silent a moment, studying her. "You say that like I should feel guilty."

She turned to face him then, one hand on her hip. "I say it like it was just a thing that needed doing. Like something you could fix with a check in the mail."

He shifted uncomfortably. "I couldn't just—"

"I know. You were up in New York, working. Doing what you had to do. And I was here, doing what I had to do."

The words weren't cruel, but they weren't soft either. Just facts, laid bare between them.

Ida turned back to the stove, stirring in silence for a moment. Then, casually, too casually, she said, "You get anywhere looking for Daddy—or haven't you been trying?"

Redding reached for his glass again, took another sip before answering. "Ida, I—"

"Never mind."

The silence between them grew as thick as the steam rising from the pot. Then she spoke again, voice quieter.

"It's just that… I wonder, sometimes. If he's still out there. If he even remembers us."

Redding ran a hand down his face. "Ida, come on."

"No, Nate. Just tell me."

He exhaled sharply. "You want the truth? The problem ain't memory. It's that he doesn't give a damn."

She spun around, fury in her eyes. "Don't you dare! Don't you dare say that."

"Why not? It's the truth. And you, little sister, being a reporter and all, you're all about the truth, ain't you?"

He regretted the words the minute they left his mouth.

She jerked back as though he'd slapped her. "You gonna start that up again? How I shouldn't be a reporter? Or if I am, I should play it safe, stick to 'women's' issues? Give me a break!"

She slammed the wooden spoon down on the countertop and marched out of the kitchen, yanking off her apron and flinging it aside. "You can fix your own damn dinner."

He sighed, threw up his hands and followed her. "Ida, I'm sorry. I didn't mean it like that."

She whipped around. "Then how did you mean it?"

He licked his lips, took a breath and chose his words carefully, holding up his hands in self-defense. "Okay, I admit I was wrong not to support you in your career. Jackass wrong and I apologize—"

"Oh, so now you care about my work?"

"I always cared. I just didn't want you getting caught in something you couldn't get out of."

Her resentful stare annoyed him, but he understood it. He deserved it.

"Look," he took another cautious step forward, "the minute I walked in, you told me how the Bureau is after you—and I've heard stories…"

She folded her arms. "What stories?"

He opened his mouth, then closed it again. "Let's just say the Bureau has gotten damn good at grinding folks down. Destroying careers. Ruining lives."

She narrowed her eyes, skepticism written all over her face.

The sharp smell of something starting to scorch drifted in from the kitchen.

"Don't you get it?" He gripped her by the shoulders. "It's not that I don't believe in you—in your talent. Hell, I know you got it in you to be the next Ida B. Wells. I trust you. But I don't trust *them*. I know what they do, what they're capable of."

She stared up at him. Her eyebrows drew together and her eyes searched his. It hit him then, that he'd revealed more than he meant to show, exposed what the war had done to him—the war and the badge and the daily darkness he had to walk through.

He pulled her to him in a hug, spoke over her head.

"I'm sorry. And about Daddy: I'll look for him. If that's what you want, that's what I'll do. But honestly, Ida, I've been a cop long enough to know one thing."

"And what's that?" she whispered, resting her head on his shoulder.

"That some things are better left buried."

She went still. Then, after a moment, he felt her nod.

"Fine," she said softly. "Maybe they are."

Another whiff of smoke, slightly stronger now.

She gently pushed away. "I'd better get in there, before dinner burns up."

They finished supper without more talk of the past. Ida made coffee and sliced two pieces of slightly burnt apple pie. She shared the latest family gossip.

"Uncle Jimmy's got himself a new sheba. Poor man, he don't know it yet, but she's got him marked for marriage."

Good food. Good talking. The kind only family could share —where conversation could come or go without feeling forced.

Redding leaned back, took a slow sip of coffee and watched

her across the table. Then, casually, he said, "Suppose I said I might have a story for you? Something you can sink those little journalistic teeth of yours into?"

Ida raised an eyebrow, her fork hovering over her pie. "Seriously?"

"Yeah, seriously."

"What kind of story are we talking?"

"One that might ruffle some feathers. Maybe even get your paper shut down if you're not careful."

That got her attention. She sat up. "Since when are you handing me stories? What's the angle?"

He set his cup down. "Victor Grayson. You know the name?"

Her expression sharpened. "The professor who died up in New York? Yeah, I know it. There's been whispers about his death, but nothing concrete. Are you telling me it wasn't a heart attack?"

"I'm telling you he was digging into something at McAllister. And now I'm down here trying to find out what."

He gave her the details, explaining how Grayson's inquiry started, how it spread and who it ultimately focused on. "Clive Mercer. You ever heard of him?"

She thought about it, shook her head. "But since he's a back office administrator, I wouldn't have." She narrowed her eyes. "Let me get this straight. You suspect this guy, this Mercer, of not only committing fraud but homicide to cover it up?"

He hesitated. "Am I talking to my sister, Ida, or a reporter right now?"

She gave a sly smile. That was enough of an answer.

He went right into Department-mode. "No comment."

"Oh, come on."

"Ida, if you take this on, McAllister's gonna be a tough nut to crack. We both know how these institutions are—especially the big ones. They protect their own and they don't take kindly to people airing their dirty laundry. They will fight you tooth and nail. And they won't hesitate to use the public to do it. Before you know it, they could have people calling you a traitor to the race, a female Uncle Tom. So, you need to think, really think about this. 'Cause it could backfire. Badly."

She was silent, thinking about it. "I understand. I do. But you know what really worries me? It's this: What if the wrong people get wind of this first, put it out there with the wrong angle? I mean, this *is* going to come out, one way or another, right?"

"Most likely. It's part of my official investigation. If it does turn out that this guy killed Grayson, then it'll come out in court. And the papers will definitely get wind of it."

"Well, then. Depending on how you look at it, I'd be doing them a favor reporting on it first, giving them a chance to clean house before the dirty laundry gets aired in public."

He chuckled. "When you put it like that, I guess so." His look of worry came back. "But how'd you do it, Ida? You don't just walk into a place like McAllister and start looking for skeletons."

She took a slow bite of pie, considering. Then her eyes met his, sparkling and full of mischief. "You let me worry about that, big brother. Trust me, I've got my ways."

He didn't doubt it. That's what worried him. But he covered it up with an, "I bet you do."

She became serious again. "So do you have any clues at all as to what Grayson did with the evidence he collected? Because without that..."

"I know—wait a minute." He reached into his inner jacket pocket, pulled out the letter Fitzhugh had given him. "There is this."

"What is it?"

He explained.

Her eyes widened. "You mean you've been sitting on this the whole time? Give it here." She made a grab for it.

He pulled back. "I can't. It's evidence."

"Read it then. It could be the solution to the case."

He took out the single sheet inside. "It's just a lot of philosophical rambling. It's not even a letter. Not even addressed to anybody. And it never seems to get to the point. It's just...nonsense."

"I still want to hear it."

He shook his head in frustration and read:

"Wisdom demands we acknowledge what cannot be spoken openly. Honor requires that truth survive, even when its bearers fall. In these troubled times, I have witnessed corruption flourish where virtue should reign.

"When corruption takes root, good men must act decisively. Honest souls deserve protection from those who exploit their trust. In my search for answers, I have uncovered systematic deception. Truth becomes currency for those who trade in lies. Fear clouds judgment, but conscience demands courage. It is difficult to know whom to trust in these dark times. Every step forward reveals new depths of betrayal. Let this message serve as both warning and guide. Distance yourself from those who would use your name for profit.

"Knowledge is only as safe as its guardian, but I have trusted my oldest friend with its fate. It is difficult, knowing what must be done, but I leave these decisions to you. There is wisdom in the hands that move with purpose, but there is also a cost in knowing too much. The first truth I learned was this: corruption thrives in darkness. For nine years I have watched and waited. In the twenty-second year of this century, patterns became clear. The third warning may be my last. One path remains open to justice. Three witnesses could speak the truth. But only one has the courage to do so. It always falls to the knight closest to the queen's heart to guard the king's secret."

He threw his hands up. "See what I mean? I don't know what the hell this is, but whatever it is, it's beyond me."

Seeing her brother's frustration, Ida's brow furrowed. "Give it here." When he didn't move, she reached over and took it from him. This time he didn't object.

Her dark eyes went over the letter carefully, shifting visibly as they moved from line to line. A slow cheshire cat smile curved her lips. "This is beautiful, Nate. Just beautiful."

For a moment, he wondered if she'd lost her mind. "It's what?"

"Look! Look here." She scooted over to sit closer to him and traced the words with her finger. "This isn't just flowery talk—he's guiding the reader. It's a puzzle."

"You think everything's a damn puzzle."

"Because it is, Nate! It is." She slapped the paper down on the table. "You really think a man like Grayson—careful, precise, the way you describe him—would leave something this important in plain sight? He didn't just write a letter. He left a map—a map to the treasure, the evidence he collected. But it's a map hidden in words. We just have to figure out how to read it."

Redding rubbed his face. "You sure about this?"

Ida jumped up, hurried to one of the kitchen drawers and returned with a pad and pencil. "I've never been more sure of anything in my life."

He scratched his head. "I guess that would make sense. Sounds like something Grayson would do."

Grayson trusted Fitzhugh, but only so far. The mild-mannered French professor was a lamb in a wolf's den. Too green to spot trouble coming. So Grayson built in insurance—made his evidence a puzzle only the right person could solve.

Ida was studying the letter with an intensity that made him remember her as a teenager. She'd gone through this period of being fascinated by puzzles and when the war in Europe broke out, she'd gotten into codes and ciphers. Studying them, breaking them. She'd gotten good at it, too.

"So you think you can crack that?"

"I'd be more than happy to try." She glanced up. "You want to join me?"

He glanced at his watch, saw how late it was. "I got an hour, maybe an hour and a half at most. Then I got a train to catch."

"You going back tonight?"

"I was planning to. Yeah."

"But I haven't seen you in so long. You could at least stay the night."

"I got work to do, Ida. And a man in a jail cell who might get beaten to death if I don't do it."

Her eyes went over him. "Fine. But you can work on it with me till it's time to go."

He agreed, reluctantly. "You know I was never good at this."

"We're both good at puzzles. Just different kinds."

He smiled, grateful for the compliment. "C'mon. Let's get to work."

For the next hour or so, they worked together, heads bent, exchanging theories and possible solutions.

Finally, Redding threw his pencil down. "You know what? You have fun with this. I got a murderer to catch." He stood to go.

"No…"

Another glance at his watch. "It's time for me to roll, anyway. Last train out tonight and I mean to be on it."

She nodded, but her frown deepened and again her pretty face reminded him of their mother. "You always running, Nate. Always running." She shook her head. "But fine. You go on and go."

He folded up the letter, put it in his pocket—Ida had made her own handwritten copy—then went to the vestibule, fetched his coat and shouldered into it.

She followed him and stood, massaging her lower back as he put his hat on. "Mama would've wanted you to stay, you know."

He paused, hand on the doorknob. "That's not fair."

She gave a small shrug, a tired smile. "Do I care? As long as it works?"

"Well, it doesn't. Good try, though. Love you for it." He bent and gave her a peck on the cheek, then watched in amusement as she rubbed it away, as she always did. He opened the door, was about to step out, when her voice stopped him.

"Oh! Wait! I almost forgot."

"Forgot what?"

"The message. You got a message. A phone call."

He turned back. "And you're just now telling me? Who's it from?"

"Don't know. The caller wouldn't say. They asked for you. When I said you weren't here, they said to tell you to meet them tonight. And they gave a time and a place."

"Man or woman?"

"I couldn't tell. The voice was muffled. But the message, I wrote it down. Hold on."

She hurried down the hall, disappeared into the living room and came back with a scrap of paper that she thrust into his hand.

Just a time and an address.

And the one word at the bottom.

"JET."

28

Redding patted his side, felt the weapon in his underarm holster. He'd checked it before leaving. No reason to expect trouble, but in this line of work, preparation beat regret every time.

The address turned out to be a church—the Shiloh Tabernacle Baptist. It sat on a side street that branched off from U Street like a calm tributary from a churning river. The sounds that dominated the main thoroughfare—jazz from the clubs, hawkers' calls, streetcar bells—reached here only as distant echoes. This was colored Washington's steady undercurrent, where teachers and preachers lived alongside those who worked the night spots on U, and where folk walked with the quiet assurance of being on solid, familiar ground.

The church's red brick was weathered by time but well-maintained. No lights burned in the windows, but when Redding knocked, the door opened almost immediately. The pastor—small in stature but dignified, silver-haired and dressed in simple black—nodded as if he'd been expecting him.

"Detective Redding? I'm Pastor Lewis." He reached out—his fingers were gnarled, but his handshake was strong.

He led Redding through the sanctuary, under a high ceiling, past worn wooden pews and stained-glass windows gone dark with evening. The atmosphere was peaceful. Serene. They stopped at a small office. Warm lamplight spilled from its doorway.

"Someone will be with you shortly." Lewis gave another small nod and withdrew.

The room was spartan. A desk and a chair. An armchair and a sofa. Bookshelves lined with a few well-worn volumes. Everything simple. Honest. But it was chilly. Next to no heating. Redding blew on his hands, rubbed them together, and wondered who'd sent the note. Harrison Whitfield? Maybe the old accountant had decided to talk after all. Or perhaps MaryAnne Fitzhugh. Did she know something she'd been hesitant to say in front of her husband? His mind searched. Came up with nothing. Who else could it be?

Whoever it was, he hoped he or she wouldn't take long.

The door opened behind him. He turned—and went completely still.

Then he blinked, and his mind kicked back into gear. *Should've known better.* There had been clues, subtle but there. The reaction when he'd mentioned Grayson's name. The way she'd look at his card. And to how many people had he given out Ida's number? Only one.

"Miss Turner?"

She hesitated on the threshold, Pastor Lewis at her side. He gave her a quiet nod of encouragement and withdrew, closing the door behind him.

Gone was the crisp, unyielding secretary from that afternoon. Her perfect posture was still perfect, but she appeared more approachable, vulnerable. That sense of being armored was, for the moment, gone.

They sat down together—she on the sofa, he in the armchair nearby. She slipped off her gloves and neatly folded them in half before tucking them into a well-worn leather handbag. The bag was elegant but aged. Its rich patina showed years of careful use.

Her Georgia lilt was softer now. "I figured you'd know it was me. But after the horrid way I treated you, I wasn't sure you'd come. I do apologize for that, sir. I do." She loosened her collar. "But there were eyes watching, ears listening."

"It's okay. I understand," he said.

And he did.

McAllister might've been the beacon of hope MaryAnne Fitzhugh described, but like any place of power, it had its shadows.

She went directly to the point. "You're here about Professor Grayson. About what happened to him, up in New York, correct?"

"Yes."

"You think Mr. M had something to do with it."

"Do you?"

She smiled briefly. "Answering a question with a question. That's a technique cops use, isn't it?"

"And you're doing it, too."

"Yes, I suppose I am." She paused. "I don't know if Mr. M—that's what we call him, Mr. M—I don't know if he had anything to do with what happened up there, up North, but I do know what Professor Grayson was looking into. And I know what he found." She paused. "Cause I helped him find it."

Redding felt his pulse tick up. "Talk to me."

"Mr. M—he's been bleeding McAllister dry for years. At first, I thought it was just a little skimming off the top—an extra reimbursement here, a padded expense there. But it's more than that. He's been forging reimbursement requests in people's names. Forging their signatures. Disbursements for fake travel, fake research, fake whatever. So grant money, scholarship money—he's been draining accounts. For years."

"And nobody noticed?"

"For the longest time, apparently not. And if they did, I didn't hear about it."

How had Mercer managed to get this past Whitfield? For a moment, Redding wondered if the senior accountant was in on it.

She seemed to read his mind. "Mr. M was careful. He never asked for too much at any one time. And he'd make sure the requests made sense, at least on the surface. He knew exactly what kind of requests each professor and student would make, for what and when and for how much."

"And the students and professors?"

"They don't have the faintest idea what their names are being used for. And of course, if anybody did ask, Mr. M could've just acted like he'd been taken advantage of, used, like everybody else."

"But somewhere, some how, he must've tripped up," Redding said.

"I guess he must have. All I know is, Professor Grayson came to me, started asking questions. I knew what he was after.

"It started with travel forms—reimbursement requests for trips the professor never took. That was the first thing he spotted. His own expense report didn't match what he'd submitted. Receipts for hotels he'd never been to, meals he hadn't eaten. His name was on the papers, clear as day—but the handwriting wasn't his."

"How long has this been going on?"

"Years. Mr. M has built a whole system—not just fake expenses, but fake accounts, too. He sends money off to accounts tied to dead professors, students who've left, or names pulled from nowhere. Always with clean-looking approvals."

"He controls these accounts?"

"Him—or someone working under him. It's done so well, it's hard to prove it. That's what Professor Grayson was trying to do."

"And did he?"

"Well, yes and no. I collected what I could—copies of forged requests, fake invoices, statements from staff who swore they never filed those claims. Anything that didn't smell right, the professor and I documented. He was going to take it to the trustees—expose the whole thing."

"But he didn't."

"No." Her voice faltered. "He said something was still missing. The final piece. He wanted that one more piece. Something that showed exactly where the money went. A letter. He said that once he had it, Mr. M wouldn't be able to deny a thing."

"Was he able to get it?"

"I don't know. The last time I saw him, he said he was close. Said someone in New York had it. And now..." She shook her head. "He's gone."

She swallowed hard. "I tried to warn him. Told him it was dangerous. But he wouldn't listen." She paused. "And then I, like a fool, gave him everything I'd collected. I shouldn't have. I should've kept back something. Made a copy. But at the time..."

"You didn't think he'd be killed for it."

"No." She wrung her hands. "I thought we were doing the right thing."

"You were."

Redding sat back, mental wheels turning. "This proof, do you know what he did with it?"

"No." Her voice trembled. "He didn't say anything. Just walked off with it. Maybe, he thought it would be safer that way. For me. For him. I don't know."

Redding considered her for a moment. She'd already helped by confirming his suspicions. Maybe now, she could help in another way. He told her the date Grayson died. "Was Mr. M in New York?"

Her eyes widened with understanding. "Oh, Dear Lord. I

booked a train ticket for him to go there. For the day before Professor Grayson died. And for him to stay at the same hotel he always uses." She named the hotel.

"You've helped me a lot tonight, Miss Turner."

"I hope so. But I think you already knew what I had to tell you."

"Some of it. Not all." He paused. "One question, though. Why did you decide to help me?"

"I'm tired. Tired of seeing Mr. M do wrong. Before Professor Grayson came to me, I'd already started keeping track of Mr. M's dirty dealings. I didn't know what I was going to do, but I knew I was going to do something. Some day. Then Professor Grayson came along. And I thought, 'Here's my chance. He's the one who can stop him.'"

She sagged. "Then I found out what happened to him."

"And then I showed up."

"Yes. Yes, you did, Mr. Detective. You scared me, showing up like you did. Suddenly, I understood why Mr. M told me he wasn't coming in today. I knew the truth and I knew you knew it. But we had our roles to play. Especially there, with everybody looking.

"After you left, I thought. 'What're you gonna do, Julia? The evidence is gone. Leave it alone. Just leave it alone. You stuck your neck out once and it got a good man killed. So, just leave it be.'

"But I couldn't stop thinking about it. About Mr. M and all the mean things he's done. About the kids who've had to leave because their aid money suddenly ran out. The programs that have died. The people Mr. M's stepped on without ever looking back. And me, sitting there, watching. Staying safe and letting it happen."

She gave a small, rueful smile. "Julia E. Turner. That's what it says on my nameplate. The 'E' is for Estelle, my grandma's name. Raised me after my mama died. She was a kind woman.

And honest. Fearless, too. 'Grandma E.' That's what I used to call her. She always said the only thing you ever really own is your name. 'Keep it clean,' she told me. 'Because you'll have to answer to it.'"

She smoothed the leather of the old handbag resting in her lap. "This was hers. Makes me feel like I belong somewhere. Like I'm somebody worth listening to."

She looked back up at him. "She's the one who gave me the courage to call you—and to show up tonight."

"She gave you more than that," Redding said. "You're a brave woman."

"No one's ever said that to me before." She allowed herself a small smile. "Thank you."

They stood. She straightened her shoulders and they started out. Redding reached for the doorknob, then paused.

"One more question."

"Yes?"

"Does Mr. M have a typewriter at home?"

She frowned. "No. He always has me type everything. Letters, memos—even his grocery lists."

"Good. Then may I ask for one last favor?"

29

Redding dropped into the kitchen chair across from his sister. He rubbed his face, felt the late-night stubble on his chin. A table lamp cast a warm circle of light over the small kitchen table where Ida had been poring over Grayson's letter. She barely looked up.

"Still at it?" He suppressed a yawn.

"You say that like I have a choice."

She kept her eyes on the letter. Her pencil hovered over the margin, tapping. "This isn't just a code. It's a personal cipher. Meant for someone who knows how Grayson thought."

"Well, I never met the man. All I know is what I've picked up through the case. He was meticulous, precise."

"Hmph. Sort of surprising. He was a philosophy professor, right? They can be vague, a bit verbose."

Redding nodded. "But I got a feeling this man was different. That he kept his words lean, each one cut with a purpose."

"Okay." She nodded. "People like that are always looking for hidden meanings—and they like to create them, too." She pushed the paper across the table. "Look at this line: 'Knowledge is only as safe as its guardian, but I have trusted my oldest friend with its fate.' He's not just talking about Fitzhugh. 'Guardian' is doing double-duty. It means something else."

"Like what?"

"That's what we need to figure out."

The hours stretched deep into the night. The table filled with scraps—half-drunk coffee, balled-up notes, old envelopes with penciled guesses and dead ends. Around three in the morning, Redding slouched back and closed his eyes.

"I'm tapped out. I've got a train in four hours."

Ida didn't look up. "Then go to bed."

"You should too."

"I will."

Redding knew better. He didn't argue. Just pushed himself to his feet and went upstairs.

The room he'd grown up in. Same scents. Same furniture. Same view. But it felt smaller than he remembered. Like the walls had inched inward over the years. The bed, with its iron frame and worn quilt, still dipped a little on the left. And the closet—he opened it—held the ghost of who he'd been.

Everything inside smelled faintly of cedar and old newsprint. A pair of shoes, soles separating. A winter coat he hadn't worn since before he left for the war. And behind it—his uniform. Pressed flat, collar stiff. The sight of it gave him pause.

He touched the wool sleeve with two fingers. It brought things back. Not the war itself—but what came after. Men he'd fought with who'd made it through the trenches only to fall on American soil. Shot by deputies. Lynched in uniform. Forgotten by the government that sent them overseas and abandoned by the country they came back to. He let the sleeve drop.

On the top shelf, he found his old leather shaving kit. Ida had threatened to toss it a dozen times, but here it was. A toothbrush, cracked but clean. Razor still sharp. He set it aside, grateful to find it. He could use it in the morning.

He glanced around the room again. When had he last slept

here? 1919? Maybe early '20, before the NYPD sunk its hooks into him. He'd moved to New York. Written home. Sent postcards. Promised to come for Thanksgiving. Never did. Something always came up—cases, deadlines, excuses. Life had a way of moving, then doubling back to remind you what you'd left behind.

He didn't undress, just lay on the bed. He closed his eyes, but sleep didn't come. Worry wouldn't let it. His mind chased shadows that wouldn't hold still.

He stared into the dark, kept turning it over. Too many questions and not enough answers. Mercer's fraud and Grayson's missing file. The blank space where a killer's name ought to be.

He heard the stairs creak an hour later. The sound of footsteps and her door closing softly.

If she cracked the cipher, maybe he'd have something solid. If she didn't...

Carlisle wasn't just looking at a jail cell.

He was looking at the chair.

The early morning light slanted through Ida's kitchen window, throwing warm patterns across the breakfast dishes. Redding nursed his second cup of coffee, watching his sister doublecheck her notes and the cipher she'd worked on most of the night.

"You know," Ida said without looking up, "I think I'm getting somewhere with this. I'll keep working on it—"

"And call me the minute you have something concrete."

She straightened up and faked a salute. "Yes, sir. Will do."

"Appreciate it." Redding drained his cup and reached for the suit jacket he'd draped over a chair. "That letter could be—"

The telephone's shrill ring interrupted him. Ida went to

answer it. He heard her speak briefly. Then she returned to the kitchen.

"It's for you. Someone from McAllister."

Redding headed to the vestibule, Ida at his heels. He snatched up the receiver from where she'd laid it on the table. "Redding."

"Detective." The voice was crisp, professional—Julia Turner's Georgia lilt unmistakable even over the phone line. "Dr. Mercer has returned to campus."

Redding's eyes met Ida's. She was leaning in, openly eavesdropping—no shame.

"Is that right?"

"Yes. He asked me to contact you. To tell you he can meet with you now, if you're available."

Redding arched an eyebrow, shot a meaningful glance at Ida.

What? she mouthed.

He raised a finger, *Wait,* and spoke into the phone. "Tell him I'll be there within the hour."

Turner paused. "Oh, and about that other thing. I'll have it ready for you."

He replaced the receiver, thoughtful, worried. He'd have to miss his train. That meant getting back to check on Carlisle later than he'd planned to. He didn't like it, but he had to trust McKay to keep Carlisle safe.

He turned to Ida, gave her the news.

She cocked an eyebrow, arms folded across her chest. "Isn't that the man who ducked out yesterday? The one you suspect?"

"The same." He slipped into his jacket.

"You know he's just gonna lie to you."

Redding almost smiled. "Of course, he will. Even the innocent do. But that's okay, Ida. That's okay. It isn't that they lie. It's what they lie *about* that matters."

Dark clouds were gathering over McAllister's main administration building as Redding approached and a damp chill touched the air. He mounted the steps two at a time, ignoring the curious stares from students and faculty. Word of his identity had made the rounds. It was bad enough that he was a New York City detective. But that he was a *homicide* dick—a *colored* one at that—and that he was there to investigate the death of one of their own, one of their most distinguished, in fact—now *that* was somebody worth staring at.

Julia Turner sat at her desk, just as she had yesterday—perfectly composed, not a hair out of place. Her eyes met his briefly as he entered.

"Detective Redding," she said, loud enough for everyone nearby to hear. "Dr. Mercer will see you now."

She took his hat and coat and led him to the heavy oak door behind her. She knocked once, opened it and announced him.

"The detective is here."

Redding paused just inside the doorway, taking in the office with a single sweep. Rich wood paneling, oriental rugs, leather chairs—the kind of place where even the dust had a pedigree. A fortress built of mahogany and bound in leather. The diplomas on the wall weren't decorations; they were armor. The massive desk wasn't furniture; it was a barricade. Every object had been arranged to deliver the same message to every visitor, whether student, university president, or member of the board: *You're in my fiefdom now.*

The message was clear and on another man it might've worked. But Redding had walked tougher streets than a carpeted university hallway. Stared down men who'd kill you for your shoes, much less your silence.

Redding had already formed an image of Mercer. Seeing him in the flesh merely added color to the sketch.

Not tall, but slim and impeccably tailored. Hair black and sleek, with silver strands at the temples to add distinction.

Mustache kept thin and trimmed and lips that produced a smile on cue—a smile that didn't disturb the calculation in his eyes.

Redding knew the type: college men with soft hands and hard eyes who figured cops were just muscle with badges. And that a badge meant you couldn't count to ten without using your fingers.

Most days Redding was dealing with knife-fighters, junkies and back-alley hustlers. But every so often, he'd catch himself one of these high-class operators—suave, smooth, dressed like a bank note. Men who wore corruption like a hand-stitched vest and thought brains made them bullet proof.

Their arrogance was annoying but it could make a cop's job easier. It made them blind to the obvious: that life on the streets had taught a cop like Redding to sense a lie before it left a man's lips. That the war had taught him that bullets don't swerve around fancy degrees. And the badge had taught him that truth always leaks, no matter how tight the cover.

It was always deeply satisfying to see their faces when the cuffs came out and they realized the game was over.

Seeing Mercer, Redding made a decision: let Mercer think he had the upper hand. Let him believe this cop was just another flat-foot dazzled by five-dollar words and leather-bound books. The more Mercer felt in control, the sloppier he'd get. Men who spent their lives being the smartest in the room couldn't help showing off, even when silence would save them.

Mercer rose from behind his desk with languid elegance. "Detective Redding." He extended a manicured hand toward the leather chair across from his desk. "Please, come in."

Redding took the offered seat. He noted how Mercer had arranged matters—so the window cast the visitor's face in light while leaving his own in partial shadow.

"Thank you for making time to see me," Redding said.

"Of course." Mercer settled back, one hand adjusting his beautifully cut pants over his long legs. "Though I must apologize for not being available yesterday. University business can be...unpredictable."

"I appreciate your cooperation. Helping clear up questions around Professor Grayson's death could make all the difference."

"Yes. A terrible loss to our institution." Mercer paused. "I understand from Miss Turner that you're treating his passing as...suspicious?"

"That's correct."

A small frown drew Mercer's dark eyebrows together. "May I ask why? I was under the impression it was his heart."

"We suspect he was poisoned."

Mercer's right eyebrow arched. "Poisoned?" He stroked his lower lip, the frown deepening. "Excuse me, Detective, but I have to say that's... Well, it's hard to believe. Who would want to harm Professor Grayson?"

"That's why I'm here. To find out."

Mercer reached for the silver cigarette case on his desk, opening it with a practiced flick of the wrist. He turned it toward Redding, offering him a smoke.

Redding waved it away, holding eye contact.

The corner of Mercer's mouth lifted in a slight, half-smile. He drew a cigarette, tapped it twice against the case and lit up with slow, deliberate moves, making an elegant ritual of it. He inhaled deeply, the smoke curling up past those watchful eyes, before he exhaled a perfect stream through his nostrils.

"I'm not sure how I can help, Detective. Professor Grayson and I were colleagues, certainly. But we weren't particularly close."

"Twenty-five years at the same institution...?"

"Yes." Mercer's smile tightened. The muscles around his mouth tensed beneath that perfect mustache. "Our paths crossed professionally, of course. But..." He trailed off, then abruptly changed direction, tapping his cigarette once against a crystal ashtray. "You should know, Detective, that Professor Grayson was under considerable strain in his final months."

Redding raised an eyebrow but said nothing.

Mercer continued, gaining momentum, smoke punctuating his words like carefully placed commas. "Your desire to talk to me… I gather you've heard that there were irregularities in his expense reports. Significant ones. The Accounts Office had raised concerns." He took another long drag, the ember glowing orange as he pulled. "I'm afraid Professor Grayson was facing serious allegations of financial impropriety."

Redding wondered just how much mud Mercer would throw."These allegations: what can you tell me about them?"

Mercer sighed with obvious regret. "I'd prefer not to. You know, speak ill of the dead and all that."

Redding pushed. Just a bit. "Elaborating on the charges does not mean speaking ill of the dead—not unless you believed him guilty. Did you?"

Mercer tapped his cigarette over the ashtray. "These things are always difficult, especially with someone of Professor Grayson's standing." He paused. "I can say that the accusations unnerved him. Totally sent him over the deep end. Why, he even tried to lay the blame on me. Can you imagine?" His left eyebrow arched dramatically. The mustache quivered with suppressed indignation. "Came to my office, threw all kinds of accusations at me. Totally unfounded, mind you. Totally unfounded."

"What kind of accusations?"

"That I was somehow manipulating his expense reports." Mercer let out a small, incredulous laugh. "As if I had the time or inclination to do such things." He again tapped ash from his cigarette with a deliberate flick of his wrist. "It was really unfortunate. Created an atmosphere in which people felt they had to choose sides." He adjusted his French cuffs, a gesture that drew attention to his expensively understated gold cufflinks. "Thank goodness, my people, the people I've been working with for nearly twenty years and know me well, they chose me."

"So, these allegations, they were evolving into a showdown between the two of you?"

"Detective," Mercer smiled. "You make it sound like we were about to draw swords or indulge in a shootout at the OK Corral. We're much more civilized here. No, I mean something else entirely."

"Explain."

"Isn't it obvious?" Mercer spread his hands, cigarette poised elegantly between his first two fingers. "Here, you had a man facing disgrace, the end of a long and distinguished career and potential criminal charges… Well, sometimes people make desperate choices."

"You're suggesting suicide."

"I'm merely noting that he was under enormous pressure." Mercer's voice softened with sympathy. His head tilted as though in contemplation. "If he had nothing to hide, why would Accounts suspect him in the first place?"

Redding nodded, thoughtful. "You have a point, one I have to say, I hadn't considered. But a perfectly valid one. Thank you for sharing it."

"Of course. Now, if you—"

Redding raised a finger. "If you'd humor me a minute longer." He reached into his jacket pocket and removed a folded piece of paper. "I'd like to ask you about this."

He unfolded the blackmail note and placed it on Mercer's desk, sliding it toward him with one finger.

Mercer looked down at it. His eyes moved over the words, lingered on the initial at the bottom. When he looked up, that asymmetrical half-smile had returned, but it was tight around the edges.

"I'm afraid I don't understand."

"It was found among Grayson's possessions," Redding said. "A blackmail note. Threatening to reveal secrets."

Mercer slid the note back across the desk. "I know nothing about it."

"The letter 'C,'" Redding persisted. "Your first name would fit that initial."

Mercer's laugh was short, dismissive, accompanied by a dramatic arch of his left eyebrow. "As would countless other names. Charles, Carl, Christopher." He took a final drag from his cigarette before extinguishing it. "Our university president is a 'Craig.'"

The side of his mouth quirked upward. "I always respected Victor. He was a genius in his own way, but like many brilliant men, he had a dark side. I suppose it caught up with him."

Redding noted the shift in Mercer's tone, how he was making less and less of an effort to conceal his disdain for the dead man.

"Were you in New York around the time of Grayson's death?"

The question caught Mercer off guard, but he recovered fast. "I was here in Washington. Faculty meeting on Thursday, budget committee on Friday. I'm sorry if that complicates your investigation, but facts are facts. Check with Miss Turner. She keeps very thorough records of my whereabouts. Ask her."

"Well, she'd say whatever you tell her to, wouldn't she?"

Mercer laughed. "You don't know Miss Turner. She's as straight-arrow as it gets. Absolutely incorruptible."

"Not that you would've ever tried to corrupt her." Redding smiled.

Mercer's eyes flashed cold and reptilian. Just for an instant. "Of course not."

Redding was satisfied. He'd gotten what he came for. He rose to his feet. "I appreciate your time, Dr. Mercer."

Mercer stood as well, his face showing relief before he

caught it. “Of course. Anything to help bring closure to this unfortunate situation.”

He extended his hand. Redding shook it, handed him his card.

“If you remember anything else…”

Mercer glanced at the card, then dropped it back on his desk as though it were of no consequence. “I doubt I’ll have anything to add, but certainly.”

Redding turned to leave, but paused. “One more thing.”

“Yes?” That left eyebrow arched upward again.

“When was the last time you saw Professor Grayson alive?”

The question brought a moment of silence.

“At a faculty function about three weeks ago,” Mercer finally said. “We exchanged pleasantries. Nothing more.”

Redding gave it one more beat, then nodded. “Thanks again.”

He left with one thing settled in his gut: Mercer had the titles, the respect, the protection that came with power. What he didn’t have was innocence.

In the anteroom, Julia Turner fetched Redding’s hat and coat, and held them out for him.

“I hope your meeting was productive.”

“Very.” Redding slipped his arms into the sleeves.

Her fingers brushed against his shoulder as she adjusted the coat—and her eyes met his for a fraction of a second.

“Have a safe journey back to New York.”

Redding nodded his thanks and left.

Outside, the campus was alive with students hurrying to morning classes. Redding paused on the steps, drew in a deep breath of crisp autumn air.

Almost absently, he patted his coat pocket, felt what hadn’t been there before—a small sheet of paper. He drew it out, unfolded it and quickly scanned its contents.

A slow, satisfied smile spread across his face.

30

Union Station was a zoo. Early morning commuters packed the marble floors. Their footsteps echoed off the high ceiling in a steady roar. The place was all arches and columns—built to impress somebody, but right now it was just another crowded terminal full of people trying to get somewhere else.

Redding cut through the crowds, collar turned up against the cold. Missing his early train had landed him in the middle of the morning stampede, but he wasn't sweating it like the rest of these poor schmucks. The delay was a damn nuisance, sure—but it also meant he could poke around, ask questions.

He headed toward the colored ticket windows, where a middle-aged agent was rapidly processing a line of passengers.

"Records of specific passengers?" The agent barely looked up from his paperwork. "No sir, we don't keep track of every person who buys a ticket. And as you can see—" he gestured to the growing line behind Redding—"we're rather busy this morning."

Redding wasn't deterred. He'd expected resistance. He pulled out his badge, keeping it low between them.

"NYPD Homicide. This is about a murder."

The agent's demeanor shifted from cooperative to wary. "I'm sorry, but I still can't help you. Even if I wanted to, those records wouldn't cross my desk."

Redding got it. From his breast pocket, he withdrew a photograph of Mercer—crisp, dignified, unmistakable.

"Distinguished gentleman from McAllister. Takes the Congressional Limited to New York fairly regularly."

The agent glanced at the photo, then nodded to his left. "You'd want to ask at the main booking office. That's where the, uh...other customers purchase their tickets."

Redding got the message. Mercer wouldn't have bought his ticket at the colored window—not with his tailored suits, university connections and first-class habits. He was the kind of man who moved through back doors and side channels, where race took a back seat to money and pedigree. In a station built on separation, Mercer had bought his way across the line. The Pullman desk didn't care what color you were, so long as your bills were pressed and your manners polished.

Redding moved across the concourse, approached the white ticket counters. He knew the drill—wait until acknowledged, keep his tone deferential, lead with his badge to establish authority before they could dismiss him. Two agents turned him away immediately, citing the morning rush. The third, an older man with wire-rimmed glasses, at least examined Mercer's photograph.

"We see hundreds of passengers every day." The agent handed the photograph back as he gestured to the next customer in line. "Even if I did remember him, I couldn't officially confirm it."

Near the colored waiting room, a group of porters were changing shifts, the night crew handing off duties to those working the morning trains. Redding approached them, showed his badge first, then Mercer's photograph.

"Any of you gentlemen remember this passenger? Would've traveled to New York last Friday, maybe. Thursday or Friday."

They passed the photograph between them, shaking heads until it reached an elderly porter with silver hair and shoulders still straight despite his years.

"That's Professor Mercer." He squinted at the image. "From over at McAllister."

"You know him?"

"Know of him. Carries himself like royalty, that one." The porter handed the photo back. "Always sits in the Pullman car. Reserved seat, same one every time."

"You remember seeing him late last week? Heading to New York?"

The porter shook his head. "Not my car that week. But Jackson might've had him." He gestured toward a younger porter organizing luggage carts for the morning departures.

Jackson was tall and lean, with intelligent eyes that assessed Redding quickly. He glanced at the photo and gave a curt nod.

"Oh yeah, I remember him. Always sits in the same seat—Pullman car, window seat facing forward. Man's particular about his accommodations."

"When was the last time you saw him?"

Jackson thought for a moment. "Late last week, it was. Yeah, the Friday morning train to New York."

The day before Grayson died.

"You sure about that?"

"Positive. He had me bring him coffee twice, complained it wasn't hot enough both times. Man like that, you remember."

Redding folded the bill once, then slipped it into Jackson's palm. The transaction dissolved into Jackson's pocket with the smooth efficiency of men who understood the economics of respect.

Near the colored entrance, Redding noticed an older man at a shoeshine stand, busy with the morning clientele. He waited until the businessman in the chair had paid and left before approaching.

"Excuse me, sir. Detective Redding, NYPD." He showed his badge, then Mercer's photograph. "I'm wondering if you've seen this gentleman recently."

The shoeshine man—"EARL" embroidered on his jacket—squinted at the photo, then broke into a wide grin that revealed a gold tooth.

"Professor Fancy Shoes! Sure, I know him." Earl tapped the photograph with a calloused finger. "Got the shiniest shoes at McAllister and that's saying something."

"You remember when you last saw him?"

Earl nodded emphatically. "Yes sir, I do. Last Friday. Remember 'cause he was in a rush, but still stopped for a shine. Said he had to catch the 9:15 to New York."

"You're certain about the date?"

"Clear as day. He always gives me a dollar tip—most folks give a nickel, if that." Earl's eyes crinkled at the corners. "But that day, he handed me two. Said one was for that day, one for next time." He chuckled. "Ain't never had a man pay up front for a shine he didn't sit for."

Redding felt the case clicking into place. "He say anything else? Mention why he was going to New York?"

"Not to me." Earl shrugged. "Man like that don't share his business with the likes of me. But I can say, he did keep checking his watch, real fidgety-like. Not like him at all."

"Thank you." Redding slipped Earl a dollar.

The old man pocketed it with a nod. "Hope you find what you're looking for, Detective."

"I believe I just did."

Redding made his way back to the colored ticket window to purchase his return fare. The morning rush had subsided slightly, but the agent still processed his ticket with brisk efficiency.

As he waited on the chilly platform, Redding mentally cataloged what he'd learned. Mercer had definitely traveled to New York the day before Grayson died. He'd been agitated, unusual for a man who prided himself on his composure. He'd expected to return quickly—hence the prepaid shoeshine.

Most damning of all, Mercer had lied about it. Claimed he was in Washington, attending faculty meetings, when witnesses placed him on a train to New York.

The Congressional Limited pulled into the station, steel wheels screeching against the rails. Redding boarded, found his seat and settled in for the journey. He had what he needed from Washington. Now it was time to follow Mercer's trail in New York.

Who might've seen him—and what had they seen?

31

Redding took the Lenox Avenue line up to 145th Street. He knew he should go straight to the precinct, check on Carlisle. But he'd spent the whole ride back knowing he wouldn't. Telling himself the best way to help Carlisle was to stay on the trail, get the evidence. He only half-believed it, but that was enough. Once he caught a scent, it took over. Everything else dropped away.

In the back of his mind, Carlisle. He pushed it down.

The Hotel Olga rose before him. Its modest brick facade stood three stories tall. It possessed a quiet dignity that emphasized its purpose: to be the premier accommodation for colored travelers of means—entertainers, intellectuals and entrepreneurs who were unwelcome at Manhattan's downtown establishments.

Inside, the lobby was sedate, protective, an immediate respite from the brutal, teeming life of the city. The space was handsome but not ostentatious—gleaming mahogany furnishings and comfortable seating. Reading rooms branched off from the main space, their shelves lined with selected volumes that spoke to the hotel's intellectual clientele.

Redding approached the front desk. The clerk, a young man with carefully pressed clothes and a professional demeanor, looked up expectantly.

"Good afternoon, sir. How may I help you?"

Redding produced his badge. "Detective Redding, NYPD. I need to speak with the manager about a recent guest."

The clerk's posture straightened slightly. "Of course. One moment, please."

Minutes later, a middle-aged man emerged from a side office. He wore a well-tailored suit and carried himself with the practiced grace of someone used to managing both crises and dignitaries.

"Mr. Walter Sanford, assistant manager." He extended his hand. "How can I help you, Detective?"

Redding shook his hand. "I'm investigating a death. One of your recent guests might have information on the matter."

Sanford gestured toward his office. "Please, let's discuss this privately."

The office was small but stylish, furnished with the same attention to detail as the lobby. Sanford closed the door and indicated for Redding to take a seat.

"Now then, which guest are you inquiring about?"

Redding placed Mercer's photograph on the desk. "Dr. Clive Mercer. Academic from Washington, D.C. Would've stayed here sometime late last week."

Sanford studied the image. "Yes, Dr. Mercer. He's one of our regulars."

"I need to confirm the dates of his most recent stay."

Sanford hesitated, then nodded. He pulled a leather-bound ledger from a drawer and carefully turned its pages.

"Here we are. Dr. Mercer checked in Friday afternoon and checked out Sunday morning."

Friday to Sunday. The timeline fit perfectly. Grayson had died Saturday night.

"Did he receive any visitors during his stay?"

"I can't say personally," Sanford replied, "but Miss Peterson at the front desk was working those days. She might recall."

Miss Peterson turned out to be a sharp-eyed woman approaching forty. She had an efficient manner and the keen observation skills developed by years of hotel work. She recognized Mercer's photograph immediately.

"Oh yes, Dr. Mercer from McAllister University. Room 721. He always requests a room on a higher floor with a view of the avenue, the same room when possible."

"Did you happen to notice if he had any visitors?"

"He did receive a gentleman on Saturday. Early afternoon. Distinguished man, about his age. I remember because they greeted each other in the lobby—not exactly like old friends, but they definitely knew each other."

"They met in the lobby? Not in his room?"

"That's right. Dr. Mercer was waiting when the other gentleman arrived. They spoke briefly, then left together." She adjusted her glasses. "They seemed...professionally acquainted, if that makes sense."

It did. "What time did they leave?"

"Around two o'clock. I remember thinking they were heading out for a late lunch."

"And did Dr. Mercer return alone?"

She reflected. "Yes, he did. Early evening—perhaps five or six o'clock. He seemed...preoccupied. Didn't stop to chat as he usually does."

Redding remembered to check one last detail. "For lunch, did they eat here, at the hotel restaurant?"

"No," she shook her head. "He rarely does. He prefers the Wells Restaurant down the street. Says their coffee is better than ours." She smiled slightly. "Between us, I think he's right."

Sanford, who had been listening, added: "The Wells is quite

popular with our academic guests. More affordable than our dining room, but still respectable."

"Thank you both," Redding said. "You've been extremely helpful."

Once outside, Redding took stock. He should get back to the station. He knew it. But the Wells was a short walk away. With any luck, someone there would remember the two distinguished men who'd dined together on what would be Grayson's last day.

Redding set off for the restaurant. He pushed thoughts of Carlisle aside. The leads were pointing in one clear direction.

Mercer had lied about his whereabouts. He'd met with the victim hours before his death. The timeline, the opportunity, the motive—it was all falling into place.

Now, Redding thought, just needed one more witness to place them together at the restaurant. One more thread to pull before Mercer's carefully constructed alibi unraveled completely.

The restaurant occupied the ground floor of a well-maintained brownstone. A tasteful sign announced its hours and a small placard in the window proudly declared: "Serving Harlem's Finest Since 1917."

Inside, the restaurant struck a careful balance—upscale enough to attract professionals and academics, yet not so expensive as to be prohibitive. White linens covered the tables, but the atmosphere remained welcoming rather than stuffy. Jazz played softly from a phonograph near the bar, and the aroma of coffee and freshly baked desserts filled the air.

The afternoon lull had set in. A few tables held late lunchers, early dinner patrons. A hostess approached with a polite smile that faltered when Redding identified himself.

"I'd like to speak with the manager."

She nodded and disappeared through a swinging door to the kitchen. Moments later, a stout woman emerged, wiping her hands on a pristine apron. Her gray hair was pulled back in a severe bun and she carried herself with the authority of someone who ran a tight ship.

"I'm Dorothy Wells." She extended her hand. "This is my establishment. How can I help you?"

Redding shook her hand, noted her firm grip. "I'm investigating a death—a professor from McAllister. I have reason to believe he dined here with a colleague shortly before his passing."

Mrs. Wells' expression turned somber. "You must mean Professor Grayson. Yes, we heard about that. Terrible business." She gestured toward a quiet corner. "Let's sit."

They settled at a table away from other patrons. She folded her hands on the tablecloth. She told Redding that Grayson had been one of her favorite customers.

"He was always polite, always left a proper tip." A grave look crossed her features. "Heart failure, wasn't it? Though I suppose that can't be the case if you're here asking questions."

Redding produced Mercer's photograph. "Did you see him with this man about two weeks ago? Wednesday afternoon."

She barely glanced at the photograph before nodding. "Dr. Mercer? He's another regular. Though it was the first time I'd ever seen them here together."

"Do you remember anything about their meeting? Their demeanor?"

She considered this. "They took that corner table." She gestured to a spot near the back, partially obscured by a decorative screen. "More private. Looked like it was serious. Not an argument exactly, but whatever they were talking about it didn't look pleasant."

"How long were they here?"

"Perhaps an hour. They ordered coffee and sandwiches. Though—" She paused, recalling something. "Professor Grayson barely touched his food. He seemed distracted."

Redding made a mental note. "Who was your waitress that day?"

"Lucille." Mrs. Wells glanced toward the back. "She should be setting up for the dinner service now."

Lucille turned out to be a woman in her twenties with observant eyes and a quiet confidence. She remembered the two academics clearly.

"They asked for a quiet table. Professor Grayson was easy to satisfy. Dr. Mercer, less so. He's always particular about where he sits, the temperature of his coffee. Everything has to be just so."

"Did you overhear any of their conversation?"

She hesitated, glancing at Mrs. Wells, who nodded permission.

"Bits and pieces. They were speaking quietly, but sometimes Professor Grayson would get animated—not loud, but intense." She lowered her voice. "I heard something about money. Professor Grayson kept saying, 'I have proof now' and 'It's all there in black and white.'"

"Anything else?"

"Dr. Mercer stayed very calm, even when Professor Grayson seemed upset. He kept saying things like, 'You're misunderstanding' and 'This isn't what you think.'" Lucille frowned, concentrating. "Then, near the end, Dr. Mercer said something that made Professor Grayson go quiet. Real quiet. Like the fight had gone out of him."

"Do you remember what that was?"

She shook her head. "No, I was clearing another table. But when I came back, the mood had changed. Professor Grayson looked... I don't know. Sad, maybe. Or worried."

"And Dr. Mercer?"

"Still calm. Too calm, if you ask me. Like somebody who thinks they've won something."

Redding had the feeling she didn't like Mercer all that much.

"Did either of them order anything unusual? Or did you notice anything strange about their food or drinks?"

Mrs. Wells frowned at the implication but Lucille merely shrugged.

"Dr. Mercer ordered his usual—black coffee and our club sandwich. Professor Grayson had coffee too, with cream. And our chicken salad sandwich, though like Mrs. Wells said, he barely touched it." She paused. "The only unusual thing was that Dr. Mercer insisted on pouring the cream for Professor Grayson. Said something about the proper amount for a good cup."

"Really?" Redding narrowed his eyes. "Did Professor Grayson drink the coffee after that?"

"Yes. All of it, eventually."

"Hm-hmm," Redding absorbed this. "And how did they seem when they left?"

"Dr. Mercer was perfectly composed, as always. But Professor Grayson..." She hesitated. "He seemed distracted. Nearly forgot his hat. And as they were leaving, I noticed his hand trembled when he reached for the door."

Early symptoms of poisoning or just the stress of confrontation? Redding made a mental note to ask the medical examiner about timing. How long after ingestion would—

"Detective," Mrs. Wells said, "are you suggesting that Professor Grayson was poisoned? Here? In my establishment?"

"We don't know. I can only say that he died later that evening. And this meeting may have been significant."

She nodded, looking troubled. "If there's anything else we can do to help..."

"Just one more thing. After they left, did either of them return later?"

Lucille shook her head. "Not that day. But Dr. Mercer came back the next morning. Right after we opened. Didn't seem in a hurry. Just sipped his coffee, read his paper. Like a man with nothing to worry about."

The morning after Grayson's death. Redding wondered if Mercer had already known about it when he stopped by for coffee, or if he'd been waiting to hear the news.

Outside, the streetlights were beginning to flicker on as dusk settled over Harlem. Redding paused on the sidewalk, fitting the new pieces into the puzzle.

The picture was becoming clearer: Mercer had traveled to New York. He'd met with Grayson at the hotel, then gone with him to the Wells. There, they'd had an intense discussion. Redding believed it was about the evidence Grayson had gathered—evidence that implicated Mercer in financial fraud.

And during that meeting, Mercer had insisted on pouring cream into Grayson's coffee.

Hours later, Grayson was dead.

The blackmail note, the train ticket, the hotel register, the restaurant witnesses—the evidence was mounting. Not proof of murder. But more than enough to justify putting Mercer under the spotlight. It was certainly as much as he'd had when he pulled in Carlisle.

Carlisle.

That tap at the back of his skull—the one he'd been ignoring since D.C.—was louder now. Insistent.

He'd delayed long enough.

He just hoped it hadn't been too long.

32

The station house: telephones, typewriters, someone raising hell in the drunk tank. Redding pushed through the doors and didn't stop walking.

"Detective."

Officer Perkins, still wet behind the ears, hurried toward him. "Messages came for you. Urgent." Perkins handed him the notes. "And that lawyer's been calling. McKay."

Redding quickly went through them. Lena: *McKay called three times. Sounds worried. Call him immediately.* Then Ida: *McKay's trying to reach you. Says it's about Carlisle. URGENT.*

His gut locked up. He didn't need the details. McKay wouldn't chase him down unless something had gone bad.

Redding broke into a run, barreling through to the cell block.

Carlisle's cell was empty. Cot: bare. Blanket: gone. No sign he'd ever been there.

Redding turned and headed for Egan's office. Cops saw his face and stepped aside. He didn't knock. Just pushed the door open and marched inside.

Egan looked up. Cool. Expecting him. "Detective," he said. "Back from your unauthorized field trip, I see."

"Where is he?"

Egan settled back, hands folded over his mountainous gut. "Funny thing. Chief Robinson in D.C. rang me. Told me one of my boys had forgotten to notify the locals before shaking the trees in his city."

"Where. Is. He?"

Egan smiled. "That's a serious violation of protocol. Could end a man's career."

"You gave me your word. He was to stay here. You said so."

Egan sighed, took out some gum. Unwrapped it. Popped it in his mouth. Folded up the wrapper, dropped it in the trash can. "We had to move him."

"To where?"

Egan chewed with his mouth open. "Harlem Hospital."

Redding stiffened. "When?"

"Last night. Intensive care."

Redding fought to tamp down the rage. "What happened?"

"Unfortunate incident during processing."

"I'd already 'processed' him. Prints taken. Picture taken. All you had to do was leave him be."

"Well, it was decided we had to process him some more."

"You mean Benedict."

Egan gave a small mean smile. "I mean your suspect resisted. Officers had to respond."

"With what, a lead pipe?"

"With appropriate force."

Appropriate force? "Enough to put him in intensive care?"

"He's lucky he's getting any treatment at all. You can thank your lawyer friend for that. I gotta say he raised hell. Burst in here like he owned the place."

"McKay was here?"

"Oh yes. Making demands. Waving papers. Like it meant something."

"And yet Carlisle's at Harlem Hospital, not dead in a holding cell." Redding gave a grim smile. "Seems like it did mean something."

Egan's face hardened. "Your pal got lucky. McKay brought in people from that colored paper across the street. Some lady reporter and a photographer."

So that's how McKay had done it. Cameras. Witnesses. Leverage.

Smart move.

"You're too close to this." Egan stood, drew himself up. "It's clouding your judgment. Take a step back. Do it—or I'll make you."

"Insubordination?"

"Nothing like it to ruin a cop's record."

Redding smiled. The last card in a weak man's hand. "Go ahead. Threaten me. But you'll be the one blinking in the headlights if Carlisle dies."

"Nobody gives a damn if a nig—"

Redding raised a finger. Just one. "Margery Davenport. Her reputation's on the line and she's not taking chances. You taint her name—make her look bad—and..." He didn't need to finish.

Egan held the line. "He's guilty."

"You want to wrap this up? Fine. So do I. Let's get our man. But get the right one."

"I'm not about to start over again."

"You don't have to. I've got somebody else in my sights."

Egan stared at him. "Get out of my office. Get out and go see your boy. What's left of him. Then we'll talk about who's in your sights."

Redding turned to go.

Egan called after him. "Oh and Detective? Once he's stable, he's still being transferred."

"To where?"

"The Tombs."

That shit-hole in lower Manhattan? It was a place where men disappeared and inconvenient truths got buried.

"We'll see," Redding breathed. "We'll see."

Egan's laugh followed him out. "You think McKay's little stunt will stop it? He bought you time. But not much of it."

Redding shut the door, let that laugh die behind the wood.

The bullpen clattered on as if nothing had happened. Like a man hadn't been beaten within an inch of his life two doors down.

Outside, Redding flagged a cab. "Harlem Hospital—and step on it."

His thoughts tore loose as the cab pulled away. What had Benedict done? How bad was it? And what was McKay planning to stop the transfer?

One thing was certain: time was bleeding out.

If he didn't find Grayson's proof soon—Mercer would walk, Carlisle would rot and Grayson would be dead for nothing.

33

Redding hit the doors of Harlem Hospital at a near run. "Carlisle. Everett Carlisle," he told the first nurse whose attention he could catch. "Where is he?"

Her eyes took in the bulge of his holster beneath his jacket. "Police?"

"Detective Redding, 32nd Precinct."

"Intensive's on three. Room 4."

Redding nodded his thanks.

The corridor stretched ahead, fluorescent lights casting everything in a sickly pallor. Room 4's door was ajar, voices drifting through the gap. One he recognized.

"—Doesn't matter what they say. You hear me? Law says they can't move you without medical clearance and Dr. Wilson isn't giving it."

Redding pushed the door open. A private room? He was relieved to see it, but wondered who was paying for it.

McKay stood beside the bed, suit jacket draped over a nearby chair, sleeves rolled up as if he'd been in a battle, his eyes exhausted.

Hayward sat on the other side of the bed. Unlike McKay, he

wasn't dressed for battle, but he had the look of a man who'd settled in for a siege: a book open on his lap, a black thermos on the side table, his vest unbuttoned. He looked up at Redding's entrance, his eyes narrowing.

Between them, Carlisle lay still and barely recognizable. His face was a landscape of bruises, right eye swollen completely shut, split lip stitched in three places. His left arm was splinted and bandaged, fingers poking out like broken twigs. His right hand, also bandaged, was manacled to the bed rail. Beneath the thin hospital sheet, his chest rose and fell in shallow, pained breaths.

McKay turned at the sound of the door, tense until he recognized Redding. Relief washed over his features. "About damn time. I've been trying to reach you since they brought him in."

Redding clasped McKay's hand, then nodded to Hayward.

"Detective," Hayward acknowledged. He rested a hand near —but not touching—Carlisle's uninjured arm. A protective gesture, Redding realized.

"How bad?" Redding's gaze shifted to Carlisle.

McKay answered. "Three broken ribs. Fractured orbital bone. Internal bleeding they're still monitoring. Left wrist broken in two places. And those are just the highlights."

"The doctor says he's stable," Hayward added. "Though that word seems inadequate, given the circumstances."

Redding started to reply, but Hayward spoke again. "I saw your people take him. Right outside my store. I had a bad feeling—pushed it aside, tried to trust the system, if you can believe that." He gave a short, humorless breath. "Didn't take long to realize how foolish that was. I got to his building just in time to see that bastard Marchetti tossing his things into the street. Like garbage."

He looked down at Carlisle's hand. "I saved what I could. Not much. You people made him lose what little he had. But at least he'll have something to come back to—if he gets the chance."

Redding heard the accusation in his voice and didn't argue. He moved to the bedside. Carlisle's eyes—the one that could open—flickered toward him, recognition dawning slowly through a haze of pain and morphine. "Detective," Carlisle managed.

"I'm here," Redding said. "I'm back."

Carlisle's good eye found him. Took him in like he knew the score. No blame. No fear. Just a nod before the drugs pulled him back under.

The knot in Redding's chest loosened.

"He's been in and out," Hayward said, closing his book. "They have him on morphine."

Redding noted the title—*Baudelaire.* The same French poetry he'd seen in Carlisle's apartment.

"We need to talk." McKay nodded toward the door. "Not here."

"I'll stay." Hayward's gaze returned to Carlisle.

Redding followed McKay into the hallway. They found a quiet corner where the bustle of the hospital seemed distant. McKay ran a hand over his face, betraying his fatigue.

"Thank Officer Perkins," he said. "He's young, but he's smart —and gutsy. I represented his brother last year when some shopkeeper tried to frame him for theft." He rubbed his eyes. "Perkins called me when he overheard Benedict talking about 'teaching your boy a lesson.'" He made a gesture for air quotes around the word 'boy.'

"When?"

"Around six last night. I got there as fast as I could, but—" McKay shook his head. "Not fast enough."

"You couldn't have stopped it." It wasn't empty comfort; it was fact. They both knew the reality of what they were up against.

"Maybe not. But I made damn sure they paid for it." McKay's expression darkened. "Called Lanie Price at the *Harlem Chronicle* before I even left my office. Told her to meet me at the station. By the time I got there, Benedict and his boys had already worked Carlisle over, had him bleeding on the floor."

"Yeah, my captain was pretty smug about it. But apparently, you got the best of him."

"Not me. Lanie. She had her photographer with her. Egan tried to keep us out, but she made such a ruckus that half the precinct came to see what was happening. Hard to deny medical attention when you've got a reporter and a camera pointed at you." McKay smiled grimly. "Egan tried to claim he was already planning to send Carlisle to the hospital. But we knew it was a lie. They'd have let him bleed out in that cell."

"And the guardian angel back there?"

"Hayward showed up not long after," McKay said. "Someone from the neighborhood must've told him. He's been here ever since."

Redding glanced back toward the room. "He and Carlisle—they go back."

"Way back, from what I gather. Barely said two words to me, but he wouldn't leave Carlisle's side. Even when the nurses tried to clear the room."

Redding braced himself against the wall, exhaustion finally kicking in. "Thank you. You did what I couldn't."

McKay waved it off. "Don't thank me yet. This is just the first round. Once he's stable enough, they're planning to transfer him to the Tombs."

A gay man in a violent prison. It was a death sentence—and Egan knew it. "What's the play?"

"Already started. Called Mrs. Davenport from the hospital phone about an hour ago."

"You actually called the ice queen herself?" Redding raised an eyebrow; he liked the idea.

"Desperate times. I laid it out for her. A colored writer is about to die in police custody after being beaten half to death. And why? Because she applied pressure for a quick arrest due to fear for her reputation. How would it look if Lanie's story ran in tomorrow's paper? 'Negro Writer Dies in Police Custody After Guest Poisoning at Davenport Soiree.'"

Redding chuckled. When he'd pushed that threat to Egan, he'd just been bluffing, hoping Egan wouldn't see through it. But apparently McKay had had the same idea—and he was deadly serious. "How'd she take it?"

"Oh, she didn't like it. Didn't like my nerve. Not one bit—but she understood the danger." McKay's smile was thin. "Said to get him a private room. She'd pay for it. And that she'd make some calls."

"Will it be enough?"

"For now. Between Davenport's influence and the doctor I convinced to declare Carlisle medically unfit for transfer, we've managed to get some breathing room." McKay's expression sobered. "But only a day—two, at most."

Redding rubbed his chin. "I've got something cooking in D.C. My sister's working on it."

"Your sister?"

"Ida. A reporter. She's got a knack for puzzles." Redding lowered his voice. "Grayson left something behind. Something that points to where he hid his evidence against Mercer."

Hope flickered in McKay's eyes—small, cautious, but there. "You think she can crack it?"

"If anyone can." Redding straightened. "She said she'll call as soon as she has something."

"That's good, but we can't afford to wait." McKay took an envelope from his jacket breast pocket. "Lanie's got the photographs ready. Her paper can't run them till next week's edition, but she's making sure Davenport gets an advance look."

Redding opened the envelope and examined the prints—

harsh, undeniable evidence of Benedict's brutality. Carlisle being loaded into an ambulance, his face bloody and swollen. Another showing McKay standing at his side.

"Lanie's showing these around," McKay said. "The real power is in the threat. Davenport knows these exist."

"And she doesn't want them published."

"Not with her name attached."

Redding closed the envelope, handed them back. "You're putting yourself at risk."

"Someone has to." McKay put the images away. They walked back to Carlisle's room. McKay turned back to Redding. "You look dead on your feet. Go home. Check in with Lena. Then get back to finding that evidence."

"I don't like leaving him."

"You're not." McKay gestured to a chair he'd set outside Carlisle's room. "I've got people coming in to keep watch. An old army buddy is stopping by in an hour. And an old client's taking the night shift. Former heavyweight. Nobody's getting past him. Just do your part. Solve this thing."

Ida pushed back from the kitchen table, stretched her arms. They had grown stiff from hours hunched over the cipher. Her notes and Grayson's letter were spread out, a mess of paper that finally made sense.

She'd gone to the newspaper office after Redding left, worked her shift, then rushed home, her mind churning with fresh ways to approach the cipher. The moment she'd thrown her coat over a chair, she'd reheated some of last night's beans and rice, wolfed them down and spread her notes across the table again.

That was six hours ago.

Now, her eyes burned and the kitchen clock read 2:47 AM,

but sleep was the furthest thing from her mind. Because she'd done it. She'd broken the code.

"I did it," she whispered to the empty room. "I did it. I did it. *I did it!*" The secret to the sauce was simple but effective—just the kind of subtlety a philosophy professor would appreciate. She checked her work again, making sure the sequence held. It did.

When corruption takes root, good men must act decisively. Honest souls deserve protection from those who exploit their trust. In my search for answers, I have uncovered systematic deception. Truth becomes currency for those who trade in lies. Fear clouds judgment, but conscience demands courage. It is difficult to know whom to trust in these dark times. Every step forward reveals new depths of betrayal. Let this message serve as both warning and guide. Distance yourself from those who would use your name for profit.

Yup. The answer stood out clearly. But that wasn't all. The text held one more secret.

She glanced at the clock again. Redding often worked late cases, but even he would probably be home by now.

Should she wait until morning? A long-distance call at this hour would cost a fortune—nearly a day's wages. Half a week's groceries.

It was money she didn't have. But stories didn't wait. And neither did the dead.

She grabbed her pencil and notes, then hurried to the phone and snatched up the receiver.

"Number, please." The switchboard operator's voice was alert despite the late hour.

"I need to place a long-distance call to New York City."

"New York?" The operator's voice reflected mild surprise. "It's quite late, ma'am."

Ida swallowed her irritation. "It's an emergency."

A sigh. "I'll connect you to long-distance."

There was a series of clicks, then another operator's voice.

Ida repeated her brother's number, drumming her fingers on the table while she waited, refusing to think about how much this call would cost. It was worth it.

Several minutes passed with only the occasional click and distant voices as operators along the line made the connections. Finally, there was ringing on the other end.

A groggy "Hello?"

"Nate, I've got it." Her voice dropped, edged with triumph. Party lines had ears.

"Ida?" Sleep thickened her brother's voice. "What time is it?"

"Almost three. Listen, I've cracked the cipher."

The line went quiet. She could picture him sitting up, rubbing his face, forcing his mind to sharpen. "You're sure?"

"It's an acrostic. The middle paragraph. Take the first letter of each sentence. They spell a name."

"What name?" Redding was fully alert now.

"W-H-I-T-F-I-E-L-D."

A shocked pause. "Harrison Whitfield? The university's senior accountant?"

"And there's more." She read from the last paragraph:

"The first truth I learned was this: corruption thrives in darkness. For nine years I have watched and waited. In the twenty-second year of this century, patterns became clear. The third warning may be my last. One path remains open to justice. Three witnesses could speak the truth. But only one has the courage to do so. It always falls to the knight closest to the queen's heart to guard the king's secret."

He was silent, obviously not getting it.

"Don't you see? It's right there," she said. "Hidden right out in the open: The *first* truth. For *nine* years. The *twenty-second* year. The *third* warning. *One* path. *Three* witnesses. And—"

"Only *one* has the courage..."

"Exactly. There's a numerical pattern hidden in the text: '1-

9-2-2-3-1-3-1.' Could be a date, a combination, maybe even a phone number."

The line went quiet. She could feel him thinking.

"Is that all?" he asked. "Nothing else?"

"There is that last line. 'It always falls to the knight closest to the queen's heart to guard the king's secret.' I still don't know what it means."

"Hmm. Maybe something tied to Whitfield?"

"Or to something he knows." Ida's mind was already working. "I can go see what I can get out of him."

"Ida—" A warning.

"Don't worry. I'll be careful. But I've got to do this, Nate. Grayson scattered these breadcrumbs for a reason."

Another silence. Longer. Then a resigned breath. "All right. But you call me the minute you learn anything. The minute."

"I will." She hesitated. "I'll crack this, Nate."

After hanging up, Ida stared at the pages on her table. Sleep was out of the question. Her nerves had too much to say.

Tomorrow, she'd knock on Whitfield's door.

Would he let her in—or shut her out like he had Nate?

34

Redding had told her that Whitfield's office was tucked away in Linley Hall's east wing, a warren of administrative departments that smelled of floor polish and old paper. She followed the brass nameplate signs down the marble corridor. Finally, she stood before the one she was looking for.

The frosted glass door stood half-open. Through it, she could make out a tall, thin figure moving between filing cabinets.

She adjusted her hat and smoothed her best wool skirt. She'd spent precious time on her appearance that morning—polished shoes, pressed blouse, her mother's pearl earrings. The costume of respectability.

She knocked lightly and went in.

Whitfield was exactly as her brother had described him. His jacket hung without a wrinkle. His bow tie was impeccably knotted, his collar rigid against his neck. A walking depiction of exactitude and discretion.

"Yes?"

Ida stepped forward, gloved hand extended. "Mr. Whitfield? I'm Ida Redding with the *Capital Tribune*." She'd thought of several cover stories on the walk over but now settled on one that was the closest to the truth.

"I'm working on a piece about McAllister's history of financial excellence. I know it's mighty uncouth of me to stop by with no appointment, but I do hope you'll spare a minute to speak with me."

Whitfield's eyes—sharp, assessing—moved over her face. For a moment, she thought he might refuse. Then his expression shifted, softened.

"Redding," he repeated. "Any relation to a Detective Nathaniel Redding?"

Ida had a sinking feeling. She'd thought about using a fake name, but he might call the paper to see if someone under the name really worked there. "My brother," she admitted.

Whitfield eyed her. "I see."

She tensed, sure he was going to throw her out. Steeled herself against the coming humiliation.

He gestured to a chair across from his desk. "Please, have a seat."

Relieved, she sank down in the chair and took a moment to absorb her surroundings. The office was immaculate—ledgers arranged by year on shelves behind him, papers stacked in perfect alignment on his desk. A photograph of a younger Whitfield stood beside a woman Ida assumed was his wife, both of them smiling stiffly at the camera in the way people did when photographs were still an event.

"I must say," Whitfield began, settling into his chair, "I was surprised to receive a visit from your brother. We don't often see New York detectives at McAllister."

"He's investigating a death."

"Professor Grayson's," Whitfield nodded. "A terrible loss. He was one of our finest minds."

"Did you know him well?"

"Only professionally. But one develops a sense for character in my position. Professor Grayson was thoughtful. Meticulous. Modest."

"Honest?"

He paused. "Yes."

"So you believe the allegations against him were false?"

He was quiet a moment, his eyes moving over her face. She felt like he was looking right through her.

"Why are you here? Really?"

Ida hesitated, then decided to trust her instincts. "I came across a letter Professor Grayson wrote—something he thought important enough to encrypt."

"Interesting." He frowned. "And what exactly did you find?"

She paused. "A name. Yours, in fact."

Whitfield's eyes widened in surprise. "Mine? Why?"

"I'm guessing it was because he thought you knew the answer."

"To what?"

"A puzzle. A number. That you could explain the meaning behind it." She took out her notebook, where she'd written the sequence. Read it aloud. "1-9-2-2-3-1-3-1. Does that mean anything to you?"

Whitfield rose and closed his office door.

"You recognize it," she said.

He returned to his desk, his voice lowered. "It's an invoice number."

"Invoice number?"

"Number 3131, processed in 1922."

"And do you keep track of such transactions?"

Whitfield looked mildly insulted. "Of course, we do." He gestured to the rows of ledgers behind him, each labeled by year. "Every penny that passes through this university is accounted for."

She thought that rather darkly funny, given what they were investigating. She wondered briefly—as her brother had—

whether Whitfield was a part of it. How could so much theft have occurred right under his nose otherwise? He could've decided that it was getting out of hand. That Mercer was getting too greedy, too careless. That discovery was inevitable. It would be smart to get out in front of it. And the accusations against Grayson could've been his way of doing exactly that—pointing the finger elsewhere while quietly distancing himself from Mercer.

But it didn't matter. Not right now. Whether Whitfield was complicit or simply outmaneuvered, Grayson had pointed her here. Either Whitfield himself was the answer—or he had it. And she meant to find out which.

The old accountant reached for a leather-bound ledger on the shelf behind him. Placed it on his desk between them. It was marked "1922" in clean, gold lettering.

He turned several pages, then found the one he wanted. "Apparently, Professor Grayson purchased an item through the university. So we invoiced him for reimbursement."

"What item? Can I see the ledger, please?"

"No. Absolutely not."

The refusal was unexpected. For a few minutes there, he'd seemed surprisingly cooperative, helpful even. But now Ida remembered her brother's warnings.

"Please. This could be the clue that solves the case of his death."

Whitfield arched an eyebrow. "Aren't you being a bit dramatic?" His voice had become oddly loud.

"No. I'm not. I—"

"Look, young lady. I wish I could help. I really do, but I'm afraid I can't. It's hard for me to believe you thought I would, that I'd just let you browse the university's confidential financial records."

He was looking past her, beyond her shoulder. She turned,

saw a shadow behind the frosted glass of the door. Someone was out there, hovering. Listening.

"I—"

Whitfield raised a finger to his lips. She hushed. After a moment, the shadow moved on.

Whitfield rose. Took out his pocket watch, checked it. "I'm afraid I'll have to ask you to leave, Miss Redding. I have to step out now. I expect you to be gone when I get back."

His voice was still overly loud. Upset by the change in his demeanor, she started to get up to go. But he waved her back down. Then he stood and walked out. She sat there for a moment, bewildered.

Then she understood.

She scooted over to his seat, pulled the ledger closer. He'd left the book open. Her finger slid down the column. There it was.

Invoice #3131.

A line item for a "Trojan Horse Chess Set." Purchased for Prof. Victor Grayson. Reimbursement requested.

She jotted down the details in her notebook, closed the ledger and slipped out the door.

She glanced down the hallway. There was Whitfield, returning with a fresh cup of coffee. He glanced up. She gave a tiny nod and mouthed the words, *Thank you.* He gave a subtle smile, then masked it with a sip of coffee.

Once outside, she headed south on Georgia Avenue, scanning storefronts until she found what she was looking for—a narrow drugstore with a red and white awning. The kind of place professors ducked into for aspirin, cigarettes, or a quick sandwich.

Most importantly, it had a phone booth in the back.

She started inside, then hesitated. There was a time she'd liked shopping here. The place always smelled sweet—hair tonic and bath salts—and they still carried the French-milled soap she'd splurged on once and never switched back from.

But then it became the place to get her mother's prescriptions—those final months when the clerk would meet her eyes but never ask questions.

She'd avoided it since her mother died. The place brought back too many memories. But now, for this, she had to push all that aside.

The store was warm, crowded. It still smelled sweet, but a faint edge of alcohol hung beneath it all—sharp and familiar.

She took a breath and plunged ahead, hurrying past the display counters. Hopefully, no one was using that phone. She meant to get in and get out.

It was less crowded toward the back. She was relieved to find the booth empty. She pushed inside the folding glass door, dropped a coin and gave the operator the New York precinct number. She tapped her foot as she waited.

Sometimes, it felt like these connections took forever.

Finally, her brother's voice came through the static. "Redding."

"Nate, it's Ida. I've got it." She leaned close to the mouthpiece, barely able to contain herself. "The number was an invoice—for a chess set. A 'Trojan Horse' set Grayson bought in '22."

"Wait—I saw that set. In his home. Hand-carved knights shaped like Trojan horses."

"That must be it. Whatever Grayson hid—it's got something to do with that set."

"You need to get in there. Fitzhugh has a key. He's your best bet."

"I'll call him next."

A pause.

"Be careful, Ida. This isn't just about a story. Someone killed to keep this secret."

"I know." She gripped the receiver tighter. "I'll be careful."

She hung up, pushed the folding door open and was hit by the smell of her mother's medicine. That scent had permeated every corner of the house, had only recently faded. Now, here it was again. Just a whiff. But that was enough. Enough to bring back memories of death and loss. To make them real.

"Be careful, Ida... Someone killed to keep this secret."

Her brother's warning. Her mother's ghost. Both of them, at once.

She didn't want to die. And Nate—he could barely handle their mother dying. She couldn't make him face burying her too.

Back away. Stay clear. Stay safe.

That would be the smart thing to do.

But this was a story she could sink her teeth into. The kind she'd been waiting for, prayed for. And it was her brother, of all people, who'd dropped it in her lap. She wasn't about to let him down—let herself down.

Harold Fitzhugh was her next stop. She squared her shoulders, thinking it through. He'd let her brother into Grayson's home. Sure. But he'd done it because a cop asking isn't a choice. A reporter asking is.

Would he do it again—for her?

35

It was mid-morning when Redding reached Hayward's shop. The bell above the door gave a single dry jangle as Redding stepped in. No customers. Just the soft scent of old paper and lemon oil.

Hayward looked up from the counter, spectacles low on his nose, hand resting beside a teacup. His expression hardened the moment he recognized his visitor.

"You again."

"Carlisle's things. Where are they?"

"You still trying to railroad him? Haven't you done enough?"

"I'm doing what I have to do. Now show me his things."

The bookstore owner stared at him for a long moment, then pushed back from the counter. He grabbed his teacup and headed toward the back room.

The storage space was small and cramped, with overstuffed shelves of paperwork and a cluttered desk pushed against the back wall. In the corner, a battered Underwood typewriter sat on a side table beside a cardboard box marked "E. Carlisle."

"Is this all of it?" Redding asked.

"That's it. Just his typewriter. Some of his manuscript. What clothes Marchetti didn't ruin—or steal."

Redding nodded, but his attention had already shifted to the Underwood. Its keys were still faintly dusted with grime from the street.

He pulled out a folded sheet of paper—the blackmail note—and a similar but blank page from his coat pocket.

"I need to test something."

Hayward tensed, watching with a frown as Redding rolled the blank sheet into the Underwood. The clack of keys broke the stillness as Redding typed. Same message. Same signature. One letter: C.

Redding pulled the fresh page from the roller and held both sheets up side by side. His eyes shifted from side-to-side, comparing them. When done, he passed them to Hayward.

"No match," Redding said.

Hayward took the pages. His expression changed as he examined them. The anger drained from his face. Instead, there was concentration, then growing realization.

"Good God." He pointed to the fresh sheet. "Different pressure. Different spacing entirely."

"And here," Redding pointed. "The 'r' on Carlisle's machine rides high. The note doesn't have it."

Hayward continued comparing the two sheets. His breathing grew quieter as the implications sank in. When he finally looked up at Redding, his demeanor had changed.

"Someone's trying to hang him."

"Yeah. And I think I know who."

Hayward stared at the detective. "You're not here to build a case against Ev."

"No. I'm here to catch a killer."

"But you don't think that's Ev."

"It doesn't matter what I think—only what I can prove."

The older man sank into a nearby chair, the papers still in his hands. He shook his head slowly.

"I owe you an apology."

"You don't owe me anything. You were protecting your friend."

Redding retrieved the pages and tucked them into his coat. As he turned to leave, his eyes caught on a photograph propped against the shelf: Carlisle, years younger. Sharp suit. Trim mustache. Montmartre behind him. One hand curled near his mouth, the other resting on a café table. And that look—direct, unflinching, almost amused. As if he'd already outlived whatever the world planned to throw at him.

Redding didn't touch the frame. Just studied it.

So this is who they tried to erase.

He turned back to Hayward and gestured toward the Underwood. "Keep it safe."

Hayward nodded and lifted his teacup. "Good luck, Detective."

Outside, the wind picked up, newspaper pages scraping along the curb like whispers. Redding turned up his coat collar against the chill. He had evidence now. Not just suspicion.

He wasn't surprised that Carlisle's typewriter had failed the test. He'd thought it would—hoped it would. Because he already knew which typewriter had produced the note.

Was pretty damn sure of it.

That little sheet of paper Turner had slipped into his pocket before he left Mercer's office? She'd typed the blackmail note's message on her office machine at his request. It bore the same quirks as the original, right down to the crazy 'r.'

Mercer was running out of shadows to hide in.

Grayson's study was smaller than Ida expected but still impressive. Ida dropped her purse on a nearby chair and stood there for a moment, hands on her hips, taking stock.

Fitzhugh lingered in the doorway. "What exactly are we looking for?"

"A chess set. A special one with Trojan horses."

His brow lifted. "Ah. The Greek set. That was one of Victor's prized possessions." He gestured toward a side table near the window. "He kept it over there."

She followed his hand and saw it—an ornate chess board with carved wooden pieces, polished and worn at the edges. The pieces stood mid-game. Not knights marching but riding astride ancient horses, rearing upward.

She crossed over to it. The set was clearly valuable, the craftsmanship exquisite. Black knights in dark ebony, white in pale maple. Hand-carved, no shortcuts. Each one was a labor of precision.

"He loved that set," Fitzhugh said behind her. "Bought it during his sabbatical in Europe. Said it reminded him that the most dangerous threats are the ones hidden inside gifts."

It held a secret, but how to access it? Through a secret compartment inside the board itself? Or was it through one of the pieces? That seemed unlikely. They were large, those pieces, but it was still hard to imagine any of them holding Grayson's evidence—or even something as small as a key to a lockbox.

But then that line, that last line from Grayson's note, came to her.

It falls to the knight closest to the queen's heart to guard the king's secret.

She'd dismissed the note as mere flourish. But now...

Her gaze traveled across the board, noting the position of the pieces. "Knight closest to the queen's heart..."

The white queen stood in the center of the board, and there

—just one square away—was a white knight. Closer to her than any other piece. She picked it up.

It was heavier than expected. Solid in the hand. The carving intricate—tiny details along the flank, the lines of the mane, the suggestion of a trapdoor beneath the saddle.

She turned it over. "There's got to be a mechanism." Her fingers traced the grain.

Fitzhugh stepped closer. "What are you doing?"

She didn't answer.

Just the shape. The feel of it. The way the base sat uneven. She shifted her grip. Pressed the edge of the head. Waited.

Then—

Click.

Twist.

Open.

The neck was hollow. Inside it, a thin slip of paper, rolled tight as a cigarette.

She eased it out and spread it flat on the table.

Grayson's handwriting. Neat, precise. A single line:

The key to all lies in the safe place where wisdom is weighed and pondered.

"What does that mean?" Fitzhugh peered down over her shoulder.

She read it again. "It's another clue. Another step in the trail."

He looked confused. "I don't understand."

She wasn't listening. Her gaze swept the room. The bookshelves. The stacks. The line felt deliberate. Too pointed to be metaphor.

Then it hit.

"He means the library. The philosophy section."

Fitzhugh nodded. "Yes, that would make sense. Victor was a philosopher. If he wanted to hide something significant, he'd put it somewhere meaningful."

She moved to the shelves, checked titles. Searching for—

"Something symbolic," she murmured, her fingers trailing along the spines. "Something that would matter to him."

There. A row of well-worn volumes—Aristotle, Descartes, Kant. Anchored by a thick copy of *The Republic.*

The other books were aligned with military precision. Not this one. The Plato jutted out. Just a bit. Not enough to catch the eye—unless you were looking.

"Are you the one?" she murmured. "Come to Mama."

She pulled the volume free. It was heavy—heavier than it should've been. The pages had been hollowed out. Inside the cavity, an envelope.

She slid it out. No name. Unsealed.

She hurried to the desk and spread out the contents. Bank statements. Travel receipts. Signed authorization forms.

Fitzhugh craned forward to peer over her shoulder. He inhaled sharply. "Good Lord."

The documents showed a pattern. Money rerouted through accounts held by "Educational Services Inc." and "Academic Consulting Corp." Grants redirected to something called "Scholastic Advancement Fund." The money was moving in and out of these accounts, back and forth between them, with suspect speed. Funds appearing here, then there, as though someone behind the scenes was playing a shell game shuffle. She'd seen this type of con before—that rapid shuffling of funds never tied to anything regular like paying rent or utility bills. The money would appear on a deposit slip, like an apple bobbing to the surface, then just as quickly disappear—sometimes the same amount, often broken into smaller amounts, but in withdrawals still big enough for the careful eye to see the pattern.

Then she noticed the signatures. The same careful handwriting across multiple authorization forms, just with different names: "C. Morrison," "Charles Mills," "C.M. Davidson."

She glanced at the shelf, searched the spines until she spotted what she needed. She pulled out a university directory from Grayson's shelf and flipped to the faculty page. There it was: Mercer's signature on a memo from last year. The handwriting was identical.

The telephone sat at the edge of the desk, tucked beside a stack of papers. She reached for it.

"I need to call my brother."

Behind her—

A click.

Not the phone. Something sharper. Mechanical. *Cold.*

She turned.

Fitzhugh stood near the shelves, just a few feet away. The gun was already up. His grip firm. No tremor in the wrist. No hesitation.

"I'm afraid, Miss Redding, I can't let you do that."

36

The bell over the door gave a halfhearted ring as Redding stepped into the shop. Wood counters, amber glass bottles lined the shelves, the faint scent of liniment and lavender colored the air. Your typical neighborhood pharmacy, a place that operated on trust as much as the law.

A thin man in a high collar came in from out back, wiping his hands on a cloth, and walked behind the counter. "Can I help you, sir?"

Redding's gaze moved across the room, past the shelves of powders and bottles, until it landed on the leather-bound logbook by the register.

"NYPD." He flashed his badge. "Tincture of aconite. You sell it?"

The man's eyes flickered to the badge, then to Redding, surprised and a little nervous. "Not often."

"But you have."

The man gave a reluctant nod. "On occasion. In small amounts. Always for legitimate use."

Redding tapped the edge of the counter. "Mind if I take a look at your poison register?"

The pharmacist hesitated, then turned the book toward him.

Redding flipped through the pages slowly. Dates, names, doses. Some signed. Some not. The handwriting varied—shaky old men, neat nurses, scribbling housekeepers.

He recognized none of them.

There was nothing here he could tie to Grayson or his associates. No initials. No handwriting. Nothing at all.

He'd known it was a long shot—that there might be an alias he didn't recognize. Or an entry with no signature. Or even no entry at all if the pharmacist had failed to properly record the sale. Still, he felt a sinking sense of disappointment.

Redding closed the book and slid it back across the counter. Then he pulled a photo from his coat pocket, leaned on the counter and held it up. "You recognize this person?"

The pharmacist glanced at the photo. Shook his head almost immediately. "Can't say as I do."

"You sure? It's an old photo. The face might've changed a bit. Take your time. Look closer."

The pharmacist rubbed his nose. After a second, his eyes slightly widened. He looked up at Redding. "No, I, uh...I don't think so. Sorry, but a lot of people pass through here and I—"

"That's okay.

Redding put the photo away. He straightened up, giving the man a polite but flat nod. "I'm over at the 32nd on West 135th. Let me know if you think of anything."

The pharmacist swallowed and nodded quickly, too quickly. "Yeah. Sure."

"Thanks."

Redding left, the doorbell ringing softly behind him. The man's face had told him what he needed. Trouble was, suspicion didn't go far. Not without something he could put on paper.

And he didn't have it. Not yet.

Ida froze. Her mind struggled to catch up. Fitzhugh standing five feet away. Gun raised. Grip solid. Eyes steady.

That gun—

The way it caught the light. Lined up on her chest. The way it made every breath feel like a risk.

"Put the phone down. Slowly."

The words snapped her out of it. She swallowed hard. Fingers hovered over the handset. "You don't have to do this."

"Step back from the phone. Hands raised."

She lifted her hands. Just enough. Just enough to keep thinking.

"You knew," she said. "You knew what Mercer was doing. Maybe you were helping him. Grayson found out about you, didn't he?"

"No, he...he trusted me."

A pause. A flash of guilt. Even regret. Then it vanished.

"He was getting too close."

Her stomach twisted. "So you killed him?"

"It was Mercer. He did it. What had to be done." His hand trembled. Just a bit. Not enough. "I tried to warn Vic. He wouldn't stop."

The gun dipped. Barely.

She needed time. Distance. A chance. "What now?" She glanced toward the door.

"Now? Now, you hand over those papers."

Her brain snapped into gear. Cataloging facts, risks, likelihoods. Give in, then Grayson would've died for nothing. Mercer would walk free.

And Fitzhugh would kill her, anyway.

She moved fast, deliberate. One sharp motion. She flung the pages toward the bookshelf. They caught the air, fluttering like falling leaves.

Fitzhugh cursed. Turned. His aim shifted.

That was enough.

She lunged. Slammed into him. Hit him high. Shoulder to ribs.

The gun jerked up. A flare of heat. A single blast. Louder than thought. Pain didn't come, but sound vanished. Everything muffled. As if she'd been shoved underwater.

She tasted smoke. Felt cloth tear. Caught the blur of his wrist. She grabbed it. Twisted. Hard.

His fingers opened. The gun dropped.

Both of them dove, collided. He shoved her sideways. She hit him hard and kicked out. The gun skidded under the desk.

She crawled—breath ragged, heart slamming. His hand caught her coat, yanked her back. She tore free and dove again. Her fingers found the gun. Cold. Real. Closed over it. He lunged.

"Harold?"

The voice stopped them both.

MaryAnne Fitzhugh stood just inside the doorway. Outwardly poised. Composed. But her face was pale. Her mouth opened, then closed. She gripped the doorframe as if it was the only thing holding her up.

"I got worried. You were taking so long."

Her bewildered gaze swept the room—from her husband, disheveled and bruised, to the papers strewn about, and then to Ida, crouched on the floor, with the gun pointed at Fitzhugh.

"MaryAnne," Fitzhugh started, but his voice died.

She stepped inside, moving like someone in a dream. Or a nightmare. "What–what's happening? Harold, what—?"

Ida kept the gun steady on Fitzhugh. "Your husband was helping Mercer steal from the university. And when Professor Grayson found out, they killed him."

"That's absurd." MaryAnne's eyes darted to her husband. "Harold, tell her."

Fitzhugh's lips parted, but nothing came.

"Harold, what is she talking about? What does she mean?"

"MaryAnne, please." He reached for her. "This girl—she's dangerous. Came after me out of nowhere. Call someone. Call the police."

"Stop lying!" Ida said. "This is *your* gun. You're the one who pulled it. Now tell her the truth—or I swear I'll use it."

Fitzhugh looked to his wife, eyes pleading. But MaryAnne just stared back at him, confusion and growing horror written across her face. No help there. His gaze returned to Ida, to the gun in her hands, to whatever he saw in her expression.

Fitzhugh sagged. "MaryAnne, I didn't want him to die. But Victor wouldn't stop."

"Tell her how you killed him!" Ida snapped.

"It wasn't me. It was Mercer. I swear."

"Liar!"

MaryAnne's voice cut through. "Harold, is it true? Were you really helping that man to-to destroy our university? Everything we built up? And when Vic came to you—trusted you, told you everything he was going through—did you—?"

His face gave her the answer.

She pressed her hand to her chest. "But he was our friend—*your* friend." Her voice cracked. "My god! *He was one of us!*"

Fitzhugh winced, as if the power of her grief hit harder than a bullet ever could.

"Say something," she whispered. "Anything."

He couldn't.

She let out a small, broken laugh—part disbelief, part despair. "No. Maybe it's better you don't."

No one spoke. Fitzhugh sat on the floor, a man unmade, his composure shattered before the only witness who mattered. Ida lowered the gun, careful not to drop it. Her fingers stayed tight, stiff from holding on too long.

A distant siren cut the silence.

Fitzhugh looked up at his wife. For a moment, their gazes

locked. She shook her head once, her lips pressed tight, then looked away.

Ida glanced toward the phone on Grayson's desk. She'd been about to call Nate before this clown pulled a gun on her. Now she had a much more urgent situation. She wouldn't be just reporting her findings. She had a confessed accomplice to murder sitting in front of her.

Should she call the local police instead? But suppose Fitzhugh lied? And they believed him over her? Arrested her instead of him?

Then there was MaryAnne. After the shock of Fitzhugh, Ida couldn't be sure about her either. Was MaryAnne an innocent bystander—or just pretending to be one? Ida's mind sped through the options.

It hit her that the sirens were louder now.

They all jerked up, exchanged glances. Fitzhugh's knuckles went pale against his knee. MaryAnne's hand flew to her throat. Ida felt her blood turn cold. Had a neighbor heard that shot? Called it in?

Two seconds of intense listening. Yes, the sirens were drawing nearer.

Ida's thoughts snapped into focus.

The evidence—the papers—if the police took them, they could disappear into some backroom box. Misfiled. Ignored. Lost to McAllister's influence. She couldn't risk that.

She swept up the scattered pages and folded them into a tight bundle. Saw her handbag on the chair. Hurried over to it, stuffed the papers deep inside and snapped the bag shut.

MaryAnne and Fitzhugh were watching her with dazed fear. They knew what cops meant, what an arrest would do to their neat little lives.

Ida knew them, knew their type.

MaryAnne presented the picture of perfectly refined womanhood. Of subservience and respectability. But Ida saw through it, recognized the steely pragmatism that lay beneath the velvet poise. MaryAnne was the real powerbroker in the Fitzhugh marriage. Convince her. She'd convince him.

"No time for debate," Ida said. "Listen up—and listen good. If the cops are coming, we're going to tell them this was a lovers' quarrel. You and me, Professor—we've been stepping out. Your wife here caught us and things got ugly."

MaryAnne recoiled. "That's absurd."

"It's ridiculous," Fitzhugh muttered.

"Maybe it is," Ida shot back, "but it's the only story that'll keep this out of the papers. Sure, the gossip will be ugly but it'll be even worse if those cops get nosy and I have to tell them what this is really all about."

"You mean that if we lie, then you won't say anything about —well, about this?" Fitzhugh asked.

"No. A man's dead and somebody's gonna have to pay for it. What I'm talking about is the difference between the cops arresting you now and you turning yourself in tomorrow."

"Are you crazy?" That was MaryAnne.

"You tell me," Ida said. "You want the university to hear about this mess before you two can speak with a lawyer? Or let Mercer get out front with his version?"

Silence. Indecision.

"Look, I'm not going to try to snow you," Ida said. "The truth's gonna get out. One way or another, the truth about the fraud and Grayson's death is gonna hit the front page of every colored paper in this country. And your name, Professor, is gonna be a part of it. But this way, you've got time. To call an attorney. To talk to the university. To turn yourself in—quietly, with dignity."

Fitzhugh glanced at his wife. What did she think? She said nothing, still holding out. The sirens stopped. His gaze darted to the door, panicked now. They could hear the sound of car doors being slammed shut.

"We do it my way," Ida said, "or Mercer wins right now."

Fitzhugh turned back to his wife. *Please. What do we do?*

Footsteps coming up the driveway.

MaryAnne closed her eyes. Then gave a single, tight nod.

Fitzhugh slumped with a relieved sigh.

The knock came—sharp, official.

Ida nodded to Fitzhugh. "You'd better be the one to answer. They may or may not know this isn't your house. But at least you can say you have the key."

Fitzhugh nodded. Dragged himself to his feet. Patted down his hair, straightened his sweater. Then limped out of the room.

Ida looked to MaryAnne. "You should go with him."

MaryAnne waved her off and turned away.

Voices now—low conversation, clipped. Then boots on hardwood. Ida positioned herself to see the door. Two cops stepped inside. D.C. municipal. One graying and pot-bellied, the other barely old enough to shave. Both armed. Both wired tight.

Family disturbance. Possible gunshot. At a campus address? They weren't taking chances.

More conversation. If Fitzhugh was trying to sell the story Ida had concocted, he wasn't doing a good job of it. The cops were looking past him, hands near holsters.

Ida looked back at MaryAnne. The woman had backed against the wall, her arms crossed tight, as if bracing against a cold wind, as if she wished she were anywhere but here.

Useless.

Ida shoved the gun into her purse and hurried out to the hallway. She came up behind Fitzhugh, smiling warmly, her hand hovering above her chest, her demeanor coy and flirtatious.

"Officers. Y'all didn't come all the way out here because of little ole me, did you?"

The younger one gave her a once-over. Smiled. "Well, miss, we got a report that—"

The older one stepped forward, thumbs hooked in his belt, belly thrust forward in a swagger. "Gunshot. Possible violence."

"Oh, no, nothin' like that, officer. It's just that—" She gave Fitzhugh an adoring look. "Well, me and the professor here, we're...close friends, if you get what I mean. Nothin' untoward, y'understand. But that woman back there—" She glanced over her shoulder and jerked a thumb toward the study, where MaryAnne could be plainly seen.

"My wife," Fitzhugh said.

"Yes, *her*," Ida said. "She's got this crazy notion that he and I might be indulgin' in some impropriety. Can you imagine that?" Ida leaned close to Fitzhugh and blew him a kiss.

The cops exchanged a look. The kind that said, *Yep, we've seen this before.*

"What about the gunshot?" the older one said.

"Oh, that!" Ida fluttered a hand. "Silly of me. We got into a little bit of a tiff. And I admit it, things got out of hand. But as you can see, nobody's hurt, officers. We're all doin' just fine."

The younger one glanced at Fitzhugh, who shifted uneasily. The older one sighed. Ida could read the reluctance in his face—colored folks' domestic affairs, no blood visible, probably more trouble than it was worth. Still, he asked: "And the gun?"

"In there."

Ida jerked a thumb over her shoulder and turned to see MaryAnne emerge from the study.

The professor's wife sailed past them, headed for the door. Posture straight, chin lifted, her white-gloved hands clutched her purse tightly. And what with the way she carried herself, with such firm dignity, the cops let her walk right on by.

As Ida would tell her brother later, "I could tell something was wrong. For the life of me, I don't know what it was. But I could just feel it in my bones."

She glanced down the hall to the study. Her bag. The clasp was open.

Ida reached out, tapped MaryAnne on the elbow.

MaryAnne stopped. Turned. The look she gave Ida said it all. *Don't you dare stop me. Don't you even try.*

Ida's eyebrows shot up and her mouth grew tight. She held a hand out. Palm up. Fingers curled.

MaryAnne hesitated. Ida didn't need a crystal ball to know what MaryAnne was thinking. Miss Respectability here had spent her life protecting her husband's name, his place, his reputation. Those papers weren't just evidence that threatened it all—they were leverage that could be wielded to protect it. Bargaining chips. Something to use with the university, then the police. She'd nearly gotten away with them. But now—caught—did she dare risk it? Try to bluff her way out?

Ida put a hand on her hip, then slid her eyes over toward the cops. *You want me to tell them what's really going on? 'Cause I will. You know I will. I've got nothing to lose—but you do.*

One glance. Less than a second. But that's all it took. Message sent. Message received.

MaryAnne's jaw set with frustration.

But after a beat, she opened her purse, drew out the folded papers and slapped them in Ida's hand.

Then she turned and stalked out the door, shoulders back, head high. A proud, if wounded, queen. She hadn't looked at Fitzhugh. Not once. She'd walked past him like he wasn't there. And now she was walking away, without even a backward glance.

As for Fitzhugh, he didn't call after her. Just stood there, eyes following her like a man watching the door close on the last chance he had.

Ida turned back to the cops, flashed a bright smile. "Officers, if you don't need me..."

Before they could answer, she returned to the study, grabbed her coat and bag. The gun was gone—probably tucked into MaryAnne's purse along with her dignity. Ida wasn't worried about it.

She checked the bundle. All there.

Time to get out of here.

She headed toward the door, hips swinging. Dropped a smooch on Fitzhugh's cheek and threw the cops a wink.

"Toodle-oo, boys."

Then she was gone.

At the corner, she didn't stop walking. Not until she was out of sight. Not until the tension in her chest finally let go.

Grayson's evidence.

Safe.

At last.

37

Ida's hands trembled as she turned the key in her front door. Grayson's papers were buried deep inside her bag, pressed against her side. She glanced behind her twice before slipping inside and firmly locked the door.

Finally. Back in the safety and silence of her own home. She pressed her back against the door and let out a long breath. Only now, alone, could she feel the full wash of adrenaline leaving her—cold, clenching, cruel. Her knees wobbled, but she pushed upright.

No time to fall apart. Nate needed to know.

She crossed to the phone in the entryway and picked up the receiver.

"Number, please?"

"Long distance to New York City." She gave the number and waited as the line crackled and clicked. Voices came and went—distant, half-formed, like ghosts on a wire.

"Thirty-second Precinct, Officer Daniels."

"This is Ida Redding. I need to speak with Detective Nathaniel Redding. It's urgent—family business."

"One moment, miss."

More waiting. More clicks. The sound of distant voices, a door closing. Then finally—

"Redding."

"Nate, it's me."

"Ida? You all right?"

"I'm fine now. I'm home." She steadied herself. "I found it, Nate. The evidence."

"That's great—"

"No, listen. There's more." She took a breath. "Fitzhugh pulled a gun on me."

Momentary silence. *"What?"*

"He's been working with Mercer. Said Grayson was getting too close. Told me Mercer 'did what had to be done.'"

"Jesus Christ." The shock in his voice was palpable. "Ida, I sent you to him. I—"

"You couldn't have known. I'm okay. That's what matters."

"How did you get away?"

She told him, kept it short. The confrontation, the fight, MaryAnne's arrival, the cops. She didn't elaborate; he'd get the full story later. What mattered was that he understood what she'd discovered.

"The evidence. It's all here. Fraud. Stolen scholarship funds. Grayson's notes, the paper trail—everything."

A beat of silence. "What about Fitzhugh? Is he in custody?"

"No. I had to act fast." She explained the story she'd spun—about a lovers' quarrel. "I told him to turn himself in. That it would be cleaner that way."

"You think he will?"

"He's got no choice. MaryAnne'll see to it."

She told him about MaryAnne's attempt to steal the evidence. "She's looking for room to maneuver. Trying to make a deal before the devil gets his due."

"Well, good thing you caught her." He let out a breath. "You did good, Ida. Real good. Send me the bill for these calls. I'll cover it."

She gave a small laugh, relief flowing through her. "That's what you're worried about?"

"No." His voice softened. "I'm worried about my little sister getting shot at because of my case."

"I'm fine, Nate. Really." She paused. "What do you want me to do with the evidence?"

Redding went quiet. She could almost hear the gears turning in his mind.

"I need it. But sending it through the mail is too risky."

"I could bring it to you. Come up to New York myself."

"You'd do that?"

"Of course. This matters."

He sounded relieved. "That would be perfect. When can you come?"

"There's a train leaving at five. I could be there by ten tonight."

"I'll meet you at Penn Station. And I'll cover the fare."

"Don't be ridiculous. This is family business."

She could imagine him smiling. "Is that what they're calling police work these days?"

"In this case, yeah. See you soon, big brother."

"See you."

She hung up, threw clothes into a bag, and headed out. She had just enough time to make the train.

Union Station was packed with the rush-hour crowd. Ida loved it, the sense of being in the middle of it all, feeling the rush of life around her. Each face told a different story, and the clues were all right there. You just had to have the eyes to see them.

She glanced at the newspaper headlines. Evening papers

hawking half-truths in bold print. Headlines that missed the story by a mile. How many tales went untold because the right people weren't there to tell them? Couldn't see them, didn't have the guts to voice them or weren't allowed to print them?

On the train, Ida pulled out her notebook. Her fingers traced the worn cover. Inside were leads and fragments her editor never let her touch. Stories he'd deemed "not quite suited" for her to write—code for "stick to women's issues."

There was the story about colored soldiers sent home to nothing. The story about housing covenants forcing families into crumbling tenements. The story about colored schools being shorted year after year while white ones gleamed.

Pitch after pitch, she'd been brushed aside.

"Great idea, Ida—Johnson will take it."

"We've already got Roberts on that one."

"This one needs someone they'll actually let through the door."

Not this time.

This story was hers. She'd done what not even her brother could do. He was a bona fide, streetwise, tough-talking New York City homicide detective. But she was the one who'd found the evidence. Dug up the proof.

She had *earned* this byline. Risked her life for it. And she wasn't about to give it up.

She put pen to paper. A professor silenced. Donors deceived. Students cheated. Names. Numbers. Blood and betrayal in ledger lines.

This was a story Ida B. Wells would've chased, pen in one hand and fire in the other.

The words came fast now, her hand moving fast across the page. How many young men and women had lost their chance at education because of Mercer's greed? How many families had sacrificed everything to send a child to college, never knowing the money meant for their futures was lining someone else's pockets?

She paused. Looked at what she'd written. Then kept going. The words poured out—precise and purposeful. She wasn't doing this just for Nate. Not anymore. She was doing it for the young men and women whose futures had been sold. For every editor who said "not quite right." For every woman told to stick to "softer" stories.

Some truths didn't need permission. They needed ink.

And this one was going to run under her name.

Ida Redding, front page.

No compromise.

PART IV

END GAME

38

Redding pressed the receiver to his ear and gave the number to the operator. A faint hum crackled on the line as she patched him through. The precinct was quieter than usual, save for the murmur of voices from the evening shift and the occasional clatter of a typewriter. He glanced out the window. Already dark outside. He'd chosen this time deliberately. Fewer distractions. Fewer ears.

There was a click, then a pause. The connection pulsed with distant static.

"Clive Mercer speaking."

Smooth. Cultured. Controlled. The voice of a man who never let anything slip.

Redding settled back in his chair, his grip loose on the receiver. "Dr. Mercer. Detective Redding, here. I trust I'm not catching you at a bad time."

A pause. Then, polite amusement. "Detective Redding. I must admit, I wasn't expecting to hear from you again. To what do I owe the pleasure?"

Redding let a small smile touch his lips. "Thought I'd extend a courtesy. Your information proved useful. Helped put some key pieces together. I figured you'd like to know that the case is nearly wrapped up."

Another pause. This one a fraction longer.

"That's excellent news. I imagine you'll be making an arrest soon?"

Redding glanced at his notepad, though he didn't need to. The names, the locations, the connections—he had them all mapped out. "That's the plan." He let the words settle before adding, "But before I do, I need one last thing from you."

Redding heard Mercer exhale. He could picture the slight tilt of the head, the practiced deliberation.

"Detective, I assure you, I've already told you everything I know."

"Maybe, but I'd rather be certain. If this is the last step, I'd hate for anything to be left open to interpretation. You understand."

Silence. Brief. Controlled.

"I see," Mercer said at last. "And how exactly do you propose we ensure that?"

"Simple," Redding said. "You come to New York."

Nothing but the clock. Tick, tick, tick.

"To New York," Mercer repeated.

"That's right. Sit down with me, go over everything in person. Just a final conversation to close things out. Won't take long."

"Detective, surely you don't require my presence for that. I can clarify anything you need from right here in D.C."

Redding smiled again, this time without warmth. "Now, that's where we disagree. A man in your position—respected, educated—you'd want to make sure nothing gets misrepresented. Nothing left unclear."

"And do you feel my name requires clarification?"

Redding waited a beat. "I think a man like you wouldn't want to take that risk."

A pause. Then Mercer chuckled, a quiet, knowing sound. "You have a rather unique way of making a request sound like an expectation."

"I do my best."

"Very well." The reluctance was just faint enough to be mistaken for grace. "If it sets your mind at ease, then so be it. When would you like to meet?"

"Noon. Tomorrow. The 32nd Precinct. We're on West 135th, between Seventh and Eighth. I'll be expecting you."

"Then you shall have me."

The line clicked and Redding set the receiver down, gaze resting on it.

The bait was in the water. He just had to watch Mercer swim toward it.

Penn Station after dark carried a special kind of energy—still bustling, but with a sharper edge, the grand concourse's shadows longer, its echoes deeper. Redding rested his back against a marble pillar, hat tilted low, eyes fixed on the platform where the Congressional Limited was due any minute.

The station clock read 10:17 PM. The train was running late.

Redding checked his watch, a gesture more of nerves than necessity. Tomorrow morning he'd be facing Mercer and he needed what Ida was bringing. Without Grayson's evidence, the entire case might crumble. Everything—Carlisle's future, Grayson's justice—hinged on those papers.

The arrival announcement finally crackled over the loudspeaker. Its distorted echo bounced off the vaulted ceiling. Redding straightened, adjusting his coat as he moved toward the gate.

The passengers emerged in a slow, tired stream—businessmen with rumpled suits, women clutching sleeping children, sailors with duffel bags slung over shoulders. And then —there she was. Ida moved with purpose, her burgundy coat buttoned tight against the night chill, a travel valise in one hand and a small leather satchel tucked securely under her arm like it contained the crown jewels.

In many ways, it did.

Her eyes found his. No smile, no wave—just a small nod of recognition as she navigated through the thinning crowd.

"Long ride?" he asked.

"Long enough." She sounded tired. "But worth it."

He reached for her valise. "Car's outside. Lena's waiting at home."

Ida relinquished the bag but kept the satchel pressed against her side. "Good. I'm starving."

They fell into step out of habit, the way siblings do. Redding instinctively took a protective lead as he cut through the crowds. Ida—smaller, but nimble and quicker—kept up with him, at ease with it all, though the sheer press of people was unlike anything back home in D.C. Neither spoke until they reached Redding's car, a modest Ford sedan parked near the station's main entrance on Seventh Avenue.

The moment they were inside, doors shut against the night, Ida reached for her satchel.

"Here." She withdrew a manila envelope. "Everything Grayson collected."

Redding pulled a small flashlight from his coat pocket and clicked it on, holding it between his teeth as he opened the envelope.

His fingers moved through the pages—bank statements, travel receipts, authorization forms. Mercer's signature showed up often, neat and confident, always on the final approvals. But Redding's eye caught the real tells: not only the aliases that always included Mercer's initials but the signatures on the original requests. Forgeries every one. Professors and staff who, if asked, would swear they never signed a thing.

The money moved to accounts none of the real professors controlled. Accounts that didn't belong to anyone with a classroom, a syllabus, or a student to teach. Shell accounts—ghost faculty on paper only, just empty names tied to full coffers. And eventually to phantom companies with generic names meant to launder Mercer's ill-gotten gains.

This wasn't just a portrait of fraud. It was of a man smart enough to look like a fool instead of a thief. A man who'd claim, if cornered, that he was no criminal—just too trusting. Fooled by bad paperwork. Misled by those he was told to honor. All while pocketing every dollar and leaving the ghosts to carry the blame.

The car's interior became a detective's office. The flashlight beam sliced through the dark as Redding examined each page.

"This is it." He tucked the envelope inside his jacket. "This is what I needed."

Ida studied his expression in the dim streetlight glow. "Enough to nail him?"

Redding's smile was thin, a hunter's smile. "Enough to set the trap."

"What kind of trap?"

"I'll tell you about—after."

"Don't want to jinx it, huh?"

"Yeah, that's right. I don't want to jinx it."

"Riiiiight." She gave him a look of disgust.

He laughed and started the engine. "How long you staying?"

"Need to catch the early morning train. Have to be at the paper by noon." She settled back into the passenger seat, tension visibly easing from her shoulders.

Redding pulled out into the Manhattan night. "Cutting it close."

"I'd do it all over again." Her gaze stayed on the passing lights. "For Grayson. For the story."

The drive to Bedford-Stuyvesant was quiet, both of them lost in thought as they crossed the bridge into Brooklyn. The borough's streets were more subdued than Manhattan's frantic pace, rows of brownstones and townhouses standing shoulder to shoulder under the glow of streetlamps.

Redding finally broke the silence as they turned onto his street. "You're going to like Lena's got cooking."

"I always do." A hint of warmth crept into Ida's voice. "She still making that sweet potato pie?"

"Got one in the oven for you."

A small two-story house came into view, modest but well-kept, with warm light spilling from its windows. Redding pulled up in front, killed the engine and reached over to squeeze his sister's shoulder.

"Thank you for coming all this way."

Ida nodded, understanding all he wasn't saying.

The front door opened before they reached it, revealing Lena Redding—petite, beautiful, and no fool. She had the wise eyes of an old soul and the luminous smile of a young one.

"There you are." She embraced Ida. "Was starting to think you'd missed the train with how late it's running."

"And miss your cooking?" Ida laughed. "Never."

Lena ushered them inside. The small dining room table was already set. The aroma of chicken and dumplings enriched the air. "Food's ready. Go wash your hands. Then sit down, both of you."

As they settled around the table, Lena brought steaming dishes from the kitchen. Redding's hand occasionally drifted to his jacket, touched the envelope. Still real. Still there.

"So," Lena finally took her seat, "I assume you two have already talked business?"

Redding nodded, passing Ida a bowl of cooked cabbage. "All squared away."

Ida glanced at her brother, then back to Lena. "He's up to something and he won't tell me about it."

Lena rolled her eyes. "Of course he's not. That's Nate for you."

Ida pressed her lips together, annoyed. She turned back to her brother and narrowed her eyes at him. "Why don't you just tell me what you've got planned?"

"Some things are just better left unsaid."

"That's not an answer."

"No," he agreed. "It's not."

"So you're really not going to tell me?"

"Nope." He forked his last piece of chicken. Popped it into his mouth. And chewed with gusto. "I'm not telling nobody. Not yet."

She swatted him with her napkin. He ducked and laughed.

"You two behave and stop acting like children." Lena set three slices of sweet potato pie on the table. "Your favorite," she told Ida with a warm smile. "Fresh from the oven."

The conversation shifted then, to lighter topics—Lena's work at the school where she taught, news from her family, Ida's battles with her editor. But beneath it all, the envelope remained, a silent presence.

Later, as the clock neared midnight and Lena prepared the spare room, Redding followed Ida into the small sitting room.

"I'll wake you at five. Get you to the station for that early train."

She nodded, stifling a yawn. "This plan of yours, when do you put it into motion?"

"Already have."

She stilled, gave him a look that said, *All jokes aside*. "Be careful, Nate."

"Always am." He squeezed her shoulder.

"No. You're not." A small smile.

Redding let out a soft chuckle. "Get some sleep. It's a short night."

He headed to his study and spent the next several hours poring over Grayson's evidence, mapping out his strategy. Slowly but surely the key pieces were clicking into place.

The next morning, he drove Ida back to Penn Station in the predawn darkness. They said their goodbyes on the platform and when he hugged her, the embrace was tighter, lasted longer than it used to. She'd risked her life for his case, something he'd never foreseen, never meant for her to do.

As her train pulled away, Redding turned toward his car, toward the precinct, toward Mercer.

The trap was set. Now, to spring it.

39

Mercer had spent his life among men who used their voices like scalpels, carving out influence with carefully chosen words. He'd studied them, watched them deliver lectures in university halls and charm donors at society dinners. He'd spent countless hours honing the same skills of polished detachment and calculated ease. He knew how to control a conversation.

But in this Harlem police interrogation room, reeking of stale cigarette smoke and dim under a sputtering overhead light, Mercer felt disoriented, unmoored. It was an unfamiliar feeling. He didn't like it at all.

He sat straight-backed, hands resting on the table. His black leather gloves lay beside his hat, both placed with precision—the hat centered, the gloves aligned, their fingers pointed toward him. His hair was perfectly conked, gleaming like polished ebony. The suit was sharp. The gold watch subtle. His tic knotted just so. Control lived in the details.

The chair wobbled beneath him, one leg shorter than the others. At first, he'd chalked it up to what one would expect in a place like this: cheap, beat-up furniture, institutional walls, harsh light. But the longer he sat, the more suspicious he became. This chair was no accident. It was cheap all right—a cheap trick meant to keep him off-balance.

He wouldn't let it. The secret to handling the chair was simple. Don't move. Each move brought a jolt. So you just didn't move. The chair might be unsteady; he wasn't.

That ceiling light, though—that was another matter. It wasn't just that it was glaring or even that it was ugly (and ugly it was). It was, of all things, the sound it made that annoyed him. It ticked. The sound ate away at him, took him back to that damn refrigerator they'd had when he was a kid. The one that never worked, that let the food rot. There wasn't that much to eat, but on those rare days when there was—when they even had something left over—it made more sense to feed it to the pigs than try to save it.

Across from him, the detective was not rushing. He moved like a man who'd played this game a hundred times before. Sleeves rolled. Tie loosened. Comfortable. Not slovenly.

Worse, Redding had the look of a man who had done this before, who had seen too many men sit in that chair and think they were about to talk their way out of something.

Calm. Patient. Dangerous.

"Long way from Washington," Redding said. "I hope you had a smooth trip."

Mercer gave a slight nod. "Uneventful."

"Good." Redding flipped open a file. "Let's go over a few things, just to be sure I've got them right. Your whereabouts, to start. For the record, where were you on the day Professor Grayson died?"

Mercer adjusted his already-perfect cufflinks. "Saturday, was it? I was in D.C. Worked in my office. I like weekends. They're quiet."

"That's what you said before, but you know how it is. Gotta verify."

"Of course."

"So, I spoke with some folks at Union Station, ticket sellers and porters, and..." Redding let his voice trail off.

"Yes?"

"They remember seeing you that Friday. Said you boarded a train to New York."

Mercer tilted his head. "I'm there often. Hard to say exactly when."

The ceiling light stuttered overhead. That mechanical tick-tick-tick was boring into his skull. He forced his breathing to remain even.

"So you think they're mistaken about the day?"

Mercer opened his palms in an eloquent gesture. Forgetting himself for a moment, he shifted his weight—just slightly—and the chair landed with a sharp jolt. He kept the smile in place.

Redding continued: "But then we have the hotel to consider."

That one hit Mercer harder. Not the chair jolt, the comment. To steady himself, he reached inside his jacket for his cigarettes —and got another jolt from the chair for the trouble. His neck stiffened. His lips tightened. He forced them into a confident smile, produced a monogrammed silver cigarette case and a matching lighter. Started to light up.

"No smoking." Redding's eyes said the rest.

The lie was obvious—the room stank of old smoke. But it served its purpose: reminded Mercer whose house this was.

Mercer's smile turned brittle. He lit up anyway, took one long drag—his small rebellion—then dropped the cigarette to the floor and ground it out with a black polished toe.

"You were saying?" He pocketed the case, careful not to move otherwise.

"The Hotel Olga. The folks there remember you. So does their register. You checked in. Stayed overnight."

A pause. Then another shrug, practiced to perfection. "What

can I say? You found me out. I was in New York. So were a million others. Doesn't mean I killed him."

Redding turned a page. "You ever been to the Wells Restaurant?"

"I assume you already know the answer."

"A witness saw you there. Said you weren't alone."

That relentless ticking grew louder. Mercer adjusted his tie without thinking. The chair shifted again—a spine-rattling jolt this time. He closed his eyes for a moment, grimaced. A headache was forming.

"Detective, I—"

"You were with Grayson. She recognized him from the papers. Said you two were having coffee."

Mercer's fingers grazed the edge of his gloves. "We exchanged pleasantries. That's all."

"He died later that night."

Mercer gave a careful nod. "Yes. A terrible loss."

"Poisoned," Redding said. "Know what kind?"

Mercer paused mid-gesture, tried to ignore the sinking feeling in the pit of his stomach. "No."

"Aconitine. It's bitter. Rare as a poison. Works best in something hot—like tea. Or better still, coffee."

Mercer's throat went dry. He swallowed. Too late, he realized the risk of that gesture. Any throat movement could suggest guilt.

"Water?" Redding asked.

Mercer almost nodded. But pride and paranoia held him back. Was Redding mocking him? Offering him something to drink after having accused him of poisoning Grayson via liquid? It was decidedly inappropriate—too inappropriate for a man like Redding to have done by mistake.

"Thank you, but no."

Was that a faint smile he saw on the detective's face?

"Not easy to trace," Redding went on. "Paralyzes the lungs.

Works slowly in small doses. Just enough to make a man feel sick at first—tremors, nausea, weakness. Breathing gets harder. Then it stops."

Silence.

"You had coffee with him."

"That hardly proves—"

"He was fine when he left you. Still fine when he got to Davenport's. But not by the time he left."

The light above stuttered. Shadows shifted across the table. The ticking drilled into his skull.

"This is—" Mercer stopped. Recalibrated. Forced a quiet laugh. "Detective, this is circumstantial at best. You're making leaps."

"I'm connecting dots."

Redding slid a sheet across the table. Mercer didn't touch it. But he knew what it was. That note. *That damn note.*

His hand went back to his gloves. Adjusted what didn't need adjusting.

"We traced the typewriter that was used to type it," Redding said. "Your department. Your secretary's office."

"A communal machine. Anyone could've used it."

"But not anyone did."

Mercer drew the gloves closer. The chair wobbled again. Tension clamped his shoulders.

"You were in New York. With Grayson. You had coffee. Then he was dead. And a blackmail note found with his body, bearing your initial, was done on your office machine." Redding slapped the file closed. "So you tell me. What should I be thinking?"

Mercer opened his mouth. No words came.

The light ticked on. *Tick. Tick. Tick.*

He could feel the sweat beneath his collar; the sharp, sickly churn of his stomach. He tried to breathe. To come up with a slick answer. But his thoughts scattered. His mind flailed. For the first time in his life, his glib tongue failed him completely.

Say something. Anything.

What trick was left in the deck?

Then he found it. The one question any innocent man would ask.

"Why would I have killed Victor Grayson? What possible motive would I have had?"

Redding told him.

The answer was devastating.

The cop knew. He knew...*everything.*

Sweat broke across Mercer's forehead. He crushed the gloves in his fist. Forced himself to breathe, to hold steady under Redding's gaze, to maintain what little control he had left.

"You have no proof."

"You think I brought you up here to bluff?"

The door opened.

Mercer startled. The chair pitched again. Another flat-foot entered—young, lean, sharp-eyed. Plainclothes. He handed Redding a manila envelope.

"Looks like what you've been waiting for."

Redding tore it open. Yanked out the contents. Three crisp sheets. No folds.

Mercer stared. Blood pounding in his ears. The ticking overhead slowed, each click stretching into eternity.

What was in that envelope? More evidence? Grayson's files? Witness accounts? His mind spun. His pulse throbbed at the base of his throat.

The cop read. No reaction. Checked the pages again.

Mercer knew, with a cold, nauseating certainty, that this was it, the beginning of the end.

But then—a faint tightening of Redding's lips.

Mercer held his breath. Was that frustration? Even anger? Something was off.

Redding looked up and fixed him with a stare. His jaw worked like he was chewing bad news.

"You can go."

Mercer blinked. "What?"

"I said, you can go—for now." One sharp nod toward the door. "Just don't leave town."

You can go.

Three words. Hard as bullets. End of story.

It didn't make sense.

Not unless... Was it some kind of trick?

He didn't dare to ask. To hesitate. He snatched up his gloves and hat. The desperate motion triggered one final, mocking jolt from the chair.

He stood. His knees nearly buckled, but he forced them to steady. Made himself walk out with dignity, without a backward glance.

The hallway hit him like a slap—typewriters clacking, phones ringing, voices everywhere. After the isolation of that room, it was chaos.

No one was watching. He sagged against the wall, took out a handkerchief, mopped his brow and neck.

What the hell had just happened? Moments ago, he'd been finished. Now?

A reprieve.

Something in that envelope had saved him.

But what—and for how long?

40

She had spent the past few days burying him in pieces. Each day brought a new confrontation with a harsh reality. Grayson's office at the *Commonwealth Review* had been first: boxing his papers, sorting through the detritus of a brilliant mind now stilled. Packing away books still open to the last page he'd read. Stacking letters he would never answer. Each item was a reminder of what had been, a whisper of what could have been.

Now, she was doing the same in his sublet—and it was turning out to be worse.

The borrowed rental still held his scent—tobacco and old books and that particular cologne he favored. As if, at any moment, he might walk through the door, tired but pleased with himself, murmuring about some new philosophical concept that had captured his imagination.

But the space was silent now. Cold in a way it had never been before.

His notes left out in careful order. A sweater slung over his chair. His glasses folded neatly on the writing desk, as if he had only stepped away for a moment and might return at any time.

Except, he wouldn't.

For twenty-five years, her life had been about him. His wishes, his needs, his...everything. He had been the core of her life. Now that core was gone. She felt hollowed out. Gutted. She had never let herself think about what life would be like without him. Had never dared to.

Yet, here it was. A reality. One she was entirely unprepared for.

Vaughn sat at his desk, staring at the itemized list she had meticulously compiled. She had organized and numbered each possession with care. It was the last, quiet duty of a life devoted to him. Soon, it would all be packed away in boxes and shipped back to D.C. Back home.

Except—home was gone.

The chasm of ache opened again. And with it came the ghostly sound of her mother's voice, singing that tune—the one that marked years of misery, soft and sad and weighted with despair.

"What am I gonna do with all that love now? What am I gonna do?"

She closed her eyes, let the memory wash over her, too tired to fight it.

"Gonna put it in that box where it belongs.

"That's what I'm gonna do.

"Back in the dark where it belongs.

"That's what I'm gonna do."

She opened her eyes. Swallowed hard.

Not now. Not yet.

Too much left to do.

The coffee cup beside her had gone cold, untouched. The past few days had been a terrible exercise in dismantling a life. She had kept busy, kept moving, desperately trying to distract herself with the endless tasks of death.

But nothing distracted her from the waiting.

For the NYPD to release his remains.

For his lawyer to settle his estate.

For McAllister to say whether she still had a place there.

But those weren't her only problems.

She rose from the desk and moved to the window. She parted the thin curtains just enough to peer down at the street below. A black sedan had been parked across the way since dawn. Most cars looked the same to her, but instinct said it was the same one she'd noticed outside yesterday. And the day before.

Someone was watching Grayson's apartment.

No. Someone was watching *her*.

Because that same car—or one just like it—had also appeared outside her apartment.

At first, she'd told herself she was being paranoid. That grief was twisting her mind, clouding her judgment. But now, standing there, gripping the curtain, her alarm sharpened. She wasn't imagining it. There was that man who'd shadowed her steps when she walked to the corner market. And now the car that had parked outside and stayed for hours.

Redding. It had to be him. The detective had been asking questions—and some of those questions were no doubt about her. She hadn't seen or heard from him since that day he'd called her to ask about Victor's friends at McAllister. She'd bristled at the idea of him digging into her professor's private affairs, possibly ruining his name. Redding had wanted names. She hadn't wanted to give him any, but in the end she'd mentioned Harold Fitzhugh. One of her university contacts had confirmed that Redding had gone down there. He'd been seen nosing around in Victor's office, then going in to see Whitfield. Word was he'd even managed to talk to Mercer and Fitzhugh.

What had they told him?

Redding was looking into the fraud allegations against Victor. Obviously. But was it just that—or something else? She hadn't known about the allegations. Surely, Redding must've seen that in her reaction to the news.

Or was it…? No, that was improbable. *Impossible.*

She let the curtain fall back into place and stepped back from the window. She pressed a hand against her chest. Her heartbeat was shallow, rapid. Could they really think she had something to do with Victor's death? *Her?* The person who had cared for him in a way no one else could?

Why couldn't Redding just be satisfied with Carlisle?

Carlisle's arrest had been a relief. She felt a deep, bitter satisfaction at the thought of him behind bars, locked away for the rest of his life. He had tormented Victor, demanded a place in his life long after Victor had tried to move on. And then, he'd sent Victor that note.

Everett Carlisle deserved to be put in jail and the key thrown away.

She'd banked on the police seeing the blackmail note, having slipped it into Grayson's pocket as she arranged his lapels. She'd hoped they would see what she saw, that they would recognize the threat for what it was. A desperate man's last attempt to force Victor back into his life.

When she'd learned of Carlisle's arrest, she'd thought they had.

But now she wasn't sure. Had she given Redding what he needed to solve the case? Or had she, in planting that note, unwittingly made herself a suspect? She couldn't see how. She really couldn't see how.

Her suitcase sat half-packed back at her apartment, waiting for the moment when she would leave. Once this was over. Once they released his remains. Once they let her go.

What if they never did?

What if they kept her here, tangled in a web of suspicion she couldn't escape?

41

Like most hotels, the Hotel Olga had its dark side. That November night, its windows threw amber rectangles onto the rain-slicked pavement. Behind them, mahogany-paneled rooms had borne witness to their share of secrets—handshake deals that made or ruined careers, whispers about fixed fights and crooked games, the careful maneuvering of men who knew that survival meant knowing which shadows to trust.

Ed Wilson had built more than a hotel. He'd constructed a sanctuary for men who needed their secrets kept and their questions unasked. The elite, he called them. He'd built it for them. Kept it for them.

Mercer was one of those elite.

His room was quiet, save for the muffled sounds of the city beyond its thick curtains. A clock ticked on the desk, patient and steady. Outside, a neon sign from the barbershop across the street pulsed red through the fabric, striping the ceiling in blood-colored flashes. He tried to ignore it as he paced the carpet.

He'd taken his time calming himself after leaving the

precinct. After escaping. Because that's what it had been—a slip from the executioner's blade.

Now, in the soft glow of the bedside lamp, he dropped into the room's sole armchair and touched his throat. As if to make sure it was still whole. His hands were trembling. He pressed his fingers together beneath his chin. Forced them to be still.

He wasn't safe.

Not even close.

The reprieve was just that—a reprieve. Redding wasn't finished. The detective had practically thrown him out, then yanked his chain with that qualifier: *For now.*

Redding could haul him in at any minute. New evidence. A new witness. A new thread. Any one of those could unravel everything.

A horn blared below. Mercer flinched—then hated himself for it. He stood, adjusted his collar in the mirror. Even now, alone, appearance mattered. Control mattered.

Redding knew about the scams. The cons. But apparently he didn't care about them. All he cared about was the dead man. Grayson.

Redding was one of those single-minded cops. Like a bloodhound, so focused he dismissed everything else.

Maybe, Mercer thought, he could use that, work it to his advantage.

All he had to do was give Redding fresh meat to chase.

He ran a palm over his slick hair.

The cop already had Carlisle. That much was public. But for some reason, he wasn't satisfied. He was still sniffing. Still circling.

He paced. Burning off nervous energy so his mind could work.

He'd tried selling the suicide angle. Hinted Grayson might've taken his own life. Redding hadn't bought it. Too sharp for that.

So who else?

He ran through names. Faces.

Fitzhugh surfaced.

Mild-mannered. But as crooked as they come. Willing to do anything to keep his wife in pretty what-not. Mercer had caught him skimming travel reimbursements. They'd come to an understanding. Then an arrangement. Then a quiet alliance.

Mercer didn't mind cutting him loose. But he knew better than to touch that wire. Fitzhugh would talk. The man had already gone quiet in a way Mercer didn't like. MaryAnne had sounded odd when Mercer rang. And Fitzhugh hadn't returned his call.

That kind of silence meant trouble.

No, not Fitzhugh. Not unless he had no other choice.

So *who?*

Who made sense on paper? Who could take the fall and stay down?

And then—

It came to him.

Perfect.

Absolutely perfect.

The pieces snapped together so cleanly he almost laughed. Of course. It was so simple. So elegant.

He sat down, turned the idea over, tested it for cracks. Found none. The story held. And if it didn't—he'd make it.

He picked up the phone. Asked the operator to place the call. By the time he heard the line connect, his voice was smooth, composed.

"Detective Redding," he said. "I believe I may have been mistaken earlier. There is something I neglected to tell you. Something that might change everything. Interested?"

A pause.

Then Redding's voice, slow and wary. "Maybe."

Mercer smiled. As far as he was concerned, the game was over. And he had the winning hand.

"Good. Because I know who really killed Victor Grayson."

A soft click. The line disconnected.

Redding kept his hand on the receiver, fingers curled loosely around the smooth surface. He sat still, staring past his desk, past the precinct walls, past the city itself. Thinking.

Clive Mercer had just made his move.

Redding had counted on it. Had even anticipated the call, the controlled urgency in Mercer's voice, the polished act of a man trying to sound like he had nothing to gain—while trying, desperately, to gain everything.

Redding let out a slow breath, finally pulling his hand away from the phone. His gaze returned to the pages on his desk, the ones that had put the brakes on everything.

That had arrived on cue.

He picked them up again, though he already knew what they said. He'd first received them that morning and read them immediately—well before the Mercer interview.

The toxicology report.

Aconitine.

There was no doubt about it. The poison that had taken Victor Grayson's life had a name. The symptoms fit. Numbness, nausea, weakness. Gradual paralysis leading to respiratory failure. It was textbook. Too textbook to be denied.

Grayson hadn't just been poisoned. He'd been executed.

And that should've been the nail in Mercer's coffin. Should have been everything Redding needed to pin the whole thing on him.

It wasn't.

Because the timing was all wrong.

Redding exhaled, flipping through the pages again. The

report was definitive. The dosage? Lethal. The time frame? Absolute.

Grayson couldn't have been poisoned at lunch. Not at the Wells Restaurant, where Mercer had shared coffee with him. If he'd been poisoned that early, then he would've been dead long before Davenport's party. But he wasn't. He was, in fact, to all appearances perfectly fine when he arrived. Yet, by the end of it, he could barely stand.

So he must've been poisoned during the party.

Which meant that whoever killed him had been there.

And Mercer?

Redding had checked with Davenport. She said the name sounded familiar but she'd confirmed that he wasn't among the guests. Shown his photo, she'd raised an eyebrow and quipped, "Now, that's a man I wouldn't forget."

His case had holes in it.

But he'd already come to suspect that. Davenport's statement and the toxicology report merely confirmed it.

The news was a terrible disappointment—at first. But then he'd reconsidered. Seen it differently. As an opportunity.

And so he'd sat across from that man for the better part of an hour, laying the trap, already knowing the case had a hole in it big enough to drive a train through. Mercer hadn't known that. And Redding had made sure he wouldn't.

Redding glanced back at the telephone.

And allowed himself the smallest of smiles.

42

Mercer stroked his neatly trimmed mustache as he gazed out his hotel window. For the longest time, when he thought about his years at McAllister, he'd been quite pleased with himself. What a con! The only thing sweeter than the payoff was the deception itself. That he could fool all those supposedly clever, bright people! So smart. So educated. Yet still too dumb—too damn superficial—to look beyond the surface and see that everything about him was a lie. From the framed degrees on his walls to the calm cadence of his speech.

Clive Mercer wasn't born—he was built. Hammered out behind a shotgun house in Macon, Georgia, where his mother scrubbed floors and his father guzzled moonshine. Got outta there at fifteen. No high school, no diploma. Just two cents in his pocket, a gift for mimicry and a name lifted off a gravestone.

And the minute he got out, what did he do? Hopped a freight train and rode the rails north. Got off in Philly. Stole a library card. Read till his eyes bled.

Meanwhile, he learned to talk the talk and walk the walk by shining white folk's shoes at the Broad Street Station. Watched how men with trust funds lit their cigarettes—and copied them down to the match strike.

As soon as he could, he bought himself a secondhand suit. Taught himself to sign with a flourish.

Then came the day he saw that mention in the papers. McAllister was expanding—adding arts, law, philosophy. Expansion required money. Money required a man to secure it. The university wouldn't say so outright, but he could read between the lines. They weren't just building departments. They were building a money-making machine.

For that kind of post, he wouldn't even need to fake a degree. All he needed was polish, a fake history of donations that impressed and the nerve to promise more. The paperwork he arranged. Letters from a "business associate," a church trustee, a civic league no one in D.C. knew. He hadn't had to fool anyone. They'd needed him so badly they hadn't bothered to reference check.

And once he got into McAllister—there was no stopping him.

Month after month. Year after year. He built his persona brick by brick. The right suits. The right clubs. The right introductions. He knew which fork to lift and when to laugh. A towering Talented Tenth fantasy. Light-skinned and savvy, generous with charm and ruthless with ambition. The kind of man the movers and shakers were too proud of—or invested in—to question.

There was only one slip. An old woman in Macon who still sent Christmas cards to her Lewis. He hadn't been back in years. Couldn't risk it. But he sent money—small envelopes, no return address. Just enough to keep her in canned goods and kerosene. He told himself it was respect. Gratitude. Duty, maybe. But it was guilt. And it festered.

Sometimes, on quiet nights, or when the train whistle cut sharp through the cold, like it had the night he left, he thought of her. She was the last person alive who knew him before. Knew his voice before he rounded the vowels. Knew his real handwriting. His real name.

He did love her—as much as he could love anyone. But not enough to see her. Not enough to tell her out loud.

And so he waited. Waited for her to die. For the last thread to snap, so he could finally be free.

Mercer sighed, his breath fogging the window glass. Everything had been going so well. Then the university started the trouble. It began with that old goat, Whitfield. He'd known trouble was brewing when Whitfield had asked to speak with him privately one day, taken out the ledgers, gone over the claims and reimbursements.

Mercer denied everything. What else could he do? Grayson was a trusted faculty member. If the professor said he'd incurred such and such expense, who was he, Mercer, to suspect him?

Mercer had walked out, relieved to have talked his way out of that one. But he'd known then, as he did now, that he'd really only bought himself time.

Grayson would fight any charges. What man wouldn't? Innocent or guilty. And Grayson was innocent, of course. Innocent and naive and so damn trusting. Men like that were meant to be played, delivered up as suckers.

Unfortunately for Mercer, the university's allegations had alerted Grayson to the fact that he was being used in a con.

The professor had fought like hell to clear his name. And he'd no doubt gotten Vaughn to help him. Of course, he had. She'd always been his protector, his second mind.

Mercer turned from the window, his hands shoved deep in his pockets, his head bent in thought. He stood just beyond the table lamp's pool of light, his face in partial shadow.

For twenty years or so, he and Vaughn had dwelled in the same circles but never truly occupied the same space. They were part of the academic and intellectual world of McAllister, but they moved through it differently.

Vaughn was already established as Victor Grayson's right hand by the time Mercer began climbing the ranks of McAllister's administration.

Mercer knew of her. Everyone did. She was the gatekeeper to the esteemed Professor Grayson, the woman who made sure his schedule ran smoothly, his work was protected and—most importantly—that no one wasted his time.

For the most part, Vaughn had never displayed any interest in Mercer—in anyone other than Grayson.

Mercer, however, had at first been quite interested in her. Not as a woman—never *that*—but as a potential foe.

His quiet financial manipulations at the university meant keeping certain eyes away from certain records. Vaughn, while not involved in finances, had a mind for detail and an ear for gossip. If anyone was going to notice something strange about McAllister's accounts, it wouldn't be Grayson. It would be her.

Grayson, being the methodical, cautious man he was, had Vaughn handle many of his financial transactions—tasks like arranging his travel, overseeing research budgets, keeping up with paperwork related to university funding.

Mercer, as faculty research coordinator, had control over grant allocations, travel stipends and reimbursements.

Vaughn was meticulous. She double-checked details that most secretaries wouldn't think to question. Mercer was calculating. He needed fraud to go unnoticed.

That put the two in direct conflict.

However, for years, they existed in an unspoken détente.

Mercer had always wondered how much Vaughn knew. And he'd waited—cool, curious—to see what she would do. Turn him in or ask for a cut?

She did neither.

Why? Was it possible he'd outplayed her? Maybe. The fake

claims he created she never saw. The dummy accounts to receive the funds—she never saw those either.

The signet ring on his pinky finger caught the lamplight as he lit a cigarette. He drew in smoke, held it, let it out slow.

Just how much did she know?

That was a hard core of it, wasn't it? It was the kind of question that kept a man up at night. He cursed himself for not asking it sooner—for letting ego convince him he was in the clear. It took a nosy cop with decent instincts to force him to look at the situation with fresh eyes. That was the real irony. He'd built an empire on seeing through people, betting on their weaknesses. But he'd been blind to the possibility that Grayson had confided in her. Too confident, too arrogant, too sure of his own brilliance to see the threat staring him in the face.

And yet—

He wasn't done. Not by a damn sight. He'd always been a gambler. A man who staked his future on the right lie told at the right time. And gamblers, real gamblers, paid attention to signs. He took Redding's warning as just that—a sign. A reminder that the game wasn't over. Just that the stakes had changed.

And in Mercer's experience, that was often when the best hands were won.

He exhaled smoke, watching it twist in the lamplight.

Beatrice Vaughn. He had to find a way to stop her. Permanently.

He hesitated. Just for a moment. What if she didn't know anything? What if she had nothing at all?

He turned the thought over, looking for weak spots—and found plenty.

Even if Grayson hadn't confided in her—and he couldn't believe Grayson hadn't—then she still must know about the allegations, must've heard of them by now. And if she had access to Grayson's private files—and no doubt she did—then she'd probably gone through them. And if she had—and no doubt she had—then she must've found something damning against him.

Had she turned him in?

A coin dropped. He'd assumed that Redding had let him go because the cop didn't care about the fraud. More likely it was because he didn't have the evidence.

And that meant, she hadn't turned it over.

The fact that she hadn't handed Grayson's evidence over to the cops wasn't good, either. In fact, it was bad, quite bad. Because it could mean only one thing: she meant to hold it over him.

After all, now that Grayson was gone, what did she have left? There was no guarantee that McAllister would offer her another position.

She'd need money. She'd need it quick. And now she had a way of getting it—easy.

Blackmail.

That was the thought that settled it. Beatrice Vaughn had to go. He had to get rid of her—*now*—before she got rid of him. This wasn't just about framing her. It was about surviving.

The tension left his shoulders. He went to the small desk and reached for the bottle he'd picked up from a bootlegger earlier.

He poured himself a drink, took a swallow and grimaced at the bite. It was cheap stuff, nothing like what he had back in D.C. But it would do for now.

He stood, swirling the amber liquid.

Vaughn. Such an obvious choice when you thought about it. The perfect patsy, really.

She'd had access to Grayson at the party.

She had motive. Twistable, but plausible.

She had Grayson's trust. That made betrayal all the more gripping, sensational—and, oddly enough, likely.

It made for an excellent story, a great one if he sold it right.

And framing her would kill two birds with one stone, both deflect suspicion and eliminate a threat.

He paced the room in tight circles.

The possibility that she really did have something on him was too great a risk to take. Yes, she was a loose end all right—and a dangerous one at that—but one he could tie up neatly.

And the detective, ironically, would be the one to help him do it.

He took another swallow, thought some more.

His conversation with Redding had gone well, quite well, in fact. Better than he'd expected.

That's all I need, Mercer thought. *A shift in focus. A little breathing room to maneuver.*

And making her the patsy would give it to him.

Of course, it would take more than his word to get Redding to move against her—the detective was too sharp for that. He'd have to provide convincing 'evidence.' Something he could manufacture. Something even the detective couldn't ignore.

If he failed, it wouldn't just mean prison. It would mean the complete collapse of the façade he'd spent decades building. His name, his reputation, his very identity would crumble. And that was a fate worse than prison for a man like Clive Mercer.

He downed the rest of his drink and picked up the phone. Seconds later, he had her on the line.

"Miss Vaughn? Clive Mercer here." He infused his voice with warmth. "Sorry to be calling so late, but I just got in."

He paused, listening. She sounded surprised, was polite but distant—as he'd expected her to be.

"Yes, I'm here, in New York. Had to come up to take care of some business."

He let a beat pass, as if considering the impact of his next words carefully. "I know Professor Grayson's death must've been a terrible shock for you. So I wanted to call, extend my condolences, see how you're doing."

He paused again, making appropriate noises of sympathy as she spoke, not that she said much. When she finished, he went on, sounding both humble and hopeful.

"I thought, maybe, we could get together. Share memories of the good professor."

He smiled to himself. Soon she'd be rotting in a New York City jail cell. She'd never see it coming.

"What do you say?"

43

Vaughn filled the kettle at her kitchen sink and set it on the stove. Dead center on the iron square above the flame to be exact. The preciseness helped her feel anchored, in control. A small mercy, because at this moment she felt in control of nothing else.

She was stuck here. Adrift. Everything about this city reminded her of her professor. She couldn't wait to leave, to go back to D.C. Though she wasn't sure what awaited her there.

Her apartment would be just as she'd left it—tidy, orderly, quiet. But it would be different now. Empty in a way it had never been before.

She returned to the window. The watcher was gone, but the black sedan remained.

Protection rather than surveillance? The thought was appealing, almost comforting. But then a colder logic intervened: if Redding thought she needed protection, he believed someone wanted her dead. The same someone who'd killed Victor.

But that was impossible. It couldn't be true.

Why would he even think that? What had he heard? Who did

he think would want to harm her? She didn't pose a danger to anyone, no one she could think of.

She drew back from the window and turned away. Twenty-five years of perfect composure and now she was quailing at shadows.

The kettle's thin whistle rose like a warning. She took it off the heat before it could scream. She went to a cupboard, reached for a teacup and paused, arrested by the question that had been haunting her: Who was Beatrice Vaughn without Victor Grayson?

She had spent so long being an extension of him—his hands, his voice, his memory—that she wasn't sure where he ended and she began.

She made her tea, took it to her small writing desk and sat down. She rested her forehead in her hands, wondering.

What would happen to her now? Where would she go? Did she still have a place at McAllister? And if so, as what? Where would they stick her? With Grayson, she'd had—

The telephone rang. Sharp. Demanding. Grating. She stared at it. Listened to its insistent, mechanical blare. And was gripped by the strangest certainty: that if she answered it, nothing would ever be the same.

One ring. Two rings. Three rings. Four.

She snatched up the receiver. "Hello?"

The voice on the other end was smooth, cultured. Unmistakable.

Mercer.

Her fingers tightened around the receiver. The surprise lasted only a second before annoyance set in. Mercer. In New York.

Of course, he was.

She listened, lips pressed together, as he spoke—too smoothly, too politely. Going on about Grayson's death, about what a terrible shock it must have been. He extended his condolences, voice rich with that manufactured warmth she'd never trusted.

She wasn't fooled. Mercer didn't give a damn about her grief.

Then, an invitation for a meeting.

Her irritation deepened.

Mercer had never sought her out before. Not once. Not in all the years they'd known each other had he ever reached out directly.

Why now?

When Grayson was gone.

When the police were trying to ruin his reputation.

When everything was falling apart.

"Miss Vaughn?" he prompted. "Are you there?"

"Yes, yes. I'm here." She paused. "How did you get my number—or know where to find me?"

She could sense his surprise.

"The university switchboard," he said. "They told me." He paused, again, then hurried on. "I hope you don't mind. My asking them."

"No. No, of course not."

She did, of course. She minded very much.

"Excellent," he said. "How about tomorrow evening? Would that work for you? Say, six o'clock? We could meet at the Wells."

Tomorrow?

"Miss Vaughn?"

"Yes. Six would be fine," she said at last. "I'll see you then."

"Wonderful. I look forward to it."

Vaughn replaced the receiver slowly, instincts on alert. She'd been invisible to Clive Mercer for decades. And now, suddenly, in the wake of Victor's death, he wanted to "share memories"?

She didn't believe it for a second.

Her professor was dead. Redding was digging. Carlisle was locked up.

And now Mercer had shown up here.

Clearly, he wanted something. But *what?*

The dream returned that night. The street, the wind, the hurrying figures. But this time, there was a man. Tall. Dark. Standing at the end of the block, perfectly still while everyone else rushed past.

She turned down a side street to avoid him. Walked faster. Turned again. He was there. Waiting. As if he'd known where she was going before she did.

He didn't speak. Didn't move toward her. Just watched, with the patience of someone who had all the time in the world.

She woke with her heart slamming against her ribs. Her mama used to say dreams were omens.

She was beginning to believe her.

44

The next evening, Vaughn stood before the mirror in her apartment vestibule, adjusting her cloche hat. The face of the woman staring back at her looked anything but naive.

Vaughn normally prided herself on her emotional detachment, her ability to be logical even under the worst circumstances. But now, looking back, she realized she'd failed miserably in one instance—one where she'd allowed her feelings to eclipse her ability to think.

At first, she'd been too hurt to see it clearly.

That moment when she'd learned that her professor had been accused of fraud had been a terrible one for her. How could he have kept that burden secret from her? It must've been one of the darkest moments of his life, yet he'd shut her out.

That wound stung deeper than seeing him with Carlisle.

But now...now she had some distance.

And she had that call from Mercer. No question—her relationship with Grayson was the reason behind it.

Had she suspected Mercer before?

Not consciously. Not fully.

She'd always disliked him. Just not enough to pin a crime on him. Slick, self-serving, too precise by half. He kept his hands clean, made himself useful and always landed on top. Courted the right people, avoided the wrong ones, never left fingerprints.

But fraud?

She wouldn't have put it past him to scheme, manipulate, make backroom deals. But steal from McAllister? Set up her professor to take the fall?

That took something else.

Something dangerous.

Did she suspect him now?

Yes. More than ever.

CONFIRMED SCHOLARSHIP DISCREPANCIES...MERCER'S TOUCH ON ALL...NO DOUBT NOW.

That's what the entry in Victor's journal had said, the one Redding had let her see.

Victor had apparently uncovered definitive evidence, evidence that would not only exonerate him but most likely incriminate someone else.

Mercer.

And right after that, Victor had been silenced.

Redding must've made this connection. He'd questioned Mercer in D.C. Now, Mercer was in New York, saying he wanted to meet.

Of course, he did.

Mercer must be feeling the heat. Must be wondering: What did she know? What had Victor told her? More importantly, what had he *given* her? What documents, letters, vouchers that might be used against him?

The bitter, stinging irony was that her professor had told her nothing.

But Mercer didn't know that and now he was here to cover his tracks.

Maybe even to make sure she didn't pick up where her

professor had left off. Where 'making sure' meant silencing her —permanently.

Vaughn adjusted her coat, smoothed the lapels with precise, neat strokes.

Mercer was an opportunist. He saw the world in terms of leverage, in terms of who could be used and who could be discarded.

If he thought he could manipulate her, he was mistaken. And if he thought he could threaten her... Well, he'd learn he was mistaken there, too.

For a few minutes, she regretted having agreed to meet him. But there was no point in avoiding him. No point in running. Because if she was going to get out of this city, she needed to know exactly what Mercer knew.

She buttoned her coat, adjusted her collar and opened the door.

Downstairs, a gust of wind, sharp and bitter, hit her the moment she stepped onto the street. It sliced through her coat, cold and damp from the gray Hudson River. All around her people were hurrying home, collars up, shoulders hunched, eager to put locked doors between themselves and whatever prowled the dark. She paused on the stoop, struck by a chill that had nothing to do with the weather. The wind. The hurrying figures. She'd seen this before—

Don't go.

The thought came from down deep. The part of her that had learned to read danger before she ever learned to read words.

She brushed it aside. Pulled her coat tighter, squared her shoulders and walked, head first, into the wind.

Blandly respectable by day, the ground-floor areas of the Wells flirted with scandal at night. It wasn't just the music the jazz band played—songs with lyrics that could make a call girl blush —but the company it kept. Toward that end, it opened a back room to select customers.

That room was small, private, dim and close. The low ceiling made it feel hidden. A chandelier threw soft, scattered light over a scarred mahogany pool table and a circle of worn burgundy armchairs slouched around it. Velvet drapes lined the walls, thick enough to silence regret.

Privacy here had a price. Intimacy bred secrets, and secrets turned dangerous.

Shadows crowded the corners where the sconces couldn't reach. This was where debts got called in. Where truths surfaced. Where the masks of daylight came loose.

The Wells' daytime patrons wouldn't recognize it. Not this room. And not what it knew.

Vaughn stood near the far wall, where a narrow vent let in a thin breath of cold air from the alley. Her hands were tucked inside her coat pockets. Still. Composed.

She eyed Mercer. He leaned against the pool table, smoking. At ease. Confident. A man who enjoyed the game as much as the win. His heavy-lidded eyes tracked her, measuring the space between them. Calculating how close he could get before she pulled away.

"Miss Vaughn—May I call you 'Beatrice?' It's such a lovely name."

"It is, but only my good friends get to use it."

The verbal slap landed with the sting she meant it to. Mercer's smile went limp for a second and a spark of anger flashed in his eyes. He recovered quickly, though. Flicked the ash from his cigarette. Pasted that smile on again as if her rebuff was nothing more than a temporary stop sign.

"As you wish. I just wanted to say that I've always admired you, been fascinated by you. That icy exterior… I've always suspected there's fire underneath. Passion. I saw it the moment I met you."

Vaughn had heard it all before. She knew exactly what he thought of her—an old dried-up spinster who'd do anything for male attention. Well, she wasn't old. She definitely wasn't dried up. And she sure wasn't a spinster. There'd been a husband once. And lovers before him. Men who'd peddled the same slick drivel Mercer was selling now. It bored her then and it bored her now.

"You didn't bring me here to flatter me."

Mercer's eyes narrowed for a heartbeat. The edge of his smile turned brittle, then softened again as he took a slow drag from his cigarette. He stubbed it out carefully, the motion languid, unhurried. His posture shifted—more calculated now, more deliberate—as he straightened up and crossed the room to stand behind her. She could feel his warmth at her back.

"Of course not." His breath touched her skin, brushed the soft hairs on the nape of her neck. "But it's not just flattery, Miss Vaughn. I find you...intriguing. And the reason I brought you here?" His voice dipped lower, as if he were sharing a secret. "It's because I know you did it. You. Killed. The professor."

Vaughn went still.

There it was. The accusation, hard as steel, wrapped in velvet.

"That's ridiculous. I never would've harmed him. Why I-I cared for him."

Mercer bent close. His moist breath gently buffeted her ear. "No, you *loved* him—loved him so hard you put him down—right into the grave."

Mercer had scored a hit. She felt it land—sharp, uninvited—but gave him nothing. She straightened, took a deep breath, and buried the sting where he couldn't reach it. She would've died before letting him see it.

She turned slowly, her expression calm, assessing. "You're crazy."

His gaze swept over her face, lingering just a little too long—like a lover tracing a familiar path. His voice dropped even lower, intimate now, as if he was coaxing her closer rather than confronting her. As if he loved her.

"Am I? Excuse my French, *Miss* Vaughn, but you're a jealous bitch and everyone knows it. I don't know when it happened, but somewhere along the line you found out that Grayson had special tastes and realized you'd never qualify. It got to be too much for you and you snapped."

If Mercer thought his crass language and insolent tone would get to her, he was wrong. But the *intent* behind them? That she suddenly understood. And *that* did hit hard.

He was in Redding's crosshairs, suspected of murder. So he'd come up with a neat little frame—a story of innuendo and spite, one that pointed at her, one that Redding might believe.

Her body tensed, rock-hard with fear and anger. But she quickly quashed those emotions. Reclaimed her composure. She knew how to deal with men like him. Life had taught her that game early on.

She took several steps away from him, putting distance between them, and raised her chin. "Do you have proof? Evidence? Or is it all smoke and no fire?"

"I don't need proof. I have you. You and your history. Maybe you don't know this, but Redding went down to D.C.—"

"To investigate *you*."

"And find out more about you. I can tell you right now that people had plenty to say—about your obsessive control over Grayson."

"I was his secretary. Protecting him was my job."

"It was your passion. Your longing for a man who didn't want you—couldn't want you—who would've never made you his wife."

"You're talking about gossip. Not evidence. It would never stand up in court."

"Not a court of law perhaps. But the court of public opinion? That's another story. And we both know how one drives the other. Just think of the damage it would do, to you, to Grayson's memory. The papers would eat it up. Why I can see the headlines now: *Esteemed Professor Murdered in a Three-Way Love Triangle*."

She felt a surge of rage and choked it down. "You'd burn down the whole world if it got you five minutes of safety."

Mercer laughed. Threw his head back and let it rip. "Safety? Hell, no. I want the win. And look who's talking. I'm not the one who lit the match." Before she could respond, he held up a hand. "Never mind. I'm not here to swap insults with you."

"Then why *are* you here?" She had a mental image of a slug. And her foot, poised to crush it.

Mercer smiled, smug and confident, like he'd just laid down the ace. "As you may know, the cops have me on the hot seat. So, I've decided to take a little vacation. Leave town. Go somewhere far, where no one knows me."

"And?"

"You're going to pay for it." He named a figure, ludicrous by her standards.

Vaughn laughed—short, sharp, scornful. "My god, you're so insufferable. So damn predictable. And greedy. But you've forgotten one thing."

"And that is?"

"Who you're talking to. I'm just a lowly secretary. You know what I earn. That I don't have that kind of money."

"Don't try to con a conman. A woman like you? You've been socking it away for years. So, hear me when I say: I'll take the money. Or I'll take you down with me."

He meant it. She didn't doubt it. Time to acknowledge that he had the upper hand—or pretend to.

"Please. No. It would take everything I have."

"Your problem, not mine. It's the money or the hot seat. Either way, I'm not taking the fall for this one."

Silence.

She contemplated him. "So, that's your angle, is it?"

He shrugged. "No angle. Just the bill coming due."

She considered her options. There were none. Not really. He'd removed them all—except one.

She reached into her coat pocket and withdrew a small .22. She was an excellent shot. Growing up the way she had, she'd had to be. She pointed the gun squarely at his heart.

Mercer's gaze dipped to the weapon. His eyes flashed wide. He fell back a step, grin fading fast, and let out a nervous chuckle.

"That's a nice little pea-shooter you got there. Real cute."

"I think of it as efficient. Of course, it won't do much harm at a distance, but when it's up close..." She took a step toward him. "Like this..."

Mercer raised his hands slowly, palms facing her, his face stripped of everything but fear.

"W-wait! You don't need to do this. Let's just talk this over. We can work something out—"

"Can we?"

A faint sound echoed from the hallway beyond the room—a soft creak, barely perceptible against the heavy silence. Mercer didn't react, but Vaughn did. Her gaze flickered to the door. She listened intently but heard nothing, so she refocused her attention on Mercer.

He seemed frozen in place, a state she found profoundly satisfying. Was Mercer the one, the dark man who haunted her dreams? If so, he was a disappointment. Dreams were nonsense, anyway. And this one? He'd soon be mist.

Her finger curled around the trigger. It was almost a shame to have to kill him. She was so enjoying the fear in his eyes, the way they darted from her to the gun, then back again. He was beginning to understand that he'd misjudged her. He'd seen only the frigid, lovelorn secretary. But now, facing the barrel of her gun, he saw something far more dangerous: resolve.

He swallowed. Hard. "You–you're serious."

"Did you think I wouldn't be?"

He started spilling words like a broken bucket. "You're making a mistake. Killing me won't solve your problem. It'll make it worse."

"Oh, really? How so?"

"Redding already suspects you. Thinks you're the one who submitted the false claim vouchers."

That came as a surprise, but it made sense. It explained the sudden appearance of surveillance. Her eyes narrowed. Had Mercer put that idea into Redding's head?

"Go on." She gestured for him to continue.

"I thought Grayson told you about his little problem, but now I suspect he didn't. And the fact that he didn't means only one thing—that he suspected you of being behind the rip-off."

She could see where this was going. A double frame. He was setting her up not only for the murder, but the fraud, too. It might work and that worried her, but she hid it. All she gave him was a shake of her head and a look that said she almost pitied him. "Good try. But it won't fly."

"You sure about that? You pull that trigger and Redding will see it as a show of guilt. That you did it because you thought I had something on you."

She inclined her head. Amused. Detached. "I have to admit you always did have a certain cunning, an ability to think on your feet. But again, you miscalculated. Redding may suspect me. But it doesn't matter. Because he suspects you, too. Just so you know, when you're dead, I'll claim self-defense. I came here because you asked me to. I was scared you'd try to blackmail me —not because I had anything to hide, but because you had information on Professor Grayson, information that would ruin his good name. So, I came prepared. And unfortunately, things went south—fast."

He chewed that over. "Redding won't believe you."

"Of course he will. He has that threatening note. Signed with the letter 'C'—'C' for Clive, not Carlisle. So, he knows you have blackmail in you. I'll say that when blackmail failed, you turned to violence, tried to kill me. Why? Because it turned out that you thought I had evidence against you, documents Professor Grayson gave me. So you see," she smiled, "in the end, I'll get all the sympathy. A little woman. Up against a big, strong blackmailer and thief. Case closed. Open and shut."

She wanted to laugh. His expression was priceless.

He stared at her. When he'd picked her for a patsy, it had been because she fit the bill. And when he'd accused her outright, it had been all talk, no substance. He'd meant to rattle her, break her, bend her to his will. But now he saw the truth.

His jaw sagged. "You really did do it, didn't you? You killed Grayson."

She allowed herself a faint smile. "What do you think?"

"Come on," he said, "If you're going to kill me, you can at least tell me the truth."

He was stalling. A cornered rat, hunting for a crack that wasn't there. She let him sweat for a full ten seconds. "Fine. Why not? Not like it's going to save you."

And so, she told him what she'd done and how she'd done it, taking him back to the hours before Davenport's party, when she'd made her preparations.

45

Beatrice Vaughn never left anything to chance. That night she'd gone to extra lengths to make sure everything went exactly as planned. It began with her visit to the pharmacy. What had she told him?

"My boss in Washington—he's a professor—suffers terribly from neuralgia. His doctor prescribes tincture of aconite. It's the only thing that gives him relief. We were in such a hurry to get up here, stupid me, I forgot to pack his medicine. And now, he's in such pain. I was hoping you might help."

"I'm sorry to hear that. Would you like to wait or pick it up later?"

"I'll wait. I'd like to take care of this now. He needs his medicine as soon as possible."

Back home, after getting dressed, she'd opened the small bottle, poured a single drop onto her finger, pressed it to her tongue. Bitter. Potent. It would need to be masked.

She paused, turned over ideas. What about his favorite drink? Yes, that would do—rye, sugar, bitters, with a twist of citrus. Satisfied, she wiped her hands with a cloth and tucked the bottle into her purse.

At the party, she'd made Grayson his favorite cocktail—an Old Fashioned. Made it twice, in fact. First round, before dinner. He took it eagerly, drained it fast. She saw the signs by the time the salad hit the table: that little tremor, the glazed look, the forced smile. But her professor was tougher than he looked. So she gave him another after dinner. This time, he barely noticed the glass in his hand—just smiled absently and wandered off, chatting with one guest then another.

Watching him, she'd willed him to drink, drink, drink! It looked like he never would.

But then Carlisle had come to her aid. He hadn't meant to. But he had.

That hissy fit he threw shook Grayson right down to his spats. The bitters were sharp enough to raise suspicion, but Grayson downed the drink in two swallows. He was too shaken to notice the taste—never realized that the cocktail in his hand was a death sentence.

And how pleasingly ironic that Carlisle had helped her destroy the man he supposedly loved.

Vaughn's lips pressed together. *All done neatly. A perfect plan perfectly executed—until this.*

Mercer.

Instead of being smart and staying silent, he chose that moment to be snide.

"So the devoted secretary finally snapped. All these years, watching him from afar, knowing you'd never have him..."

She nearly put a bullet in him right then and there. But her face must've said enough. He stopped cold. Fell back. Jerked his hands up high.

"S-sorry! I didn't mean—Look, I just—I want to hear all of it. I mean, there *is* more, isn't there? There has to be."

She stared him down. "There isn't much, actually."

But there was. Actually.

There was the trip home—watching Grayson struggle, seeing the pain in his face. After that, the ambulance. The hospital.

She hadn't counted on anyone suspecting poison. Grayson was older, tired, already showing signs of ill health. Obviously he'd a stroke. Or a heart attack.

Obviously.

However, just in case someone looked too hard, she'd slipped that note into his pocket. Let the blame fall where it would fall most easily.

But then, the bad luck—that detective. The one cop in the whole goddamn NYPD who didn't settle for easy answers.

There was that one really bad moment—when he'd offered her a ride. She'd nearly turned him down. The idea of sitting beside a homicide cop, trapped in a steel box under his control, made her stomach roll.

But refusing would've raised eyebrows. Made him curious. So she got in. She'd expected questions. Small talk. A little pressure dressed up as concern. But he said nothing. So neither did she.

She watched the streetlights slice across his face and thought about what was in her purse.

A small amber bottle. Poison dressed as medicine. The end of Grayson, tucked between her lipstick and a handkerchief. It was right there, close as a kiss. A secret so deafening it pounded in her ears. And the detective sitting beside her hadn't the faintest idea.

Once home, she took the bottle out. It was empty now, dry around the rim. She went to the building corridor and dropped it down the incinerator chute. A muffled clatter. Then silence.

She stood a moment longer, listening. Then she went back inside. Drew the curtains. Got ready for bed.

That night, she slept better than she had in a month of Sundays.

There was a lull when Vaughn finished telling her tale. A soft murmur of voices drifted from the hallway beyond, indistinct and muffled. Vaughn's gaze darted toward the door, remained there for a fraction of a second, then slid back to Mercer.

She thought she had a good handle on him. Thought he couldn't surprise her. But Mercer, being Mercer, proved her wrong. He expressed no empathy for the dead man. Instead, he criticized her plan.

"The note," he said. "That was a mistake. Thinking it pointed to Carlisle, not me."

Vaughn felt a surge of irritation. Did this man's ego have no end?

"A miscalculation, perhaps. Not a mistake. I wanted the police to suspect Carlisle. And they did. They still would, if it hadn't been for you. You're the reason the cops kept looking. You're the reason this whole damn thing has gone off the rails."

It hit her then, how much she despised him. The superciliousness. The arrogance. The affectations and fake charm. She'd sized him up the moment she met him—known exactly what kind of hole he'd slithered out of.

He stood across from her now, throat working as he groped for a lifeline. The surface sophistication he'd cultivated so carefully—the expensive suit, the over-precise diction, the calculated pauses—none of it was worth a damn now.

"You won't get away with this."

That again. She nearly yawned. She'd expected more from him—or perhaps less. Either way, something different than this predictable struggle to maintain dignity while facing the barrel of her gun.

What truly sickened her wasn't the fraud or the theft, but the presumption. That he thought himself untouchable. That he believed he deserved what he took. That he saw her professor—brilliant, principled—as nothing more than an obstacle to remove.

"You know what your problem is?" she asked. "You always believed you were the smartest person in the room."

His face tensed, his eyes darting from her face to the gun.

"But you never were," she said. "Not at McAllister. Not with my professor. And certainly not now."

Her words landed. His eyes showed it. For once, Clive Mercer had nothing clever to say.

No, she didn't just dislike Mercer. She hated him with a cold, precise fury that surprised even her.

Twenty-five years of loyalty. Of devotion. And this man had tried to destroy it all.

"Killing Victor? Yes, I did it. That was my crime. But you're the one who deserves to do the time. Every bit as much as Carlisle." Her gaze didn't waver. "You framed my Victor. Used him. Tried to ruin him." A pause just long enough for it to hurt. "I should kill you for that alone." She adjusted her aim.

And then Mercer, breathing heavily, surprised her again—did something she'd never heard him do or think him capable of.

He apologized.

"W–wait. Just…look. I'm sorry. I didn't mean to—W–we can fix it. Just give me a chance to—"

Too little. Too late. She squeezed the trigger.

46

Mercer staggered back, clutching himself as blood seeped through his fingers. His face twisted in pain and disbelief.

"Y–you shot me! You shot me!"

"Did I? Seems like I missed. 'Cause you're still talking." She leveled the gun to fire again—

The door burst open.

Redding and two uniformed cops rushed in. Slammed her against the wall. Struggled to wrestle the gun from her. Finally, wrenched it away. Pinned her arms behind her back and cuffed her.

Mercer, still nursing his wounded upper arm, was furious, indignant. "What took you so long?"

Redding checked Vaughn's cuffs, then turned to Mercer. "Turn around."

"What?"

"I said turn around—and put your hands behind your back."

Mercer's dark eyes widened in shock. "What the hell? You're arresting me? But I—"

"Turn around!"

"I showed you she did it!"

Redding grabbed Mercer, swung him around. Yanked his arms behind his back.

Mercer protested. "Look, I risked my life to help you. To get you your proof. I kept my word!"

"Oh, we're not getting you on the murder." Redding slapped the cuffs on. "We're getting you for fraud."

Mercer's jaw sagged open.

Redding planted his feet, hands on his hips, and gave Mercer a look of tired disgust.

"Before Grayson died, he collected evidence. Left a letter telling us where to find it. Everything's there. Everything you and Fitzhugh pulled—the embezzlement, theft. The whole dirty trail. He, by the way, is already talking. And DCPD says he's got a whale of a story. So, yeah, you and Vaughn, you're both going down. Taking a ride—courtesy of a dead man."

Mercer's mouth opened, then closed. He blinked, eyes darting around, looking for an escape that wasn't there. For a brief, impossible moment, his usual bravado faltered, flattened by bitter disbelief. Then he pulled himself together, visibly drew himself up. "That's ridiculous! I never—"

Redding silenced him with a single, hard stare—flat and unblinking.

Then he turned to Vaughn. "Ma'am?"

She turned to face him—and froze.

The street. The wind. The man who never moved.

It was him. The shape from her dreams. Tall. Still. Watching her the way he'd watched her in the dark, with the patience of someone who already knew where she'd end up.

Just like that, she understood: She'd been walking toward him all along.

He looked like hell. Drawn. Tight around the jaw. He had

her. Had them both. But there was no triumph in his eyes. No gloating. Only weariness. Resignation. Maybe even regret. He'd had to connive and scheme, scheme and deceive. Some cops didn't give a damn how they got their man. But Redding did. The anger in his face—muted, but sharp—was undeniable.

So was the sadness.

"Beatrice Vaughn, you are under arrest for the murder of Professor Victor Grayson."

The words hit hard, but they didn't penetrate. It was his eyes that did that. She saw herself as he did: cold, calculating, utterly devoid of grace. The vision shamed her more than any man's words could. She turned away, unable to bear it.

Then Mercer was foolish enough, conceited enough, to open his mouth again. "But—"

"Tell it to the judge," Redding said.

His hand twitched—just once. Like he might reach for Mercer's collar. Or flatten him where he stood. Vaughn found herself wishing he would.

The cops she'd seen growing up certainly would've. A big meaty hand, fast as a whip. The sound of skin on skin cracking like gunfire. And a slap packed with power—enough to make a grown man stumble. For once, she would've welcomed it. For once, she'd have cheered it on.

But this cop was different. And to her deep annoyance, he held back. Took a slow breath. Let it out. His right fist flexed and released at his side.

The moment passed.

He gave Mercer one last hard stare, then jerked his thumb toward the door. "Take 'em away, boys."

One of the uniformed cops grabbed Mercer by the collar and shoved him toward the open door. The other yanked Vaughn away from the wall and did the same.

Mercer briefly tried to fight. Vaughn eyed him with derision.

Who was he trying to impress? The jig was up. They both knew it. Why pretend otherwise?

She remembered Mercer's words, the ones he'd thrown at Redding. *I risked my life to help you. To get you your proof. I kept my word.*

That cry of outrage—of betrayal. It had hit her where it hurt most—her pride. She should've known. Should've seen it. She'd been played. They both had been.

Played like amateurs.

Redding had pitted them against one another, used their pride, their egos—their *desperation*—as pawns on his very own chessboard. He'd tricked each into incriminating the other. And now, he had the evidence he needed against both of them.

That's when she heard it. Grayson's voice. One word, whispered near: *Checkmate!* The cold breath in her ear. The brush of his lips. Closer, more intimate, than he'd been in life. It wasn't real—she knew that—but the chill still landed.

She glanced at Mercer. He finally understood.

Their eyes locked and the laughter came. Just like that. Dry. Bitter. The sound of two people who'd realized, too late, that their whole game had been a sucker's bet. They laughed in perfect sync. Like only they could see the punchline—and knew it wasn't funny at all.

Vaughn paused before they took her. Stepped close to Redding. "Well played, Detective. Well played."

A small nod. Barely there. A touch to his hat brim. Not sympathy. Not pity. But something rarer. Respect. The look a man gives a worthy opponent—a foe he had to work to bring down.

And he had, hadn't he? He'd had to use trickery to catch her, to get enough to cuff her. Even then, he wouldn't have succeeded—not without Mercer.

She felt a rough shove in the small of her back. She stiffened, twisted, shot a glance at the cop behind her—a resentful, indignant, *How dare you?!* He answered with a grin and pushed her again.

She stumbled forward and that's when she heard it once more. Clearly this time. Not Mercer's laugh. Her professor's whisper.

Checkmate, dear Bea. Checkmate.

PART V

RECOVERY

47

Everett Carlisle held himself erect. He would not give in to the pain and the damage. He would not give these mutherfuckers the pleasure of seeing him bent or bowed. The bruises on his face had faded to a yellowish purple. His eye was better—no longer completely swollen shut—but it was far from right. His left arm stayed tight in a sling and he moved with careful deliberation, each breath measured against the pain of his ribs.

He stood beside Redding at the 32nd Precinct's processing desk, with McKay on his other side.

The desk sergeant avoided their eyes as he reviewed the release papers Redding had placed before him.

"Everything appears to be in order." The sergeant's stamp came down hard. Carlisle inwardly flinched.

The sergeant shoved the file aside. "You're clear."

"I'll need copies for our records," McKay said.

The sergeant muttered something about procedures and stood up slow, like it hurt.

Carlisle let the words flow past him. Said nothing. He hadn't spoken since they walked in.

The sergeant returned with copies and handed them to McKay. Then he slid a cardboard box across the counter to Carlisle. "Your personal effects."

Carlisle looked it over, checked each item with his right hand—fingers still mending but the hand usable. Keys, cufflinks, a folded scarf. Then he stopped.

"My wallet. It's not here."

McKay stepped forward. "My client's property is incomplete."

The sergeant glanced at the rear door. "I'll check." He returned minutes later. "Here it is." He handed over a beaten brown leather wallet. "Must've been filed separately."

Carlisle checked the billfold. It still held his two dollars, but he wasn't thinking of money. That had never been the point.

It was the photo, creases worn soft from years inside his coat, the only photo he'd kept through everything.

He eased it out, held it steady. It was a small image showing two young men: one lanky and confident, the other portly and earnest. A quiet corner on campus. Arms slung over each other's shoulders. Like nothing would ever come between them. Friends. On the verge of becoming more than that. Before fear and lies had done their work.

The image had faded, but his memory of that day hadn't. He could still smell the sharp green of the grass, the sweetness of honeysuckle, the rough press of Victor's shoulder against his. Grayson had looked away from the camera, pondering something only the two of them would've understood.

Hayward had taken it. He'd been an upperclassman then—Carlisle and Grayson were just starting out. It had taken careful planning: finding a time and place—quiet enough for what they felt, public enough to deny what it was. If anyone stumbled upon them, it would just look like two friends marking the moment. Even the pose had been calculated. Arms over shoulders was all they could risk, all they'd get to keep.

Carlisle looked at the image a second longer. It wasn't just a memory. It was proof. That once, they'd tried. He tucked it back into the wallet and slid it into his coat. The garment sagged against his frame, a size too large now. He hadn't realized how much weight he'd lost.

"That everything?" McKay asked.

Carlisle nodded.

"Then we're done here," Redding said.

They moved toward the door. People waiting in the lobby stared at him. But officers looked away as he passed. Carlisle didn't care. He was done being there. Had no business being there in the first place—and if they ever hauled him back, it had better be for a damn good reason.

One of his own choosing.

They'd nearly broken him in there. Nearly.

But nearly wasn't enough.

Outside, the light hit hard and clean. Carlisle stopped on the steps and breathed in. Not dust, not rot, not fear. Just air.

McKay checked his watch. "I've got to go by the courthouse before it closes. You need me to give you a lift somewhere?"

"No. You've done more than enough."

McKay looked concerned, but he gave a short nod. "You know how to reach me."

As McKay descended the steps toward his waiting car, Carlisle turned to Redding. "Is it true? About Vaughn?"

Redding nodded. "She confessed."

"And Grayson?"

"Never suspected."

Carlisle shook his head. "Twenty-five years."

He didn't look at Redding. Just kept staring down the street, as if the past might come walking up the steps.

"He pushed me away for twenty-five damn years. Made me into some ghost of a mistake. A shadow of a maybe. Said it was too dangerous. Too risky. Like loving me would've cost him everything."

A breath. Not shaky, but sharp.

"And maybe it would've. But you know what it didn't cost him? His life."

Another pause.

"She was the one he let close. Trusted. Let into his home, his work, his daily routines. All the pieces I would've killed to be a part of. And she's the one who put him in the ground."

A humorless laugh, short and dry.

"He was so afraid of the danger I posed, he never saw the one standing right next to him. That's the part I can't get past."

He gave a bitter huff of air.

"And now he's gone, and she's still here, and I'm supposed to make peace with that?"

He waved the idea away.

"To hell with that."

He exhaled slow. Rage banked. Voice even again.

"And Mercer?"

"Going away. Not for murder, but for fraud. Grayson left enough evidence to bury him."

Carlisle's face turned hard, his smile bitter. "Good. Let the bastard rot."

He felt Redding's glance. It was the same look he'd glimpsed during those late-night conversations in the hospital, when Redding had come to check on him despite having no official reason to be there.

It wasn't pity. More the silent acknowledgment of one survivor to another. The detective's face showed none of the cold calculation that had dominated their first meetings. Instead, they reflected the soul of a man who'd seen enough to empathize and had enough humanity not to judge.

"What're you going to do now?" Redding asked.

"Keep writing. But not for them. Not for respect or forgiveness or some damn place at the table. I'll write because the truth still scares people. And as long as it does, I've got work."

Redding's lips twitched. A flash of a smile. Quick, but unmistakable. Pulled back before it had a chance. But there.

And Carlisle clocked it. He'd seen that look before. Usually right before someone decided he was either crazy or dangerous. But there was something else there, too. Something like approval. Respect, maybe. Even admiration. Like tilting at windmills wasn't the worst way to spend a life.

Carlisle lifted his chin, prouder than he wanted to admit that he'd earned a cop's friendship.

And not any cop.

This cop.

Carlisle went on. "The article he turned down—Grayson—it was about authenticity. About refusing to be what others want you to be." He paused. "He didn't want it. Maybe because he knew I meant it."

Redding said nothing. Two seconds of silence—just long enough for Carlisle to recognize he'd been read like yesterday's news.

"Fine. They're publishing it." Carlisle hated the pride he heard in his voice. The hunger to be heard. To matter.

"Well-deserved," Redding said. "'Bout time someone listened."

The words caught Carlisle off guard. After all these years, someone cared. Finally understood. Twenty-five years of closed doors, rejected manuscripts and smug dismissals—all those bastards who'd told him to quiet down, to play nice, to write what people wanted to hear—and here was this hard-nosed cop cutting through it all with five simple words. No bullshit. No platitudes. Just recognition.

Carlisle felt a surge of warmth in his chest. A sense of relief he hadn't expected. He tried to fight it, then gave in. He had a *right* to feel this way. He'd earned it.

They stood still. Just the sound of cars and wind and the low rhythm of the street.

"Thank you," Carlisle said. "For taking a harder look, for believing me."

"Just doing my job."

The city noise picked up. Somewhere, a siren wailed. A lonely sound. And it conjured a lonely image. Despite Carlisle's resolve not to feel sorry for himself, he did. Victor was gone. And with him, any hope of reconciliation.

He might finally see some professional success after this. But it wouldn't be the same. Not without Victor. Not without someone to care for, yearn for, dream with.

A car pulled up to the curb and Julius Hayward stepped out. Dapper as always.

"Looks like your ride's here," Redding said.

Carlisle's shoulders eased. "So it is."

Hayward closed the door and started away, then turned back. Apparently, he'd forgotten something. He returned to the passenger side, bent into the car, and reemerged with a small paper bag tucked under one arm. His eyes found Carlisle's across the stretch of pavement and he smiled, lifting the bag like a promised prize.

"He's always been there for you, hasn't he?" Redding said.

Carlisle blinked, considered. "Yes. Yes, I guess he has."

A pause. "Why do you think that is?"

A shrug. "I don't know."

Redding looked at him. "And you never thought about it?"

Carlisle frowned, puzzled.

Redding went on. "He told me about your time in Paris. And how he went there, too."

"Yes. He didn't like it very much. Couldn't take it."

"Is that what you think?"

Carlisle didn't answer.

"He went for the same reason you did. To find you. And when you didn't see him—didn't want to—he came back. Built a life. Built a bookstore. Waited."

"For who?"

"For you."

Carlisle gave him a stunned look. "Is that what he said?"

"Not word for word. But it was all there. In the way he talked about you. In his reasons for leaving Paris and coming back here."

Carlisle felt as though the wind had been knocked out of him. He'd spent a lifetime accusing others of willful blindness. Grayson. The school administrators in Philly. The editors in Boston. Pierre in Paris.

But who was the real blind man?

Who had refused to see?

He had a sudden stark image himself, standing alone atop a pile of rubble. The rubble of his life. He'd always blamed others for the blowups, the disasters that drove him from town to town. But he'd played his part too, hadn't he?

And in a strange way, he'd fought to end up alone. Spent decades yearning for a man who never chose him—while ignoring the one who had.

Julius Hayward. Hayward, who'd shown up again and again. Silently. Steadily.

He thought of the photograph he so treasured. But for once, he thought of it differently. Realized he'd done what so many do—become so focused on who was in front of the camera that he'd forgotten who was behind it.

Hayward. Just months from graduating. He'd risked as much—maybe more—than either of them. For him, taking that photo wasn't just friendship. It was complicity. Suppose someone had seen him lugging that equipment across campus? Guessed the truth—not just about Carlisle and Grayson, but about Hayward, too? McAllister would've expelled him. Withheld his degree. Years of work discredited. Stained by scandal and shame.

All that risk. Taken why?

"He was always there," Redding said. "You just didn't see him."

Hayward taking him in. Hayward at his bedside. And now—here—Hayward coming toward him.

"I see him now."

And he did.

As Hayward approached, Carlisle saw the exhaustion in the man's eyes. Saw how much he'd taken for granted. Saw that he'd treated Hayward no better than Grayson had treated him.

Saw. And felt ashamed.

"You look terrible," Hayward said.

"You should see the other guy."

"I'd rather not." Hayward extended the bag. "Clean handkerchief. Aspirin. Cigarettes."

Carlisle accepted it. "Always prepared."

"Someone has to be." Hayward gave Redding a nod. "Detective."

"Mr. Hayward."

"The guest room's still yours," Hayward told Carlisle. "For as long as you need it."

Carlisle considered it. "Just for tonight."

"Whatever you say." Hayward didn't argue.

Carlisle started off, moving carefully. And noted how Hayward fell in beside him. Always there. Never crowding. Never controlling. But always close enough to steady him if needed.

"They say there's a new place opened on Lenox," Hayward said. "Jazz club. Supposed to be good."

"I'm in no shape for clubbing."

"Not tonight, no. But soon."

They moved toward Hayward's car.

When Carlisle reached the door, he paused. Turned back. Touched his forehead in a soft salute—and saw the cop return it.

Still hurting. But upright.

He had breath. He had work.

And this time, he wasn't writing for approval.

He was writing for himself.

And finally ready to choose the love that chose him.

48

Redding felt drained and didn't mind admitting it. He slouched in one of the leather armchairs facing David McKay's desk. He was done with the Grayson case, satisfied with his arrests. But he still had the feeling there was another shoe to drop. That somewhere out there lay something he'd forgotten. That was the only explanation for it, for the tension in his shoulders and the knot in his gut.

He was looking forward to getting home and Lena's hands massaging the tightness away—but for now, he was okay with being here, warm inside McKay's home office, away from the gloom and chill of a November evening. He could wind down. Take the edge off with conversation and a taste of the man's fine rye.

McKay moved to the cabinet and drew out two cut crystal glasses and a decanter, stopper glittering like a jewel. "My father bought this before Volstead. Laid in cases." McKay poured the rye with care. "He loved himself some Overholt. I've been saving it," he handed Redding a glass, "for special occasions. This would seem to fit."

Redding lifted the glass for a toast. "To what? Luck? Justice?"

"To getting it right." McKay raised his glass.

"For once."

The rye went down clean. Warm. Certain. Redding felt the knot in his gut loosen.

"Official word came down today," he said. "Case closed. Vaughn and Mercer both formally charged." He sighed and frowned. "I should be happy but..."

"But what?"

"That last bit of evidence Grayson said he was expecting. I never found it. It's still out there."

McKay paused, then said: "Not quite."

Redding's brows drew together. "What does that mean?"

"It means that Davenport called me today. In fact, I'd just gotten off the phone with her when you arrived."

Redding's brow lifted. "And?"

"And she read about Mercer's arrest in the paper. Saw the part about the dummy accounts. And all at once, it came back to her."

Redding straightened. "What came back?"

"Grayson asked her for a letter, days before he died. Made it sound like a simple favor. He wanted her to confirm—on paper—where her last donation had gone."

Redding's eyes narrowed. "You're jiving me."

"Turns out she confirmed to Grayson that Mercer had given her the remittance instructions for the donations himself. And like the good society patron she is, she followed them. Didn't question a thing."

Redding sat forward, elbows on his knees. "And we both know that money didn't go to any official McAllister fund." He shook his head. "Grayson's final proof. She had it all along."

"She did. Buried under cocktail invitations and thank-you notes, but she had it."

"So, why'd she call you?"

"To ask me what to do with it."

Redding was stunned. He opened his mouth, then closed it. He didn't know what surprised him more: that she didn't know what to do or that it was McKay she'd turned to for advice.

"Let me get this straight. She couldn't figure out what to do with the letter? With evidence in a criminal case? The answer's damn simple, isn't it? She hands it over. We close the lid on Mercer's coffin and she goes back doing what she does, conscience clear. Why the hell would she even have to ask—and why ask you?"

"She's worried how it'll look. The papers already love the scandal—they'll eat it up if one of Harlem's white benefactors looks complicit."

"She wasn't complicit. Just careless. There's a difference."

"Try explaining that to a city that doesn't care for nuance," McKay said. "But none of that matters now. We've got it—the final piece Grayson died for."

"Grayson's evidence was good. Davenport's letter will make it even better. It'll tie Mercer to every penny he stole—and every lie he told to cover it."

"Sort of ironic, isn't it? Grayson knew it would take a white woman's signature to bring Mercer down."

"And it cost him his life."

They sat there a moment longer, both men knowing that justice had come—too late for Grayson, too bitter to taste like victory.

McKay turned his glass slowly. "How're you doing with that captain of yours?"

"I'm guessing he's still trying to figure out whether to fire me."

McKay gave a half-smile. "I wouldn't worry too much about that if I were you."

Redding gave him a sharp look. "Why not? You know something I don't?"

"Well, I guess you didn't see it, but Lanie's article in

yesterday's paper had Egan's name all over it. Not directly, but anyone with sense could read between the lines."

"Egan won't face any official reprimand." Redding had long ago stopped expecting perfect justice.

"No, but Davenport made some calls." McKay looked faintly pleased. "Word is, Egan was up for a promotion. Deputy Commissioner had his eye on him."

"And now?"

"Now they're reconsidering. Too much attention. Doesn't look good, they're saying." McKay shrugged. "Not justice. But it's something."

Redding nodded. "I wouldn't have been sorry to see him go, though."

"Yeah, but you want him moving down not up."

"True." Redding took another sip. "You think Davenport's calls had anything to do with Benedict's transfer to Staten Island?" He'd heard about the reassignment that morning—news traveled fast when it involved someone as notorious as Benedict.

"Officially? No." McKay allowed himself a small smile. "But that kind of timing isn't coincidence. I suspect Davenport wasn't too happy about Benedict. His beating up Carlisle put her reputation at risk."

It was more consequence than most ever saw. It wasn't full vindication. And it was done for all the wrong reasons. But it was better than nothing. Far better.

"And Carlisle?"

"He's bitter—but determined to keep fighting."

"Yeah. That's what he told me, too."

A real tilter at windmills, Redding thought. If Hayward was Harlem's Keeper of Secrets, then Carlisle was its Don Quixote. Bound and determined. Was Carlisle courageous or naive? A pig-headed genius or just plain pig-headed? Redding didn't know, then decided he didn't care. Labels didn't matter. Carlisle had more guts, more grit, than half the guys strutting around with medals pinned to their chests. And if that made Carlisle a fool—then so be it. The world, Redding decided, needed more fools like him.

"He's a survivor," McKay said. "He's healing. Slowly." He refreshed their drinks. "Hayward's looking after him." He paused. "He approached me yesterday about Carlisle's future. Seems he's been talking to Davenport."

Redding looked up. "About what?"

"Compensation. For Carlisle." McKay's expression was carefully neutral. "Davenport feels responsible. Not enough to admit it publicly, but enough to offer…patronage."

Redding nearly gagged on his rye. "Davenport? As Carlisle's patron? The woman who controls her artists like chess pieces and the man who's middle name is defiance?"

"The very same." McKay chuckled. "Those two working together?" He shook his head. "I can just imagine the fireworks."

"And it was Hayward's idea?"

"Apparently, yeah. He approached her."

"The man's got nerve."

"Yup." McKay took another sip. "I've been helping with the legal side, but Hayward's negotiating the details."

"Actually, it could be good for the both of them. Teach them some needed lessons."

"Exactly. Plus it helps clear Carlisle's name of any lasting doubts."

"Helps restore some of his credibility."

McKay started to put the glass to his lips, then paused. "Funny how it works. Carlisle's spent the last twenty-five years trying to prove himself to his own people. Turns out it'll take a white woman's signature to make them listen."

They mulled that over.

Redding chuckled. "Oh, the delicious irony. She'll try to

shape him; he'll refuse to be shaped. She'll expect gratitude; he'll give her grief."

"And Hayward—quiet, patient Hayward—will be there to broker the peace, again and again."

Redding sighed. "He still cares, you know. Despite his denials, Carlisle still cares what the world thinks, still craves acceptance."

McKay looked at him, smiled. "Well, look at you. Under all that hard grit, there's just an old softie."

Redding took the teasing. A faint smile. A little grunt. "It's got to hurt, though. That acceptance isn't coming from his own people finally seeing his worth, but from a white patron's checkbook."

McKay's own smile faded. "Yeah, that stings. But he's tired of going it alone. Realistic enough, to take the deal. Survival, in this world, is its own kind of victory."

Redding stared into his glass, aware that this win, like most in his world, fell short of true victory. "Sometimes I wonder if we're just rearranging deck chairs."

McKay considered this. "Maybe. But at least this time, the right people are going to jail."

Redding nodded. "That they are."

They settled into a thoughtful silence. Strains of Bessie Smith's 'Bye Bye, Blues' faded in from somewhere, then just as quickly faded away, as if someone had briefly opened a window perhaps, then closed it again.

"I've been thinking about France," McKay said.

Redding waited.

"When we were over there," McKay said, "fighting in mud and blood for a country that didn't even want us to come home, I swore to myself that if I survived, I'd never let anyone make me compromise what I knew was right." McKay's voice was quiet, reflective. "Then I came back, went down South and ended up... Well, you know what happened."

All of Harlem did. Everyone knew about the prodigal son who had left to investigate a lynching, then disappeared. How he'd reappeared after years away to look into his sister's death and ended up himself charged with murder. The trial had shaken Harlem's staid upper class and left him a virtual pariah.

"You didn't compromise when it came to this case," Redding said. "You put everything on the line for Carlisle."

McKay looked around at his elegant office. "This place… sometimes I feel like I'm just keeping it warm until I figure out what I'm really supposed to be doing with it."

"Taking cases no one else will touch seems like a start."

"Maybe so."

They moved to the living room and took the bottle with them. McKay put on a record by the Duke and lit some logs. They sat in silence, staring at the flames and lost in thought. Just the tick of the old clock and the pop of the fire.

It was Redding who asked the question: "You ever regret coming back?" He looked over at McKay. "Be honest."

McKay didn't answer right away. Just looked into the fire like it might answer for him.

"Yeah," he said. "There've been moments. But…I came back for a reason. Thought I could do more here. Make a difference."

Redding gave a short nod. He'd thought the same thing, had the same hope, the same dream. "And have you—or do you think you have—made a difference?"

"I don't know, man. I don't know." McKay took another sip of his drink. "But yeah, on this day, at this hour, I'd like to think so."

They sank back into silence. Outside, a car passed on the wet street, its tires whispering against the curb.

Redding finally roused himself. He glanced at his watch. "I should be heading back. Lena will be wondering."

"How is she?"

"Good. Better than good." A warm smile crossed Redding's

face. "She says you should come by for dinner. Says she doesn't like the idea of you rambling around in this big house by yourself."

McKay smiled, looked surprised. Grateful. "I'd like that."

Redding held up his glass. It still held a swallow. "Still think the case was worth drinking to?"

"On this day, at this hour, yeah. I do."

The two men downed the rest of their rye. Redding stood, setting his empty glass on a side table. They moved toward the vestibule.

"Tell Lena hello for me," McKay said. "And thank her."

"I will," Redding took his coat down from the rack and shouldered into it. "But I've got one last errand to run before heading home."

"Davenport?"

Redding nodded.

"She's scared," McKay warned. "Of the headlines. Of her name showing up in the wrong column."

"I know. But that letter's the last piece and she's still holding it."

"Careful how you press."

"Says the man who put the squeeze on her first."

"Exactly. I know how hard to turn the vise."

"So do I." Redding put on his hat. He opened the front door, glanced back. "Trust me. If she hasn't made up her mind yet, I know how to help her do it."

He left, stepped back out into the cold, warmed not by rye but by purpose.

One last door to knock on.

49

Margery Davenport didn't turn when he entered. She stood at the window, arms crossed, her reflection faint in the glass. "Detective Redding."

"Mrs. Davenport." He didn't bother to sit.

"I take it you've spoken to Mr. McKay."

"I did, indeed. And I'm told that you have something for me."

She turned to face him. Cool. Analytical. "You want the letter. I'm not sure I...I don't see how it could help. Your case against Mercer is already airtight."

"That's not up to you to decide." He was too tired to play games. "Come on. Give it here. You know you're going to have to hand it over sooner or later."

But even as he said it a thought hit him. "Actually, you must've known that when you called McKay. Why *did* you call him, as a matter of fact? You knew his role in the case, his obligations as an officer of the court and you must've known that he'd talk to me."

She didn't answer, not at first. "When I first got involved with... Well, with you people, I knew it wouldn't be easy. But I never thought it would get this complicated."

"You people?" It took effort, but he kept his expression neutral, professional. "I assume you mean the police department?"

She flushed. "Yes. Of course."

"Yes, well, welcome to our world."

Lips pinched, she crossed to a small but exquisite antique secretary that stood nearby, drew a slender envelope from one of the cubicles and handed it to him. "This is the letter Victor asked for. The one he should have received. I found it tucked behind a stack of correspondence."

Beautiful stationery, faintly scented with her perfume. He opened the envelope, took out the letter. It was just a few lines, made out in a small elegant script.

"You wrote this yourself?"

"He asked me to. I offered to have the bank handle it—more official that way—but he insisted. Said it was just a formality."

"It wasn't."

"I know that now."

He reviewed the contents. McAllister Research Advancement Committee. Redding would've bet his last dollar the fund was a setup. A Baltimore bank. Clean. Respectable. Just far enough from the university's usual accounts to pass unnoticed. Mercer hadn't stolen in handfuls. He'd built himself a channel. And this letter marked the mouth of it.

"You sent the donations exactly as directed? To this bank. Under this committee name. In these amounts?"

"Yes." Her chin lifted a fraction. "Every one of them. Exactly as Mr. Mercer specified."

"Then you know what this letter does."

"I do. It puts Mercer's hands directly on the money."

"Thank you." He put the letter back into the envelope and slid it into his left inner coat pocket, where it rested over his heart. "You didn't answer my question. Why did you call McKay? You do know he's not your friend."

"I do. But I also know he's not my enemy, either." She saw his expression. "Surprised?"

"Actually, yes. I am."

"I know what happened to him. I actually attended that trial. And I heard him speak. I might not agree with everything he did, but I respect his reasons for having done it."

She was calm but tight at the corners. "I called him because I want this done. And because I don't trust anyone else to end it cleanly."

"You could've kept quiet, said nothing."

"Believe me, I thought about it."

"But?"

"I'm not in the habit of rewriting history, Detective. I leave that to the men."

He took the hit and let it pass. She wasn't wrong.

Davenport inclined her head. "I bet you came over here thinking you'd have to threaten me to get the letter, maybe say you'd charge me with obstruction of justice or get a search warrant or some such nonsense. Isn't that true?"

"It never once crossed my mind."

"Of course, it did. But you knew it would never work."

"So you thought you could afford to be generous."

"I knew I could afford to be fair. People like you don't have a chance against people like me. We both know that."

A pause. And then a quiet, "No. We're not supposed to." He looked down on her and gave her a gentle smile. "But here I am."

That stopped her. "You're a very confident man, aren't you?"

"And a very busy one." His dark eyes sparkled with mischief. "Now, I'm just gonna thank you for your generosity and take myself on outta here."

She bristled at the plantation humor. "You think I'm a horrible person, don't you? Because I care so much about my reputation. Well, let me tell you this, *Mister* Detective, there's such a thing as glass cages and I live in one."

He had no idea what she expected him to do with that. Fact was, he didn't care. She might live in a glass cage, but the people he dealt with were living in a steel jungle. Every damn day. Exposed to predators, big and small. Predators who looked and smelled and sounded just like her, who would rub you on the back one minute and stab you in the heart the next.

He knew both worlds. Had moved through mansions and tenements alike, seen how the rules changed depending on the neighborhood. And he'd made his choice about which side he served, which side he saved his sympathy for, long ago. His badge wasn't just metal—it was a commitment to those the folks in the glass-cage rarely bothered to see.

She wandered back to the window, gazed out at the street below. She was tall and thin and the room suddenly seemed vast around her. Vast and empty. A showcase, yes—but also a cell. Just with invisible bars and enough room to make it look like freedom.

She was a rich widow. Alone. Lonely.

And she was admitting it. Showing him what she'd no doubt spent years learning to hide.

He realized he felt a growing sympathy for her. He set it aside.

Fine. She had her worries and her woes. So what? What soul alive didn't? He didn't have time for a pity party. He'd gotten what he'd come for. It was time to leave.

"Mrs. Davenport, I—"

"I should've known something was wrong. I…should've asked more questions."

He didn't disagree, but he said nothing.

She turned to face him. He was amazed to see tears glistening in her eyes.

Not falling. Just there. Waiting.

"He had nothing to do with the donations. So why was he asking about them? As if he were auditing the whole thing. And then he was dead and I forgot all about the letter. It wasn't until I read about Mercer in the paper that I...that I..."

She rubbed her forehead. "Oh, God, I should've known."

Redding wanted to feel nothing. But that phrase, *I should've known*—how many times had he heard it before? From wives, husbands, mothers. Rich or poor. Didn't matter. It always came wrapped in the same twine of guilt and hindsight.

And sometimes? It came rehearsed.

She'd had the letter when they first spoke. Had suspected it mattered. Had almost told him—*"There is one more thing"*—then swallowed it. Chose silence. Chose self-protection.

She'd accused men of rewriting history. But here she was doing the same. Making a convenient adjustment that made her look less culpable, less complicit in the delay.

Should he call her on it? Be brutal about it? He chose diplomacy.

"Mrs. Davenport, it boils down to this: You didn't help Mercer commit fraud. And you're not responsible for Grayson's death."

"But if I'd given him the letter..."

You mean, if you'd given it to me...

"You've read the papers," he said. "You know why Grayson died. The letter had nothing to do with it." And now, a touch of the bitter truth. "If you'd given me the letter earlier, it would've helped us nail Mercer sooner. But it wouldn't have saved Grayson. Nothing you did—or didn't do—would've made a difference when it came to that."

She didn't answer right away. Instead, she reached into her sleeve and drew out a small, neatly folded handkerchief. Pressed it lightly to her lips. No tears—just stillness.

Then she lowered it, smoothed its edge between her fingers and folded it once more, precisely, as if restoring order to something unruly.

"I'm not directly responsible. I know that." She spoke clearly.

Not pleading—stating. "But there were things I should've done. Things I should've said. It wasn't just the letter."

She looked away, fingers tightening around the handkerchief now folded in her palm.

"I suspected. About Carlisle and Grayson. I didn't know—not really—but I saw the signs. I told myself it was none of my business." A breath. "And I knew what Vaughn was—how jealous she could be, how tight a grip she kept on Grayson."

She turned back. Lifted her chin. Voice steady, but the words coming faster now.

"I kept wondering, *Does she know? Or doesn't she? About him and Carlisle? Because if she does*...I thought about talking to him, warning him. But I didn't dare. I mean, you don't *do* things like that, do you? I told myself it wasn't my place, that I was being polite, discreet—when really, I just didn't want to get involved. But I should have. I should've said something. That's what I live with."

She finally stopped, looked toward him. Seeking sympathy? Judgment? Forgiveness? Or just assurance that he'd actually heard. Believed. Understood?

Redding took a breath. Let it out slow.

"You're not the first person to stay quiet when they should've spoken up. And you won't be the last. You made a choice. Might've been the wrong one. But it wasn't a crime."

She said nothing. Wanting absolution. Too proud to ask for it.

And not giving away more than she had to.

"If it's guilt you're after," he said, "there's plenty to go around. But not for murder." He shook his head. "That's not your cross to bear."

She looked at him long and level. "Is that your official verdict, Detective?"

"I'm just a cop, ma'am. I don't deliver verdicts. Only judges and juries do."

She was silent, thoughtful. Then she gave him a single, curt nod, folded the handkerchief and tucked it away.

She walked him to the door. At the threshold, she paused." You're a hard man, Detective. But I suppose you've had to be."

He started to answer, but she lifted a hand.

"Don't. It's not a complaint." A ghost of a grin—wry, tired, almost fond. "Knowing that about you? It's the only thing that reassures me."

He gave her the barest nod. Nothing more.

Outside, the air hit cooler. Cleaner. Like something had lifted. Redding reached into his coat and touched the envelope over his heart. The final piece of Grayson's puzzle.

Finally where it belonged.

50

The late afternoon sun slanted through the windows of Redding's Brooklyn parlor. Three days had passed since the arrests—three days of interrogations, paperwork and press conferences that had left Redding bone-tired but satisfied.

He sat in his armchair, tie loosened, a cup of coffee on the side table. Ida sat comfortably on the sofa across from him, notepad open on her lap, pencil moving in quick, precise strokes as she took down quotes and details.

"So you played them against each other." She looked up from her notes. "Mercer and Vaughn."

Redding nodded, taking a slow sip. "Had to. Couldn't get either of them to break on their own." He set his cup down. "But we got there."

Ida's professional demeanor gave way briefly to a smile of sisterly pride. "Well, I'd say we make a pretty good team."

Lena appeared in the doorway with a fresh pot of coffee. "About time someone showed him he could use a little help now and then." She smiled at Ida, then shot a gently scolding glance at Redding. "Always seems to think he has to do it all on his own." She refreshed everyone's cup, then sat down.

Ida flipped to a fresh page in her notepad. "Walk me through it again—from the beginning. I need to get this right." Her tone had shifted back to the journalist, all business.

"So when did you start to suspect her?"

"First time I met her. Ten minutes after we sat down."

"That early? Why?"

Redding raised his arms and yawned—a long, slow, jaw-cracking stretch.

Across from him, Ida cupped her hand to her mouth and yawned too.

Redding smiled a little. "You see what you just did?"

She blinked, gave a little shake of her head. "No. What?"

"You did what she couldn't."

"And what's that?"

"Express empathy."

He let that sink in. Enjoyed the puzzled look on her face.

"It's basic wiring," he said. "Somebody yawns, you yawn back. Without thinking. It's reflex. Means you can feel what someone else feels. Simple as that."

Ida was incredulous. "You mean you got suspicious...because you yawned and she didn't?"

Redding's smile faded. His eyes stayed steady. "I mean it told me what she was. That if she didn't kill him, she was damn sure capable of it."

Ida frowned, then cocked an eye at him. "Come on. You can't be serious."

"Oh, but I am." Redding's expression hardened. "You sit across from enough liars. Enough killers. You start to notice. They don't yawn. They watch."

"And she was," Ida said, quieter now.

"Like a poker player with a stacked hand. She grieved, sure. But she stayed inside herself. Every second. And that's when I knew: She wasn't grieving. She was managing her appearance. Managing *me.*"

Ida mulled that over. "But the papers said Carlisle was your main suspect."

"Yeah. That's what they said."

"So, it was what you *let* them say."

A pause. "Not only. For a while, that's what I made myself believe."

"Meaning?"

"I had a captain breathing down my neck, a rich woman with connections making calls, and a blackmail note signed with a 'C.' Brass wanted an arrest. The evidence said Carlisle."

"So Carlisle was it?"

"Yeah, he was it." Redding set his cup down. "I knew that something wasn't right. But I buried it. Told myself I was following the evidence." He shook his head. "What I was doing was following orders. And calling it detective work."

"And Carlisle nearly died for it."

"Yeah." The word came out flat. Final. "He did."

A beat of silence.

"So what happened?"

"Carlisle did. When I got him in that pressure box, I realized… It didn't fit. It didn't fit. *It didn't fit.* He's smart—but impulsive. Chaotic. Hot-headed. Whoever did Grayson was a stone-cold planner. Carlisle's never planned a damn thing in his life." Redding paused. "Then Benedict beat him. And that was on me. I'd let that happen."

"That wasn't your fault," Lena said.

"Tell that to the man with smashed fingers and a broken eye socket. The only good thing—and I hate to say it—the only good thing that came out of it is that he did start talking. Seeing him all busted up like that—and he told me about Mercer, I knew I had to backtrack."

"Let me get this straight," Ida said. "Does that mean you stopped suspecting Vaughn?"

"No. It means I knew I had to my mind open. There was a lot

going on, more than I'd suspected. Too much for easy solutions—especially the wrong ones. I had to work the case the right way. No more cheats. No more short-cuts. And no more trying to please people who would just keep asking for more."

"But why her?" Ida asked. "What made you keep coming back to her?"

"Grayson was poisoned—fast and neat—and no one else at that party got so much as a headache. That ruled out the food, the punch, ruled out the bar. It had to be something he drank. And whatever it was, it was his alone. Someone fixed that drink for him personally."

"So, it had to be Vaughn?"

"Who else? She knew what he drank. Knew how he liked it. Had probably fixed it for him a hundred times before."

Ida tapped her pencil against her palm, pensive, seemingly satisfied with his logic but not quite ready to let him off the hook. "But who's to say he didn't order the drink himself, you know, asked Davenport's bartender to make it for him? And then someone—any one at the party, actually—could've slipped the poison in when he wasn't looking."

"I checked with Davenport's staff. None of them made that drink—"

"They could've been lying."

"True—"

"But you still believed it was her."

"With every bone in my body."

"So that's why you took off to D.C." Lena said.

"Had to. I followed the trail to Whitfield, Fitzhugh and Mercer."

"What about when Fitzhugh said Mercer did it?" Ida asked.

"I'm sure he believed it."

"And that didn't sway you at all? Vaughn still stayed on your list?"

"Top of the chart. Problem was, I had no proof."

"What about the poison?" Lena said. "I don't understand how she even got her hands on it."

Redding explained that tincture of aconite was regulated but not closely tracked at every counter. "Doctors know it's poisonous, but they still prescribe it in small doses for neuralgia, rheumatism, heart conditions. Not like morphine or laudanum—strict controls there. But aconite falls into a gray zone."

"A very convenient one if you want to kill somebody," Lena said.

"Very. I had her place searched—twice. No poison. No bottle. She knew how to get rid of the evidence. Quiet, clean."

"Sounds like a dead end," Ida said.

"Would've been for anybody but my husband," Lena said.

"Ida, while you were at Fitzhugh's tracking down Grayson's evidence—and nearly getting yourself killed while doing it," (here, a big brother glance of teasing disapproval) "I was out, pounding the streets. I talked to every pharmacist within walking distance of Vaughn's place. Even the ones along the way to *Commonwealth Review*. Found the one she probably used, asked to see the poison register. Nothing."

"You showed him her picture?" Ida asked.

"Said he'd never seen her."

"Naturally," Lena said. "To admit that would mean admitting he sold her poison without making her sign for it."

"Admitting it to a *cop, no less.* A cop investigating a *murder,*" Ida added.

"So there I was," Redding said. "No bottle, no signature, no confession. When it came to hard evidence, I didn't have a damn thing." He nodded to Ida. "It was right after that, that I got your call. You'd found Grayson's evidence."

"Good timing, huh?"

"Not a minute too soon. Without it, I'd still be chasing shadows. Knowing I had it in my back pocket, knowing what it proved, it gave me room to play the long game. "

"Ah-huh! So, now do we finally get to hear about that plan of yours, the one you were all hush-hush about?"

"Sure" Redding refilled his cup. "I invited Mercer in. Let him know what I knew. Not all of it. Just enough to make him sweat. I needed him to think he had wriggle room. So, I laid out the soft angles—the train tickets, the hotel records, witness statements placing him with Grayson the day before he died."

"That was a whole lot right there," Lena said. "It must've given him a bad shock."

"It sure did. But the bigger shock came a few minutes later—when I let him go."

"Wait!" Ida sat up. "You did *what? Why?*"

"I needed him to do the dirty work for me—to nail Vaughn. To set her up, so I could take her down. And Mercer, being Mercer, did exactly that. He went looking for a patsy and went straight for her. When he called, I was waiting."

"He thought he was playing you—"

"But I was playing him. It was a gamble, but there's one thing every cop knows he can count on: the arrogance of a swindler. Mercer was quick enough to see that Vaughn made the perfect suspect. But he was too slow to see that she'd actually done it."

"Man, oh, man, brother mine." Ida shook her head. "I knew you could be sneaky but ..."

Lena teased her. "Says the undercover girl reporter." She turned to Redding. "Go on, baby."

"Y'all know the rest. When Mercer called with his theory about Vaughn, I played along. Let him think he was feeding me a new lead. Meanwhile, I had tails on both of them. Mercer reached out to Vaughn, tried to blackmail her—thinking she was innocent and would pay to avoid suspicion."

"That was so wrong." Ida said. "But so Mercer."

"When he tried to frame her for a crime she'd actually committed, she decided to silence him—permanently. She agreed to meet him. But came prepared."

"Did Mercer know you were there, waiting?"

"He knew. We'd agreed on it. Discussed what he'd tell her, what he'd demand, the kind of pressure he would put her under."

"Did you expect her to pull a gun on him?"

Redding paused, the cup midway to his lips. "Let's just say I wasn't surprised."

Ida smiled grimly, jotted down one last note, then began flipping back through her notepad. "That's some slick work. You caught them both red-handed—her admitting to the murder, him to the fraud and blackmail."

"Got everything I needed."

The telephone rang in the vestibule. Redding started up to get it, but Lena waved him to stay put and hurried out. Her voice became a soft murmur in the background.

Redding rubbed the back of his neck, felt the muscles crack. "There's a certain irony to all of this. Vaughn wasn't caught because she was careless — but because she was so precise. That intimacy she so jealously guarded, that quiet role she made for herself—not as his lover or his wife, but as the one who knew him best—that's what damned her. She was the only person who could've made him that drink. The only one who cared enough to cater to him like that. And the only one he trusted to get it right."

Ida inclined her head, thoughtful. "And the fact that she used bitters to do it—that adds a certain poetic cruelty to it, doesn't it? Love is sweet."

"Supposed to be."

"But whatever love she felt for him, it must've really turned sour. 'Cause she didn't just decide to put him down. She decided to use a sour whiskey cocktail to do it—to lace it with poison and a dash of bitters. Hmm-hmph," Ida shook her head. "Now that's what I call cold. Cold fury."

Lena stuck her head in. "Your editor," she told Ida. "Says it's important."

Ida frowned, set aside her notepad and went out to take the call. Her voice drifted from the hallway—professional, firm, occasionally rising in frustration. When she returned, her lips were pressed together with indignation.

"Can you believe it?" She paced the length of the small parlor. "Three days I've been working on this story. Three days gathering facts, conducting interviews, writing draft after draft. And Thornton wants to give it to Jacobs!"

Redding raised an eyebrow. "Your editor's giving your story to someone else?"

"Says a 'story of this magnitude' needs a more experienced reporter." She made quotation marks in the air. "Says readers will 'take it more seriously' coming from a man."

Lena made a sound of disgust. "That's rich."

"I told him I'm the one who broke this case wide open. I'm the one who risked my life getting that evidence. I'm the one with all the facts." Ida's hands clenched into fists. "You know what he said? 'That's why we need you to share your notes with Jacobs.'"

Redding headed out to the telephone. "What's your editor's name?"

Ida stopped pacing. "What?"

"His name. I want to talk to him."

She followed after him. "Nate, don't—"

"You got the evidence. You helped solve this case." He was already picking up the receiver. "That byline belongs to you."

"This isn't your fight."

"Like hell it isn't. I wouldn't have caught Mercer or Vaughn without what you brought me. Thornton needs to understand that."

The call was brief but pointed. Redding identified himself, explained his role in the investigation and made it clear that Ida alone had his cooperation for any follow-up questions. He spoke with the calm authority of a man used to being heard.

When he hung up, Ida was staring at him, arms crossed. "I didn't ask you to do that."

"I know."

"I can fight my own battles."

"I know that too." He settled back into his chair. "But some battles are easier won with reinforcements."

A beat passed between them, tension hovering. Then Ida's expression softened. "Did it work?"

"We'll see." He picked up his cup again. "But I made it clear the NYPD won't be providing any exclusive details to Jacobs."

Lena chuckled from where she'd been listening. "I'd have paid good money to hear that conversation."

Ida shook her head, but a reluctant smile tugged at her lips. "You're still the same pushy big brother, aren't you?"

"Some things don't change." He raised his cup in a small toast.

"Hmph." Ida returned to the sofa and picked up her notepad. "So what happens now? With Mercer and Vaughn?"

"Mercer's already talking, trying to cut a deal. Says he'll testify about the embezzlement scheme, implicate everyone involved." Redding rubbed his jaw. "Vaughn's different. She's not saying a word. Cold as ice, even now."

"Do you think they'll both go to prison?"

"Mercer will get a few years, maybe less with good behavior. White-collar crime..." He shrugged. "The system's always been more forgiving of men who steal with pens instead of guns."

"And Vaughn?"

"Murder's different. If she's convicted, she's looking at life."

Ida wrote this down, her pencil scratching softly. "What about Carlisle?"

"Released yesterday. No charges." Redding's expression darkened. "Nearly got beaten to death for a crime he didn't commit."

"Because of a note planted by Vaughn." Ida shook her head. "All those years devoted to Grayson and in the end, she..."

"People do strange things for love. Especially when that love isn't returned."

A comfortable silence settled between them. Outside, a young newspaper boy called out the evening edition, his voice rising and falling with practiced rhythm.

Finally, Ida closed her notepad and tucked her pencil away. "I should get going. Got a story to write."

"You're heading back to D.C. tonight?"

She nodded. "Last train leaves at nine. Bag is already packed and standing by the door."

"I packed you some pie for the ride back," Lena said.

"And I'll drive you to the station." Redding stood.

"You don't have to—"

"Of course, I do."

At the door, Lena embraced Ida warmly. "Don't be a stranger. And let us know when that story runs. We'll be cheering from the sidelines."

As they walked to the car, the evening settling around them like a familiar coat, Ida glanced at her brother. "You never did tell me if you looked for him."

Redding didn't pretend to misunderstand. "Dad?"

"Yeah."

He opened the car door for her. "I made some calls. Checked some records."

"And?" She got in.

"Nothing yet." He started the engine. "But I'll keep looking."

He pulled out and Ida fell quiet for a while. Every now and

then, he glanced at her. It was never good when she stayed silent for too long.

"Ida, I—"

"You know, I always thought if I could just find him, ask him why he left, then everything would make sense."

"And now?"

"Now I'm not so sure it matters." She turned to look at him. "Maybe knowing why doesn't change anything."

Redding nodded slowly. "Maybe not."

"Is that why you stopped looking? 'Cause you figured it wouldn't change anything?"

His hands tightened on the wheel. "I stopped because I thought I already knew the answer. And I didn't like it."

"That he didn't care."

"Yeah."

Ida nodded to herself. She went back to looking out the window, to watching the gray city landscape slide by. "And now?"

A long pause. Then, quietly: "Now I think maybe I don't know as much as I thought."

They drove the rest of the way in silence. When they reached Penn Station, Redding pulled up to the curb and cut the engine.

"Your editor," he said before she could open the door. "If he gives you any more trouble…"

She smiled. "I can handle Thornton."

"I know you can. But the offer stands."

Ida reached over and, in a rare gesture, squeezed his hand. "Thanks, Nate. For everything."

He nodded, uncomfortable with the sentiment but accepting it all the same. "Going to write a hell of a story?"

"The best you've ever read."

"I believe it."

She gathered her things and stepped out onto the curb. He

watched her walk toward the station entrance, a small figure against the grand facade, moving with purpose.

Just before she disappeared inside, she turned and lifted a hand in farewell. He waved back. Then she was gone, swallowed by the crowds, and Redding turned the car toward home, toward Lena.

A GIFT FOR YOU

Reviews help other readers discover books they might otherwise miss.

If you enjoyed Nathaniel Redding's first case, please consider leaving a brief review on Amazon.

Even a sentence or two makes a difference.

Thank you for reading.

THE MUSIC BEHIND THE MYSTERY

During the writing of *Courtesy of a Dead Man,* music became part of the story.

You can listen to the official playlist here:

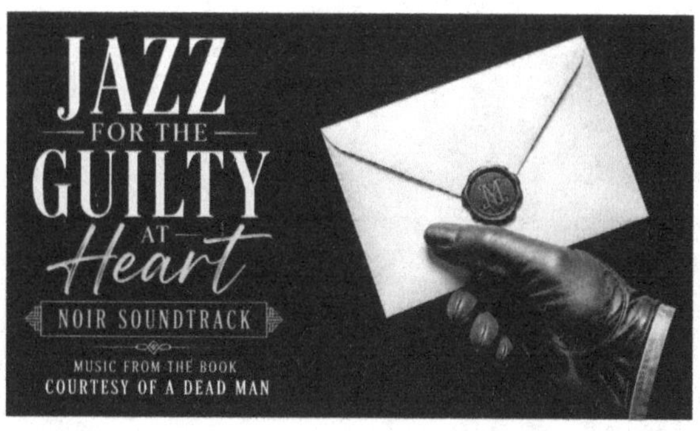

HISTORICAL NOTE

The man you've just followed through a complex investigation was drawn from life.

Wesley C. Redding, born in Atlanta on August 26, 1892, was the first black detective sergeant in the history of the New York City Police Department. He studied at Morehouse College and later attended college in New York City. During World War I, he served as a Special Patrolman at Pennsylvania Station in Manhattan. In 1920, he joined the NYPD and was assigned to the 38th Precinct on West 135th Street.

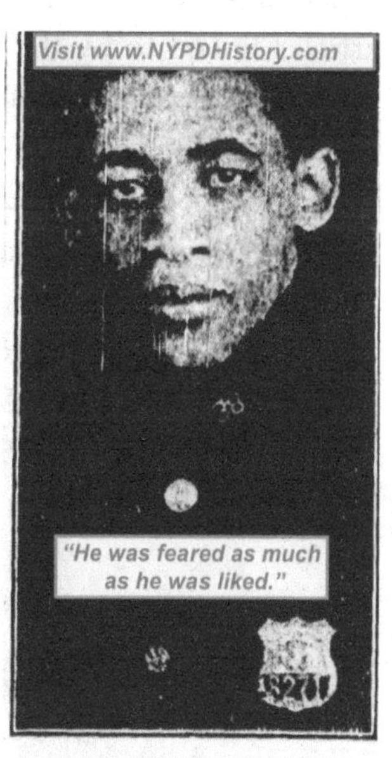

OFFICER WESLEY REDDING, First Negro Detective Sergeant of New York.

On August 26, 1921, Commissioner Richard E. Enright promoted him to the detailed rank of Acting Detective Sergeant. The promotion followed a string of high-profile arrests, including the resolution of the Capitol Theatre robbery and the apprehension of dangerous men whose presence threatened the safety of Harlem.

Commissioner Enright told him: "Officer Redding, you are the type of policeman that makes the New York cop known the world over as the finest, and it is fitting that you should be the first colored detective sergeant that ever graced the Police Department of New York City."

A few days later, a magistrate in Washington Heights remarked, "The City of New York never fails to acknowledge the able work of its employees—especially the type of work you represent."

Redding's career was brief but extraordinary. He died of tuberculosis on February 25, 1924. He was 31. According to articles linked to by the NYPD History site, the funeral drew thousands, black and white alike. "Never before in the history of the city," the press wrote, "has the white and colored population, with one accord, paid such a profound tribute to its hero-dead."

He was survived by his wife, father and two sisters. He was buried at Woodlawn Cemetery in the Bronx.

Detective Nathaniel Redding is fiction. But he walks in the shadow of a real man. Wesley Redding earned the badge he wore, and he wore it well.

ACKNOWLEDGMENTS

You had better things to do with your time. Books of your own to read, jobs to manage, lives to live. And yet, you read mine—carefully, critically and with the kind of honesty that's rarer than it should be. For that, I am genuinely, deeply grateful.

Courtesy of a Dead Man is a better book because of you. You caught timeline snags, flagged places where the story wasn't as clear as it should be. One of you even made sure I'd chosen the right poison, which is exactly the kind of sentence I never imagined writing in a thank-you note.

But what I'll remember most is the encouragement. You gave it at the right moment, and it made a difference.

This case deserved witnesses. You were good ones.

Margaret Martin
Sonia Ehrt
Renee Brown
Felicia Chambers
Maggie Covington
Ingrid Sangiwa
Emma Tracy
Jordan Walker

ACKNOWLEDGMENTS

[illegible]

[illegible]

ABOUT PERSIA WALKER

"Just the facts, ma'am. Just the facts."

Persia Walker writes historical crime fiction where glamour, race, ambition and danger collide. A native New Yorker, Walker is a former Associated Press writer and retired U.S. diplomat. She has lived on three continents and brings a reporter's eye to the hidden corners of history.

Visit her online at PersiaWalker.com. Scan the QR code to receive her newsletter, *Criminal Musings*:

facebook.com/authorpersiawalker
amazon.com/author/persiawalker
persia.substack.com
threads.com/@persiawalker

ALSO BY PERSIA WALKER

Have you read the others?

STANDALONES

Lyrics of a Blackbird

An attorney returns from the dead to uncover the truth about his sister's brutal death. His search reveals a world of lies, hypocrisy, and tragic betrayal. But each day brings him closer to ruin. How soon before his enemies uncover his own bitter secret—the sin that could destroy him?

THE LANIE PRICE SERIES

Goodfellowe House

A poor but gifted pianist is kidnapped on a snowy Christmas night. Then thieves hit the home of her rich patron. Silver, jewels, cash—gone. Coincidence or conspiracy? Was the kidnapping real or cover for an inside job? Lanie Price turns up the heat on this ice cold case.

Black Orchid Blues

Lanie Price witnesses a brutal kidnapping. Then a severed hand lands on her doorstep. What does this killer want and how many people is he willing to kill to get it? Evil hides behind the façades of genteel Strivers' Row and death stalks the ballroom of Harlem's most famous gay party.

Backdrop to Murder

A handsome photographer and a Cotton Club beauty, shot dead in his studio. The suspect: the dead man's wife, found weeping with regret over his body. Can Lanie Price save this widow from a wrongful date with the electric chair—or is this innocent not so innocent after all?

Dear Sister Dead

Vera Kincaid had everything to live for. The wife of a preacher man, she was rich, smart, beautiful. But lovely wives often have dark secrets, and Vera was no exception. For Vera, forbidden love had deadly consequences.

Shards of Betrayal

Maverick director Seth Carter wants to tell hard truths on the silver screen. But sabotage plagues his set. Someone means to kill his film—even if it means killing the people making it.

www.ingramcontent.com/pod-product-compliance
Lightning Source LLC
LaVergne TN
LVHW030915080826
845145LV00013B/2905